monsoonbooks

JAIPONG DANCER

Patrick Sweeting worked for the United Nations on issues of conflict prevention and recovery and has been living and working in Asia for over 30 years. He has spent many years in Indonesia, studying behaviour, crime and conflict and speaks several local languages. Patrick studied for a PhD in Social Anthropology at The School of Oriental and African Studies (SOAS) in London.

JAIPONG DANCER

PATRICK SWEETING

monsoonbooks

Published in 2012
by Monsoon Books Pte Ltd
71 Ayer Rajah Crescent #01-01
Mediapolis Phase Ø, Singapore 139951
www.monsoonbooks.com.sg

First edition.

ISBN (paperback): 978-981-4358-73-6
ISBN (ebook): 978-981-4358-74-3

Copyright©Patrick Sweeting, 2012
The moral right of the author has been asserted.

All rights reserved. No part of this publication may be reproduced,
stored in a retrieval system, or transmitted, in any form or by any means
without the prior written permission of the publisher, nor be otherwise
circulated in any form of binding or cover other than that in which
it is published and without a similar condition being imposed on the
subsequent purchaser.

Cover design by Cover Kitchen.

National Library Board, Singapore Cataloguing-in-Publication Data
Sweeting, Patrick, 1950-
Jaipong Dancer / Patrick Sweeting. – Singapore : Monsoon Books, 2012.
p. cm.
ISBN : 978-981-4358-73-6 (pbk.)

1. Love stories. 2. Dancers – Indonesia – Sumatra – Fiction. 3. Sumatra
(Indonesia) – Fiction. I. Title.

PR6119
823.92 -- dc22   OCN778046051

Printed in Singapore
16 15 14 13 12   1 2 3 4 5

To Ibu Zubaidah and Pak Yahya

Glossary

Batak – people of North Sumatra

Belando – foreigner

Da'eut – literally means "up and inside" but is usually used to refer to places deep inside a mountain range. However, it is also used as a place name and it can refer to the mythical origins of the Rejang people

Ibu – madam or mother

Ilir – downstream or riverine

Indo – a child of mixed Indonesian-European descent

Kebaya – formal blouse

Komrin – people of South Sumatra

Melayu – the lingua franca of Sumatra before the introduction of Bahasa Indonesia

Nona – young lady

Pak – mister or father

Ramayana – Hindu epic describing the journey of prince Rama. In Indonesia it is performed as a dance-drama

Rejang – people of the mountain areas of south west Sumatra

Rupiah – currency of Indonesia

Sarong – cloth wrapped around the lower body

Sita – wife of Rama in the Ramayana epic

Terang Bulan – title of a Malay love song

Tuan – sir

Ulu – upriver, often implying heavily forested areas

Author's Note

Jaipong dancing applies to a dance form developed in Indonesia in the 1970s based on a traditional West Javanese dance called Ketuk Tilu (three gong dance). The term Jaipong is used in this novel for ease of reference.

Prologue

South Sumatra – 1950s

It was a hot, humid evening in Linggau and the deserted streets were still wet from the afternoon downpour as Hans made his way towards the House of Young Bamboo.

The House had originally been built as a rest house for rubber planters and Dutch colonial officials working in the lowlands of southern Sumatra. It still had the fine balconies and ornate dining rooms so beloved of the Dutch but they were now used for very different purposes. When the Dutch were finally driven out of Sumatra, the house fell into disrepair until Ibu Efi suddenly appeared and renovated it into its present condition. Amongst the locals it was now known as the House of Lost Souls because many people who entered its ornate doorway were never seen again.

Hans knocked hard on the door, which was opened by a burly Madurese guard wearing a smart sarong and short-cut jacket. "You got any firearms on you, Tuan?" he said to Hans.

"No."

"Mind if I search you, Tuan?"

Hans slipped him a few coins and walked into the House.

In the entrance hall was a reception desk with a smartly dressed Chinese girl behind the counter. She looked up and smiled as he entered. "Good evening, Tuan. Would you like some company?"

"No thanks, I just want a drink. Is Ibu Efi in? I want to speak to her."

The girl glanced quickly at Hans's face while pressing a button hidden under her desk. "Does Tuan have an appointment?"

"No, but I do have an introduction. General Sirait said I should see her. Got some business to discuss."

"OK Tuan, go straight through to the bar at the back. Ibu Efi may see you later. Enjoy yourself."

"Thanks."

Hans wandered along the dark hallway leading to the back of the building. Doors led left and right; some open, revealing a girl reclining within, others firmly closed. At the entrance to the bar, under the soft red light of a shaded lamp, a young girl in a shiny blue cheongsam beckoned him to enter with an encouraging smile. "You want company?" she asked, flashing her oval eyes at Hans's damp, sweating face.

"Not now," he replied, entering the doorway.

The smoke-filled bar was half empty, it still being early evening. There was a mixed gathering of army officers, Chinese businessmen and local gangsters sitting in conspiratorial groups in the darker corners of the bar discussing gold, women, drugs, guns. These were the foremost currencies of the House and constituted the major subjects of its conversations.

"Whiskey with ice," Hans said to the dapper-looking barman. "And only use clean ice."

"Yes, Tuan. I've not seen you before. Is Tuan new here?" The barman spoke politely and slowly while pouring the whiskey; he knew how to handle foreigners.

"Never been here before," was all Hans said as he sat at the bar and surveyed the scene.

The bar was large and ornate, in accordance with its colonial heritage. At the far end was a stage where several girls were performing the monotonous but sensuous movements of the Jaipong dance. They moved slowly until someone in the audience went up to the stage and threw them a few coins or passed a banknote to one of the dancers. Then they would speed up for a few minutes before slowing down again and waiting for the next payment.

Hans took a large swig of whiskey and turned casually to the barman saying, "Go and tell Ibu Efi to come here."

The barman's eyes narrowed as he stared at Hans; no one but a fool or a general would refer to Ibu Efi in that manner. His hand shook as he poured Hans another whiskey but he kept his foot close to the emergency button under the bar.

The Chinese girl from the reception desk came up to Hans. "Ibu is ready for you now. She wants you in her office, so please follow me."

The girl turned back towards the hallway expecting Hans to follow, but he did not. He didn't even acknowledge her presence but stayed at the bar drinking and studying the dancers. She hurried back to the bar. "Tuan, you must come now. Ibu doesn't like to be kept waiting."

"Tell her to come here. Tell her I was sent by the General and I want to see her in the bar before I step into her spider's web."

The Chinese girl looked worried. "Please Tuan, come with me. Ibu gets very angry if she's kept waiting."

As she spoke, she glanced briefly at the barman who pressed the emergency button under the bar. A young, slim Chinese man strolled over and spoke briefly to the girl in Chinese. Hans studied them carefully. He guessed they were discussing him but his attention was drawn to the man. He had expected a couple of toughs to come for him, not this effeminate-looking young man. But Hans was a man of violence and he recognised in the slim young man the look of a highly intelligent killer.

"I want Ibu Efi," he said to the Chinese man. "Can you get her for me?"

The young man looked closely at Hans, a serene but inscrutable smile on his youthful face. "Your name please, Tuan," he asked with a silver tongue while keeping just the right distance from Hans to prevent any quick action with fists or knives. Hans nodded his approval; this sort of behaviour he understood.

"My name is Hans. I'm from America. I want to discuss business with Ibu Efi. Fetch her for me."

"OK Tuan. You stay here, nice and quiet, while my friend goes and asks Ibu if she will come here. But no sudden moves, OK?" He smiled as he spoke and Hans nodded his acquiescence.

Hans was worried about his first visit to Ibu Efi because he was unsure how far the name of the General or the reference to America would protect him. The politics of Indonesia were changing fast and his mentor, General Sirait, was out of favour for being too soft on rebels and dissidents, although Hans knew otherwise. General Sirait was anything but soft, but he was greedy and had tried once too often to milk all sides of the multitude of local conflicts affecting Sumatra. He would probably be killed soon but, as long as he lived, Hans could still get some attention through the use of his name.

There was a flurry of movement by a side door and Hans saw the girls step aside in silence as a middle-aged Javanese woman stepped out. Hans was immediately struck by the size of her bosom; she leant back slightly as she walked, presumably to maintain balance. She came purposely up to Hans, her large, half-closed eyes studying him intently. There was a smile on her well-powdered face but the eyes spoke of business.

"You want me, belando. You should come to my office like you were instructed."

Hans had achieved his first aim of getting Efi to come to him but he also realised the peril of his position. He needed to maintain the initiative.

"Thank you, Ibu," he said. "General Sirait suggested I come and see you. Maybe we could discuss business."

Ibu Efi frowned briefly at the name of the General, her eyelids drooping ever lower to hide any meaning her eyes might reveal. With a swing of her magnificent bosom, she turned to go back to her office with a curt, "Follow me."

Hans followed, as Ibu Efi knew he would. No one ever disobeyed a direct instruction from Ibu in her own House.

Hans felt the eyes of her effeminate Chinese killer as he followed them through the bar, studying every move he made. Hans knew he was outmatched but he would still play his cards with confidence. All he had left to lose was his life.

Once in her dark office Efi sat down and motioned Hans to sit opposite her. "With hands on the table," added the Chinese man with a malicious smile.

"You want a drink?" she said.

"No," said Hans.

Efi did not reply. She knew how to keep her prey in suspense.

Hans continued, "I want to discuss business privately, not in front of your ladyboy." He nodded towards the Chinese man as he spoke.

"His name is Lim and he's no ladyboy," said Efi. "He's special. Been with me since the start. He may look effeminate but he has ... what shall I call it ... special tastes in women, violent tastes. No one, not even I, will offend sweet Lim. I hope you understand who you are dealing with."

Efi sat back in her chair to better study the effect of her speech.

For one of the few times in his life Hans felt completely out of his depth. The General had simply told him that Efi was involved in gold smuggling, gun-running and prostitution and that she was keen to expand her empire and secure her connections. He hadn't expected such a professionally run group of gangsters in a small town in the middle of a swamp in Sumatra, but obviously the local gold trade attracted some big operators.

"You still in contact with the General?" Hans asked.

Efi remained silent, smiling back a reply that said nothing.

"I'm for sale," Hans said, while he also sat back and waited for a reaction.

Ibu Efi smiled again. "Then I shall sell you to sweet Lim. He's quite an expert with both women and men."

"I'm for sale to the highest bidder. I don't deal in ladyboys. You want to do business or not?" retorted Hans impatiently.

"Maybe. Tell me what you can do for me that Lim and his colleagues can't?"

Hans took a deep breath before he spoke. He was about to cross the Rubicon and he knew it. "I've got good contacts in the army in Padang and with the communists in Jakarta. They trust me because I get them gold, women, drugs, anything they ask for, and in return I get rich rewards, but now the General is out of favour so I need to build new contacts. I think we can do business. I need bigger backing, more capital. I want to trade guns for gold and gold for guns depending on whom I'm trading with. We can also add opium to the list, the Chinese like it."

Efi nodded at Lim who quietly left the room, leaving Hans alone with her.

"Thanks," he said. "That monkey gives me the creeps."

"He's a good boy as long as he's on your side," Efi replied. "Now, down to business."

***

It was almost morning when Hans left Efi's office. She had driven a hard bargain and had methodically bound Hans into the success or failure of her empire. He was now "her man", as she put it, and if he ever betrayed her trust, she would feed him to Lim. In return she would open her establishment to Hans's guests so that they could be trapped into political or financial deals; furthermore, she would give him trading capital to start illicit businesses in gold smuggling, gun-running, drug dealing and, at Efi's insistence, women trading. All sides of the conflicts affecting Sumatra would be bound into shady deals which would effectively mean they were funding each other, while Ibu Efi and her associates creamed off the profits. Hans was very satisfied.

Efi handed him a key. "You stay in room 13. I'll send one of my best girls to keep you company."

As they left the office, she called to the ever-watchful Lim. "He's one of us now. Keep an eye on him but give him enough room to manoeuvre."

Lim looked disappointed.

***

The following morning Hans called in to see Efi in her office before heading west, towards the mountain town of Curup, the centre for smuggling gold from the illegal mines high in the Barisan Mountains.

"Two things for you to remember," she said. "Firstly, this is not a partnership; you work for me and if you fail, you will suffer. Secondly, I need more classy women for the House, dancers preferably. Our generals are growing bored with these peasant girls I'm feeding them. Get me some pretty young dancers from Java or Manado and make sure they've got class. I'll pay a high price."

Hans left the House of Young Bamboo feeling a great deal more confident than when he had first entered.

Chapter 1

Yahyu peeped through the curtain that led into the outer room and looked in disgust at the gnarled old man sat on the mat, smoking and talking to one of her uncles. He already had two wives; she was to be his third.

"You got to marry him," said her father firmly. "No one else will marry you now, not with that thing in your womb."

"No, I can't," Yahyu cried. "I don't want to end up like that. I'd rather kill myself."

"You will shame us in front of the whole village if you don't," said her mother. "He's a rich man and he knows what you got in your womb and he's still prepared to give us gold in exchange for you. You can't expect any better. Not in your condition."

"It's all arranged," her father said. "You marry him tonight. It's your own fault. We paid good money for your dancing school and then you shame us. You should think of your younger brothers and sisters. Your future husband promised to help pay for their schooling."

"No," Yahyu screamed. "I will get money for you but I will not marry this old man. I refuse."

With a tearful glance at the stern face of her mother, Yahyu ran out of the room and into the muddy pathway but she was not dressed for flight. She wanted to run towards the obscurity of the surrounding swamps but her long, tight-fitting sarong and ornate blouse did not allow for speed. Those same expensive clothes, presented to her only a few months ago by her dancing school as a reward for excellence, were now the cause for mockery. She hurried on, eyes firmly fixed on the ground, trying to ignore the stares and comments of the old men lounging on the verandas of their meagre wooden huts.

One of her uncles, dressed in dirty shorts and tee shirt, wandered out of his hut and stood in her way. "It was a belando that got you, wasn't it?" he said loudly, looking around at the staring faces. "Bloody belando. They grab our country, then they grab our women. You're not much good to anyone now, are you? Not that you'd look at us village folk. You're just like your pa', the arrogant old fool, too good to mix with the rest of us. You dancers are all the same; just a collection of whores who dance for money. If you danced in front of me, I know what I'd give you." There was much chuckling and nodding of heads from the old men. Morality was strong amongst the impotent of the village.

She said nothing. What her uncle had said was true in its own way, so there was nothing she could say. She walked around him, without looking up into his face, and continued her hobbled flight towards the surrounding swamp. Almost blind with tears and sweat, she longed to lose herself in the tall grasses and hide from the watching faces that showed no sympathy and no pity, but the path seemed to go on forever

A group of half-naked boys followed her, taunting her. "Hey, Nona, where's your ma' now? Nona's going to get lost in the swamp. Nona's going to get her smart clothes all dirty."

The young boys grew in confidence as the village elders did not come to shoo them away. One of them picked up a stone and threw it at the departing figure of Yahyu but missed. More boys joined them as they gathered in a group and followed her more closely. Dancing down the pathway they yelled out the abuse they had heard from the elders, "Whore, slut." It was all good fun.

As Yahyu entered the swamp, there was no one to say goodbye; just the taunts and insults of the elders and the feigned indifference of the rest of the village. Nobody wanted to be seen consorting with a loose woman.She rushed on, blind to the future, but the boys would not leave her.

A stone hit Yahyu in the back and she started running, but the way was wet and slippery and the sun hot overhead. Between the tall grasses she glimpsed the dark forest that lay beyond the muddy waters but it looked so far away. She turned off the pathway and into the swamp, hoping to lose herself among the long grasses, but the mud was thick and it slowed her. She struggled to push forward but her sarong was tight around her legs and she could not run. The boys were relentless in their pursuit as they splashed joyfully behind her. One of them pushed her from behind and she fell.

"Go away. Leave me alone," she yelled, clutching her stomach with one hand as if to protect it while trying to ward off blows with the other.

The boys gathered around her, taunting and kicking. She tried to get up but they pushed her down again. "Look at her smart clothes.

Don't look so posh now she's all muddy, does she?" yelled one of the boys as he jumped in delight.

Yahyu looked desperately for an escape but the sun was bright overhead and sweat dripped into her eyes, distorting her vision. The boys appeared as vague shadows dancing in front of her like malevolent phantoms. "God, please help me," she cried towards the emptiness of the swamp.

As she struggled to get up, the boys suddenly let go and backed away, leaving her lying in the muddy waters. They gathered in a group under the shade of the grasses, quiet but expectant, throwing glances at her and sniggering. She looked down at herself. Her blouse was torn at the front and her sarong loose and dishevelled. She looked around in confusion while trying to hide her naked skin. She could not concentrate; everything was happening too quickly.

"Hi Yahyu," said a voice from the shadows, a voice of honey and menace. "So, you're running away. You got no ma' and pa' to look after you now. Maybe I can help you."

She turned towards the voice she knew well and saw her cousin smiling at her. She needed courage to face this new threat but her reserves were already low.

"Good day, Cousin Udin. Thank you for coming to help me. Please keep these boys away. I want to go." Her voice sounded strong but her knees shook as she tried to look up at him against the glaring sun.

"Where're you going, Yahyu? You haven't got nowhere to go now. You going to run after your belando boyfriend? I heard he dumped you. Expect he knew you was just a village tart. Nothing special about you now, is there? No point putting on them airs and graces, eh? Are us village lads not good enough for you anymore? You haven't got a family now. You haven't got any one. You're worse than a beggar. Maybe you need me."

Yahyu didn't need his words to know she could not trust him. He was not a good boy and he was too strong for Yahyu to handle but she needed his help.

She smiled modestly at Udin. "Thank you for coming to help me. Please take these boys back to the village and let me go on my way. I need to find another village before it gets dark." She stood still, watching him closely, waiting to see his response.

Udin smiled with his mouth but his eyes were devoid of emotion as he studied her. He's summing me up, working out how he can get me, she thought. I must be strong. Don't let him know I'm scared. Why can't they just leave me alone?

"You can't go into the forest. That's Komrin territory. They'll kill you or maybe they'll play with you first and then kill you after they had some fun. You know what they do to us migrants if they catch us. What're you going to do when they chase you, eh? You going to run back to the arms of your belando lover?" He looked at her, smiling and admiring her body. With a lopsided grin he asked, "You got any money hidden in them clothes you wearing?"

Yahyu sensed the danger. She saw Udin's angle of attack but she did not give up hope. She stood up straight and looked into his face while avoiding his eyes. "Cousin, you are a good boy; don't spoil it now. Just let me go. You're my cousin. We have the same grandmother. I know you won't harm me." She realised the hollowness of her statement. She had no mother or grandmother to protect her now and Udin knew it.

Udin turned to the boys and yelled, "Scat, get the hell out of here." The boys ran, giggling and laughing, but fearing Udin's anger. He turned back to face Yahyu, his eyes opening wide in a vacuous attempt to show his honesty, tempting her to trust him.

"Now, now my sweet, you know me. I'm your cousin; you can trust me. Your old man back in the village knows you got a belando kid in your belly and he wanted to marry you off to that old Chinaman. I'm not like that. I like you. I came to help you." He held out both hands, palms upwards in a gesture of peace and honesty, but the greater his efforts to appear sincere, the more she distrusted him. She tried to move away, step by step, but Udin followed her closely.

He placed a hand on her bare shoulder, an intimacy never attempted in the village, even amongst family. Yahyu felt him shaking. The palm was damp with sweat. She looked up at his face and recoiled at the sight of his smile twisting with suppressed desire.

"You got money stuffed in your bra. I know you women keep money in your bra; I saw my ma' doing it. I got money here too. Maybe I'll give it to you." Udin took a torn and dirty bank note from his trouser pocket. "Why don't I stuff this note in your bra? It will help you when you run from those Komrin bandits."

Yahyu backed away, her eyes flashing anger and fear. She turned away from him but he caught her around the waist and pulled her to him. With a pleading voice, he whispered in her ear, "Come on Yahyu, just let me put the money in your bra, then you go."

"Leave me alone," she screamed, trying to tear herself free, but he held her firmly. She dug her nails into his arm but his excitement protected him from pain.

"No one's going to hear you in this swamp. No point screaming.

Just come along with me for a bit. I'm not going to hurt you. Just a bit of fun and then you get the money. That's what you want, isn't it? It's what all you dancers want. Or do you prefer that foreign money from those belando bastards on the rubber plantation?"

Udin dragged her to the edge of the swamp, the sharp grasses cutting her bare legs. She stopped struggling; she wanted to protect her stomach. She didn't care much what happened to her but she must protect the baby from Udin and from everyone. She hoped that if she lay still he would be quick and would just go away when he was finished. But he was neither quick nor gentle.

No word was spoken that afternoon. Yahyu kept her eyes firmly shut and her body rigid. She wanted no movement, no expression, no action to excite Udin's passion or his anger. She just wanted him to finish but he wouldn't. He kept her, using her throughout the long, hot afternoon until she was shaking with exhaustion.

He left her in the evening lying beside the path, her clothes torn and dirty. He kept his face turned away as if shame had finally caught up with him. He said nothing as he quickly walked back down the path in the gathering dusk. His shame was not sufficient to persuade him to leave the banknote.

***

Her mind a blank, Yahyu lay beside the swamp, the wet mud cooling her bruised body. Above her she saw the tall, slender grasses against the moonlight, swaying gracefully with the gentle breeze. She felt nothing but numbness in her heart and a vague feeling of relief that it was over. Whenever she relaxed her grip and her mind flowed back to events of the afternoon, she felt a sickness arise from her stomach as she pictured the face of Udin close to her, his features distorted in ecstasy. She quickly slipped back into her stupor and stared passively at the beautiful grasses. Udin did not exist. He was a nightmare that would never be recalled.

With a sudden awakening, as if from a bad dream, Yahyu tried to get up, but her knees were weak and she slowly sank to the ground. She felt dirty; she must wash everything; clothes, body, hair, heart. She crawled towards the swamp, took off her clothes and slipped into the dark waters, oblivious to her surroundings, letting the warm, muddy water wash away the dirt and smell of him. She picked up some twigs and scrubbed her body as if scrubbing away the dirt would also scrub away the memory of him. Then she scrubbed herself harder and harder, not believing she could ever be clean. Only when her skin was stinging from the constant hard rubbing did she feel his presence was completely erased from her body.

As Yahyu slowly came back to reality, she realised she was alone and night had fallen. She had never been alone before; there had always been somebody to protect her, both in her village and in her dancing school; but now there was no one. She had longed to be alone while running from the village but now she found the loneliness terrifying, and it was dark.

Yahyu put on her wet clothes and crept slowly and silently back onto the path bordering the swamp. She held her breath as she moved, afraid the slightest noise would awaken the demons of the dark waters. She sat silently on the edge of the footpath with her head on her hands, not daring to look out at the darkness around her.

During the long night Yahyu could not sleep; she kept thinking about her mistake. Her life had seemed so straightforward, so wonderful. From her small village in the swamps of South Sumatra she had risen to the heights of her ambition. She had performed in the classical Ramayana ballet in the provincial capital of Palembang. This was achieved partly through her beauty and elegance but also through hard work and dedication at her dancing school. She was the envy of her class. She had enjoyed the adoration of the audience and all the luxuries that went with her newfound stardom. Then she left the path that was set for her and strayed into unknown territory. She was tempted by a young belando man who promised her love but left her pregnant and alone.

She felt she had betrayed her family. They had scraped and saved so they could pay for her dancing school. Everyone had gone without the few luxuries of village life so that she could succeed in her dancing career and now she had let them down in front of the whole village. She knew there was no going back now, but she must fight for survival until the birth. She would do nothing to harm the unborn baby.

Towards morning, as the sunlight dispersed the mists and gave her courage, she made her plans. I shall try to find my uncle in the goldfields of the Barisan Mountains. Maybe he is still there. If God forgives me, he will let me find him and find gold, and then my baby can live in luxury.

***

Yahyu hitched a ride on a cargo boat meandering its way slowly up one of the tributaries of the Musi River, carrying rice and dried fish for sale to the log fellers who worked in the swamp forests of the Komrin Ulu. The boat was managed by a family who claimed they never slept on land. The steersman, the nominal captain of the boat, was old, thin and toothless while his wife, who really controlled the boat, was large and friendly, with a face as wrinkled as a nut; the result of years looking upriver in the glaring sun. In return for the ride, she washed their clothes and cooked their meals as they slowly worked their way upriver.

Yahyu liked the river, although not the smell of diesel and fish that permeated the boat. In the afternoons, after washing clothes and cooking, she lay on the deck and dozed. She felt safe on the boat, away from the surrounding forest. She learnt to like the gentle chug, chug, chug of the small diesel engine as it drove the boat slowly against the lethargic current. Nothing seemed hurried on the river; the family that managed the boat lived life at the same pace as that of the river.

They were an uneducated crew and spoke mainly in their own tongue, but sometimes they spoke to her in broken Melayu (the lingua franca of the island). "Hey Nona, why have you got no man? You've got a nice face and pale skin, and you know how to cook. You'd make a good wife. Where's your man?" The old woman spat tobacco into the river after each hesitant sentence.

"Don't know Ibu. No man seems to like me much, and at the moment I prefer to be alone." Yahyu liked the old lady but did not want to encourage any conversation about men. She was too conscious of the baby in her womb and she wanted to avoid all reference to the cause of her flight.

"Ain't natural. A woman's got to be with a man, even if it's only an ugly old pig like my Pak here." The old woman pointed towards her husband at the tiller who looked up with a toothless grin.

"One day, Ibu. I want to find a prince first." Yahyu smiled to herself. In her ballet performances she had married a prince; if only that could come true.

The old lady turned to Yahyu and guided her to the prow of the boat, speaking quietly. "You won't find no princes on this stretch of the river; just leeches and mosquitoes. But you got a strange look about your face. I know what's wrong with you but I'm not going to make any fuss, don't worry. What happened to him, the man that done that to you?"

Yahyu looked shocked. There was no way the old woman could know about her pregnancy. Her stomach did not show at all. But these boat people were renowned for their skills in magic and the black arts, and it scared her.

"It's nothing. Please don't ask."

"Why not? Perfectly natural question. You go with a man and you get pregnant. I know, I've got nine of them; children that is, not men." She sniggered at her own joke. She was a large, friendly woman much taken to laughing and keeping everyone cheerful but she had little tact.

"How do you know I'm pregnant?" Yahyu asked.

"Not your stomach; it doesn't show there. It's your face, especially in the mornings. All us women on the boat notice. You can't fool us river folk. We may not be educated but we know a thing or two about folks."

Yahyu remained quiet, undecided whether to tell her story, but the woman continued her questioning. "What's wrong with being pregnant? Maybe your man left you. So what? You have the baby and then you find another man. With your good looks you'll get these river boys queuing up just to get a smile out of you."

Yahyu took the plunge. "He was a belando man and he left me. I was at dancing school. My father paid for it and he's a poor man. We are just migrants on this island. The school threw me out. Then my parents wanted to marry me off to a horrible old man so I ran away. I'm alone now."

The old woman looked thoughtfully at Yahyu's young, earnest face. "I suppose they regret the loss of money from your dancing. But all you got to do is have the baby, then find yourself another belando man. Make sure he's a good one this time. Then your family will love you again. For us river folk it don't make no difference; you can have as many men as you like and it just increases your value. It shows that men want you."

Yahyu looked doubtfully at the old lady; this wasn't how her village or her dancing school had reacted to the news of her pregnancy.

"I don't know, Ibu. My father and mother really worked hard for my dancing school and now everyone in the village is laughing at them, saying they were arrogant because they had such a beautiful daughter and now look what happened to me. I can't go home until I have enough money to restore my family's honour. I want to go to the mountains and find my uncle who is a gold miner. I can help him find gold and then I can repay my family back in the village."

The old woman snorted in derision. "No woman would go alone to those goldfields, let alone a pregnant one. They're dangerous places full of thieves and bandits. You stay with us. You can have your baby on this boat. All my children been born on this boat; over there, under the canopy. No problem for us."

Yahyu was tempted; she had found a potential family. But as

she looked at the simple face of the cheerful old woman, she realised the weight of her responsibilities. "Thank you Ibu, but I need to find money to help my family."

"Suit yourself, but we got ways of solving them problems. I can get some roots that will solve your problem once and for all, if you want it done that way. It's a bit painful but after a couple of hours it's all done. Then you can look for a new man."

"No, Ibu," Yahyu said angrily. "That's a sin. Please don't ever say that to me again."

"A sin against whom, Nona?"

"A sin against God. He will punish me even more."

"There're many gods on this river, some good and some bad. Maybe it was one of the bad ones that done that to you. You won't get a good man carrying that thing around in your stomach. Get rid of it and find yourself a new man and a new god."

***

They were travelling through a dreary stretch of forest as the sun sank below the treetops, casting long shadows across the muddy waters and shrouding the river banks in gloom. They were looking for a place to moor for the night when they came across several small boats tied to a tree on the river bank. These boats were smaller than the normal lumbering cargo boats Yahyu had seen on the river. They looked as if they were built for speed. Yahyu expected them to moor together for the night, but instead of steering towards them, the old man steered for the far bank while putting his finger to his mouth, motioning them to keep quiet as he tried to manoeuvre the boat silently past them.

"Stop," yelled a commanding voice from one of the moored boats. "Moor here. The forest gets thicker farther up river. You stay with us for the night."

The old man at the tiller looked at his family, a worried expression on his face. "I can't stop, Pak. I must go on; we're late." He tried to steer away from the moored boats, but the river was too narrow and he had to pass them closely.

"I told you to stop, old man," said the voice from inside the boat, as several young men came out of the cabin to see what was happening. One of them leapt the short distance onto their boat, took the tiller with a smile and allowed the boat to drift to the bank. "You stay with us, like the commander ordered," said the young man. He gave Yahyu a grin as he jumped back into his own boat.

Yahyu felt her heart sinking. She had been enjoying the uneventful life the river offered but this new development suggested their quiet journey was about to be disrupted.

***

The old lady told Yahyu to cook rice while the old man timidly invited the other boatmen to come and eat with them. The other boats' crew were a rough-looking group, clad in dirty shorts and tee shirts. They were all young men—no women or children amongst them—very different from the cargo boats they had met before. They spoke a strange language which the family on her boat had trouble understanding.

"Who are these people?" Yahyu whispered to the old lady.

"They're Batak, from up north," she whispered. "Be careful. They can be violent. I don't know what they're doing here; they don't usually come this far south. It's a bad omen when you see groups of Bataks coming south. It always means trouble."

While cooking dinner, Yahyu saw several of the men looking in her direction but their looks did not show friendliness or desire, just mild suspicion. She heard her name mentioned several times and the old man from her boat was arguing. She guessed it was about her but they did not approach her.

One of the men talked more than the others and everyone stopped to listen whenever he got up to speak. He looked different from the rest. He did not have their tough peasant faces or their easy-going manner. He was thin and wiry, and wore thick, round spectacles that gave him an owlish appearance, but his expression showed a rigid strength as if he was unwilling to reveal weakness. He read aloud from a pamphlet and everyone listened to him but Yahyu could not understand the language. Whatever he was saying, she did not want to get involved. She had her own troubles to think about. She kept close to her cooking stove and avoided meeting anyone's eye.

When the crew were getting ready for sleep, Yahyu clambered over the boats to get to the shore. She did not like sleeping in the boat. At night, with no wind blowing, the smell of fish was too much for her and made her feel sick. Better to sleep on the river bank, under the stars, covered by her sarong to keep out the mosquitoes but close enough to the boat so as not to be scared of the dark. She clambered onto the last boat where a small candle burned under the thatch roof of the cabin.

Suddenly there was a shout, "Stop, Nona, don't move." It was the man with the thick glasses shouting to her in Melayu. He leapt over the gap between the boats with great agility and grabbed her by the arm.

"Pak, don't. Pak, I'm not doing anything. I'm going to the river bank to sleep."

The man held her firmly by the wrist and pulled her back to his boat. "Sit and be quiet," he said.

After some discussion with the old couple from her boat he turned once more to Yahyu. "What are you doing here?"

"I'm going to find my uncle in the goldfields in the Barisan Mountains. I want to find gold."

The young men in the boat roared with laughter but the man with glasses kept staring at her.

"Anyone with such a stupid idea cannot be a threat to us. Do you know who we are?"

"No, Pak. How can I know who you are? I've never met you before and you haven't introduced yourself."

The young men laughed again but the tall man signalled them to be quiet. "My apologies. My manners are not always the best as I'm leading a rough life. You can call me Jon. This old man and his wife," he said, pointing to the family who owned her boat, "speak well of you. They say they don't know who you are. You just appeared out of the swamp and asked for a free ride but you are quiet and respectful and you work hard. Is that true?"

"I try my best, Pak. I don't want to cause any trouble."

"I think you are the one who will be in trouble if you go to the goldfields," said Jon. "And please don't call me Pak. I prefer to be called Jon." He smiled in a stiff and formal manner, as if smiling did not come naturally to him. He had deep lines engraved vertically down both cheeks and the lines had to be broken to allow a smile to appear.

Yahyu felt her fear subside as he continued to speak to her. He was a highly educated man and spoke Melayu fluently and with great power and eloquence which contrasted sharply with his austere appearance. Yahyu was more fascinated than scared; she had never met anyone like him before.

After staring at Yahyu for some time he said, "You are dressed like a pauper but you have the elegance and beauty of a Javanese princess; very interesting. There is some mystery attached to you, Nona. I don't know what it is but maybe I can guess. For some reason you are running away from family, from village, from lover, from debt. You are an outcast. Is that right?"

Yahyu thought carefully before answering. It was not her way to respond spontaneously to anyone, least of all to a man she hardly knew. She did not understand all the words he used but she felt his understanding of her plight putting her at ease. She was tempted to talk to him, but guardedly, at least at the beginning, until she knew more about him.

"Maybe you are right, Pak. Sorry, I mean Jon. Why don't you like being called Pak?"

"To understand that, you will need to know more about our movement. But I don't trust you yet and it may be better for you if you know nothing about us. There are great things happening in Java now. It will spread to Sumatra soon and then you will know who we are. We are not communists although we are close to them in many ways. We are fighting for you, Nona, and for these ignorant boatmen. One day you will all be free."

"Free from what?" Yahyu asked in surprise. She had found the freedom of the swamps terrifying and longed for the security of her family and village.

"Free from the landowners. Free from the corrupt officials and fat policemen. But I don't want to talk about me; I want to know about you. Why are you running away and where are you really running to? Can I trust you? You must speak honestly to me. I won't harm you. I often wonder if I am capable of harming anyone."

"I am sorry, but I don't want to tell you why I am running. I think I must be a bad person and God is punishing me." She looked down as she spoke, shame written over her face.

"There is no God," he interrupted sternly but seeing the shock on her face he softened his voice and smiled. "Please go on."

"I don't know where I'm going. Nobody wants to know me. I have no family now."

Jon sat quietly as she spoke, staring at her through his thick spectacles and mopping his sweating brow with a small, dirty towel that hung around his neck. Now and then he muttered, "Um, go on please," as she told him of her travels but she did not tell him of the circumstances under which she had left her village.

He was the first person she had spoken to about her adventures since running from her village, which seemed so long ago but in reality was only a few weeks. He was different from the other men she had known. He did not make judgements, he did not give vacuous advice and he was not trying to seduce her. He was trying to understand her and in so doing he gave her comfort.

When she finished her story he looked at her with sympathy. "You have not told me all, have you? There is some other deeper secret you are not revealing, but no matter. One day soon, after a great struggle, we will all be free to be ourselves. There will be no families. There will be no God. There will be no false morality. You will be my equal; you will be the equal of all men. But not yet. We still have far to go."

Yahyu wasn't sure if she approved of this kind of talk. She liked his interest in her and his sympathy for her plight, but she did not appreciate talk about no families and no God. She wanted to find out more about him but some of his ideas were frightening.

"What do you do? You are no fisherman. You seem so ... so educated. I don't understand all the words you use."

"Ha, education; it's a myth. It teaches you to obey, not to think. When I was young my father owned a small sugar plantation near Palembang. The workers travelled around the plantations selling their labour. Men, women, children, we hired them all and paid them only for the work they did. When there was no work, we pushed them out. I saw boys who fell ill being kicked out in case they infected the rest of the labour gang. It was awful, an injustice to mankind, and it was my father who was doing it."

Jon stopped talking and looked at the dark forest around them, his face drawn and haggard as if he was fighting alone against all the injustices of the world. Both his anger and his earlier animation had suddenly collapsed like a burst balloon. He sat limp and lonely on the side of the boat. He took a deep breath as if to gather strength for yet another trial but instead he spoke softly to Yahyu and, Yahyu noted with a twinge of excitement, he talked only to her.

"My ambition, when I was young, was to study and then to teach. I wanted to become a schoolmaster and teach all the children about the injustices of the world. My father sent me to college in

Padang to learn to be a schoolteacher. But what I learnt was that education taught people to obey, to accept what they are given, not to question, not to act. The worst were the religious teachers. 'God has decided,' they would say. Pah! God has decided what? That mothers should die in childbirth because they can't afford a doctor. I want education to teach people to think, to question, to act and to change the world. We must act to achieve freedom and that means we must fight and, sometimes, to kill."

He suddenly stopped his monologue. He looked at Yahyu and blushed as he realised how much of himself he had disclosed to this strange girl. But she did not want him to stop; she wanted to hear more about the injustices but not about struggles and killing people.

"Do you still teach? I think you would be a good teacher. You understand our problems. What are you doing now?"

"As you cannot tell me about your secret errand, then I also cannot tell you about mine," he said with a laugh.

"I don't fully understand you but I don't think you are a bad man. You want to do good things and to help poor people but killing is not good." Yahyu had strong feelings about good and bad and her conviction showed in her voice, for Jon looked at her with a gentle smile.

"No, killing is not good but sometimes it's better to kill one man than to allow that man to kill a hundred others. Life is not as simple as our religious teachers want us to believe. We have to make difficult choices sometimes and God is not always on the side of the innocent. If one day I am called upon to kill for the cause, I hope I will have the strength to do so." He fell silent, holding his knees close to his chest and looking into the dark river.

When he spoke she felt he was allowing her to glimpse into a different world. Or perhaps it was the same world but looked at differently; she wasn't sure. He made it all seem so simple, so obviously good. She moved to his side of the boat and sat close to him, encouraging him to confide more of his dreams to her. The other men had either gone to sleep or moved away from their leader. They were more interested in action and sex, neither of which looked promising from this private conversation.

Yahyu felt a stirring of her young, unformed emotions. No man had ever shared an ideal or a feeling with her before. It was new and it was exciting. In her village, relationships were about family unions and the bringing up of children. Her relationship with the young belando man had been based on sexual curiosity, as she now understood. But Jon seemed to offer something different. At that moment Yahyu did not care about her problem. She just wanted to prolong the moment of intimacy with this man who was so driven by ideas of justice.

"Enough of me," he said. "You have problems of your own, I can see that. What are you going to do? You can't go to the goldfields alone. There is no quick way to make money there unless you are a thief or a prostitute, and you are neither. Those goldfields are dangerous for lone women. I go there often; the gold funds our cause."

***

The boats stayed together for several days, winding their laborious way upstream. During the daytime Jon stayed on his own boat, but every evening he leapt over the side of Yahyu's boat and spent long hours talking to her about the injustices of the world, until they both climbed slowly up the river bank and fell asleep under one of the dark trees, side by side but never touching. Jon was proving to be a man of principle and iron will.

On their final evening together he took Yahyu to the river bank where they sat on a fallen tree trunk, looking at the fireflies as they danced their way over the dark river. Yahyu felt excited; something was about to happen. She could sense the tension in Jon, as if he was wrestling with a problem or a decision that he could not make. Whatever it was, she must be ready and equal to the task. She wanted to earn his respect in her own Javanese way, through staying calm, alert and in control; she would not give in to any spontaneous emotions.

Jon turned towards her. "Yahyu, you understand nothing of our cause or our work, yet I feel you are one of us. You understand with your heart, even if your head has yet to catch up with it. You are already an outcast so you have nothing to lose. Why don't you join us?"

This was not quite what she expected. She was not sure what she had expected but it was not this. She had listened to Jon for many hours and was fascinated by him and his ideas, although his intensity frightened her. It was as if he wanted to crush all the injustices of the world in one go. However, he was never frivolous, hence Yahyu was sure his offer was serious and would have been made only after much deliberation. She thought carefully before answering. She was tempted to say yes, but ... there was one obstacle which she could not overcome: she could not ignore the baby in her womb.

"If I were a man I would join you, but I am just a woman. I can't fight," she said.

He looked at her strangely before continuing. "Don't misunderstand me. I have a proposal to make which you may not like, but don't be offended. I am a straight man, if also a desperate one. These are difficult times for some of us and opportunities for friendships rarely arise." He stopped, as if to test her reaction.

"Go on, you can ask me anything. I can always say no."

"I need a woman," he said directly, although she detected a fleeting look of embarrassment on his stern face.

Yahyu was shocked. She had been expecting something a little more romantic than this. As she started to protest, he held up his hand to stop her.

"Quietly, Yahyu, hear me out before you run off to your goldfields and become so rich you forget all about me. I need a woman, yes, but not here and not now; I'm not an animal. I need a woman as a partner in my struggle, not just in my bed; a woman who supports the cause and will fight beside me. I lead a solitary life. It's hard and it's dangerous but not as dangerous as going alone to the goldfields. Why don't you join me? You can leave me whenever you like. I don't believe in marriage. I can see from your situation you are really one of us. You are also on the run from something. You don't fit in any more and neither do I. You can fight with us, fight with me, by my side." He looked at her with passion in his eyes but she could not judge if that passion was for her or for his cause.

Yahyu sat cross-legged on the ground, thinking. She was slow and deliberate in her thoughts but she was astute enough to realise that Jon was as awkward with women as she was ignorant of men, and he was probably using "the cause" to hide his embarrassment. This was a proposal of sorts and she recognised it as such and wanted to respond with as much delicacy as her immature heart could manage.

There were many implications for Yahyu to consider and her sheltered young life had not given her the experience to judge such novel situations, but she was learning fast and found the novelty refreshing. Most of the men she had met had appealed to her vanity and offered her gifts and tokens of affection. Jon was different; he was offering an affair full of blood and toil that would free mankind. Was this any more stupid than her plan to go to the goldfields? She was tempted again to say yes; what did she have to lose that she had not already lost? But she had not told him of her true situation and, if she did, he might not want her anymore. Also, the future baby bore heavily on her mind and her conscience; it could never go away and she would do nothing to harm the baby. She wanted to give the baby a good start in life, to make up for the guilt she felt about bearing the child.

"You have made me a proposal and I can see it is an honest one. I don't object; I take it as a compliment in its own way. I admire you and your cause. I think you are a wonderful man, perhaps the most wonderful man I am ever likely to meet. In any other circumstances I would like to follow you and be with you, but in my present condition I would just slow you down. I also have a mission to complete; a personal mission. It's a different sort of mission to yours and if you knew what it is you might not want me anymore. Better we part as friends for I must complete my mission alone. But if in the future we ever meet again, maybe it would be different."

She got up as if to go but lingered by the tree, hoping and praying he would call her back, and he did.

"Don't go. You don't have to decide now. Just stay close to me tonight. I need you. Tomorrow I have to do something that I don't want to do and it scares me."

"You, scared? I don't believe it."

"Don't misunderstand me. I'm not scared of death and I'm not scared of pain. I am scared of failure; failure to live up to my ideals, failure to act when I know it's right. Tomorrow I leave the river. I go on foot for many miles to complete my mission. This mission is not dangerous. To my comrades in the boat it's like a picnic. They don't care as long as they get food and drink. But for me it's a test, and I don't know if I can pass the test. In a few days I shall have to kill the god inside me if I am to complete my task. Do you understand what I am saying?"

Yahyu felt uncomfortable with talk about killing God but at the same time she felt Jon reaching out for her support and it thrilled her. She felt he was trying to reveal himself to her as a real human being, full of doubts and fears, whilst desperately trying to hold himself under control, determined to see through his task. This was a different feeling to the one she felt when she had been tempted by the belando man in the rubber plantations; this was an appeal for her emotional support as a woman.

"I don't understand what you have to do, but I think I understand you. You have to do something terrible to achieve your aim. Whatever it is, I know it's a good aim because you are a good person."

"If you knew what I am about to do, you would probably not want to know me anymore," he said.

Yahyu smiled at him, "And if you knew my situation, you might not want to know me anymore."

"I have to kill," he said. His face took on a haunted look, reflected darkly in the light from the lantern.

During the night they slept on the river bank but Jon was restless. He turned and twisted in his disturbed sleep until Yahyu got up and made him tea. She sat quietly next to him as he looked into the river, muttering words about fear and duty. Yahyu was lost for words but she sensed that her presence next to him was a comfort against his loneliness. She was so concerned for his problems that she forgot her own in her delight at being able to help another person. She sat next to him, holding his hand, until sleep once more overcame them.

***

As Yahyu's boat was being prepared for departure in the morning, Jon went up to her and spoke quietly, "You look out for me in the goldfields. I will use Curup as my base in the mountains and you may be able to find me there. You have a difficult journey ahead of you and I wish you luck. Hope to see you again one day."

He jumped out of her boat and she watched him climb the river bank followed by the young men with rifles slung from their shoulders. She knew he was hurrying so as to hide his embarrassment or perhaps to help her hide hers. Before they disappeared into the forest he turned to look at her once more and waved.

Chapter 2

"Hey, Nona," called the old women on the boat. "We're coming to a village. Do you want to get off?"

Yahyu was not prepared. She had been purposefully avoiding facing the decision of where and when to leave the boat and continue her journey to the goldfields. She liked the river and didn't want to leave the security of the simple family. "What sort of village is it, Ibu?" she asked.

"Komrin, of course. This is Komrin Ulu country."

Yahyu froze. She looked at the old woman sitting calmly on the side of the boat, biting on her betel nut with dark red teeth and spitting into the placid river. She seemed calm enough, but Yahyu remembered the terrifying tales told in her village of what the forest-dwelling Komrin did to Javanese migrants when they caught them. Most of them were bandits and they did not like intruders in their territory.

The old woman laughed. "What're you afraid of? We're Komrin too; we're Komrin Ilir and we haven't eaten you yet although one of those young Batak men last night said he wouldn't mind getting a taste of you.

"You want to go west," the old woman continued, "towards the mountains. We go north later, up towards Jambi. You get off at the next village and walk west."

Yahyu detected a note of warning in the old woman's voice, as if she didn't want any argument. She felt the smile on her face slowly disappear as the full realisation of the woman's statement hit her. She sat dejectedly on the side of the boat looking down at her feet while the family went about their business, pointedly ignoring her despair or perhaps hiding their embarrassment. Her recent boost of confidence, almost elation, resulting from her closeness to Jon suddenly evaporated as she realised she would once again be alone and she didn't like being alone. She guessed they were afraid of Jon and his armed group and wanted to be rid of any association between themselves and Jon's mission.

She regretted her bravado of the previous evening when she had rejected Jon's offer of companionship. It had seemed such an easy, almost noble thing to do at the time; to give preference to her baby and to the needs of Jon above her own needs. It was easy because she felt comfortable on the boat with the simple river folk to talk to. She had not thought beyond the following day.

She sat thinking, in her slow but deliberate way, about the problems of surviving without a family. Friends weren't like family; they came and went and there was no commitment, no loyalty, no togetherness. She wished she had accepted Jon's offer because they could at least have pretended to be married.

"OK Nona, you ready to leave now?" The old woman spoke kindly but firmly as her husband tethered the boat to a rotting wooden pier on the edge of the village of Talang Basah.

Yahyu looked around her at the now-familiar scene but the boatman avoided her gaze. Although she had only been on the boat for a week, she had grown to think of it as home. It was hard to part company with this happy, easy-going family. She meekly picked up her small bundle of clothes and followed the old lady onto the pier.

Yahyu walked gingerly into the village. The reputation of the Komrin Ulu was truly terrifying; they were fierce warriors as well as black magicians, but no one in the village seemed to notice her or even to look in her direction. She wasn't sure how to take it. It was like she was invisible. In her own village, if anyone new arrived, everyone came to see them and hoards of children would follow them everywhere. But here … there was nothing.

Talang Basah was a typical Komrin village of large wooden houses, big enough for several generations to live together, built on stilts ten feet above the ground. Livestock were kept under the houses during the dry season, and during the wet season the stilts kept the houses above water level. They were crowded together around three or four main streets which, at this time of year, were muddy but passable. During the rainy season, visits between houses had to take place by canoe.

They stopped by a small tea stall tucked under someone's house and the old lady said something to the stall owner, who motioned Yahyu to sit down and brought her tea. Yahyu looked around, feeling insignificant and scared. No one talked to her and nobody seemed to even care that she was there. She sipped her tea while trying to think of what she should do. She couldn't stay in this strange place where no one talked.

"Ibu, excuse me, can you tell me the way to the mountains, please?" Yahyu asked the stall owner but her words fell on deaf ears. The owner continued washing glasses, avoiding Yahyu's eyes.

"What's going on?" she whispered to the old lady from the boat. "Why are they ignoring us? You're a Komrin. Why don't you talk to them?"

"You don't understand us yet. I'm from the river; these folks are from the forests. We talk similar but we're different. They don't trust me anymore than they trust you. They know I'm river folk from my accent and they know you're a stranger from your face. Also, you've got class and it shows. They'll be wary of you at first. But don't worry, all Komrin are kind to strangers and they won't hurt a woman, as long as she behaves.

"Not many Javanese girls as pretty as you would ever dare come near these places. Come to think of it, no girl, pretty or not, would ever travel this area alone. They don't understand you and, to be honest, we don't understand you either. They probably think you're a witch. You certainly bewitched that Batak commander. We're a bit scared of you too, now, after Jon. But the forest Komrin are scared of witches, so you can use that to your advantage."

The lady got up to go.

"No, Ibu, stay with me please. Don't go. I don't know what to do."

"Sorry Nona, we've got to go. The river is like that, always moving. It's not like you farmers who stay in one place. We'll meet again if you ever come by this river. I spent my life on the river. I know every bend, every current and every tree along the whole length of it. We river folk can never stay still; it's not in our nature. Our home is not the boat, it's the river.

"Goodbye and may the gods help you. I expect you'll need it if you go to those goldfields."

The old lady said something to the stallholder before turning her back on Yahyu and walking away. After only a few paces, however, she hesitated and turned back towards Yahyu. With a look of embarrassment she said, "We're poor people, we haven't got much and we can't help every witch that comes our way, even one as beautiful as you. I've given this stall owner enough money to feed you tonight and tomorrow. Rice and fish she promised to give you, and tea, so make sure you get it all. And my ugly pig of a husband has gone all soft on you and wanted to give you this. It's not much but it's all we have. It was woven by his sister a few years ago."

She handed Yahyu a small, shiny green scarf inlaid with gold thread. It looked beautiful as it glistened in the late afternoon sunshine. Yahyu loved beautiful clothes and took the present with a broad smile on her face and put it around her shoulders. "How do I look?" she said.

The old lady looked embarrassed and turned away. The lady behind the stall, who had been watching them intently, smiled to herself and then looked away also.

Yahyu felt uncomfortable. "Why Ibu, what's the matter?"

"I expect such a beautiful girl as you to be accustomed to looking in mirrors and things like that. You got a beautiful face and beautiful pale skin. There's no denying it. But your clothes; they're all torn and you look like a beggar. And that scarf is so beautiful on you, makes me feel sad to see you so down on your luck. You must have been a real beauty when you were all made up."

The old lady turned abruptly and walked away, back to her boat and her river, leaving Yahyu alone in the strange village of witches and silent ghosts.

***

Yahyu ate her meal quietly. People walked by as if she did not exist. There were no greetings but also no insults. However, whenever she looked up quickly from her bowl of rice, she could see faces staring at her from open windows but they quickly withdrew. The local people were curious but were either too well-mannered or too scared to approach her. She tried to engage the stall owner in conversation but she either did not understand or did not want to speak. She smiled back at Yahyu in a bland, inscrutable way but said nothing. But neither did she leave Yahyu alone.

A large, middle-aged woman came bustling up to her, dressed in normal Komrin fashion of tight sarong and even tighter blouse. She sat opposite Yahyu, quietly waiting until she had finished her rice.

"Hello Ibu," Yahyu said as deferentially as her rice-filled mouth would allow.

"Eat your rice first, Nona. Then we talk." The lady spoke in good Melayu but with a thick accent which Yahyu had difficulty in catching.

Once the large woman had established herself opposite Yahyu, a number of children plucked up courage to gather around and people stared more openly from their windows. Yahyu found it embarrassing to eat her food in front of the gathering audience; she coughed on some mouthfuls and spat out others. Each morsel of rice accidentally dropped was greeted by sighs followed by comments in their own language which Yahyu could not understand. Wish they would stop staring, Yahyu said to herself, forgetting her previous desire to be noticed.

"Why are you here, Nona? Why did you choose to come to this village at this time?" said the large lady once Yahyu had finished eating.

"Excuse me Ibu, my name is Yahyu."

The lady looked shocked. "Please don't tell me your name. I don't need to know it. I'm not your mother. Where are your father and mother and brothers? Why are you travelling alone? I'm the headman's wife. I need to know."

"I am pleased to meet you, Ibu. It is kind of you to talk to me. I have no father or mother."

The lady looked more confused. "No father or mother? Then how did you come into this world? Has that Ilir woman brought us a witch?"

"I had a father and mother once, but not now. I'm an orphan." Yahyu justified her lie with the thought that she was really an orphan in all but name.

"There are no orphans here; everyone's got family. You're strange, you look young and pretty and you walk like a princess. We all saw that when you came into our village, but you're dressed like a beggar. We don't like strange things happening in this village and you're strange. Are you looking for a husband?"

"No, it's nothing like that. I'm just passing through. I want to get to the mountains so I can find gold."

"Gold." The lady looked up sharply and stared at Yahyu for several long seconds. "Hey, Ibu Bida, Ibu Nin, come here," she called to her friends who came quickly enough. They talked together in their own language before the headman's wife turned back to Yahyu.

"How're you going to find gold? Have you got something special, some sort of magic compass?"

Yahyu felt confused. She hadn't even begun to think about how she would find gold. She thought her uncle would show her. "I don't know yet, but I'm usually quite lucky. If God wants me to find gold, then he will lead me to it."

The three ladies looked darkly at Yahyu, which rather scared her. "What God are you referring to?" one of them said.

"Oh, Allah I suppose. If he is kind to me he will let me find gold."

"And why should he be kind to you? What have you done to deserve God's special attention?"

Yahyu felt out of her depth. "I've done nothing special. I just want to find gold. Maybe I shall be lucky."

The women looked at her suspiciously and Yahyu realised they probably thought she really was a witch from the swamp or the forest or the river.

"How long you want to stay in our village?" the headman's wife asked.

"Just one night, if I may. Then I want to go west, towards the mountains. Can you show me the way?"

The ladies talked again in their own language.

"You may sleep here, behind this stall tonight. In the morning we shall give you some rice to see you on your journey." With that they left her to sleep alone on a bamboo mat under the house. She could hear the family above talking and laughing and she could smell their food cooking but they did not bother her.

In the morning, as she was getting ready to leave, the headman's wife came up to her holding a bundle of banana leaves containing cooked rice and fish. "Go well, Nona. Don't think badly of us. We don't understand you and we don't like strange things happening in our village but we don't wish any harm to you. We will pray for you tonight. Now, please go."

All the Komrin villages were similar. They were not at all hostile, not like she had been told in her village. The villagers seemed to understand hard luck and accepted it as a part of life. They were kind to her in a rather casual way. She was never attacked, boys never threw stones at her, and no one made dirty comments about her. But at the same time she was never a part of them. She was not a member of any family hence she was not really a person at all. They gave her some rice but otherwise left her alone. She was something from the forest and she would eventually go back to the forest of her own accord. There was no need to bother her or be bothered by her. Towns, however, were different.

***

After several weeks walking through the forests and villages of the Komrin Ulu, Yahyu arrived at the small market town of Muaraklingi. Towns were always a problem; she didn't know why. She quickened her pace, hoping to get back to the countryside without attracting too much attention. People stared at her and moved aside as she walked down the side of the street. She felt conspicuous and uncomfortable. She looked at the ground and hurried on, but her weakness for beautiful clothes got the better of her and she was tempted by the bright lights in the shop windows.

She lingered outside the clothes shops, looking at the hand-woven silks in bright greens and blues with thin threads of gold and silver that glittered in the neon lighting. She forgot herself in her delight. It was like being back in her dancing school choosing her costume for the next performance. But when she raised her head, she saw a disgusting scarecrow of a woman looking out at her from inside the shop. She was wearing ragged clothes and her face was gaunt and lined with dirt.

I'm going mad, she thought. I must be seeing ghosts? She looked again into the shop window and the figure was still there, staring out at her. She scratched her head and moved to one side but the figure in the window followed her as if copying her every movement. She gave a stifled scream and clutched her handkerchief to her mouth. The figure in the window was her own reflection; the wretched scarecrow was herself.

My god, she thought, it can't be me. She put her hands to her face and saw the scarecrow in the window acting a mocking reflection of her. Yahyu slowly caressed her cheeks, feeling the sunken cheekbones and the greasy skin. Her eyes still shone brightly but they only served to highlight the gaunt and grimy appearance of her face. She looked down at her clothes: they were relatively clean but torn and badly repaired. Her hands were clean but her nails ragged and dirty and she was barefoot. Now I know why people stare at me. How can I have sunk this low?

Her knees felt weak and she began to stagger. She went to the gutter, sat down and put her head in her hands, oblivious to the stares and comments of the passersby. A peasant women dropped a coin in her lap saying in a quiet voice, "Poor dear", and moved on quickly, not wanting to be seen associating with a dirty tramp.

A couple of policemen lounging in a nearby coffee stall wandered over. "Hey, beggar girl, move on. You're not wanted here. You can't hang around this town. Move on, unless you want to give us a bit of fun first." The two policemen laughed as they moved behind her, enjoying the admiring stares of the passersby. With eyes hidden behind dark glasses, fat stomachs bulging over pistol belts, they exuded power and casual violence.

The girl didn't notice them. She held her head in her hands, looking at the ground, silently sobbing.

One of the policemen pushed her with his foot. "Beggar girl, get out before we arrest you. You know travellers in this town have to pay a tax. Give us your begging money and then get out of town and back to the forest where you belong."

Yahyu slowly came to her senses. She looked up and saw the eyeless policemen staring down at her. She knew their type; they were simple but dangerous. She must not antagonise them. She forced saliva to drip down her chin and giggled quietly to herself as she squatted in the gutter.

"You're not pissing in our streets, you animal," said one of the policemen. "Get out."

Maintaining her idiotic grin, Yahyu got up and moved slowly down the street. The policemen followed her every move with their eyes. Idiot policemen, she thought, they're easy to fool. But she was careful not to sway her hips as she walked. She increased her pace through the main street, longing for the solitude of the dark forests that surrounded the small town. She needed a quiet stream where she could wash her clothes and her body, somewhere where nobody would see her. She saw the end of the main street and began to breathe more easily, relaxing her pace, but her luck did not hold.

On the outskirts of the town Yahyu came to a mosque. It was Friday; prayer day. The men had finished their prayers and were wandering into the street, carrying prayer mats over their shoulders and chatting to each other. There were no women. This situation, she sensed, was dangerous. Men fresh from prayers tended to be in a state of righteousness and her situation was not one likely to attract much sympathy. She started to cross the road, hoping to avoid confronting or provoking them, but in her rush she crashed into a cyclist and they both fell to the ground in a clatter, tomatoes spilling over the road like blood.

Yahyu got up with the help of the cyclist, a peasant man who had been carrying tomatoes to market.

"Nona, your nose is bleeding. Here, have this towel," he said, holding a dirty rag to her nose. "And be careful," he glanced at the young men watching them from the entrance of the mosque, "your blouse is ripped. They're looking at you."

Either the blood and dirt on Yahyu's face or her bare shoulder showing through the rip in her blouse antagonised some of the young men, one of whom came up to her. "Cover yourself, you disgusting tramp," he said in a voice loud enough to be heard by his friends. "You are passing a house of prayer. Have you got no respect?"

His friends joined him in the middle of the road as he lectured her about respect for God and the modesty of women but he did not speak nicely. He was not really speaking to her at all. Yahyu knew they would not touch her as that would be immoral but they could insult her and they could throw stones. It was the stones she feared most. She had been stoned several times in the past few weeks and it always hurt. The insults she could take.

"Why've you got no father or brother to protect you? Why are you travelling alone? Are you a whore? Whores aren't allowed outside our mosque. Maybe we should beat you, teach you to dress properly, teach you to respect authority."

She stood in the middle of the crowd, trying to stop the blood from her nose dripping onto her blouse, while looking for an easy escape from the young zealots who lacked any sympathy for her or her injuries.

The cyclist bobbed his head respectfully at the righteous young man and spoke to him in a language Yahyu could not understand. The young man looked arrogantly away from him, as if a peasant was of no concern to a religious man like himself.

The peasant turned to Yahyu, speaking quietly, "Just walk slowly with me to the edge of town. I have a farm there. You can stay with my wife for the night. You'll be alright there. I can't go into town now; my tomatoes are all broken. Walk behind me."

The young men seemed disappointed that Yahyu had found a protector, even if he was just an uneducated peasant, but their moral righteousness remained unsatisfied. They lingered in the road watching the man as he picked up his buckled bicycle and Yahyu collected the few unbroken tomatoes. They were acting out a scene as the moral guardians of the town, ensuring the dangers of people like Yahyu would not defile their brothers and sisters. One or two of them, Yahyu noticed, were paying great attention to her bare shoulder.

"Me help, me help," shouted a voice from the roadside. "Me carry tomatoes for Nona."

The young men turned their attention to a new figure of fun who was jumping up and down by the roadside. He was a youngish man dressed in a filthy, torn military jacket, probably a Japanese army jacket, and torn trousers that only came down to his knees. His hair was long, matted and filthy, and decorated with bits of paper and chicken feathers. He waved the scabbard of a Japanese army sword above his head as he danced around the young men, shouting and singing.

"Ha ha, me help Nona," he said, pointing at Yahyu as he danced in delight. "Nona my sister, I pick up Nona's tomatoes. Nona be my friend?"

The young men roared with laughter. "What a pair: the beggar girl and the village idiot. What an excellent couple. Why don't they get married?"

The peasant man with the bicycle looked at Yahyu and said simply, "They're going to turn nasty soon. I think it's time to go. I don't know who this strange man is but I think he means trouble. Try to ignore him."

As she moved away slowly, the strange man caught hold of Yahyu's torn blouse and pulled her back saying, "Nona, take me too. I help Nona." She cringed at the thought of being touched by him, but she thought with some dread that he may have recognised in her someone of a similar situation to himself and was clinging to her as an ally.

She had no option but to follow the peasant man while the strange new man followed her, holding on to her torn blouse. The young men could not resist the temptation of humiliation. They followed behind, shouting, "Look at the bride and groom. What a beautiful couple. Let's escort them on their honeymoon."

Yahyu expected the stones to fly, so she kept her head low, with shoulders hunched, but instead of stones she heard the sound of a motorcycle and the young men fell silent. She kept on walking, following the peasant man and hoping that whatever was happening behind them would have nothing to do with her. The strange man, however, whimpered and grabbed Yahyu's hand. She could feel him trembling. She looked behind and saw the two policemen get off their motorcycle and walk up to them.

"OK you two, that's enough trouble. You're going to jail for the night, then we shall see what our chief does to you tomorrow. You could be dangerous rebels in disguise."

The strange man screamed, "No hit me, please, no hit me. I help you. I help girl. I help everyone. Please don't hit me." He grew crazier with fear as he knelt on the ground to hide his face in Yahyu's sarong.

"This couple stink like a shit house," said one of the policemen. "Don't think I fancy having any fun with this one, do you? I'd probably die from the smell." They both laughed as they handcuffed Yahyu to her newfound friend.

"Hey you, come here," said one of the policemen walking over to the peasant who had been trying to quietly move away but his broken bicycle had prevented him. "You're causing a public disturbance. Give me your money." He held out his hand.

The peasant bobbed his head humbly. "Sorry Pak, I have no money. I'm just a poor farmer. I can't even sell my tomatoes. They're all broken." He looked at the ground as he spoke, trying not to provoke the policeman into anger or violence.

"Don't lie to me. Give me what you've got, or else you come to jail with this pair of lovers. Maybe you're in league with them too, eh?"

"Pak, I have a few tomatoes left. You're welcome to them. Please take them home to your wife."

"Tomatoes," said the policeman contemptuously but he took them all the same.

As the couple were led away to the police station Yahyu saw the impotence on the face of the peasant man. He'd done his best to help her and had suffered as a result. She found enough courage to offer him a quick smile of appreciation as she was pushed from behind by the police. The young men jeered once more as the two policemen walked past them, showing off their prisoners. "Well done," they shouted to the policemen. "Teach the unbelievers to respect authority."

At the police station, Yahyu and the man were thrown into the same cell. It was barred at one end and looked straight onto the guard's table where a group of policemen were playing cards and smoking. The cell was sparsely furnished with a wooden shelf for a bed and a stinking bucket at one end. There was some ancient graffiti on the walls giving pornographic messages. Mosquitoes and flies flitted around the cell, getting in their eyes and up their noses.

How much lower can I sink, thought Yahyu. I make just one error in my life, just one mistake, and suddenly everything goes bad. This is a bad world. God does not forgive; he just punishes. Jon said God does not exist and I hope he's right.

The strange man squatted in a corner of the cell and looked at

Yahyu in despair while quietly jabbering to himself and scratching his chest. Yahyu did not fear him. She pitied him while also realising how close she was to his disgusting situation. She felt the need to be strong because failure was too horrible to contemplate. It could mean ending up like this strange, demented man, and that was not the way to bring a new life into the world. She must find the courage to get out of this situation and get enough money to ensure the baby would have a future.

She consciously adopted the pose of Sita, whom she played in the ballet. She sat cross-legged, arms resting on her knees with thumbs and middle fingers together, alert and in control of herself. The thought of Sita gave her strength and comfort. She was a better person than these fat pigs of policemen and she must never give in to them.

"What is your name, Pak?" Yahyu asked her fellow prisoner quietly and respectfully.

He looked at Yahyu as if he did not understand the question, but he crawled over and squatted beside her.

She tried again, "Pak, what is your name please?"

He looked at her again and then looked at the ground, scratching his head. "My name is …". He stopped and scratched his head again. Hesitantly, as if unsure of his facts, he said, "My name Rusdi, I think. My mama called me Rusdi. Maybe that's my name." He fell quiet as if deep in thought.

"That's a nice name. Brother Rusdi I shall call you," said Yahyu. "What are you doing in this town, brother Rusdi, and where were you going?"

"Want to find Da'eut. Nona nice lady. Help Rusdi find Da'eut."

"I don't understand, brother. Where is Da'eut, or what is it? I've never heard of it."

Rusdi looked confused. "Everyone wants to go to Da'eut. Everyone happy there. Rusdi's mama in Da'eut."

Yahyu did not understand, but she wanted to give her cellmate some comfort so she replied, "When we get out of here, I shall try to help you find Da'eut."

To her surprise, Rusdi jumped up and danced, laughing and singing words that Yahyu could not understand. He was deliriously happy.

"Stop that fucking row, you pair of lovers," yelled one of the police guards.

Rusdi started to shake again and saliva dribbled down his chin. He squatted on the floor, hiding his face in Yahyu's sarong. "Don't let them hit me Nona, please don't let them hit me."

As the policeman unlocked the cell door, Rusdi screamed and ran to the end of the cell, cowering behind the toilet bucket. The policeman went up to him and kicked him hard in the groin. "Now shut up, you little shit." Rusdi lay still on the floor, holding his groin, quietly moaning.

The policeman looked at Yahyu. "You little slut, you keep that bastard quiet or you'll get the same as him. Understand?"

Throughout this violence Yahyu kept her poise, sitting cross-legged on the filthy shelf, showing no expression on her face although her heart was pumping fast. "Yes Pak, I understand. He is afraid of you. If you talk to him kindly he will not cause you any problems."

The policeman looked confused when faced with such politeness. "Better be careful with that girl," he said to his colleague when he got back to the card table. "Might be something funny going on. That girl's not normal. Could be an agent in disguise. Better wait till the chief comes back next week."

In the meantime, Yahyu and Rusdi remained in forced company, locked in the tiny cell. Police cells gave no food to prisoners. Those who had family were fed by them after paying a small bribe to the guard on duty. Those who had no family and no friends starved. By the second day Yahyu became desperate; Rusdi seemed to lack the energy to get up and she was feeling faint from lack of food. She called out to the police guard, "Pak, we're hungry. You can't keep us here without food forever. You must have pity."

"You got money, you get food. You got no money, you get no food. You expect me to buy your food for you? Bloody tart. You and your crazy lover can starve."

***

The police chief arrived the next day; a young Javanese officer. He looked in the cell and laughed, "What's this pair of lovers doing here? In God's name, what a stink. Why don't you chuck them out and clean out these cells," he said to the guard.

"Something funny about this girl, Pak. Don't know what it is. She's dressed bad, looks bad, smells bad, but she talks good. Thought it best I keep them for you to look at, Pak."

"Quite right," said the officer as he walked over to the cell.

"Hey, beggar girl, what're you doing here with that crazy lover of yours?" he said, pointing at Rusdi. "And why are you sitting like that? Think you're someone special?"

Yahyu spotted her chance. She recognised his aristocratic Javanese accent and she could reply in the same way. She was probably better trained in Javanese culture than he was. She adopted a calm pose and addressed him respectfully. "Pak, I don't know this man, but he is harmless. I don't know why I am here. I have done nothing wrong."

The officer was amused and curious. Her torn clothes and dirty face did not match the politeness of her voice or the elegance of her hand movements. But the officer had been in the police force for some years and knew how to break down resistance, whereas Yahyu was still new to the game.

"Bring her to my office," he said abruptly to the guard who handcuffed Yahyu and pushed her into the officer's office.

"Why the hell you put the cuffs on the girl? You afraid of a bit of skirt," he said to the police guard. "Take them off now and don't be so bloody stupid. She's not going to attack you. Maybe you're afraid she's going to rape you. A fat bastard like you, no such luck." The policeman did as he was told and sullenly stood to attention, glaring at the back of the girl.

"Sit down and talk," ordered the officer as he sat opposite her, staring directly at her face.

Yahyu looked back at him but with her face lowered. He was young, smart, and with the fine features and long, thin nose of the Javanese aristocrat. He was obviously educated and maybe he was not a bad man. She presumed the officer would respond to good manners, so she sat quietly but said nothing. She thought to avoid any reference to her reason for running away. Any suspicion of her pregnancy would suggest she was a loose girl and she had learnt from bitter experience that she must never approach that subject with any man.

"Where are you from?" he said to her.

"I am from Palembang, Pak" she replied.

"Where are you going?"

"I want to find my uncle. He's working in the goldfields in the mountains."

"Why have you come to this town?"

"Just passing through. I want to get to Curup and the goldfields."

"Why?" the officer asked sharply.

"There's gold there. I want to find my uncle and be rich," she said.

The officer relaxed and laughed. "Nona, they will kill you. All the scum of the islands go to those goldfields. Some go to dig gold, some to steal from those who have found it and others to steal from those who have already stolen it. It's dangerous and it's no place for a woman unless you are a whore and, if I judge you correctly, you are no whore. But quite what you are I don't know yet." He sat back in his chair, relaxed but vigilant. Not much would escape his watchful eye.

"What's your relationship to that idiot in the cell?" he asked.

"None. He wants to go to Da'eut but I don't know where that is."

The officer looked at her for a long time before continuing. "What part of Java are you from?"

"My father comes from Wonosobo but I was born here."

"You're from a migrant family, I guess," said the officer.

"Yes Pak."

"OK," said the officer deep in thought.

Yahyu guessed he was torn between his disgust at her appearance and his loyalty to a fellow Javanese, even one as curious as herself, but she was wrong: his concern was with her disguise. While reading from some notes on the table in front of him, his attitude changed. He walked over to the window and looked outside for some minutes, deep in thought. Suddenly, as if he had reached a decision, he walked over to her and fired off a series of questions.

"You are not what you pretend to be. I don't believe anything you told me. Who was that peasant man, the one on the bicycle? What's your relationship to him? Why did he try to protect you?"

He moved behind her as he spoke. She could feel the menace in his voice and his actions but she could not see him.

"I cannot answer your questions. I don't know him. I crashed into him on the road. I've never seen him before."

"Nona, you are no beggar, you are no whore and you are no tramp; so why are you dressed in that disguise and why are you in my town?"

"No reason, Pak. I am here by chance. And this is not a disguise. I have no money and no family. That's why I am dressed like this. It's not from my choice."

"We shall see. Guard, bring in the idiot," he yelled in the direction of the door.

There was the sound of fighting as the guard dragged Rusdi shouting and screaming into the office.

"Shut him up," the officer ordered.

As the guard drew out his baton, Yahyu sprang to her feet. "No," she yelled. "Let me talk to him."

Going to Rusdi, she smiled, saying, "Calm down, brother. This nice officer wants to speak to you. Just answer his questions. No one's going to hurt you."

Rusdi slowly calmed down and sat on the floor by Yahyu's feet, muttering to himself, but he would not look up into the officer's face.

The officer looked at Yahyu in some surprise. "That was quite convincing. But you politicos are always convincing. It's what they teach you."

Yahyu was confused. She had never heard the word "politico" before and she failed to grasp its significance.

"I am the police chief in this district. I control everyone and everything in this town. Nothing happens here without my permission. You two come to town, a man who pretends to be an idiot and a girl who has education and is cultured but dressed like a tramp and behaving like a whore. You accidently bump into a peasant in town while running away from honest worshippers.

"These are dangerous times. We have these bloody politicos coming in from Java and agitating the peasants and estate workers. You expect me to believe your story. We shall see. Guard, sit the idiot in a chair, beside the girl, next to my desk."

Rusdi struggled when the guard laid hold of him and he clung to Yahyu shouting, "Don't let them do it. Help me." He looked at her with pleading eyes and, for one fleeting moment, Yahyu thought she detected sanity in those eyes; sanity and real fear, as if he was trying to relay a desperate message to her which he could not articulate.

"Put your right hand on the desk, idiot," the officer said as he casually strolled behind the two chairs.

As Rusdi hesitated, Yahyu said, "It's alright brother Rusdi, don't worry. The officer just wants to question us. Do as he says and answer his questions. It'll be alright."

Rusdi looked at Yahyu as he raised his right hand and placed it on the top of the desk. His expression was no longer one of madness. He seemed to be assessing whether to believe Yahyu or his own instincts.

The silky voice of the officer came from behind Yahyu's head. "Now Nona, you just tell me why you are here. Tell me your mission and then you and this idiot can go on your way. I just need a little information for my report. Nothing more."

"I have no mission. Not in the way you mean, Pak. I have a personal problem, that's all. It has nothing to do with this man," she said waving her hand in Rusdi's direction. "It has nothing to do with anyone here. I just want to run away. That's not a crime, is it?"

The officer leant down and placed his face over Yahyu's shoulder. Speaking very softly he said, "No one does something for no reason. No one leaves home for no reason. No one acts like a beggar unless she is a beggar or wants to appear as a beggar. Are you a beggar, Nona? I see the way you walk, the way you use your hands when talking to me, like you are painting a picture. You are no peasant girl, neither are you a beggar. You are something different. There's something secret about you and I'm going to find out what it is."

There was movement behind her but she did not turn to see. She wanted to offer no opportunity for the officer to react to her. All her training taught her that personal restraint and good manners were the behaviour of a good woman. She waited quietly as the tension mounted. Rusdi fidgeted but looked neither at Yahyu nor the officer. He stared only at the floor.

There was a loud crack and Rusdi rolled onto the floor screaming and writhing in pain, holding his bloodied right hand next to his chest. "Nona promised, Nona promised no pain," he sobbed as he lay on the floor nursing his broken hand.

Yahyu clutched her hands to her mouth in horror. She was not accustomed to purposeful violence and it scared her. "Rusdi, I'm sorry. I didn't know. Oh, Rusdi your hand …".

She looked over at the officer who stood impassively before them; no emotion showing on his aristocratic young face but his eyes were ever vigilant as he surveyed the odd couple before him.

Rusdi glanced up at Yahyu and she saw once again the sanity coming back into his eyes. Real pain and danger seemed to bring out the normality in Rusdi, as if he was being forced to forget his madness. Regrettably, the police officer also noticed and was quick to jump on it.

"Put the idiot back on a chair, facing the girl," he ordered the guard.

He stood behind Yahyu and put his hands on her shoulders as he spoke to her, cheek to cheek. She smelt his effeminate perfume and felt his hands firm on her shoulders. He was in total control of himself.

"Nona, that wasn't a nice thing you forced me to do, was it? To hurt that poor idiot. He is innocent, I think. What do you think? Is he an innocent man?"

She looked at Rusdi sitting on the chair, nursing his broken hand, his face pale with pain and fear. He would not look at her. He kept his eyes firmly on the ground so she could not see his eyes.

"I don't know. I have never seen him before. I know nothing about him. He is mad, as far as I know. He helped me pick up the tomatoes that were spilled on the road." She began to panic, to lose control, and the officer, ever alert, noticed.

"Are you innocent? I am a man of the world. I understand these things. Young girl, innocent of the world, maybe seeking adventure, maybe seeking a lover. You were tempted by a cause, by money, by a man. I understand all these things. Just give me names and locations of your contacts and you will both be free to go. No one need know. Just tell me."

Yahyu looked at Rusdi. He still hung his head down, refusing to look at either her or the officer. She could feel the expectancy. They were both waiting to hear what she had to say.

She opened her mouth to speak but before she could utter a word, the officer slapped her hard on the cheek from behind. There was no pain but the shock was dramatic. She clutched her face with one hand while looking around her; she could not see him but she could smell him, ever-present and menacing. She sat still, too stunned to react.

Rusdi looked up. His eyes had taken on their madness again. He tried to get up but failed. He tried to shout at the officer but his attempts were weak and pathetic. He waved his good hand in the air as if to try and slap the officer. He whimpered, "You leave Nona alone; no hit Nona. She's my sister."

The guard smashed him hard on the head with the butt of his revolver and Rusdi fell on the floor, bleeding from the head but, thankfully, unconscious.

Yahyu put her hands to her face to hide herself. She wanted to cry but she could not; she was too terrified. I must keep control, she told herself, don't give in. But for all her brave thoughts, she was at a loss for what to do. She felt the world closing in around her. The little prison office was slowly squeezing her to death. She felt sweat trickling down her face and, worst of all, she smelt her own fear. She tried to speak but her mouth was dry. She mouthed a few words at the officer but nothing came out.

The officer walked around the desk and stood nonchalantly by the window, admiring the view outside. "Guard, these two are innocent. No one would employ two such weak idiots as these. Take them to the edge of town and throw them out, but give them some food first."

The officer had his back turned to Yahyu as he said, "You are still a mystery to me but you are too stupid to be a danger. I expect you have a personal problem in which case I offer you my apologies, which I hope you will accept. These are dangerous times and I am responsible for the safety of everyone here. In safer times I would not have treated you as I have but these are not safe times. Take my advice and don't go anywhere near those gold mines. You don't understand what is happening up there.

"Now, get out of my town and if I ever see either of you again, I will really hurt you, both of you." He did not turn around but stayed looking at the scene outside the window.

Yahyu tried to stand up but collapsed. Her legs had turned to jelly and she could no longer control herself.

"Guard," yelled the officer. "For goodness' sake get them both out of here and clean up that mess on the floor."

***

Yahyu and Rusdi were cast out on the edge of the town and they quickly walked away, following footpaths that led deep into the forest as they both wanted to hide from the urban horror. After bandaging Rusdi's broken hand, she hurried on to find somewhere to wash away the dirt of the prison. She had disgraced herself in the police office and she needed to bring some normality back to her life. There was little she could do about her tattered clothes, but at least she could be clean and tattered.

The first stream she came to was enough to satisfy her needs but she had difficulty in telling Rusdi to leave her alone. He was not trying to impose. He was simply following her wherever she went and he did not understand her desire to be alone while bathing. In the end, she accepted his presence, sat on a rock by the stream as she covered herself with her sarong and slipped into the cool, refreshing water and let it lap over her as she revelled in hours of clean, refreshing luxury. She had no soap but she did her best to scrub herself and her clothes with twigs and stones, and to drown the lice that had set up home in her hair. She only had one set of clothes so she put them on immediately. They would dry quickly in the midday sun. She turned to Rusdi who sat patiently on the river bank looking at her and, with a more confident smile on her face, said, "OK brother Rusdi, let's go to find Da'eut."

***

Rusdi proved to be a surprisingly easy companion, always following, always obedient, never causing trouble. He kept his damaged hand in the makeshift sling and it did not seem to cause him much pain, although it was unlikely he would ever be able to make much use of it. The lucidity that Yahyu had seen fleetingly in his eyes in the police station never returned. He had reverted to his old self, idiotic but happy.

When they walked on quiet footpaths through the swampy forest, he would dance and sing to himself, never going far from Yahyu. When they were in small towns, he performed a ridiculous dancing act and collected a little money from the mocking audience, although sometimes given with a kindly smile. The money was important now. Since Rusdi had joined her, the villages she passed through were less willing to give her food. They were too suspicious. She never begged herself; she swore to herself she would never do that, but she saw no harm living off Rusdi's begging for a little while, until she got to the goldfields. He, in his turn, trusted everything to Yahyu. He never kept any of the begging money for himself.

After several weeks of hard walking, they could see the distant blue peaks of the Barisan Mountains, where lay the illegal mines and pits of goldfields.

"Nona, Nona, look over there, mountains. I go find Da'eut." Rusdi danced and jumped in the air, swinging his sword scabbard above his head. "We go Da'eut together."

"No, brother Rusdi," she said. "We cannot go their together. You must find Da'eut alone. I cannot come with you. I have another errand which I must do."

"No, Nona. Nona not understand. Da'eut is ... it's ... it's ...". He looked confused and could not go on. His voice was strangled with emotion as he tried to explain what Da'eut was, what it meant to him and what it could mean to her. In the end he hung his head and said very simply, "Everyone happy in Da'eut. I want Nona to be happy too. We could have picnic in Da'eut." He walked ahead of her, head hanging down, until he regained his composure and started singing to himself again.

The closer they got to the mountains the more agitated Rusdi became. She noticed him giving her sidelong glances, checking to see if she was looking at him. Sometimes she even suspected he was keeping some of the begging money but she had no proof. He had become secretive, talking to himself in a whisper, not involving Yahyu in his secret conversations. Yahyu questioned him many times about Da'eut. What was it? Where was it? What happened there? But Rusdi was always evasive. He just gave his idiotic grin and said, "Rusdi happy in Da'eut. Nona also be happy in Da'eut."

***

After several days, Yayhu realised they were lost. They were in a long disused rubber forest and there were no villages. The land was flat and overgrown and they rarely saw the sun because of the dense forest canopy. People had obviously tapped the wild rubber trees sometime in the past as she could see from the V-shaped scars on the tree trunks. And there were endless small footpaths that wound around the forest for many miles, only to end in small clearings with the remains of a bamboo hut in it. But everything seemed to be old and deserted; there were no people. The rubber forest was dark and forbidding, and Yahyu and Rusdi had started whispering to each other, as if afraid to wake the dark secrets within. The feeling of suspense was beginning to unsettle both of them and Yahyu felt fear rising up inside her once more, slowly but insidiously undermining her courage.

Equally worrying was the behaviour of Rusdi. For the past few days he had been moody, often looking behind him. Sometimes he would jump behind a tree and lie still until Yahyu could coax him out again and they would continue their journey. She questioned him often but he said nothing clearly and just jabbered to himself. She thought the dark forest must be getting to him, depressing his volatile spirit.

"Maybe the rubber is too old," she said to Rusdi as they arrived at yet another deserted hut in the forest. "But there must be some people still here. They can't have deserted all the trees at the same time."

"Rusdi know why." He looked scared. He sat on a tree root, his eyes staring out at nothing. He started dribbling again and his good hand was shaking.

"Why brother, why are there no rubber tappers here?" she asked. But Rusdi remained silent and wandered off into the forest, looking sad and depressed.

Yahyu was worried. Since they had entered the rubber forest, they had seen no one. She opened her sack to check their rice supplies once again. Enough for two days, she calculated, if we only eat once a day. They also had some fruit Rusdi had collected; he was good at that. But the baby in her stomach was affecting her stamina. Previously, she had had the strength to eat once a day and still go on, but now she felt her strength waning as the uncomfortable feeling in her stomach started to grow and gnaw at her consciousness. She thought endlessly of food as if someone else, someone inside her stomach, was telling her to eat.

"Rusdi, I think we really are lost." She spoke as lightly as possible. She did not know how Rusdi would react to the new danger. He seemed to depend on her judgement in all things but she had failed this time.

Rusdi did not look worried. "Rusdi find way out for Nona. Nona not worry," he said.

"Brother Rusdi, yesterday you looked worried. Today you look happy. How can I ever understand you?" He looked up at her with uncomprehending eyes. "Tell me, why are there no people here? Where have they all gone?"

Slowly, Rusdi's expression changed from idiocy to fear as his knees shook, causing him to squat. Then he lay on the ground grovelling and howling, "No, no, no, don't, don't do it. Please, don't do it." He let out a long, stifled moan of terror.

Yahyu shook him. "Rusdi, stop it. Stop it, you're scaring me. What's the matter? What are you scared of?"

"They come for us. They come for us. Everyone run away. Everyone scared. We must hide. Nona hide me." His pleading look filled her with pity but also dread.

"Who are they, Rusdi? What are you afraid of? You can tell your sister."

Rusdi tried to speak, "U ... U ...". He looked at her, pleading with her not to force him to say the words that he feared so much. He hung his head, trying not to catch her eye. Then she heard him whispering to himself. She moved closer and heard words that had an ominous ring. "The uniforms, they have guns; everyone run from them. They are coming. They hunt people in the night. They hunt us too."

He would say no more. He squatted on the ground, murmuring to himself and hiding his face from Yahyu's stare.

***

When she awoke in the morning, she was cold and wet. It had rained most of the night and steam was rising from the forest, giving the trees a ghostly beauty. She had slept in a disused rubber tapper's hut but the roof had collapsed long ago and although she had done her best to cover it with leaves and branches, she was soaked. She got up, shivering, and looked around her but could not see Rusdi. She went outside the hut and called him but there was no answer. He's probably gone looking for fruits again, she thought, but she knew in her heart that she may have lost him, her only companion in the forest.

As the day wore on, Rusdi did not return. She called and shouted but her voice fell flat amongst the damp, forbidding trees. She waited all day, calling his name but he never came. As evening closed in, she realised how fond she had become of him. He was mad but he was also friendly. Since leaving the river he was her only companion. They had been together for several weeks and she had grown used to him but now he was gone and she was alone, and she was scared of loneliness. Worse still, she was scared of the dark and night was coming on.

During the night Yahyu could not sleep. She felt a strange sensation in her stomach, as if a giant pomegranate lay there. She craved fruit but there was none to be had. She craved meat but their supplies were exhausted. Worst of all, she craved company; she was scared. She hid her head under her sarong. She could not look out at the darkness beyond the area lit by the glow from her small fire. The noises of the forest, quiet during the heat of the afternoon, came alive at night with screeches, slitherings, croaks and grunts. She heard them all, or thought she did, and she was terrified.

The next morning she moved on. She didn't know the right direction but she could not stay still and wait for hunger to slowly kill her and her ever-growing baby. She hoped she would come across Rusdi but the forest guarded its secrets. She came across neither him nor anybody all day. Her only company were groups of monkeys who circled above her in the trees, but she rarely saw them because of the density of the foliage. She just heard the sudden crashes and swishing of branches as they swung around.

As she plodded slowly along another winding path, she realised she was quickly weakening. Hunger and the baby in her stomach were draining her strength and she doubted she could continue many more days with no food. She wanted to move quickly because she was scared of spending another night alone in the forest but she could not. Even small efforts cost her pain and she had to kneel and fight for breath. Getting up to walk again, she felt weak and faint. She was losing control and losing touch with reality. She saw faces looking at her from deep in the forest and she would shout and run towards them only to find there was nothing there. At night she lay huddled in a ruined bamboo hut, slowly crying herself to sleep, hiding her face in her arms and dreaming of waking up to find Jon sitting beside her, telling her everything was alright.

On the third day of her lonely trek, as the sun was falling, Yahyu thought she saw beams of light shining in the sky. In her weakened state she did not recognise them for what they were but instead doubted her sanity. She thought she was seeing illusions in the sky but she moved closer to them because they at least offered hope. In her weakness she fell over roots and into muddy pools. She became covered in mud and her limbs were cut and torn by thorns, but she had ceased to notice or to care. She walked on slowly, like a robot programmed to keep going until the batteries finally ran out. Gradually, as if waking up from a dream, she heard the sound of engines in the distance; the lights were from the headlights of vehicles on a road.

Yahyu was past caring. Lights meant people and that, potentially, meant food. She pressed on.

Chapter 3

I love the misty beauty of the Gaja Tiga Tea Plantation. I am self-contained here and I rarely visit the outer world beyond the cloudy boundary that surrounds the plantation. I don't often seek company beyond that of my workers and staff, but every few months I force myself to become a social being for a few days. I descend the mountains and head for the dubious delights of Linggau; the gateway to the swamp lands of South Sumatra. Amongst the motley collection of foreign rubber planters, smugglers and the occasional over-earnest American trying not to look like a CIA agent, I cease to be Tuan and become simply Jim Robinson, manager of the only tea plantation in South Sumatra. We drink the nights away in exaggerated friendship at the bar of the House of Young Bamboo; a house of elegance and debauchery in equal proportions. I don't really fit in there but neither does anyone else. It's a place for the displaced, the flotsam of the Second World War looking for … whatever it is that flotsam looks for. For myself, I had found a solitary kind of beauty in my mountain kingdom and that was enough for me, or so I thought until I saw a young tramp skipping through the rubbish of Linggau bus station.

My Jeep had broken down in Linggau so I needed to get a bus back up the mountains; a tiresome journey. Sumatran buses are unlike any other buses in the world. They are built and operated like battle tanks but are twice as uncomfortable and a great deal more dangerous.

The bus station was bustling with activity; passengers jostling to get seats amidst the mud and litter that is endemic in any Sumatran bus station. It's like the base camp for major expeditions going into the mountains. Each bus is packed with luggage strapped onto the roof, the sides, the backs and the fronts. Passengers can pay half-price to sit on the roof, together with the chickens that are tied there. Inside the buses the wooden benches are so narrow and close together that despite rough roads and sharp bends, the passengers cannot be thrown around because they are packed too tightly. The drivers drive fast and hard on the potholed roads and around the sharp bends that wind up the mountainsides. It's always best to sit by a window to breathe fresh air and get out fast if they crash.

"How much longer before we depart, Pak?" I asked the surly-looking driver of the only bus going to Curup. "I need to get there before nightfall and it's going to rain later."

"Not full yet, Tuan," the driver said, but although his words were polite, his look was hostile. "Why doesn't Tuan take another bus? Maybe we shall be another hour or two here."

"You know as well as I do there's no other bus to Curup today. What the hell are you talking about."

"Suit yourself, Tuan. I'm just trying to help. Our bus will be very crowded and maybe Tuan wouldn't like it."

The driver had a particularly nasty sneer to his voice but I ignored it. It's only a six-hour ride to Curup and a surly bus driver was hardly a novelty. I told the driver to reserve a seat for me near the window while I searched for a tea stall to sit and read while waiting for the bus to fill up; always a tedious task. The bus left the station and toured the town looking for passengers and then returned to the bus station only half full. After another half an hour, they toured the town again and so it went on until the bus was nearly full. It could take several hours between reserving a seat and the bus actually leaving and I had no intention of spending those two hours squashed on a bus looking for passengers.

While drinking tepid tea and idly watching the buses as they slowly filled up, I saw a young girl, probably Javanese, judging from her fine features, approaching the bus for Curup. I was immediately struck by the contrast between the elegance of her movements as she tiptoed through the mud and rubbish that littered the station and her tattered clothes and bare, bleeding feet. She seemed very young to be alone in a bus station and she was hesitant, as if afraid to get on the bus. The driver, seeing her hesitancy, came slowly up to her, lighting a cigarette as he walked. I couldn't hear what was said between them but the driver's assistants laughed as the girl walked away with her eyes fixed on the ground.

She came past my tea stall, not looking at anyone. She looked exhausted but had an expression of determination on her face as if she wasn't going to give in whatever the odds. My friends always say I'm a soft touch, that I can never ignore the underdog, especially when it involves an attractive girl. I suppose it's true and I view it as a weakness sometimes, although considering the difference between my wealth and the local poverty, I think a certain amount of softness towards bad luck in others is justified. There were already a number of women throughout the island who were living on my monthly remittances.

I was once accused by an irate belando woman of being a womaniser, but that's not true. I just find it hard to ignore an honest appeal for help. Some of the women I am supporting are old enough to be my grandmother, ex-workers on the plantation who were never my lovers, but people aren't interested in truth; gossip is much juicier. In this case I was definitely struck by her beauty and elegance, even though it was well hidden under her emaciated and weary face. But more interesting than her beauty was the story that might lie behind her expression of exhausted determination. It was not common at that time to see such strange phenomena in Sumatra, where large family groups protected their own and young women rarely travelled alone, although it was to become less unusual in the years ahead as political upheaval divided families and friends.

I had nothing much to do while waiting for the bus and I was attracted by the romance of a beautiful tramp. I stood up as she passed my table and spoke to her in polite Melayu, "Nona, would you like to sit here with me and have some tea? It's quite safe."

The girl looked at me in surprise, her face such a mixture of conflicting emotions that I couldn't read her reaction. Was it fear, suspicion or relief? She hesitated, uncertain whether to stay or continue walking by.

I called out to the tea lady, "Ibu, bring the Nona some tea and you join us, please. I think she's scared of big belando men like me."

The old lady came over and spoke to the girl briefly in Javanese, which I don't understand, and the girl relaxed a little and sat down next to the lady but she still looked downwards.

"Where are you going Nona? Are you off to find your fortune in the goldfields?" I spoke jokingly, so as to put her at ease, not knowing then that that was exactly what she was planning to do.

She continued looking at the ground and said nothing.

"Come on Nona, tell us where you're going? I can see from your face that you aren't from around here. You're Javanese and you weren't born to be a tramp. I can tell from your expression and the way you move." I spoke softly so as not to scare her.

The girl looked up as if to speak but then saw the driver and his assistants looking at us. She blushed and shut her mouth, looking again at the ground.

After a few minutes, and to my complete surprise, she said very quietly but without looking up, "Please speak more slowly. Your accent is strange to me and I cannot catch all the words. Please don't embarrass me. Everyone is looking at me but I have nowhere to go and I am very tired. I want to sit here for a little while until I get my strength back. But I thank you for your kindness."

I hesitated on hearing the girl's dignified little speech. I was fascinated to find such good manners, as well as such beauty, behind her tattered and haggard appearance. "You are a stranger here. Do you realise this is a very rough town? All the criminals from the outer islands come here to look for gold. You don't look to me like the sort of girl that visits these areas. Do you know what you are doing and where you are going?"

She gave a long sigh and sipped her tea but said nothing.

I saw several of the drivers making obscene gestures in our direction. It was obvious what they thought she was doing but I was equally sure they were wrong. It's not unusual in Linggau for women to come up to strangers in bars and restaurants offering a good time, but this girl was definitely not of that type; her actions showed control and a kind of natural grace as if every movement of her limbs was guided. She was obviously holding herself in, trying to control herself and her situation, trying not to let her exhaustion get the better of her. She was very different from the smiling peasant women milling around the bus station or the streetwise Javanese women who inhabited the bars of Linggau.

"Nona, how old are you? You look too young to be travelling alone. Tell me please?" I said slowly.

"I am seventeen," she said. She looked up as if to say more but then stopped and looked once again at the ground.

"What is your name?" I asked.

"I am Yahyu. I need the bus fare to get to Curup. It's too far for me to walk and I'm already exhausted. I'm going to look for my uncle in the goldfields; he went there some years ago. If you lend me the bus fare, I will pay you back twice as much when I am rich, but don't expect anything else from me because I'm not that sort of girl."

The laughter died on my lips. One look at the purposeful expression on her classical Javanese face and I realised laughter was misplaced. She meant what she said, although she could not have understood the impossibility of carrying out her plans. She resumed sipping her tea and once again the contrast between her dress and her actions was striking; she held her tea cup with great delicacy, like the old matrons in the tea shops of Cheltenham when I was a boy, fingers arched outward as she delicately and silently sipped her tea, but her hands were scratched and bloody.

"OK Nona, I will pay your fare," I said, expecting her to look relieved and a bit friendlier but again I was wrong.

"Then please give me the money now as I don't want to get on the bus with you."

I must have looked shocked because she quickly qualified what she had said.

"You need to understand my position. I cannot get on a bus with a strange belando man or people will think badly of me. Just give me the money now and give me your address. You will get the money back with interest when I have saved enough." She then showed her complete mastery of the situation by saying, "And please don't worry. Although I don't trust you, you can trust me and you will double your money." I saw then the first hint of a smile twinkling in her clear black eyes.

When the driver signalled that he was finally ready to depart, the girl got up and walked towards the bus without a word. The driver's assistants spoke laughingly to her as she climbed in but I could not hear what was said and she ignored them. The other passengers seemed to be trying to avoid her, as if some of her beggarliness might rub off on them. It was obvious what they thought of her.

As I climbed into the bus, one of the driver's assistants stopped me, saying, "Mister, you're not wanted on this bus, get off." He was sniggering as he spoke. I told him to go to hell in English and I think he got the point, for he let me on. Swearing in Melayu is not satisfying; it doesn't have the vulgarity of good English swear words. I always revert to English when I am really angry.

Yahyu was sat in front of me but she never looked behind and I was content to admire the back of her head. She had a long, elegant neck and small, finely carved ears; points of little importance, perhaps, but there's not much else to do on a Sumatran bus other than study people and she was certainly worthy of study. However, other passengers seemed to be uneasy and the atmosphere was tense. Maybe I should have sensed trouble was coming but trouble comes in many shapes in Sumatra and it didn't worry me too much.

The bus wound its tortuous way up the side of the Barisan Mountains. On the few occasions we came across a bus going in the opposite direction, the driver stopped, leant out of his window and chatted to the other driver, much to the annoyance and discomfort of the passengers. As the road got worse and the bends got tighter, some of the children were sick, which added to the stench of so many sweaty bodies crammed into too small a space. The passengers, however, seemed more agitated than normal, constantly fidgeting and looking towards the back of the bus which was curtained off with a large sheet hanging from the roof. A few of the young men were sniggering but most passengers looked confused or embarrassed.

"They got one of them girls in the back of the bus," the passenger next to me said. "This driver is not a good man but what can we do? And my daughter's here too." He nodded in the direction of the child next to him.

When I looked back I saw one of the driver's assistants coming out from under the curtain, doing up the zip on his trousers, a dirty grin on his face. He swaggered up the bus, leapt through one of the windows and pulled himself onto the roof. Immediately, another of the assistants went under the curtain. This was a bit extreme, even by the standards of Sumatran buses, but it was none of my business so I ignored them and went back to dreaming of food, women and tea;

the three essentials of life for a tea planter.

"Never satisfied, these drivers. They'll be doing this all the way to Curup. Wonder who she is? The girl in the back," my neighbour said to me but I ignored him. I was thinking about what was going to happen to Yahyu when we got to Curup. It's a rough town and very cold at night; not a good place to be sleeping rough. Although she was sat just in front of me, she never turned her head or showed any interest in me or any of the other passengers. She had spent the whole journey looking down towards the floor, avoiding contact with anyone.

One of the thugs that collected fares called something to the driver who braked hard and brought the bus to a stop. Laughing, two assistants pulled a woman out from behind the curtain. She was rather old, her blouse hung drunkenly from one shoulder and her hair was dishevelled as if she'd been sleeping rough. They pushed her through the rear door, threw a few coins on the road and drove off. She didn't seem to object. I looked back and saw her picking up the coins as if this was just another part of a normal day.

One of the assistants who had been sitting on the roof climbed through the window next to Yahyu and sat on the window sill, his bare feet on the back of her seat. I saw Yahyu flinch and her body stiffen as he did so. He was smiling while talking to her and nodding in the direction of the back of the bus, but she turned her head away and looked out of the opposite window, the elegance of her posture contrasting sharply with her ragged clothes and the vulgarity of the young man. The passengers next to Yahyu inched away, as if to avoid contamination or involvement in what was likely to be a nasty scene.

I wasn't too worried at this stage because the bus was so

packed they couldn't have got her to the back of the bus without a struggle and her body language suggested she had seen all this before and knew how to handle it, unpleasant though it may have been. However, things took a turn for the worse when a second man descended from the roof and they started pulling her up towards the window and, presumably, the roof. I hardly knew Yahyu at that stage but I had an ill-defined feeling of responsibility towards her, as if our brief conversation at the bus station had established a bond between us. However, it was difficult to intervene because we were too tightly packed and I couldn't move towards her. The girl started to struggle but the young men just laughed and the passengers turned away in disgust.

The man next to me looked at the girl. "What else can she expect dressed like that? Looks more like one of them sort of women anyway, travelling alone with no father or brother to look after her. Wish they would just throw her off the bus."

This was getting out of hand so I yelled in English, "Hey, stop this bloody bus," and tapped the driver on the shoulder but he continued as before and lit another cigarette as he took a tight bend at high speed. This was too much even for my relatively mild manners, so I leant forward and grabbed the back of his dirty shirt and yelled at the top of my voice for him to bloody well stop, which he did, violently.

Once the bus had slithered to a stop amongst the mud and potholes of the Barisan highway, there was an audible sigh from the passengers who slowly crawled out of the door and onto the earthen road. Some went off to the forest to relieve themselves, one or two were sick on the spot, most of them looked sheepishly at me as if to say thank you but were afraid to incur the wrath of the tough-looking bus driver and his assistants.

One of the older men took me aside. "Be careful, Tuan. This driver is a Batak. He's violent. Don't anger him."

The driver and his crew looked more like a bunch of bandits than a bus crew and they were glaring at me in a most unhappy way and talking together in whispers. The best way to handle this sort of situation is to bluff it out. One sign of fear and they would have the upper hand and then anything could happen. Most of the bus companies had the police in their pockets so there was no point in expecting help from anyone; not that there was anyone on this isolated stretch of road.

I strolled over to the driver and his crew and said politely but firmly, "Pak, you leave that girl alone. She's paid her fare. Tell your men to lay off. And don't give me any more trouble. Understand?"

The driver laughed, spat on the floor, took another drag on his cigarette and said something to the young man perched on the roof of the bus, but I couldn't understand what he said.

The girl stood alone by the side of the road everybody avoiding her. She looked ragged and dirty but she still had poise and elegance. I've seen the rough side of life in Burma during the war and I recognise toughness when I see it and I admired her for her calm composure. She wasn't going to give in, not to a crew of down-at-heel bus drivers. Whatever it was she had been through or done she still kept her pride. I felt myself drawn towards her, more because of her courage than her beauty, or so I tried to convince myself.

As the passengers got back onto the bus, one of the young men stopped me and laughed, pointing at the young girl. "Hey Mister, you can take her now. Enjoy." Then, to my surprise, my bag was hurled off the roof of the bus, the door was slammed shut and the bus started to move.

"Hey, stop. What the hell are you doing?" I yelled, running after the bus.

The bus slowed down, and the driver stuck his head out of the window, grinned at me and yelled in English, "Fuck you, Mister," then threw his cigarette butt in the girl's direction and drove off.

I gazed after the departing bus as it sped around a bend, the young men on the roof laughing and making obscene gestures in our direction, and then it was gone. The muddy, potholed road was deserted and the noise of the badly maintained bus was replaced by the sounds of the jungle that signal the end of the afternoon heat and the start of the night. Natural beauty replaced the ugliness of a dilapidated Sumatran bus but natural beauty can be deceptive. It can hide many dangers that are not at first apparent. The Sumatran forest at night is not a place for the faint hearted.

The girl was sitting by the roadside, staring blankly into the forest, ignoring me and the departing bus, apparently deep in thought. I went up to her, but to my great surprise she slowly got to her feet and, without even glancing in my direction, started walking up the road in the direction of Curup.

"Hey Nona," I called. "Where are you going? It's nightfall; there're no more buses on this road. It's dangerous." I ran after her but she continued walking, ignoring my calls. She was barefoot, had no luggage and her sarong was torn at the back. If anyone needed help it was her, but she did not ask for anything. She seemed not even to notice me.

I caught up with her and stood in her path, not sure whether to smile or look concerned. I didn't want to frighten her but also, noting her pride, I did not want to appear condescending. Turning to walk beside her, and with a big smile but a quiet voice, I said, "Nona, we're both in a spot of bother. Let's talk while we walk, shall we? Let's try to work out what we're going to do."

The girl looked at me and then looked at the dark forest on either side of the road but kept walking, neither answering me nor avoiding me. I had the feeling she was tolerating me, rather than me helping her.

I walked beside her up the long incline into the mountains. I kept quiet and we walked together in the gathering gloom of the overcast evening which suggested yet another tropical downpour. It seemed that my silently walking beside her was somehow acceptable to her. Her previous graceful but aloof stance was growing softer as she occasionally glanced in my direction.

The road was deserted; there were no vehicles, no villages and no people. It was more of a wide muddy track than a road and it wound up the mountainside for another twenty miles before getting to the mountain town of Curup. The likelihood of any further vehicles coming on the road at this late hour was remote. It was not safe to travel at night in this part of Sumatra. Gold smugglers used the road at night to avoid police, and local gangsters set ambushes to steal the gold from the smugglers.

After passing several small paths leading off the road, Yahyu stopped by one of them and looked into the forest. She looked worried. Turning to me with a searching stare, she said, "We can't stay on this road. It's not safe. We need to go into the forest to hide till morning." But she stayed still, not moving towards the path or walking up the road. She looked at me as if summing me up. She was a small, slim girl dressed in tattered clothes, her bright clear eyes looking up at me as if to say, "Can you be trusted?"

She looked me straight in the eye before speaking. "I'm not scared of you but I am scared of the dark. You can come with me into the forest if you want. I don't want to be alone in the dark." She looked up at me again and, for an instance, I thought I saw the ghost of a smile come to her face, as if she saw the absurdity of her statement and was mildly embarrassed by it. She could face gangsters, smugglers and bandits without turning a hair but she was afraid of the dark!

"If we go into the forest, we shall be stuck there all night and it looks like rain," I told her, looking at the darkening sky. Already there were distant flashes of lightning and the occasional roll of thunder. "Let's continue up the road until it's dark. Maybe we shall come to a farm."

Yahyu stood by the entrance to the pathway thinking. I saw the concentration on her face. She seemed to treat all decisions with great deliberation. She raised her head, a sign that I was already beginning to recognise as meaning she had come to a decision. "No. You are wrong," she said, looking away from me and into the forest. "There will be no farms and soon it will be too dark to see our way into the forest. If we stay by the road, we shall be caught by the bandits. These paths usually lead to woodcutters' huts. I expect we shall find a hut where we can stay till morning."

She looked briefly at me as if to say, "Take it or leave it", and without any further word, she walked gracefully off the road and into the forest. I had to either follow her or abandon her, so I followed and, thinking about what she had said, I had to admit she was probably right.

I stared at her back as she skipped over the rough track. Despite the cuts and sores on her legs, she never faltered and never complained but walked as if she was gliding on silk, her hips gently swaying to the rhythm of her steps as she nimbly negotiated the tree roots. I also noticed her figure. She was young and slim, in a very Asian way, but I tried to put this to the back of my mind. I was in too awkward a situation to get distracted by her figure.

After some time we came to a clearing in the forest. The girl immediately slipped behind a tree and motioned me to do likewise. She knew how to anticipate danger.

After some minutes silently watching, I quietly slipped out from behind the trees and approached the clearing from an angle. I saw her watching me intently, alive to the dangers around us, alert and not flinching. In the clearing was a small bamboo platform with no walls but a thatch roof, partly collapsed. There were some logs lying over the ground and a lot of wood chippings. It had obviously been a woodchopper's hut but it must have been deserted for some time and there seemed little likelihood the owner would return that evening, so I called her to join me in the clearing as I started collecting wood to make a fire.

Before the fire was ready the rain started. A distant patter of rain drops falling heavily on the leaves of the forest trees, creeping ever nearer, a dampening of the atmosphere, a sudden darkness and then a deafening roar as a wall of water fell on us. The partly thatched roof was of little use. Tropical storms of this intensity in the mountains usually only last a short while but the volume of water can be terrifying if you're not used to it. We sat there, side by side, drenched to the skin and unable to talk for the noise of the rain.

The rain stopped as quickly as it started, leaving us cold, wet and shivering. "No point trying to light the fire," I said, looking around at the dripping forest. The girl did not reply. She sat silently on the platform, shivering and looking mournfully at the water dripping off the forest leaves.

"Where do you come from, Nona? Where's your home?" I said quietly.

She looked at me as if surprised to find me still there. "I come from nowhere particular," she replied. She spoke without self-pity, as if stating a rather obvious fact to an ignorant foreigner.

"OK. So where do you want to go?" I asked again, still speaking softly so as not to alarm her.

"Tuan, I don't know exactly where I am going. All I know is that I cannot go to where I used to be. You do not need to know why." She neither smiled nor looked sorry for herself but had an expression of tired resignation on her face. I don't think she was trying to be evasive. Perhaps the enormity of what had happened to her was too difficult for her to comprehend or to explain to a stranger. I decided to persist, but gently.

"Excuse me Nona, you are dressed like a tramp but I can see you were not born to be a tramp. I can also see that you are not from around here. Can you tell me what's happened to you?"

She seemed surprised at my comments. Her eyes opened wide as she studied my face and a hint of a smile came to her eyes but she quickly turned away. "Why do you ask?" she said.

"We are here for the night and it's going to be long and wet. We may as well get to know each other. I mean no harm and you don't have to answer my questions. But you interest me; you are not what you appear to be and that's interesting in itself."

She didn't answer directly. She spent some minutes looking into the dark forest as if searching for inspiration. But then she raised her head and turned towards me.

"Not many people ask me questions. Not now. I used to get men coming up to me all the time, before I became like this. I didn't really like it although it was a compliment in a way, but they don't ask anymore." She looked down at her filthy clothes as she spoke and I thought I detected a tear sliding down her cheek but we were both so wet I could not tell if she was crying or if it was just rainwater.

She tried to dry her face on a green scarf she kept hidden in her blouse and continued. "Dressed like this and with my hair so messy, everybody tries to avoid me unless they want to do bad things to me like those nasty men on the bus. So why are you interested?" She gave me a sharp enquiring glance. She may have been distressed and down on her luck but she was also streetwise; she wasn't going to let her guard down. She must have had some nasty experiences to make her speak with such bitterness and suspicion. But I suppose it's not usual for any young girl to be suddenly stuck in a forest with a foreign man in the middle of the night. Under the circumstances she was acting with great maturity. I felt sorry for her. She seemed so cultured in her manners and it contrasted so vividly with her appearance. She realised it and it obviously hurt her.

"I would like to hear your story. Why don't you tell me? I see you as a cultured young woman who is down on her luck. There's no need to be ashamed. I've been down on my luck once or twice and I know the feeling."

She raised her head once more to look at me. I could tell she had come to a decision to talk.

"I am ..." she hesitated, as if unsure how to go on. "No, no, that's not true anymore. I was a dancer, a classical Javanese dancer. It seems so long ago now. I once danced in front of the military commander in Palembang."

I saw her eyes brighten as she recounted her tale and her face started to relax. "I was top of my class at dancing school. My teacher said I was the best dancer in my generation. I remember the first time I danced on stage. I played the part of Sita in the Ramayana ballet. Before the performance started, I was shaking and sweating but when I started dancing it was like ... I don't know how to explain. It was like I lost myself. It was like it wasn't me at all but someone else dancing. It was like I really was Sita. I shall never forget my first performance. I love dancing."

She looked at the ground and then looked around her at the dark, dripping forest. "But I don't think I shall ever dance again." Her face took on the bleak and haunted look that had so attracted me from the beginning; a face of lost dreams.

After a long silence I said, "Why won't you dance anymore? What happened?"

She seemed not to hear me or even notice my presence. She was thinking and I was not a part of her thoughts. Maybe she was still dancing in her dreams.

"I think you should get some sleep if you can," I said as I got up to stretch.

She seemed startled. She looked at me with a kindly smile, saying,

"You seem a good man. I shall trust you. I'm very tired and need to sleep. Don't disturb me please, but also don't go far away. I don't like to be alone in the dark. I've spent weeks alone and I don't like it. When I was lost in a rubber forest some weeks ago, I slept next to a gentle madman called Rusdi, simply because I'm afraid of the dark. If you do this for me, I shall be grateful." With that, she curled up on the edge of the bamboo platform and went to sleep but I noticed she lay facing me. She had not turned her back. In sleeping, however, she kept her hands always over her stomach as if protecting it; an unusual posture for someone sleeping rough.

We were in the jungle miles from the nearest habitation and I was sleeping next to one of the most beautiful, albeit emaciated, women I had seen for a long time but there was nothing I could do about it. I could not betray her trust in me but I also enjoyed the denial of contact. I have a very contradictory streak in my character. It's probably why I like the loneliness of my kingdom in the mountains. I love women's company but I also enjoy being deprived of it because the expectation of pleasure is often greater than its satisfaction; like a thirsty man longing for a glass of pure mountain water and spurning the chance to drink from a muddy stream. Yahyu seemed to be that mountain spring and I didn't want to eventually find that she was not what I had expected. I think it's better to spend life constantly searching for paradise than to find only disappointment. I thought at that stage that it was best to simply help her to Curup, earn her thanks, and then go off on my own and keep my vision of her as a dancing princess from the forests and maybe to dream of what might have been.

The night was long and damp. I noticed Yahyu constantly waking, looking at me as if to check I was still there and then, reassured, falling back into a fitful sleep. It was a rather strange feeling for me, after so many years of freedom from dependence from anyone, to be suddenly thrown into the position of guardian. I can't say I didn't like it, because I did, and I took the role very seriously. I adopted a trick I learnt in Burma of half sleeping while keeping all senses alert to the slightest sound, smell or movement. I was a very good guardian that night, although nothing happened to disturb us, which was a shame. I rather fancied myself in the role of knight in shining armour, instead of which I was just a very wet tea planter protecting a young tramp from the non-existent demons of the dark forest.

***

Next morning we returned to the road and, after a long wait, caught a dilapidated bus for the rest of our journey. We finally reached the mountain town of Curup in the evening and it was getting cold. Yahyu was shivering; she was not dressed for the mountains.

We walked the short distance from the bus station to the market centre, now closing for the evening. It was extremely dirty and full of litter. Dogs were pulling down the rubbish bins looking for scraps and chickens wandered through the garbage. The market square was surrounded by two-storied wooden houses looking down onto the market. Only a few people were around, braving the damp, overcast evening. It rains most evenings in Curup and it looked as if that evening would be no exception. A few coffee shops still had lights on and the Padang restaurants had a few furtive-looking customers, probably discussing gold. Everyone in Curup discussed gold.

Passersby looked at us strangely but kept their distance. People were obviously afraid of the big belando man but they stared mainly at Yahyu, the ragged tramp. I could see the question in their eyes, "Why are these two together? Can't he afford a better woman than her?" I am sure she noticed the unfriendly stares but she had learnt how to cope with it. She kept on walking with her head down, looking at the ground in front of her.

We found a tea stall still open and I ordered tea for both of us. The old man in the shop looked askance at Yahyu but my presence stopped him saying anything and he went away to get the tea. In this town I was known as the manager of the only tea plantation in this part of the mountains and that position carried a lot of prestige among the local Rejang people.

I told Yahyu to stay in the tea stall while I wandered around to buy a few things and find some suitable accommodation for her. She looked at me strangely before I left; it was only later, whilst shopping, that I realised I hadn't yet paid for the tea and she may have suspected that I was not going to come back. When you are completely penniless, even the cost of a cup of tea can lead to disaster and leave you vulnerable to abuse. It said a lot for her trust in me that she was prepared to let me go.

When I returned I could see the immediate relief in her face. I was rather chuffed to see her concern; the first time she had ever shown any real interest in me. When I offered her the clothes parcel I had purchased for her, she looked even more surprised and I was rewarded with a long searching look, followed by a smile, the first full smile I had seen and it lit up her face, her eyes almost laughing in delight.

"I love beautiful clothes," she said, as if that were explanation enough for her change of attitude.

She looked carefully at the woollen shawl and a bright red sarong I had bought to replace her torn and dirty clothes. She spent many minutes studying the cloth and tracing the flora pattern with her figure, oblivious to the shop owner hovering behind her. "Now I can look like Sita again," she said with a glint of humour in her eyes. I thought then that if only she could see herself as I saw her, she would not have made such an incongruous statement. No one could have looked less like the beautiful Sita than this half-starved scarecrow in front of me. But, I had to admit, her face and eyes were those of a classical beauty if only she were better fed and better washed.

She turned to me and with great seriousness said, "If you buy me a kebaya, a red one to match this sarong, I can look very beautiful again. Please buy me one. When I find gold, I will repay you."

I wanted to laugh again but I couldn't. She was so serious, so focused. She meant what she said.

"I will buy you one later, but first we have to decide what to do. What were your plans?"

"I was told that when I reach Curup I must turn north towards Lake Tes and then go west, high into the mountains to Lebong Tandai and ask about my uncle." She spoke without embarrassment, as if describing a simple journey. I had to remind myself that despite her apparent maturity in some matters, she was still a complete baby in others.

"Please believe me when I tell you that your plan is ridiculous. Those goldfields are many days' walk into the mountains, the path is dangerous and the goldfields are worked by criminals and bandits. You will not last one day. You can guess what they will do to you when you get there. I don't need to tell you."

"It's not for me that I go. I need money for ..." she hesitated before continuing, a slight blush on her cheeks. "I need the money for someone else. I don't care what happens to me." There was no hint of defeat or false drama in her voice. She spoke as if stating a simple fact, as if she accepted her responsibility and her fate.

I had been thinking while I was shopping whether I should offer her the chance to stay on my plantation for a few days and get her strength back. But at the same time, there was a nagging thought in my mind that her presence, beautiful though it would be, would spoil my solitude. I liked my life and my plantation. I lived there from choice and wanted to go on living there until I died. Then I thought to myself that such selfishness was unbecoming an educated man when faced with such hard luck as represented by Yahyu, so I took the plunge.

"Why don't you come to my plantation for a little while? There are always jobs to do there. Maybe you can help my maid with the cooking for a few weeks until you have sorted yourself out." I said this with some trepidation but what else could I have done? I couldn't leave her there with nothing but a plan to get herself eaten by a tiger on the mountain paths or killed by bandits in the goldfields. But also I was fascinated by her. In all my years roaming around Sumatra and the outer islands I had never met anyone quite like her before. I was probably already infatuated with her, but my years of bachelorhood would not let me recognise or admit it.

She sat, looking at the ground with her chin resting on her delicate hand. She looked to be deep in thought once more. She never made a spontaneous decision as long as I knew her. She was always careful and deliberate before coming to any decision but once her mind was made up, she could act with great decisiveness and, when necessary, great courage.

"I shall work for you. That is good," she said. "But first you must lend me money to do my hair. I can't arrive at your plantation looking like a beggar." I am not sure if she noticed the irony for she continued immediately. "I have no money but I will repay you with hard work. I'm a good cook as well as a good dancer." She smiled as she spoke and, I think, she almost laughed but had sufficient sensitivity to my feelings not to do so. Perhaps she was afraid of appearing greedy or too happy with success. Javanese think it rude to express emotions too openly; success or failure should be taken in the same way, with a controlled acceptance.

I took Yahyu to the local Catholic hospital and handed her over to the care of the good sisters who did not look too pleased to be presented with a dirty tramp, especially one brought along by me. My unjustified reputation for loose morals carried much weight with the good sisters—negative weight. Before I left I gave Yahyu some money to get herself smartened up while I went to one of the few places in Curup that sold beer, where I drank a toast to the prim Sisters of Everlasting Virginity. I spent the night in the only reasonable hotel in town: a rambling old wooden structure that dated from the colonial era, with plumbing to match.

Next morning I went to pick up Yahyu from the mission hostel but she kept me waiting over an hour. Whilst I was walking around the gardens, the Dutch priest, Father Tomas, came up to me. We were on familiar terms; I occasionally dropped him a bottle of scotch, usually around Christmas time, and he was always pleased to see me, sinner though I am. He never discussed religion; he was always too busy managing his hospital on very limited resources to worry too much about theology. But he liked to get drunk occasionally and I was one of the few people in the mountains he could safely drink with. "Two sinners together," he would say as he poured himself yet another scotch. "But please don't tell the sisters."

"Hello Jim, nice to see you. Who is the tramp girl you brought here last night?" he asked.

"Don't know, Father. Someone who was thrown off a bus with me. Why, is she being a problem?"

He smiled and said, "See for yourself when she appears. She may not be what you think she is but she is certainly not a bad person. She helped the sisters washing the patients. It's not a nice task, you know; not unless you're used to it. If you don't want her, I could always employ her here. I don't care what she may have done. She's proved to be very useful, even in the short time she's been here."

When Yahyu eventually turned up, I could hardly recognise her. She was dressed in traditional Javanese style in her new tight sarong and kebaya with her hair tied into a bun and decorated with flowers. She was smiling in a rather modest way. She still had a gaunt and hungry look in her face but her eyes were bright and confident.

"Ok Tuan. I am ready to travel with you." This was all she said with her mouth but her eyes said much more. I think she was enjoying the shock she had given me. She knew the power of her beauty but was sufficiently prudent not to show her confidence too openly.

***

Yahyu fitted in well with my domestic arrangements. She worked hard, much to the surprise of my existing maids, and charmed most of my domestic workers with her extremely good manners and elegant behaviour. The plantation workers, who were mostly Javanese, fell in love with her at first sight. They liked the sense of culture she brought to the plantation. I saw her one evening in the workers' dormitory area performing part of a Javanese ballet by the light of a small lantern, much to the delight of the workers. Happy workers are usually good workers and her presence added something light and happy to the plantation. I could feel it amongst the tea pickers when I toured the plantation every morning.

With me, Yahyu was always considerate but cautious. She seemed to genuinely enjoy the position of high status that she very naturally slipped into, both in my house and within the plantation. None of the staff had seen her as I had first seen her: a barefoot tramp in Linggau bus station. She glided smoothly from tramp to princess in just a few weeks. All she had needed was a new set of clothes, a good hairdo, a bath and a bed, the rest she did herself as if born to the part.

Most evenings she joined me on the veranda and sat on a bamboo mat watching me and talking of events happening on the plantation. She also talked a lot about herself at that stage; about her dancing school, her adventures on the river, Jon and the policeman, but she never alluded to the reason for her abandonment and I never asked. I was too enchanted with her presence.

I thought often about our unusual relationship. It was so easy, so pleasant, even though completely unphysical. I think we were both afraid of breaking the magic spell we were weaving around each other; neither of us wanted to see the spell evaporate. Living in expectation is always exciting; why end it?

Every morning she bathed in the river. The rivers in these mountains are freezing. I bathed in them every morning but few of my staff ever attempt to. After months of vagrant wonderings, I think she found the feeling of being clean a real delight and she spent many minutes standing in the clear, rushing water, pouring buckets of it over her body as she modestly covered herself with her sarong.

I bathed quite close to her most days. The Javanese are not particularly prudish, and men and women bathe in the same area, although never touching and always covering their bodies with strips of cloth. I couldn't stop myself admiring her body when she left the water with her wet sarong clinging to every curve of her smooth figure. She had filled out a lot since she had arrived. She ate enormous quantities, sometimes five or six times a day, according to secret reports from my buxom chief maid, Ibu Wati. Yahyu must have put on three or four kilos over the few weeks she had been with me and it showed in her curvaceous figure. The sharp edges and bony limbs had all disappeared and been replaced by a smooth suppleness that was exquisite to look at.

Whilst bathing I always tried to look at her figure obliquely and I suspected Yahyu also tried to show me her figure equally obliquely. We both knew that at some stage we would have to approach the big question of a relationship but neither of us wanted to spoil what was, at least temporarily, a kind of paradise of expectation and promise.

**

I was lying in bed under my mosquito net, reading a novel that was slowly getting damp with sweat when I heard suppressed shouting from the domestic quarters. I got up to investigate, knowing that Ibu

Wati had gone to Curup for her day off. There was nobody around but I could hear noises coming from Yahyu's room, as if she was fighting. I opened her door quietly and saw her struggling on her bed but there was no one else there. I cautiously walked towards her sleeping form and gently shook her awake. She was damp with sweat. She looked up in shock and then grabbed me tightly.

"I saw my mother," she panted. "She was running through a forest calling for me but I couldn't move. She passed by without seeing me. I tried to call after her but I couldn't speak; no sound came out. Then I saw ... I saw someone I don't want to remember. Don't leave me, not now. Sit with me for a little while."

I sat in a chair by her bed while she fell back on the mattress looking at the ceiling.

"Do you often have bad dreams?" I asked her.

"Sometimes, usually when I start to relax, I dream I'm lost and can't find my way home. I suppose it's true in a way." She spoke softly as if still in the land of nightmares.

"Go to sleep again," I said. "I shall sleep here tonight, in the chair. If any tigers try to attack you, they will have Jim to deal with." I received the glimmer of a smile as she turned towards me.

"Thank you, Tuan. I hope I shall dream of you tonight."

I awoke early the next morning, as I always did. I saw Yahyu's beautiful face relaxed in sleep and her curvaceous body lying peacefully on the bed. I stared at her for some minutes until I saw her eyelids flutter and I turned away in embarrassment.

"You still here, Tuan?" she said as she awoke.

"Still here. I've been sleeping in the chair."

"You shouldn't have stayed all night. I feel very guilty," she said as she slowly climbed out of bed. She turned as if to look out of the window then suddenly turned back, put her hands on my shoulders and kissed me lightly on the cheek. "No other man would have done that for a simple tramp. You kept all the tigers away. I wish you could always sleep by my bedside."

I kissed her forehead and quickly turned away. I am not sure who was more embarrassed but I think it was me.

That day I couldn't concentrate on my work; Yahyu occupied my thoughts as I trudged between the neat rows of tea bushes. I was thinking: shall I or shan't I? Do I really want to spoil my independence? Do I really want someone constantly in my home? Do I want to spoil the romance of the mysterious tramp girl? I decided on nothing except to go home early and discuss it with Yahyu. When I got home, I found her waiting on the veranda dressed in her finest clothes.

"You're early," she said. "I'm glad. I've been thinking about you all day."

We spent the evening casually chatting whilst avoiding the big topic that was foremost on both our minds. In the end, it was Yahyu who plucked up the courage to approach the subject. "You aren't relaxed tonight," she said. "I can feel the tension in you and I know the reason. You are afraid of starting something serious with me." She smiled at me before continuing, "I feel the same. I want to keep my image of you as an independent man who doesn't give in to desire. I respect you as being different from other men. I don't want you to change."

She looked up at me, her face a mixture of emotions, tears not quite forming under her eyelids.

I poured myself another drink and sat looking at Yahyu's beautiful but haunted face. Although she had never spoken of sex, I expected she had had some awful experiences as a tramp, which must have turned her off the physical side of love. Perhaps she could not see me in that role; that of a lover. I wasn't sure if I could see myself in the role either.

"I want to love you from a distance," she said quietly, as if to herself. "I never want to lose the picture of you sitting here, on the veranda, looking over your tea gardens. I can't think of you in any other way."

I plucked up courage; alcohol helped. I approached the subject obliquely, "Do you want me to guard you against tigers again tonight?"

She blushed deeply as she replied, "Yes, please."

I walked over to her and pulled her to her feet. She smiled and held her face up to mine, as if asking to be kissed; we didn't stop till early morning. By that I mean we didn't stop kissing till early morning. I forget when we actually started making love. It must have been some days later; it didn't seem to matter.

My self-imposed solitude had ended in a way I could never have planned.

Chapter 4

Several weeks later Yahyu suddenly disappeared.

I had been away for a few days visiting one of our farthest tea gardens and came home late afternoon expecting to see Yahyu on the veranda waiting for me, but she wasn't. As I entered the door I could feel the emptiness in the house. Everything was in place but unused and lifeless. In the bedroom I saw Yahyu's smart clothes neatly folded on the bed as if left there for me to see, but the cupboard which contained her working clothes was open and the shelves empty. I opened her mahogany jewellery box and found everything in place, even the earrings which she never took off. Her purse lay on one of the shelves but with no money in it. Yahyu had gone out in the evening with all her spare cash but no purse, no jewellery and wearing her working clothes; maybe not a cause for concern but a bit of a mystery nonetheless.

I waited on the veranda until the sun finally set, expecting to see her appearing out of the clouds that were swirling around the plantation, but she did not come. I called the maids but they either didn't know where she was or were being evasive. They had not seen her since yesterday. I walked over to the dormitories and asked the workers. Several of them reported seeing Yahyu walking towards the main gate the previous evening but when they waved to her she just ignored them and walked on.

I wandered back to the veranda to think, when Ibu Wati came hurrying up to me. "Tuan, I found this letter on your bed, under Nona's clothes." I immediately recognised Yahyu's large, childish script. It wasn't really a letter, just a few short sentences that read: "*Tuan, I have to go. I'm sorry for everything. Don't think badly of me. I may be able to come back again one day. Will you wait for me? Yahyu.*"

Yahyu never did anything spontaneously; this was a planned exit. She had said several times that her presence on my plantation was temporary, but I had never believed her, thinking it was just her way of exerting independence. I should have known Yahyu better. She didn't need to show her independence to me because we both knew she didn't want to be independent. She enjoyed being part of a family and she viewed both me and the whole plantation as her new family. She must have left because she still had some task to complete which did not involve me. The only clue I could think of was from our very first conversation, when she told me she was going to look for her uncle who was supposedly digging for gold in the mountains. I remembered laughing at her when she said she was going to head for Tes and then turn west into the mountains where she hoped to find him. Would she really be stupid enough, or brave enough, to go there? I knew the answer even though I did not understand the motivation.

I had to get to Tes before she did. Once she entered those remote mountain paths, anything could happen and no one would ever find her or even know what happened to her. I prepared the Jeep for the long journey to Tes but as I was leaving, Ibu Wati climbed purposely into the back and sat down with an immovable expression on her face.

"Ibu, you can't come with me and I'm in a hurry. Please get out," I ordered her, more sternly than I had intended.

"I'm coming with you, Tuan. This is women's matters; you won't understand. I don't know where we're going but I know we need to go there fast, so stop wasting time." Then, as if she suddenly remembered her manners, she added, "... Tuan." If I hadn't been so stressed, I would have given her a hug but, on second thoughts, maybe I wouldn't. She was a formidable woman.

The journey to Tes takes about fourteen hours by Jeep when it's not raining. The road is truly awful; just a muddy track that runs through endless streams and rivers that can cause lengthy delays when they are in flood. In many places buses unload their passengers and harnessed them into pushing the bus out of deep potholes or through the thick mud. It's not a fun journey.

I turned around to speak to Ibu Wati who refused to sit in the front, next to me, because it would be unseemly. "Did Yahyu say anything to you before she left? Do you know why she left?"

Ibu was very direct in her answers. "That's two questions, Tuan. Which one do you want me to answer?"

I would have given her a quizzical stare but I couldn't turn round far enough. "Just tell me what you know, Ibu, please."

"She said nothing to me. And I don't know why she left but I can guess." I waited for her to continue but she didn't.

"Are you going to tell me what your guess is?" I asked, impatiently.

"It's women's business. Can't expect you to understand. Leave it up to me." Then, as another afterthought, she added "... Tuan."

It had started raining heavily which made the road extremely dangerous and I had to yell at Ibu so she could hear me over the sound of the rain on the canvas roof. "Ibu, why did you come along with me if you're not going to tell me what you think?"

"Because when you meet Nona Yahyu, there's going to be a scene and if people see you, a belando, trying to get her into this Jeep, they are going to get suspicious. This is women's work; you let me handle Nona Yahyu. You just get me there before she does. That's all you've got to do." I was her boss but it appeared that in "women's matters" I was just a common driver.

We passed several small towns and villages on the road to Tes. Buses were parked in the scruffy little stations allowing the passengers a chance to stretch their legs and eat but I decided not to stop. It would waste too much time.

Tes is a truly strange place; it's a cowboy town in a Sumatran setting. It's immensely dirty, it's rough, it's full of transients furtively drinking in small, dark stalls discussing gold. All faces have an expression of suspicion, as if everybody is a potential criminal, which, in this town, is probably correct. But Tes is situated in the most spectacular country; standing by a large lake and ringed by enormous cone-shaped volcanoes. It is truly dramatic when seen from a distance and truly nasty when seen close up. You can feel the danger in the air. It's not a place for the faint-hearted.

I parked in sight of the small bus terminal but, on Ibu's

instructions, I stayed inside the Jeep so as not to attract too much attention. Ibu strode into the bus terminal and sat herself rigidly on a stool by a tea stall. She stayed there for several hours, immovable, her ferocious expression sufficient to frighten even the most hardened of criminals. She was never bothered; she was a rock in the midst of a sea of furtive figures rushing by in the misty gloom that precedes a Sumatran rainstorm.

I saw Yahyu as soon as the bus drew in. She climbed nimbly off the bus, ignoring the comments from some of her fellow passengers and immediately started walking towards the end of the town as if she knew exactly where she was going. She had never been here before but it's the best way of avoiding suspicion; hesitancy is a recipe for disaster. But Ibu Wati was ready for her.

Yahyu walked, as always, looking directly at the ground as if oblivious to her surroundings but in reality to ensure she avoided anyone's eye when Ibu caught up with her and grabbed her arm. Yahyu looked startled at first, but on seeing the familiar face of Ibu she immediately looked around and spotted the Jeep parked amongst the evening litter of Tes market. She tried to walk on, skirting around Ibu, but she was no match for the formidable commandant of my staff. Ibu gently, but firmly, held her arm and guided her towards the Jeep.

I leapt out the Jeep and opened the door as Ibu pushed Yahyu silently into the back seat and followed her inside, immediately locking both doors so Yahyu could not get out. I was glad Ibu had come; I could never have done that in public, not in a town like this. I drove off immediately, before the startled passersby could gather their wits.

On the long ride back to the plantation hardly a word was spoken. I had to stop for a few hours to get some sleep and when I awoke, I saw Yahyu lying on Ibu's lap, sleeping. I drove on, trying not to disturb her, but I think Ibu did not sleep at all; she kept a quiet vigilance throughout the long journey. We arrived at Gaja Tiga in the early hours of the morning where Ibu took hold of Yahyu and guided her to the domestic quarters. I left them to it; Ibu would be a good guard and I was too tired to try to understand what was happening. I collapsed in bed and slept.

***

For several days Yahyu did not appear although I had regular reports of her progress from Ibu Wati. At first she wouldn't eat, but on the second day she started eating and wouldn't stop. She talked to no one but Ibu Wati, but what they discussed Ibu did not tell me. I kept myself busy on the plantation while waiting for Yahyu to pluck up enough courage to confront me once again. I didn't want to rush her; she had been through enough hardship already, so I let her take her time.

Several evenings later, Ibu Wati came to see me while I was sitting on the veranda drinking.

"Tuan, I need to talk to you." She spoke with concern. I presumed I was going to hear about Yahyu.

Ibu Wati stood as if to attention. I don't think she ever sat in my presence; it was not allowed in her book of protocol. "Nona Yahyu is pregnant," she said.

"OK," I said slowly while thinking it through. "But I doubt if you're right. We've only been together for about a month. Far too early to tell and, even if she is pregnant, it's hardly a disaster."

Ibu gave me one of her looks which suggested she was dealing with an idiot and took a deep breath, which only succeeded in further enhancing her enormous iron-clad bosom, almost bursting the seams of her tight kebaya. "You're not the father, Tuan. The father is another belando but she doesn't know where he is."

Her statement came as a real blow. I wasn't sure if I was just shocked or, perhaps, a touch jealous that somebody else had a prior claim on her. The news suggested the end of my dream and, I suppose, it had ended her dreams several months ago. I should have noticed her pregnancy without being told. I had seen a bulge in her stomach while she was bathing but I put it down to her improved diet. She was eating enormous quantities at this stage, probably making up for lost time, and her body was filling out and this camouflaged the growth of her stomach. I had also tasted an occasional tingling sweetness on her nipples which I had presumed was Javanese love potion but I now realised it was just milk. I think my total absorption in her had blinded me to reality, but now that I knew the reality, I had to decide how to respond to it.

Ibu still stood in front of me, waiting for orders which I was not yet ready to formulate, when she took the initiative. "Do you still want to see her or shall I prepare something else for her? You tell me what you want, Tuan."

"What do you mean; prepare something else?"

Ibu Wati sighed deeply; foreigners were obviously too stupid. "Tuan, this is not the first unwanted pregnancy in the world and it won't be the last. You can't let her stay here or the workers will lose respect for you. Sleeping with a girl who is pregnant from another man is not the behaviour of a good manager. But we can't let her go with nothing, so we have to do something to help her. You're a rich man. Give me some money and I can find a good family in Bengkulu to look after her until the birth. If you give them more money, they will also look after the baby and she will be free to return to you or go back to her family in Palembang or do whatever else she wants. Money can do anything Tuan, if you know how to use it properly."

Judging from her tone of feigned deference, I think she was inferring that although I had the money, it was her that had the good sense, so I should let her take control. Ibu Wati was eminently practical. Like many Javanese, she was not so concerned with the emotions of a relationship but with the protocol and status that went with it.

"Ibu, I need to speak to Yahyu. Tell her I'm not angry but we need to talk. We need to work out the best solution. Please ask her to come here?"

Ibu Wati gave another sigh and asked, "Why?" I didn't immediately respond but waited several moments until she reluctantly added "... Tuan", but she showed her agitation in her raised eyebrows and contemptuous expression although her appreciation of her position as employee forbade her from saying outright that she thought I was a fool.

"Because I want to hear what she has to say," I said.

Ibu responded with an exaggerated show of patience. "You know what she has to say. She ran away in shame. That means she's a good girl at heart and will not cause you any trouble. Let me handle it Tuan; I know what to do."

If I had taken Ibu Wati's advice, the subsequent events would never have happened and we could have both led safe but separate lives. But I didn't. I acted in a way I thought was noble but was probably based more on my self-interest; I loved Yahyu and wanted her back.

***

It was several hours before Yahyu appeared on the veranda. She was dressed modestly but smartly. I noticed she was wearing the earrings I had bought her which, I suppose, Ibu Wati had surreptitiously taken from the jewellery box in my bedroom. She looked at the ground as she sat on a bamboo mat at the back of the veranda but she did not passively wait for me to start the conversation. Without looking up into my face she started speaking, so softly that I had to lean towards her to catch the words.

"Tuan," she started. Despite our intimacy, she insisted on calling me Tuan. "I did not run away from you. I left to complete my duties to my baby and my family. I wanted to find gold so the baby could have a good life and so I could pay back my family for all the sacrifices they made for me. If God was kind to me, he would let me come back to you. I don't want to be a problem to you or to anyone; this is my burden and my duty and I must find a solution to it myself.

"I don't know about your past and I don't care. I know you are a good man and that you have a good life here. The workers respect you; everyone respects you. If they knew about me, you would lose their respect and then you would hate me. I don't want that. But if I stay here, I cannot keep my condition a secret much longer.; it's beginning to show. I have to leave you but I don't want you to pay for my baby. It's not fair."

I looked out over the veranda. The sky seemed to reflect Yahyu's mood, sombre and forbidding. Already the mountaintops were lost from view as the clouds crept over the valley. I looked back towards Yahyu and saw her looking up at me, studying my every reaction.

"This is what I shall miss the most when I leave," she said, staring out at the gathering storm. "Every day I look forward to this time, when I am with you on the veranda. I never wanted this to end; it's like a storybook and I wanted to pretend we would live happily ever after but we won't. This story can't have a happy ending, but I still wanted it to go on as long as possible. I wanted to live this dream until the last minute and then leave you with happy memories of me. So many people hate me now, so many people are disappointed in me; I don't want you to hate me or be disappointed. But now you know the true story. Tell me what you think of me, please."

I was still undecided what to do or say. Did I really want someone else's baby in my life; my exciting, beautiful, solitary life? I looked at Yahyu's earnest young face, a face that should have been destined to enchant a thousand audiences as she enacted the legends of old Java. Instead, she had been cut off in her prime and was trying desperately to come to terms with her fate.

"All I know is what Ibu Wati told me; that you're pregnant from another belando. I think you should tell me the whole story and let me be the judge of what I should do."

She spent a long time looking out over the tea gardens towards the mountains, deep in thought. I was waiting for the moment when she would raise her head. I waited a long time, but when she eventually spoke, it was with bitter pride.

"Before I graduated from my dancing school, I was already

performing in towns around Sumatra. People asked specifically for me to perform and my dance school released me to go touring with dance groups and I earned money. I was very proud. Several times important government officials requested I dance for them at their garden parties. They sometimes gave me tips which I hid from my teachers and bought presents for my younger sisters. I loved dancing. And my sisters loved me because of the presents I brought them."

She hesitated again, taking a deep breath before continuing. It was obviously causing her a lot of pain to explain. "I'm not proud of what I have done. It was a mistake. Do not judge me too harshly." She fell silent again and I had to prompt her to continue.

Yahyu sat still on the wicker chair, wringing her hands. I think she wanted to share the burden but was still sufficiently inexperienced with men to know how I would react. I think I was also insufficiently experienced because I wasn't sure how I would react either. My major fear was to hear the words that she was still in love with the father of her child.

"My family had been paying my dancing school for six years. They are poor farmers; we are migrants in Komrin country, upriver from Palembang. They grow peanuts and maize and do some fishing in the swamps. It's hard to make a living, scratching it from the earth. It was a big sacrifice, a big investment for them to send me to dancing school.

"Because I was so good at dancing, everyone expected me to become rich and to marry a rich man, and then support all my brothers and sisters through their schooling. When I went home to my village, the family was so proud of me that they took me around people's houses to show me off. I danced in the village hall and everyone came to watch, not just from our village but also from neighbouring villages. They said I was like Sita come down from heaven to protect their crops.

"All the fathers brought their sons to our house as potential marriage partners for me but my father refused them all, even when they offered land as part of the marriage arrangements. Maybe he was too arrogant, but he was so proud of me, he wanted me to marry a rich government official."

Tears flowed down Yahyu's cheeks as she recounted the story of her family and her village in the swamps of Komrin Ilhir, many miles from here. For a young girl with no money, she had performed an amazing feat of strength and ingenuity to have travelled so far through very rough country and survived.

"My dance group was asked to dance in front of the belando managers of a rubber plantation near Perabumulih. After the performance, we were given a big meal and the belandos started drinking. One of the young managers talked to me all evening. He spoke Melayu quite well. He said he came from Holland and he wanted to get to know me better. I felt complimented by his attention. We didn't often speak to men; our teachers wouldn't let us, but he was a belando man and a manager, so I trusted him. When we got back to Perabumulih, one of the older women dancers asked me to see her in her room. She told me that the young man who had talked to me, Wilhelm his name was, wanted me and that if I went with him, he would pay for all my schooling and also help my family."

Yahyu hesitated; she was coming to the point and it was obviously embarrassing for her. I had already guessed the rest of the story but I decided to stay quiet and hear her out.

"The lady explained in detail what I would have to do. I was still a virgin then. I didn't understand anything, and I was delighted that someone wanted to support me. I could imagine the joy on my sisters' faces when I went home carrying presents for them all, and I could hold feasts where my father would be seen as a great man in the village.

"The lady said that many of the dancers did it and they often ended up marrying the man. To marry a rich belando would give great status and wealth to my family. She said it was normal for belando men to do this before marriage."

She was studying my face, looking to see any reaction to her story, but my face remained blank, I think, although my heart was pounding. I wanted to hear everything before making judgements but an insidious jealousy was creeping inside me like a cancer. I already hated Wilhelm, although I knew nothing about him.

"All I said to her was that I would meet the man again but I would not promise to do more. I met him many times, and each time he gave me money. I had never met a man before that gave money. I thought he must really love me to give me so much money. He told me he had wanted a village girl who was pure and beautiful, rather than the other girls that hung around the plantation trying to catch one of the belando managers. And I believed him.

"When I went home to my village, I gave money and presents to my family. They no longer had to support me; I was supporting them and they were so happy. But I lied to them: I told them the money was from my dancing. I wanted to believe it was true but it wasn't really true, was it? The money came from Wilhelm and it wasn't given for my dancing."

Yahyu fell quiet, in embarrassment I think. She looked at me but I remained quiet, not quite knowing how to react.

"Every weekend when I left him to return to dancing school, he put his hand in his pocket and gave me whatever money he had. I had never in my life seen so much money. I thought him a very rich and generous man. But I never really looked at him as a person. I never asked myself if I even liked him. I thought he was madly in love with me and that was all that mattered."

She looked up at me as if asking a question. I think she was asking whether I thought this was bad, but I did not respond. I wanted to know everything, although my feelings were a mixture of disappointment at such naivety and jealousy of this man Wilhelm. I kept forgetting she was only seventeen and I was ... older.

"Then I found I was pregnant."

Although I already knew about it, the phrase hit me in the face. Those words, "I found I was pregnant", have such finality about them; it was the end of all her dreams. It was the end of her life as she knew it.

Yahyu started crying again but when I went over to her, she waved me away and continued her story despite her tears. "I went immediately to tell Wilhelm. He was kind and considerate and he asked me to stay the weekend with him. He said he needed time to sort things out but that I shouldn't worry because he would take care of everything. I believed him." These last three words were said with great bitterness and her face took on the haunted look that had first attracted me to her in the bus station in Curup.

"As I was leaving after the weekend, he said he needed to go to Jakarta for a few weeks but when he got back he would finalise arrangements for me. I believed him again. He had been so kind and generous in the past. I thought he would marry me after he returned, although he never actually said that."

There was no stopping Yahyu now. I think she forgot I was sitting next to her. She was recounting the whole sorry tale and there was a look of shock on her face as if she still couldn't believe what had happened. She looked down at her feet as she spoke, as if speaking to no one at all.

"After two weeks had passed," she continued, "there was still no word from Wilhelm, so I went to his rubber plantation to ask after him. When I got there, no one would talk to me and the office guard told me to leave. One of the domestic staff said that Wilhelm had been moved to another plantation in Kalimantan but she would not tell me where it was. I asked her what I should do and she just shrugged her shoulders and said there was nothing to do. Wilhelm had gone and would not be back.

"He had left me with nothing. *Nothing.*" Yahyu almost yelled the last word whilst glaring at the gathering clouds, oblivious to my presence. I had never seen Yahyu angry before.

Yahyu's story created mixed emotions in me. I was angry that Wilhelm had got her pregnant but, in a rather perverted way, I was really pleased he had turned out to be such a bastard. My greatest fear had been that she was still trying to find him because she still loved him but that seemed not to be the case. However, her story had not finished; she turned back towards me, anger still showing in her flashing eyes.

"What was I to tell my family and my village? I no longer had any money to give them because dancing paid very little in comparison with the money Wilhelm had given me and, in any case, I would not have been able to dance much longer because of my stomach. I had lied to my family and let them all down. I was too ashamed to tell my teachers and my school friends and too ashamed to go home. I wandered around Perabumulih for some days and was tempted to get money in bad ways but I couldn't do it. I met a man who offered me money to stay with him for the night, but I just couldn't go with him. I ran away. In the end I decided to go home because I had no money left and nowhere else to go.

"When my family saw me carrying no presents and looking depressed, they knew something was wrong. They brought me quickly into the house so no one could see me. They were distraught when I told them what had happened. They had told everyone in the village that we were rich and now ... what were they to say?

"My father flew into a rage and my mother cried for hours. My brothers and sisters saw their education disappearing. The village would laugh at us; from rags to riches and then back to rags again in only a few months. I had caused them so much shame. I didn't know what to do.

"After my father had calmed down, he told me I must marry immediately, before anyone in the village knew I was pregnant. He sent one of his brothers to my dancing school to see if they knew anyone who wanted me. Within a few days an old Chinaman came to the house. He said he had seen me dancing in Palembang and had sent his agents to my dancing school to find me. He would give gold to my father if he could marry me.

"He already had two wives. What could I do? I said no but my father went ahead with the arrangements. I ran away when they were still negotiating the marriage arrangements. I couldn't marry that horrible old man. It was the end of everything."

Yahyu stopped talking and looked at me enquiringly. She was only seventeen; how could I possibly judge her? I was about to speak when she suddenly burst out, "I refuse to sell myself again to any man as I had done to Wilhelm. I hate him." I was delighted to hear her words. The more she hated Wilhelm, the more contented I became, although I tried hard not to show it. Love can be very selfish.

Yahyu looked at me again, anger still pushing her monologue onwards. "I *will* get gold and I *will* pay for my baby to go to a good family and I *will* repay my family and I *will* repay you." She punched the table with her delicate hands in a show of aggression at her fate and in her determination to fight that fate.

After her sudden outburst, her shoulders slumped in exhaustion and her head began to droop. Tears flowed down her cheeks and fell onto her bosom. "I'm sorry," was all she said as she dried her tears, "I didn't mean to be angry with you."

I had not guessed that gentle, kind, graceful Yahyu could possess such depths of anger and hatred. This was a side of Yahyu I had not seen before but I respected her for it.

Yahyu got up and walked towards my chair. "I'm sorry," she said again. "This is not your problem and I didn't want you to have to deal with it. What are you going to do now?"

Looking into Yahyu's sad eyes, I knew then I couldn't leave her, despite what Ibu Wati said. I held her hand as I spoke, "I don't know but I think it's more a question of what you're going to do. You can stay here as long as you like. We can sort something out although it may take me a bit of time to get used to it all. But you can't go to the goldfields."

She once again hesitated briefly before continuing. "When you found me, I was desperate. I was hungry and the baby weighed heavily inside me: I couldn't have kept going for many more days. When you brought me to your plantation, I thought you were going to use me. I would have accepted it because I thought all men behaved like that and better you than anyone else because you seemed to be a good man. But you didn't use me. For two weeks I slept alone, expecting to hear your knock on my door but you never came. I respect you, Tuan. You are not like other men. You are a solitary man, you love your mountains and your jungles, and you are ... I don't know how to say it properly, but you are different. You don't follow or lead. You are just yourself. There is no other man on earth like you; not in my experience. I think the gods sent you to help me."

I smiled at the thought of myself being a gift from a god, however, Yahyu was not joking. She continued, "But I misled you. I was not thinking of the future; I was living in a dream. I wanted to pretend I was not pregnant. I wanted to forget about it just for a few days or weeks and enjoy myself with you. I wanted to live the life of your Ibu even if it was only for a short while. I wanted to feel the pride of being with a good man. But I realise the situation I have put you in. I don't want you to suffer and I don't want you to hate me for destroying your reputation. I want to leave you so I can remember you as you are now; proud and thoughtful and kind."

I stroked Yahyu's cheek before I spoke. She was so young to have experienced so much hardship whilst managing to keep her essential goodness in tact. "I feel like you have been with me for years," I said. "I can't let you go to your death searching for gold that you'll never find. Promise me you will stay here for the next few weeks until we can work something out. I shan't desert you and I appreciate your thoughts for my reputation, not that I care much about it myself."

That evening we parted company for the night, more in emotional exhaustion than anything else. I asked her to come to my room later and she said she would think about it, but she never came and I did not call her. We both needed time alone to think.

***

Over the coming few days I saw little of Yahyu; I worked from dawn till dusk on the plantation. She always joined me in the evenings on the veranda but only for an hour or so before disappearing into the domestic workers' quarters. She said little and was rather distracted. Our conversations were constrained, as if neither of us knew what to say. Her main concern was to protect my reputation. So far only Ibu Wati knew she was pregnant, but she could not keep it secret much longer. My concern was largely for Yahyu's welfare; to prevent her doing something stupid out of desperation. Neither of us wanted to part company, but neither of us knew what to do about it.

Several days later we had a visit from Bunggo Tucker, one of my very few long-term friends. In Burma, in between fighting the Japanese, Bunggo ran an illegal whiskey trading business, selling through our Karen irregulars who carried more whiskey into the jungle than ammunition. Bunggo said they sold it to the Japanese before they ambushed them. "My contribution to the war effort," he said. "Get the buggers drunk and then shoot 'em; that way we win the war and make a profit." He was a natural trader, if always a little on the shady side, and was now trading in tea based out of Medan in north Sumatra. He came to see me three or four times a year to test our tea production and drink my whisky. Bunggo was as fat as a pig and twice as ugly but a great friend.

On his first evening we sat on the veranda discussing the price of tea and the quality of the crop when Yahyu came to join us. Rather than sitting on a stool as she usually did, she brought out a bamboo mat and placed it at the back of the veranda and silently watched us.

"That's a nice-looking girl," said Bunggo appreciatively. "Who is she?"

I could tell from Yahyu's expression she knew we were talking about her although she couldn't understand English. Bunggo spoke Melayu fluently, as I did, but we always spoke English together.

"I don't really know how to answer that. She's a phantom from the clouds come down to earth to make me into a good man."

Bunggo gave me a quizzical look. "She'll have her work cut out to do that," he said as he purposely looked away from Yahyu. Bunggo was a tactful man behind his bluff and hearty exterior, and he quickly changed the subject.

Throughout that long and rather drunken evening Yahyu never took her eyes off us. She said nothing and only went to bed when we eventually disappeared. She had never met any of my friends before, not that I had many, and I could only guess at what she thought of Bunggo. On the outside he looked like a shady wheeler and dealer, which he was. All evening he had sat back in his rattan chair with his shirt undone and his enormous hairy belly sticking out, dripping with sweat. He could not have been a very attractive picture for a young girl. However, Yahyu was different and maybe she saw things differently. She certainly gave him a friendly smile as he staggered off to bed, although I doubt if he was in any fit condition to notice it.

Early next morning as I was leaving to tour the plantation, Yahyu came up to me and asked, "Is Tuan Bunggo a good friend of yours?"

"Yes," I said. "One of my few friends. Why do you ask?"

"Can I talk to him, please?"

I thought it very sweet that she should ask my permission to talk to Bunggo, but on second thoughts I realised she probably wanted to ask him questions about me and possibly about our current situation. I had few secrets from Bunggo and was happy to share the secret of Yahyu with him. Maybe the three of us could come up with a solution.

I did not return that night. I visited the outskirts of the plantation and it rained so badly, the Jeep could not get me back to the house. I spent a wet and uncomfortable night in one of the tea-drying huts, wondering what Yahyu and Bunggo would be discussing. The following morning involved a long, wet, muddy hike back to the house and I thought as I was walking how much I loved life on the plantation. I loved the rain and the muddy potholed tracks, I loved the mountains and the jungles, and I loved the smell of tea from the drying factory that greeted me as I got close to the house. I came towards the house dirty but content. However, I could tell from the atmosphere when I arrived that something had been decided in my absence.

As soon as I sat down, Yahyu and Bunggo glanced at each other in a conspiratorial way, which annoyed me; it was my kingdom and nobody was going to arrange my life here but me. But when I saw the concern on Yahyu's face, I melted. She had picked up my irritation immediately and wanted to compensate for it. But Bunggo, as so often happened with fat, pig-like Bunggo, came to the rescue first. He came straight to the point and spoke in Melayu so Yahyu would understand.

"She told me a lot last night, about her meeting you and about her being pregnant. She thinks you're sent by the gods to help her; funny taste some people have but I'm not a woman so I can't judge." Bunggo laughed into his gin but on seeing the serious expression on Yahyu's face, his laugh changed into something akin to a hiccup and a yawn.

"I can help her with the birth. That's easy," he said. "I can place her in the Catholic orphanage in Medan. They take in pregnant women regardless of religion. You will need to pay but it doesn't cost much; a few dollars a month is all you need. She's happy to go to the orphanage and work there till birth so as not to embarrass you but she says she will not leave her baby in an orphanage. As she's got no money, I don't know what the hell she will do afterwards if she's alone. She can't live with a young baby and no money, but the convent will solve the temporary problem."

We both turned to Yahyu who was looking at me, trying to read my expression. I could tell from her face that she had made up her mind on something but was uncertain how to say it. I helped her along the way. "You can return here with the baby and stay, if you want," I said.

"Thank you, Tuan. I know I can do that, but then I could not be with you. You cannot be seen to have a concubine who already has somebody else's baby. I could not live here and see you every day knowing that I was an embarrassment to you."

I could tell from her stance that she was slowly coming to the point but it might take her a long time to get there. She knew I did not like people interfering in my life, so she was probably trying to get me to come up with a suggestion that she and Bunggo had already worked out. I could already detect the understanding formed between them and I was wary as to its meaning. I didn't mistrust Bunggo at all, and I had no reason to mistrust Yahyu, but they were obviously sharing a secret and this continued to annoy me.

Then Bunggo came out with it and, like a bullet, it struck home. I was never to learn whose idea it was, Bunggo's or Yahyu's, but it was brilliant in its simplicity. "We will say the baby is mine," said Bunggo, holding up his gin and tonic as if to study the wildlife living inside the glass. Yahyu sat on the mat staring intensely at me, willing me to say yes.

Bunggo continued with studied calm, as if discussing tactics for selling out-of-date sardines to an unsuspecting Japanese army. "I will take Yahyu with me to Medan now, before her stomach sticks out any further, and I will place her in the convent until birth; you pay, of course. Yahyu can come back to you a few months after the birth and then, some weeks later, I shall turn up with a baby. I shall say it's mine from one of my women in Medan and I want you to look after it for me, as I am too embarrassed to show it to my mum." Bunggo laughed. He had never been embarrassed about anything, least of all about his harem, which only existed in his imagination.

He continued, "You will need someone to look after the baby, so you keep Yahyu as your housekeeper-cum-nanny. Voila, you have the most beautiful housekeeper and bed-keeper in Sumatra. People will gossip a bit but as long as they don't know the truth directly, it doesn't matter. Yahyu will have you, God bless her and good luck to her for that, and she has the baby. Your name will remain as pristine as your socks on washing day and mine as black as the hole in Calcutta, which is how I like it." He pulled a rueful face before laughing out loud. "All you have to do is tell St Peter when we get to those pearly gates that it wasn't me that did it, and can he please let me in as I don't fancy eternity in the other place, although most of my friends will probably already be there."

I looked at Yahyu. "I want you to say yes, Tuan," she said. "I want this more than anything. I will work hard for you and the baby won't bother you. We can sleep in the domestic's quarters if you want. And there will be no obligation, Tuan. You will be free to ask me to leave at any time and I will go. You know I keep my word."

I had never heard Yahyu ask for anything before, so this came as a surprise. I suppose she suddenly saw a light at the end of her dark and dangerous tunnel and didn't want to let it slip away. I believed her when she said I could ask her to go at any time; she understood my love of freedom and she didn't want to restrict me. She just wanted to be given this one chance to prove to herself and the world that she was a good woman.

Bunggo said that the ancient Persians always made important decisions twice; once while sober and then again while drunk and then compared results. We tested the drunken one that night, long into the night, and Yahyu joined me in bed once more. I don't think we ever made a decision; we just let it happen with the minimum of fuss.

***

When the time came for Yahyu to go to Medan I was loath to let her go. It would be another four or five months till the birth and we would be parted for all that time. I had decided to escort her to Palembang and put her on a boat to Medan; a journey of about five days. Bunggo would meet her at the other end and take her to the convent. The journey to Palembang took us back through the regions where Yahyu had previously walked on her long, hard journey to the mountains. She now fervently believed that I was the goldfield she had been searching for (in a non-materialistic way) and, indeed, she had found me in the mountains, so she was convinced her instincts had been right from the start. It also gave her proof of the basic goodness of the gods who had rewarded her honesty after punishing her for her misdemeanour. This is a very Javanese logic, not to be taken too literally; it's a kind of active fatalism where the gods offer you a chance at redemption but you have to strive to achieve it. I suppose my tea plantation, and myself, was her reward.

On the way to Palembang, Yahyu was in a sombre mood. She was worried about parting from me, as if the dream would suddenly vanish and she would wake up on the roadside again as a tramp. On the way to Muaraklingi she tried to find the spot where she had eventually found her way out of the rubber forest but she could not identify it. She kept her eyes glued to the window, hoping she might see Rusdi but he never appeared. When we passed through Muaraklingi, she cowered in the back of my Jeep, asking me to go through quickly; she was still scared of the police chief.

As we approached the outskirts of Palembang, Yahyu said, "I think I should visit my village before I go to Medan. I want to tell them I shall pay them back one day."

This was a suggestion I had not been expecting but, on reflection, it made sense. It would be the start of her rehabilitation back into her family.

On the journey to her village she was very nervous; I could tell by her silence. She was probably unsure of her reception when we got there and, I suspected, she was uncertain how she would behave if we met Udin again. I knew how I would behave and I expect Yahyu would have joined me, which would not have been a very dignified entrance into her village and her family.

"You are going to come into the village with me, aren't you?" she asked as we stopped the Jeep by the roadside.

"Of course I am. Why ask?"

"I don't want to meet Udin again but I do want the village to see you. I know I'm not your wife, we have a different relationship to that, but I am still proud of you and I want to show you off. I want them to understand that my family are not just failures to be laughed at. I shall not pretend you are the father of my child. I shall just say you are my protector. They will understand what that means and respect you for it. We will sleep in the same room but not in the same bed, then they will respect you even more as a man of great pride and control."

Yahyu's village was very isolated. From the small muddy track where we left the Jeep it was a day's hike through forest and swamp to reach it. Yahyu said very little during the journey but her silence showed how difficult it was for her. Despite the relatively short time she had been away, she seemed uncertain of the direction and several times we took wrong turnings, wandering off into the forest and ending up in small jungle clearings, only to retrace our steps once more. So much had happened to her in the few months she had been away, she had forgotten her past.

Her village was a typical migrant village: a collection of wooden shacks built on stilts to protect them from flooding, very different from the grand wooden houses built by the indigenous Komrin which smacked of pride. This village exhibited poverty and decay; migrants far from their homeland, lost in the middle of a swamp. The children were ragged and dirty, the houses looked ill kept; there were no signs of wealth or of any rich men in this miserable place.

As we walked into the village, Yahyu in front of me, as was the custom in Sumatra, people stopped and stared, open-mouthed. I don't know if they recognised Yahyu or not. She had changed her clothes just outside the village and was wearing her smartest kain and kebaya with her hair pinned up and decorated with an ivory comb. She had also told me to smarten up but I just laughed; it would take more than a migrant village to force me to look smart. Nobody greeted us on our walk through the village. I think they were all too shocked and didn't know how to respond.

When we got to Yahyu's house, I saw her hesitate before entering. I left her to it and wandered around the village. Everybody tried to avoid me. Afterwards I learnt they were afraid I had come to seek vengeance for their dismissal of Yahyu but I didn't know that at the time.

The evening passed well enough. Yahyu distributed presents amongst her immediate family and in the evening a large gathering of people came to the house to see the strange belando man whom Yahyu had brought with her. It was fun, in a way, although language was difficult as these migrants spoke Melayu badly and Yahyu had to keep translating from their native Javanese. Yahyu's father was humble and polite and, I suspect, a little scared. Her grandfather, however, boldly sat next to me with a happy smile on his gnarled face.

"You have rescued my granddaughter," he said. "She is the love of my old age and the most beautiful dancer I have ever seen. I want you to protect her. Beauty is a dangerous thing for a young girl." He patted my leg as he spoke; his age gave him the confidence for intimacy.

"She will be safe with me, Grandpa. She can live on my plantation and I will look after her." I spoke loudly so all the family could hear. Already I could detect their growing respect for Yahyu. They probably believed her previous failure was just a test from the gods and she had won their favour.

We left the village the next morning. Yahyu's rehabilitation in village life was complete. Few people understood what had happened. All they knew was that Yahyu was in the care of a big man and therefore she was a big woman. Many of her relatives walked with us for several hours on the journey back to the car. Udin, we were told, had run off to the swamp as soon as he saw us coming and had not returned; a shame, for I had been looking forward to meeting him.

***

I saw Yahyu onto the ferry for Medan. It was a difficult parting. We had only known each other for a short while and Yahyu was hesitant to leave, being uncertain as to whether I would really have her and her baby back. She boarded the ferry with the words, "If you don't want me back, you must say so before I come." I knew she didn't mean it.

I had mixed feelings on the journey back home. I was tempted to stop in Linggau and visit a few friends but decided against it; I wanted to be alone again. During the next few months I got back into the rhythm of my previous life, but there was an emptiness in the evenings. Sitting on the veranda admiring the mountains was still appealing, but the loneliness struck home; a feeling I was not accustomed to.

I wrote to her every few weeks, care of Bunggo, and I got simple replies written in large, childish script. Obviously writing was not an art they developed at the dancing school. However, I learnt that the nuns were very nice but disapproving of Bunggo, the supposed father who would not marry her. That her stomach was growing by the day, and she was looking forward to the time when it would all be over. That Bunggo came to see her every few weeks and occasionally took her out on picnics but the nuns insisted on sending along one of the servant girls from the convent in case Bunggo started to "act in the manner of all men". That she missed me and prayed for me every night. I wondered which particular god she was praying to; probably all of them, just to be safe. That she also missed our evenings on the veranda with the view of the mountains.

***

Several months later, close to the expected birth time, I had visitors on the plantation. A new police chief had been appointed to the region: Captain Supriyono. He came roaring up the potholed road to my house in his new American Jeep, accompanied by an overweight belando passenger dressed in civilian clothes. The Captain was very polite and precise in his speech.

"Hello Tuan Jim. I am your new police chief, based in Curup. May I introduce my adviser, Hans. He's from America."

Hans may have been American but he spoke English with a strong German accent. "Hi. You're that English tea gardener I heard about. You'll be seeing a lot of me in the future." He didn't smile and didn't explain his presence but he portrayed a studied contempt for me. I ignored him but invited the Captain in for tea.

He was surprisingly well-educated and articulate for a policeman. He spoke at length about local politics, a subject on which he was very knowledgeable, before turning his attention to my affairs. "You have been here for almost ten years. You live on your own but there are several women you send money to. Why do you do that?"

I was surprised at his knowledge but also a bit baffled as to why a policeman would be interested in such trivia. "Why do men send money to women?" I said flippantly.

"Let me explain," he continued. "Hans has been lent to me to help in our fight against provocateurs who want to destabilise us. His job is to check up on all foreigners in South Sumatra to see what they are doing and why they are doing it. Money is a powerful weapon in the hands of the wrong people. Hans has orders to report everything to me."

"I'm a plantation manager. I'm not a likely candidate for joining a revolution."

"There is more that one party trying to destabilise our country and use our problems for their own ends. My job is to help protect you, not to accuse you." The Captain spoke with such sincerity I almost believed him; he was certainly not a typical policeman.

Hans intervened, "You brought a woman here a few months ago

and now she's gone. Who is she and where did she go?"

"She's just some girl I picked up in Linggau and now she's gone. Nobody important. What the hell's it got to do with you? Why are you snooping into my affairs?"

"Good bit of arse, was she?" sneered Hans, who was sat at my desk casually going through my papers.

"You are a foreigner here," the Captain said. "You are a guest of my government. I must protect you; plantations are prime targets for agitators, and your wealth is a prime target for … anyone. I'm sure you will help; it's in your interests."

Hans wandered up to the Captain and spoke loudly. "I think I will stay here tonight. I want to speak to the workers tomorrow."

"Like hell you will," I said. This was my plantation and I didn't want some sleazy snooper prying into my affairs.

The Captain turned round immediately and looked me in the face. "Why not? There may be things happening on your plantation that you don't know about. Hans has a way of finding out these things. Not everyone here likes foreigners; they interfere in our internal affairs."

"What's going on, Captain? Why this sudden interest in my plantation? I've been here for ten years and I run a commercial plantation. I'm an unlikely recruit for the communist party, or any other party, and there are no agitators amongst my workforce."

Hans wandered over, his unshaven face glistening with sweat; he obviously wasn't accustomed to the tropics. "Name Jon mean anything to you?" he said.

"Jon's a pretty common name in Sumatra. If you knew your job better, you wouldn't ask such stupid questions."

"Got any friends in Medan, have you?"

"Yes, I do. So what?"

"Jon comes from Medan. We believe some political parties are trying to control the gold smuggling to finance political activities. Know anyone involved in the goldfields?"

Hans was looking into my drinks cupboard as he spoke and he pulled out a bottle of scotch. I looked towards the Captain who immediately intervened.

"Hans," the Captain said. "This is not your house and you will not stay without Tuan Jim's permission. You can question his workers now if you wish." Then, looking at me, he continued, "My apologies for my colleague; he has no manners but he does have the skills I require in my struggle to maintain law and order. We will often come back to visit you."

As they were leaving, Hans turned to me and quietly whispered, "Be careful, we are watching you. There are greater forces at work here than Captain Supriyono. If you hear anything useful, let me know. "

I was glad to get rid of the smell of his unwashed body.

Chapter 5

Yahyu gave birth to a boy whom she named Peter.

We had decided that a couple of months after the birth Yahyu would travel alone to Palembang, while Bunggo and the baby, together with a nurse, would come a few weeks later. Peter was to start life with a strange collection of non-parents; an assumed father in Bunggo, an anonymous non-existent mother somewhere in North Sumatra, a stand-in father in myself and a true mother pretending to be a nanny in Yahyu. He would need to be a tough character to come to terms with all that.

Although I was excited by the imminent return of Yahyu, I had a strange feeling of unease which I could not entirely escape. I wondered whether I was worried about my reaction to Yahyu's presence or whether the social unrest in the surrounding villages was undermining my confidence in the future. The earlier visit of Captain Supriyono and the unwashed Hans had not been by chance. The workers on my tea plantation were worried and refused to travel anywhere at night. There had been several serious gunfights on the footpaths and small trails leading from the goldfields, only a few days' walk from my plantation. It was said that a revolutionary group was battling with the gangsters for control of the gold trade. Even more ominous was talk of the army's involvement, which could have far-reaching consequences for the brittle politics of Sumatra and their leanings towards independence. It was an ominous time to be starting a new family, particularly one as peculiar as mine.

***

I went to Palembang to meet Yahyu from the ferry. As the ship drew close to the dock, I saw her standing by the deck railings waving in my direction; she looked stunning, dressed in a bright red sarong and matching silk kebaya. I knew the moment I saw her descend the gangway we had made the right decision. She almost danced the last few steps to meet me, no longer the frightened and confused girl but a mature and confident woman. She took me by the arm and led me out of the dock area saying, "I want to go straight to the plantation. I don't want to stay in Palembang. I want to start our new life together. The baby will be arriving in a few weeks and we need time together before he arrives. He's beautiful. I'm sure you will like him."

On the journey, Yahyu never stopped talking about her time in the convent, the antics of Bunggo and the birth of the baby. "Bunggo played his part with the nuns to perfection," she said. "He showed only a disdainful interest in the proceedings and refused to come and see the baby for several days after the birth. The nuns thought he was a really disreputable type and asked me why I wanted to be with such a bad man. He was so funny. When the nuns came into the room, he looked bored, but when they turned their backs to us, he winked at me and put his tongue out at the nuns. He made me laugh but the nuns never understood why."

After talking for several hours about the convent and Bunggo's antics, she suddenly turned to me and exclaimed, "I want you to get everything you want from me. I don't want you ever to look at another woman. I'm yours now." She looked away in embarrassment, her cheeks reddening, before returning to the story of her adventures in the convent.

***

We had several happy weeks together before Bunggo and the baby arrived. Every day Yahyu came on my tours of the plantation, leaving early morning and arriving back in the evenings dirty but contented. On Friday evenings she organised cultural events for the workers in their dormitory area. She was very popular and within a few weeks the hint of social discontent brought about by the presence of political agitators subsided, at least on the surface.

Bunggo, Peter and the nurse arrived several weeks later. Bunggo tried, unsuccessfully, to look dejected and embarrassed, but it didn't last beyond the first gin as he embarked on a series of old stories about the war, all of which I had heard before but they never lost their fascination or their humour. He always managed to rekindle that almost affectionate friendship that can exist between men who have had to rely on each other in extreme situations. But after only a few days, Bunggo announced his immediate departure.

"Sorry chaps," he said. "Time I left my offspring in your good care and went back to my harem. I've got my living to make and my women to keep happy."

"You shouldn't say that, Tuan Bunggo, even in fun," said Yahyu, seriously. "You should get yourself a proper wife." Turning to me, she continued, "Why don't we find a wife for Bunggo? One of my sisters would make a good wife for him."

Bunggo reacted immediately with a forced laugh. "No need to do that. I'm too young to settle down."

I was a little surprised at her suggestion although it was very much in keeping with her values. "Why do you think Bunggo needs a wife now? He's managed without one for the past ten years."

"Every man needs a wife, and if he married my sister we would always be together."

"Well Bunggo, do you fancy having a try with one of Yahyu's sisters?" I asked him jokingly.

Bunggo took a big swig of gin before continuing, "Does Yahyu know of my past?" he asked.

"No, of course not. I wouldn't tell anyone your secrets."

Bunggo emptied his glass but when Yahyu offered to refill it he declined; a sure sign in Bunggo that he had something important to say. He looked at the ground for some minutes as if summoning the courage to face up to his past.

He turned to Yahyu. "Jim knows my past. We served together in Burma, as I told you. When I was there I got this Burmese girl pregnant. We were on active service then and the army didn't like us mixing, so I couldn't marry her properly. We did a sort of local ceremony secretly, with Jim as witness, so the baby could at least be legitimate in local eyes. The girl followed us everywhere, all the way through the retreat from Rangoon to India. She walked most of the way, following the refugees, trying to keep up with my brigade, with her stomach growing by the day. She was tough and beautiful."

Bunggo, despite his constant humour, was also surprisingly emotional and both Yahyu and I noticed a wetness around his eyes as he stopped speaking, refilled his glass and took several big swigs before he continued, facing Yahyu as if she was his confidant. "Near the Indian border, there was an ambush. The Japanese found the refugees and some British soldiers together and they opened fire. Then they moved in and did what they always do to women prisoners."

"No need to go on, Bunggo. I think Yahyu understands now," I said.

"No, let me continue. If Yahyu's going to live with you, then she'll have to get used to me too."

Bunggo looked at Yahyu with embarrassment written over his fat, serious face. "What they did to her and the foetus was pretty awful. Since then I've sort of ... lost interest in women, if you know what I mean. Can't get excited anymore. I don't even like thinking about it."

There was silence on the veranda; nobody knew what to say. I had been with Bunggo when he found the girl. She was a real mess and must have died in agony. As for the unborn child ... some things are best left buried and forgotten.

Yahyu showed great sensitivity that belied her youthful age. "Javanese girls like men who are faithful. You've been faithful to the memory of your wife all these years. When you feel ready, you tell me and I will arrange for someone to come to you. It's never too late to start again."

She took Peter to bed while Bunggo and I stayed till the early hours of the morning, only retiring when the gin was finally finished.

As Bunggo was leaving the next day he took me aside. "She's a wonderful girl," he said. "I might take her up on the idea one day. If her sisters are like her, then maybe I could try again."

***

Yahyu spread the word around the plantation that Bunggo had left his unwanted baby with us. Everyone took it as very natural and much in line with the character he liked to portray. The domestic staff were delighted with the arrangement; I suppose my bachelor existence with its lack of any social activity, whilst being easy, must have been boring for them. The baby and Yahyu added a new dimension to everyone's life.

Slowly but surely Yahyu made her mark on both on my domestic life and on the plantation. I retained my freedom to roam around the plantation as before and everyone on the plantation seemed to be happier with her around. After several months, it was difficult to imagine I had ever lived without her, so completely had she become integrated into our discrete society. I even started coming home earlier in the evenings so as to spend time with Peter before he slept.

I had expected there to be problems with Ibu Wati, of whom I was extremely fond, but they didn't arise. Yahyu understood Wati's position well and treated her like her own mother, which ensured that all staff maintained sufficient respect for Wati's position. I could tell from Wati's body language that she slowly and rather grudgingly accepted Yahyu into the family. Ibu Wati was the only person on the plantation who knew the true situation of Yahyu and Peter and this gave her a privileged position which she never abused.

***

Several years went by, during which time Peter grew into childhood and Yahyu grew into full maturity as Ibu of the plantation. The problems outside the plantation rumbled on, but we withdrew into ourselves, forming an island of sanity and culture. Few visitors ever came, except Bunggo on his three-monthly visits, and he informed us of disquieting events in Jakarta and conflicts in the outer islands. But the events didn't touch us and we lived largely for each other.

I sometimes took Peter on my tours of the plantation and he turned out to be a tough little character; happy to sleep anywhere, eat anything and play with anyone. He was a remarkably good-looking boy, having inherited the best characteristics of both races, with olive-coloured skin and shining black eyes: he was the darling of all the Ibu on the plantation. He had very quickly learnt the art of Ibu seduction. When his mother was angry with him, he went in search of Ibu Wati and got her to play with him. When Ibu Wati got angry, he went back to his mother. On the few occasions they were both angry, he demanded to come with me so he could play with the women tea pickers. I admired his skill with women: I wish I had it.

Peter had a secret life, which was amusing. He had somehow found a deep hole under the mango tree in the back garden where he hid all his most precious possessions; mainly his tin soldiers but there was also a small jade Buddha which Yahyu had once bought to increase the number of gods who were supposed to protect the plantation. We saw him one night slip out of the window of his bedroom and creep over to the tree to check they were all there. He was only four. We were full of admiration and never let on that we had seen him.

In many ways it was an idyllic time, but I never completely lost my sense of unease although I put it down to fear of losing something precious which I had only just gained. I often discussed my feeling with Yahyu but she had no such qualms and, on the surface, the plantation seemed to be quiet despite the news from "out there".

We began discussing marriage plans, not so much as a decision but more as a natural progression of our relationship. I didn't see the need for plans. It was just a question of a quick trip to Curup and getting it done. Yahyu, however, had grander ideas. She wanted a wedding in Palembang with all her village invited. I understood her reason although I didn't like the idea of a complicated wedding ceremony. Yahyu wanted the social value of a public marriage ceremony to give her the status that is so important here. She also hinted that Peter needed a more active social life which she would organise, but she couldn't do it until she had the status of wife. She was developing into a woman of strong character who was subtly, but very decidedly, changing my lifestyle.

***

Once a month we travelled to Bengkulu to buy supplies. Bengkulu is a sleepy port on the west coast of Sumatra, an ex British colony fallen into decay. It consists of a tumbledown fort covered in mildew, which had once housed a future president of Indonesia, a graveyard full of the remains of eighteenth century British soldiers and a drowsy but surprisingly well-stocked Chinatown. It also boasted one of the most beautiful but rarely visited beaches I have ever seen.

I always made a point of staying overnight in Bengkulu so I could wander along the beach. The evenings are spectacular when seen from the beach, as the sun quickly sinks behind Rat Island with its isolated lighthouse sending lonely beams of light into the empty night. Ships no longer called into Bengkulu because the harbour had silted up years ago, but this had not lessened the enthusiasm of the local authorities. The lighthouse was still manned, possibly in the hope that one day a ship might try to call in to this most lonely of ports. More likely, no one had thought to cancel the lighthouse's budget, so the lighthouse keeper kept his job and his chickens on his isolated rock off the coast of western Sumatra.

Yahyu also loved Bengkulu. Nothing much happens here but, during the cool of the evenings, the town comes alive as the gold shops open their doors and the streets are lined with cloth shops, shoe shops and food sellers. While I wandered down to the beech to see the sunset, Yahyu browsed around the clothes shops and chatted with the Javanese shopkeepers who controlled the trade in batik cloth. Yahyu always took Peter with her and, being an Indo, he was of great interest to the local Ibu in the market who totally spoiled him.

As I walked slowly along the beach where the conifer forest reaches almost to the sea, the sound of the pounding surf was suddenly shattered by a shriek, followed by the charge of what appeared to be a mad Japanese soldier wielding the scabbard of a samurai sword. He attacked from behind a tree, but it was not an attack that any self-respecting Japanese soldier would be proud of, his charge being interspersed with twirls and jigs and much dramatic stamping of feet.

Before me stood a parody of ferocity. He was a youngish man, wearing the tunic of a Japanese officer, much torn and dirty, with a grimy loincloth that did little to hide the sores and cuts on his legs. On his face he wore the type of drooping black moustache favoured by Javanese actors playing the part of ancient Hindu kings, but he was no king. His long, wild hair was covered in feathers and his face smeared with sweat and dirt. He spent several long seconds casting sly, sideways glances at my face before announcing very formally, "I'm going to Da'eut. Tuan come with me to Da'eut. We have picnic in Da'eut." His request was no less strange than his appearance.

After regaining my wits and my dignity, and trying not to laugh, I continued walking along the deserted beach, hoping the madman would lose interest in me, but he didn't. With a look of inane happiness on his face, he danced in front of me, occasionally turning to see if I was still following. On my way back to the Chinatown to find Yahyu he continued to follow me while he in turn was followed by a group of taunting young men. Ignoring their comments, we trudged on, me pretending we were not together, and he pretending we were; it was ridiculous.

Yahyu, as always, was surrounded by a group of doting Ibu playing with Peter. In Bengkulu, which I only ever visited once a month and where I was not well known except amongst the Chinese gin sellers, everybody presumed Peter was my son because he looked an Indo, hence Yahyu was either my wife or my concubine. I think she secretly encouraged such beliefs, maybe not consciously, because she wished it to be true. Yahyu had a strong romantic streak that could turn a sordid reality into a beautiful dream and a beautiful dream into an equally beautiful reality. I think she imagined, or possibly even believed, I was now the real father of Peter.

Yahyu came up to me, beaming with the pleasure of her child being the centre of admiring attention, when she suddenly stopped and her eyes grew wide in disbelief as she stared behind me. "Rusdi," she shouted as she moved towards him but then hesitated, clutching

Peter to her side.

Rusdi's mad eyes took on some measure of recognition. He slowly grew quiet and squatted on the road, putting his head in his hands as if deep in thought.

"It's Rusdi," Yahyu said to me. "What shall we do?" She looked at him in disbelief for some minutes. "He looks in bad shape but I don't want to go near him with Peter. I don't know how he will react. I'm not sure he even recognises me."

So this was the famous Rusdi whom Yahyu had talked so much about. I should have made the connection, but several years had passed since her vagrant travels and, with all the complications and delights of having a new family, many of her earlier stories had completely slipped my mind.

I knew that Yahyu would want to help him but her situation had changed whilst his had not. I drew Yahyu away from the young men milling around us so I could speak to her privately. "I've seen people like this before. There's nothing you can do for them except give some charity and leave them to their own devices. To try and care for him would probably destroy him; he couldn't cope with a sedentary life in social care. Let's give him some money and then leave him."

"No," Yahyu said. "We can't just leave him. I know what will happen to him. Look at his left hand; it's still deformed from what the police did to him."

I looked at Rusdi who was sat on the floor staring at us. I don't think he recognised Yahyu at first. She was a much-changed person from the scarecrow he would have known several years ago, but perhaps he sensed some familiarity with her. I looked at his crippled hand and then at his face, which was full of bruises and cuts which I presumed had been picked up in a fight. He was scratching his head with his good hand, as if trying to get his memory to work.

Slowly Rusdi raised his head and focused for some moments on Yahyu's face. "Nona," he said suddenly. "It's Nona come to rescue poor Rusdi." He leapt to his feet and danced up to Yahyu, much to the amusement of the spectators.

Peter took great exception to Rusdi. He didn't cling to his mother for protection but took the offensive immediately. He grabbed Rusdi's sword scabbard and shouted, "Leave my mama alone. She's my mama, not yours." He stood defiantly in front of his mother as Rusdi stopped in confusion. In other circumstances I would have laughed, but the situation was getting embarrassing for Yahyu who was torn between wanting to get Peter away from Rusdi and her residual feelings of loyalty to someone who had been, in his own crazy way, her companion through some difficult times.

I took hold of Yahyu and Peter by the hand and led them away, knowing that Rusdi would probably follow us, but at least we would be away from the prying eyes of the Ibu in the market place. Rusdi indeed followed us to the Jeep, dancing and singing all the way, and he was followed by the ever-present group of young men who had nothing better to do.

I tried to usher Yahyu into the Jeep but she either refused to go or Rusdi refused to let her go—I couldn't tell which. I managed to get Peter into the back seat and turned back to see Rusdi clutching Yahyu's blouse and the young men smirking and sniggering behind them. I told Rusdi in a very stern voice to back off, which he did, looking at me in fear, which was not quite the effect I wanted.

Yahyu looked at me and then back at Rusdi. She was not

somebody who could readily desert a friend, even one as strange as Rusdi. "Let's take him to the plantation for a few days to get cleaned up," she said, "and then we take him to Father Tomas in Curup. Maybe he can help. I don't think I can desert him just because I'm now rich."

Back on the plantation my staff looked askance when we arrived with Rusdi sitting in the back of the Jeep. As soon as we stopped, he leapt out and started his ridiculous sword dance in front of a group of shocked workers and a very disapproving Ibu Wati. It seemed to be his way of introducing himself, although it may also have been a way of showing his madness early on so people would keep their distance from him and hence he would not have to interact directly with anyone. I was not as certain as Yahyu as to the genuineness of Rusdi; mad he certainly was, but I thought there was also a touch of shrewdness in his madness.

During his stay with us he followed Yahyu everywhere, which was rather upsetting for Yahyu although she tried her best not to show it. In the evenings he kept a silent vigil over us as we sat on the veranda chatting. He never interfered or said anything, but I could feel his eyes studying us as he squatted at the back of the veranda. At bedtime I had to forcibly, but gently, stop him following us to the bedroom and I locked the door at night.

Rusdi kept his distance from Peter, never interacting with him in any way. In return, Peter kept his eye on Rusdi and whenever Rusdi got too close to his mother, he stood defiantly between them as if daring Rusdi to touch her.

On the night before we were due to take Rusdi to Curup, he fell seriously ill with a high fever. There was no doctor on the plantation and it was not safe to drive to Curup at night, so I tried to treat Rusdi myself. I kept a good supply of quinine-based drugs in the house, but Rusdi would not take them. As his fever quickly rose and hallucination set in, Rusdi's madness began to subside and something akin to a fevered normality took hold of him and he talked about himself. It was as if the fever was fighting against the mask of madness and he no longer had the strength to keep up the effort of maintaining the mask.

"I want to find Da'eut," he whispered. "It's important, everyone's happy in Da'eut. Tuan and Nona happy also in Da'eut. Help me find Da'eut. Mama's waiting there for me." Despite his fever, he spoke with urgency, although it cost him much effort. He gripped my shirt as he spoke and I could feel the fevered sweat on his hands. His voice was faint but desperate.

I looked at Yahyu and asked what he meant by Da'eut. It sounded like local Rejang language which I only partly understood.

"I don't know," Yahyu said. "He talked about Da'eut in the police cell, but I didn't understand what he was talking about. The police chief was suspicious at first but decided he was just a madman and it meant nothing, but I am not so sure. When he talks about Da'eut, even in his fever, it seems to have meaning for him. But I don't know where it is and neither does he."

I wanted to get the pills into Rusdi's mouth but the chills had started and he was shaking so violently I couldn't get his mouth open. It's difficult to talk during malarial chills. The body shakes and the teeth chatter and it's impossible to keep still because of the cold. Rusdi's hand waved in front of his face as if he was trying to grasp something floating before his eyes; a common enough action in high fevers. The local people call it the grasp of death, as if the patient is trying to grasp his soul to stop it leaving his body and floating away to never-never land. Without medicine, it's a sign of impending death. I needed to force the pills into Rusdi's mouth but he still fought against me. In the end, it was Yahyu who came up with the answer.

"Rusdi," she said. "I've got some sweets here from Da'eut."

Rusdi's eyes completely lost their madness for a fraction of a second before he realised what had happened and reverted to his madness. But during that second I saw an agony on his face which I cannot describe. It was as if the reality of Da'eut raised a memory of fear within him. I had expected it to have the opposite effect of calming him by referring to his favourite, although probably mythical, paradise. However, as he reverted to his madness, I was able to force the pills into his mouth. They would start to take effect after several hours, but in the meantime his fever rose and with it his lucidity increased or, perhaps more accurately, his madness subsided.

Rusdi, we were to learn that night, was not quite what he appeared to be. He was a walking tragedy that summed up the horror of warfare. He was the kind of beneficiary of competing ideologies that nobody likes to talk about; one of the hidden casualties that are never put on public display during victory parades.

As the pills began to reduce the severity of the chills, Yahyu talked to him again. "Rusdi, tell me about Da'eut and your mama." She spoke to him quietly, almost affectionately, and it seemed to strike a chord within his mad soul.

"I go Da'eut with my mama and my sisters. All village go Da'eut and we all happy. But now I lost Da'eut. I don't know where to find it."

Tears flowed down Rusdi's cheeks as he spoke. Maybe Da'eut really was a place; somewhere he had been happy as a boy. In his madness, I think he meant it was just a place of happiness, like nirvana. When you found it, you would be happy, and Rusdi was desperate to find happiness.

Suddenly he screamed. "No, *no*. Don't do it. Give me back my mama, leave her alone." He fidgeted and fought me, so we both held him down. Despite his malnutrition, he was still a strong man.

"Must run to Da'eut. Mama says run to Da'eut," he repeated but now in a whisper of appeal.

I noticed again the madness slowly leave his eyes as weariness overcame him. There's a limit to how far anyone can fight a fever. It's hard work.

"When we going home from Da'eut, they came for us," Rusdi began in a weak but desperate voice. "There were many of them and they wore uniforms and had hard, slanting eyes; they carried big guns. Mama told me to run, but they caught me and my sisters and they dragged us into a clearing. They took my mama into the forest. I heard her screaming but I didn't know what to do. I tried to follow, but a soldier hit me with his rifle. When Mama came back she looked frightened and she wouldn't look at anyone. She sat on the ground holding her head in her hands, and the soldiers laughed at her. Mama didn't want to talk to me. No one wanted to talk to me."

Rusdi's eyes now showed a fierce determination; whether induced by fever or by his memory, we could not tell, but he was fighting the fever so as to get his story out. He gripped my arm like a vice and his face dripped with sweat.

"Some days later they took us to a camp. There were many

people in the camp; men with their hands tied behind their backs. I saw my papa. I hadn't seen him for a long time so I called to him, but he turned away as if he didn't want to know me. Then a soldier came running up to us and yelled at me in a hard language. I didn't understand him. They came and tied me up with my mama and my sisters. All of us tied up and a man told us they would shoot us."

Rusdi was talking in a high-pitched, fevered voice and we could not stop him. The story was coming out despite his resistance to it, like a dam had burst inside him and the agony of a life of madness was suddenly spilling out after years of suppression.

"They brought us to a field where there were two trucks. They take my papa and tied him to the trucks and the trucks drove in opposite directions and tore him apart. My papa screamed. Mama screamed and screamed until a soldier knocked her to the ground. I put my hand in front of my eyes but a soldier hit me. Rusdi not want to talk anymore."

As he spoke, his eyes looked into the far distance. There was a look of total horror on his face. Contrary to his desire not to talk, we couldn't stop him. He gripped me even tighter and continued but in a quieter voice, almost whispering, as if he did not want anyone else to hear.

"The soldiers took us through the forest; many days walking and no food. Rusdi hungry and my sisters cry. In the evening the soldiers always take my mama into the forest, and sometimes she came back bleeding and she would sit and cry. One night my mama gathered us together and told us we must all run away or else the soldiers will kill us. She tell us she would walk up to one of the guards and take her clothes off and then we should run fast all night and not stop running till morning. One day, she told us, when this madness is all over, we will meet again in Da'eut and have a big picnic together. There are no uniforms in Da'eut, she said. We will all be happy again. My sisters started crying, but Mama tell me not to wait for them. We must all run. She went up to the guard and took her blouse off and I ran. I heard gunshots behind me, and then there was shouting and screaming, but I ran and ran. I don't know how long I ran. It was days and nights. I ran until I collapsed.

"When I wake up, I was surrounded by men. They carried guns but not wear uniforms, and I could understand what they said. They laugh at me and call me orphan boy. They take me with them and try to teach me how to clean rifles, but I couldn't learn. I couldn't forget what happened; I kept on crying. Then they called me mad boy, and they lost interest in me and told me to walk down the path until I get to a road.

"They lie to me. The path not lead to a road but deep into the forest and Rusdi lost once more. I ran again until I was captured by more soldiers who took me to a new camp. They beat me and ask questions about rebels. When the soldiers realised I was just a mad boy, they laughed at me and told me to dance for them. I stay with them for long time as their mad dancing boy. I hate them.

"One day, when we passing through a town, they told me to go away. Get lost, dancing boy, they told me. We've got man's work ahead. Get lost before we shoot you. They aim rifle at Rusdi, so Rusdi ran. Everyone in town call me mad boy and tell me to dance in the street. So Rusdi become mad dancing boy and no one bother Rusdi ever again. Rusdi not want other people; only want to find Mama in Da'eut.

"Mama promise Rusdi we all meet again in Da'eut, but I can't find it."

Rusdi was exhausted and his voice grew weaker, but he still had the strength to grab my shirt collar and pull my face down close to his mouth. I could smell the decay on his body that often accompanies the very sick in the tropics. "Tuan, help me," he pleaded. "My mama is waiting for me in Da'eut but I don't know if she's dead or alive."

Rusdi's final plea really upset me; I couldn't decide if he was totally insane or deeply exotic. What did his mother really mean? Was Da'eut a place in this life or the next? Did Rusdi understand the difference or was that difference his real dilemma?

Rusdi did not die, but it took him many days to recover and he was never quite the same man again, at least not with Yahyu and myself. His eyes quickly took on their vacant expression and he adopted his idiotic grin and dancing antics once more, but I also detected a kind of animal shrewdness in the way he looked at me. It was as if he was trying to assess how much I had seen through his mask of madness or how much I realised that the mask he had adopted had really become himself, albeit with a small window still open into his soul which the fever had managed to open.

I thought then that Rusdi may have wanted to become a real person again, at least with Yahyu, for whom he had a special affection, but the madness had taken such a hold, he could not shake it off. He no longer understood how to relate to people and his madness ensured he never had to. That way he was protected from any suspicion of political activism. He had survived the ordeal but at what a price.

***

During Rusdi's recovery we had a surprise visit from the Captain and Hans; they had not been to see me for several years and I had forgotten about them. It was a Sunday afternoon and I was doing some paper work while Yahyu was in the domestic quarters looking after Rusdi who was still very weak. As before, the police roared up the muddy roadway, stopped directly in front of my bungalow and calmly strolled up to the front door and walked in, unannounced and uninvited. They were not welcome visitors although I did my best to hide my annoyance.

The Captain was polite, brisk and efficient. He leant against the table and, after a brief greeting, started to question me. "Pak Jim, it's been a long time since we last met. You never come to Curup anymore. Are you trying to avoid me?"

"Captain, I'm a busy man as you know, but I'm not too busy to forget my manners. Would you like some tea?"

"Of course, I would love some tea. You are the grower of some of the best tea in Sumatra. I hope you are thankful to our government for allowing you to stay here and enjoy the delights of this wonderful island."

Hans turned towards me. "Make mine a beer, will you? A large one. Can't stand your English tea." I ignored him but noted the embarrassment on the Captain's fine features.

The Captain adopted a bland smile to hide his annoyance as he continued. "Your plantation is very quiet; your workers seem to be too quiet. There has been a lot of fighting recently. The rubber plantations near Muara Enim have been disturbed by agitators and the foreign manager's house burnt down. Some of the workers in the rubber factories have gone on strike. Our police force has stopped that." He rested his hand on the butt of his revolver as he spoke. I don't think it was an intentional attempt at intimidation—the Captain was too subtle to use such a vulgar gesture—but the effect was striking.

"Why is your plantation not affected," he continued. "You are on one of the main gold routes from Lebong Donok to Bengkulu. The communist agitators are active here and there are rumours of a separatist movement; the gold attracts all the opportunists. But I know the names of some of the local leaders. Hans found them for me." He turned to Hans who leered in reply as he stuck his feet on my table in an overt show of contempt. However much I disliked the attitude of Hans, I had a nasty feeling he was not all he appeared to be. His bad manners were too forced; I thought he was play-acting, trying to appear like a stupid thug whilst perhaps hiding something more sinister. He gave me the creeps, and I am not easily frightened.

As the Captain was talking, one of the domestic staff came in carrying a tray of tea and cakes, followed by Yahyu leading Peter by the hand. As Yahyu walked through the door and saw the back of the Captain, she froze and, for one moment, I thought she would scream but I couldn't imagine why. The Captain continued talking to me. He had his back to the door and did not see what was happening. However, Hans immediately picked up on something in Yahyu's manner. He casually walked up to her and spoke softly but just loud enough for me to hear.

"You're a sweet little creature, aren't you? We heard about you; many different stories." He grinned at me as he spoke. "You're quite a celebrity. What're you doing here with this English tea worker?" he said, pointing at me. "And whose child is that you're holding? I've heard he has many fathers? Looks like an Indo child to me. You like belando men, do you?"

Yahyu glared at him but still hesitated by the door, uncertain whether to come in or quietly retire, but the Captain turned to see what was happening. He looked searchingly at Yahyu as if trying to remember something while Yahyu looked at the ground, blushing. I was shocked by her behaviour. I thought she had lost the habit of looking down in public as if she was ashamed of whom she was. Perhaps policemen scared her, which was news to me. Eventually the Captain turned back to me, still with a slightly puzzled expression on his face.

Hans put his hand on Yahyu's shoulder, saying, "Come and join us for tea. I'd like to get to know you better."

"Get your hands off my mama," demanded Peter in a loud voice, much to the amusement of the Captain, but not of Hans.

Yahyu shrugged off Hans's hand; men do not touch women in public and Hans had made an overtly obscene suggestion to her. She gave Hans a look of disgust as she turned to go back out the door when Hans stopped her. "Not yet, my sweet little Nona. I want to know who you are. Come in here."

This was pushing his luck. It was my house and Yahyu was more or less my wife. I marched forcefully over to the Captain. "Can you tell this animal of yours to mind his manners? You're welcome in my house and I respect your position as police chief, but please don't bring him with you."

The Captain looked embarrassed once more and turned back to Yahyu. "My colleague doesn't mean any harm. He's got an important job to do for our government. Please come in and tell us who you are. Your face looks familiar but I don't recall from where I have seen you."

"Don't go in, Mama. I don't like these men. They're not good. Let's go in the garden." Peter glared up at the two men as he spoke, defiance written in his posture.

The Captain was amused. "Good boy. It's good to protect your mama. But I want to ask her some questions, with your permission."

Peter looked at me and I nodded back to him; he was a real tough customer. "OK," Peter said. "But no touching her like that other man did."

"Ha ha, what a young knight in armour." The Captain laughed as he offered Peter some sweets from his pocket.

"Thank you," said Peter as he took a handful.

Captain Supriyono turned back to Yahyu and continued, "I heard someone had come here to stay with Pak Jim and that a man by the name of Tucker had also come with his baby some years ago. I didn't take much notice at the time but things may have changed now." He stared at Yahyu who kept her eyes fixed on the ground. I could see her body tense as she gripped the arms of her chair to stop her hands shaking, but at least she had the sense to keep her mouth shut.

Hans brought over his chair and sat in front of Yahyu, staring straight into her face. "Our English tea picker has good taste in women. Do you have a nice sister who can come and cook for me?" He laughed as he spoke, but his face was so close to Yahyu I thought he was going to eat her. Yahyu recoiled from him but still kept her mouth shut and refused to look him in the eye. Peter, however, got very upset.

"You go near my mama and I'll kick you," he screamed. Hans ignored him.

"Where are you from, Nona?" Hans asked.

"It's none of your bloody business where she's from," I said. "She's here with me and she's not interested in you."

Peter joined in quickly. "Mama's sister is going to marry Uncle Bunggo, so you can't have her. Go away." He turned away in a sulk and looked to me for support.

"Hans is only doing his job," the Captain said. "He's here to help us, although his manners are not quite what I had expected. But most of you foreigners are uncouth." He looked over at me as he spoke, "But you're different. You're not like the other foreigners here and that interests me; it interests me both personally and professionally. You live alone, or did live alone before this delightful girl came out of the mists to join you, you don't go to bars, you treat your workers well and you cause no trouble. This is all good but maybe it's too good.

"Why is your plantation protected from the agitators and the gangsters when all the lowland plantations are in uproar? Why do they leave you alone? Why have you suddenly got this beautiful girl to stay with you after years of living alone? For a policeman, Pak Jim, you raise many questions. Believe me when I say that I like you. I respect your love of these beautiful mountains, but please remember that my duty will always come first; friend or no friend." With that he turned and nodded to Hans who turned back to Yahyu.

"The Captain says you came out of the mists. I wonder which mists they were. There are so many secrets about you that not even I know the truth. I salute your subtlety. Now tell me how you met this romantic tea gardener with the quiet workers? And why are you looking after Mr. Tucker's child, or is it your child? Maybe you sleep with Tucker and the English tea gardener and you don't know who the father is. What are you doing here, apart from sleeping around with belando men?"

Hans then made a fatal mistake. He walked behind Yahyu's chair and bent down as if to whisper into her ear and in doing so he put both hands on her shoulders to hold her still while he spoke. He was probably so accustomed to doing as he liked with frightened women in police cells that he was not expecting any reaction except fear, but Yahyu was made of sterner stuff, even though she was extremely scared.

As I moved towards her she waved at me to stay still, wriggled out of his grasp, stood up and spoke, not to Hans, but to the Captain.

"Captain, why do you allow this belando to interfere with Indonesian women?" She spoke with great precision and she hit a raw nerve in the Captain's armour. This was more than the good Captain could take, but being a man who practised the art of good manners, he quickly retrieved his pride. He dismissed Hans with a wave of his hand and a curt, "Wait for me by the car."

"Of course, my great Captain. I am here to help you and I will report to Jakarta and to Padang about the excellent job you are doing in controlling the agitators, the separatists and the communists." He smirked at the Captain's apparent discomfort as he spoke.

Turning to Yahyu, he said, "We will meet again, sweet Nona. There is more to you than meets the eye and I would enjoy talking to you privately." His threat, with its suggestion of seduction, was not lost on either Yahyu or me.

The Captain prepared himself to leave but took a final look at Yahyu. "Don't worry about Hans, unless of course you have something to hide. I will be in touch now and again. If you have trouble with him you can report to me. And as for young Peter here, I congratulate you on having such a loyal son. He does you both credit, if he is indeed your son."

As the Captain opened the door to leave, he saw Rusdi hobbling up the steps, wearing his torn army jacket and carrying his sword scabbard. The Captain looked at me and then at Yahyu, and suddenly his manner changed and I saw the ruthlessness behind his smile. He came striding briskly back into the room.

"Ibu, you were a beggar girl whom I released from jail in Muaraklingi some years ago. You are now living with Pak Jim on this plantation and you have brought with you that dancing monkey who, I suspect, is not a monkey at all."

The colour faded from Yahyu's face as the Captain spoke and I finally realised who the Captain was. Perhaps I should have guessed, but Yahyu had never mentioned his name and I hadn't made the connection. Although Yahyu had nothing to hide, in these times of madness and suspicion, her story was indeed incredible and not one a local policeman would be likely to understand.

I looked out at Rusdi as he turned to run away, but he was still weak from the fever and he fell down the steps of the veranda.

"Stop him," the Captain shouted to Hans, who walked over to Rusdi and kicked him hard. Hans strolled back up the steps of the veranda as a couple of policeman dragged the struggling Rusdi to the police Jeep and threw him in the back. I could hear him shouting from inside the Jeep, "Nona, Tuan, don't leave me, they'll hurt me.

You can't leave Rusdi. You promised to help me find Da'eut."

I went back into the house to find the Captain and Hans standing in front of Yahyu who sat in a chair looking at the ground. I intervened quickly.

"Captain, this girl is with me. I know her father and she is to be my bride."

Hans answered in English, so the Captain could not understand him. "That won't protect you or her. This policeman can't protect you either. This girl is either very clever or very stupid, but she is also very attractive, so I'm going to take her with me to the police station." He turned to leer at Yahyu whose face slowly grew pale.

I turned to the Captain and, using Yahyu's clever tactics, said, "Captain, is Hans really in charge here? I think he's overstepping his authority; he can't arrest anyone in this country."

The Captain took the bait, but in doing so us that he was only nominally in charge. Hans must have had some powerful backing somewhere.

"Hans, wait. I have not made any decision yet. But you may question the idiot for me."

Despite her fear, Yahyu again showed her courage. She stood up and, deferentially bobbing her head to the Captain, spoke directly to him whilst pointedly ignoring the hovering Hans. "Please don't hurt Rusdi. You questioned him before in Muaraklingi. You know he's only an idiot. Do you think your original judgement was wrong?"

The Captain looked at Yahyu with an amused smile. I think he also secretly admired her courage although he would never have admitted it. "No, my judgement was not wrong but there is something strange about you and about this plantation. As I don't want to offend my friend, Pak Jim, by questioning you, then I must question the idiot, unless, of course, you want to cooperate and talk to me now."

I intervened once again. "Captain, you can question Yahyu now, here, in front of me, but not with Hans in the room. We've got nothing to hide from you but your pet ape gives me the creeps." I said this slowly to make sure Hans could understand. "Then, if you are satisfied, you can release Rusdi."

The Captain, with a tinge of triumph in his voice, told Hans to wait outside.

Yahyu told the Captain the true story, including her pregnancy, her meeting with Rusdi and with me, and the role of Bunggo. I noticed she did not mention Jon, whom we had discussed often and who we presumed was in some way mixed up with violent politics. The Captain listened quietly, never saying a word but concentrating hard.

"You were right to ask Hans to leave. He can be hasty and he doesn't always obey my orders," he said. "This story is too extraordinary not to be true. I salute you, Ibu Yahyu, on your survival skills. Pak Jim, my judgement of you seems to have been correct. Let's part as friends and as allies, but please be careful; enemies are everywhere and it's hard to tell friend from foe." He stared out at Hans as he spoke but I could not tell if that was by chance or if he was giving me a message. He continued, "Trouble will come here one day and then you must tell me. Hans already has informers on your plantation and he hears everything; both what is true and what is not true. If I hear that you have rebels operating here and you have not informed me, then I will withdraw my support of you. Both you and your beautiful bride will go to prison where Hans will deal with you. Neither of you will want that to happen."

He turned to Yahyu with a smile. "Ibu, I will keep my word and release Rusdi, and please believe me when I say that had I recognised your beauty when you were in the jail in Muaraklingi, I would probably never have let you go."

I was beginning to like the Captain; it was unusual to find an honest or even an intelligent policeman in Sumatra in those times, and the Captain was both.

We all went out to get Rusdi from the Jeep. He was still shouting but quietened as soon as Yahyu spoke to him and we helped him down. His weakness from the fever and his fear of the police was so great he could not stand, so I carried him inside. While I was doing so, I saw Hans go up to Yahyu and whisper something in her ear. She later told me he had said, "You may fool the Captain but you don't fool me. One day soon you will ask for my help and you will do anything to get me to help you. That superior English pig with all his romantic dreams won't be able to protect you, and neither will our aristocratic Captain. Soon you will all realise who is really in charge here. Maybe then you will be glad of my company." He had pinched her thigh as he left.

Chapter 6

Yahyu and Jim were worried by rumours amongst the workforce of growing strife in the surrounding villages. At night they often heard gunfire in the distance, and sometimes dead bodies were dumped by the gates of the plantation; who they were and who had killed them was never clear. So far, the violence had not spread over the plantation boundaries and Jim remained confident they would not be directly affected, but he never travelled without his revolver and neither of them ever travelled at night.

As the violence grew in frequency, Yahyu's visits to the outside world declined and she became more immersed in the life of the plantation. However, she needed to solve the issue of Rusdi and that meant a quick journey to Curup to see Father Tomas. She left the plantation in the early morning, taking Peter with her, hoping to be able to return before dark. She arrived at the church complex by lunchtime and spotted the Father rushing between the orphanage and the hospital. She called out, "Father, can I talk to you please?"

Father Tomas waited until Yahyu reached him. "You must be proud of young Peter," he said as he resumed his brisk walk through the gardens of the hospital, Yahyu trying hard to keep up with him. Father Tomas never had much time for social activities, except drinking whiskey late at night, and he preferred to conduct conversations on the run.

"Father, we're getting married soon. It will be good for Peter's future if his parents are married," Yahyu said proudly, whilst planting a seed of belief in the good Father's mind that Jim may have been the natural father of Peter and herself the mother. Yahyu was never a liar, but in her strong desire to form a family with Jim, she almost believed that he had become the real father of Peter through an act of one of the Javanese gods whom she prayed to when Jim wasn't looking. Genetic science could not compete with Yahyu's beliefs; an act of faith that Father Tomas would probably have understood and approved of, if he had known about it.

"Jim's a good man. I don't see him much but on his few visits he usually gives me a bottle of whiskey; says it's a charitable gesture. Anyway, Nona, or should I say Ibu, what can I do for you? Do you want me to marry you? I can't do that because you're a Muslim, albeit a very Javanese one. You need the civil courts for inter-religious marriages unless, of course, Jim wants to become a Muslim, which I doubt. He likes his gin too much to change religion, presuming he has one in the first place, which I also doubt." Father Tomas giggled; his usual reaction to embarrassment.

"No Father, we shall get married in Palembang. Do you think it's bad for a Muslim and a Christian to marry without changing to one religion?"

Father Tomas stopped his high-speed rush and looked at Yahyu. He didn't like answering questions like this because he was torn between his doctrine and his instincts, and he had little time to spare for doctrinal niceties. Life was a constant battle against disease, poverty and prejudice. He no longer really cared what religion his patients or his staff were. He didn't even bother to ask anymore.

"I don't know. All I can say is that Peter needs a family and you are both much better off now than when you first came to see me. Jim has much to offer both of you. I can't believe that God wants to divide your family. Is that an answer for you?"

Yahyu smiled as she held Peter close to her. This was the answer she wanted to hear, and the fact that she had manipulated it out of the good Father didn't worry her in the least. It added to her belief that she and Jim were destined to be together; that the Javanese gods, or Muslim God, or Christian God, or Sita had arranged in some mysterious way for her and Jim to meet under the extraordinary circumstances of the Linggau bus station so as to save Peter, who was therefore destined to be a special man. Yahyu's mission in life was to prepare Peter for the great things he would do in the future and Jim was inextricably involved in this mysterious godly plan for Peter's future. Yahyu was the link between Peter and Jim and she would maintain that link with her life if she had to.

"Father, I need your advice about something else and it's a little complicated. It's about a madman called Rusdi."

"Everybody seems to have complications at the moment. Can you stay the night? I shall have more time later this evening; I can't stop now. You can stay in the convent. The nuns will love having Peter with them." The Father strode off in the direction of the wards with a friendly wave.

***

In the evening, Yahyu left Peter in the care of the nuns and went searching for Father Tomas. It was a cold, wet night with a bracing wind sweeping down from the Barisan Mountains, bringing with it the damp but fresh air which is characteristic of Curup. She went over to the church offices but they were locked, so she walked quickly towards the priest's quarters. On her way she saw that the front gate, normally open to everyone, was firmly locked and there were a couple of young men dressed in dark jackets casually hanging around outside. They glanced at Yahyu as she hurried by but otherwise ignored her.

She knocked on the priest's door but there was silence from within; the complex seemed to be in suspense. She knocked again and heard shuffling inside.

"It's me, Yahyu. Are you there, Father?"

There was silence again but she could feel the tension emanating from behind the door. There was someone inside, listening.

She knocked again. "Father, it's me, Yahyu. Let me in please. I want to discuss something with you."

"Come back tomorrow," Father Tomas said from behind the door, but his voice was hoarse, as if he was talking under great stress.

"Father, are you alright? You sound worried. Let me in please."

"No, please go. You can't come in now."

Yahyu turned to go but spotted a small window looking into the darkened room. She went over and tapped on the glass whilst trying to peer inside. When her back was turned, the door flew open and a stranger dressed in dark clothes came out. "Get inside, Nona, quickly," he ordered as he turned her around and pushed her from behind. She fell into the room with a thud as the door was slammed shut behind her. Strong hands lifted her up and carried her to a chair.

Yahyu was too confused to feel scared. She sat on the chair and looked around the room; it was dark with only a small hurricane lamp hanging from the ceiling. There was a group of men gathered around the dining table, on top of which was a body covered in blood. In the corner, standing in the shade from the hurricane lamp was a tall, thin man, but Yahyu could not see his face. The atmosphere was subdued but tense.

Father Tomas sat beside Yahyu. "Sorry, there was nothing I could do but don't worry, these men don't mean to harm us." He looked around him at the dark-jacketed and heavily armed fighters. "But be careful. They are nervous and they can react violently if you do anything unexpected."

"Shut up you two," said one of the men in black.

Dr Sirait stood up from his examination of the body and walked over to Father Tomas, nodding to Yahyu. He did not look scared, which gave Yahyu some confidence, but he looked very tired and rather disappointed.

"He's dead," the doctor said. "Nothing we could have done for him. He was shot twice in the chest. He'd lost too much blood before he arrived here."

Father Tomas stood up and walked over to the body on the table. Instead of a prayer, he offered an apology. "Sorry, whoever you were. I should have come to you sooner. May God have mercy on your soul." Then, turning to the tall man standing in the shadows, he said, "Jon, you must hide the body. I can't bury a man without permission and the police will ask questions about a man killed by a bullet."

The man called Jon was tall, lean and wiry. As he came out from the shadows and turned towards Father Tomas he glanced at Yahyu but showed no recognition. Yahyu, however, recognised him although it was several years since she had last seen him. It was the same Jon she had met on the river while running away from her village. It was with mixed emotions that she viewed him talking to the Father. They had spent a mildly romantic time together on the river bank, but she did not want any complications from her past to interfere with her marriage plans, so she showed no recognition and allowed his glance to slide away.

"Father, you and the doctor have tried your best even though you failed. Now we need to get out of here with the corpse or else you'll all get trouble from this new police chief." He paced the room as he spoke, as if afraid to stand still in case he was caught. He smoked continuously, lighting one cigarette from the stub of another.

"Father, there's a Jeep outside; I need it. Who's got the keys?

The Father nodded towards Yahyu with an expression of helplessness.

Jon turned to Yahyu. "The keys, where are they?"

She decided to feign fear and hope Jon would not recognise her. Looking down at the floor, she spoke to Father Tomas, "The keys are with the driver; he's sleeping in the guest house."

"Go with one of my men to get the keys," Jon said to her. "And don't do anything silly. I've no respect for the church or any damned religion but I like the Father; he helps the poor, and I don't want him to get into trouble."

Yahyu went to the door as meekly as her pounding heart allowed, her eyes fixed firmly on the ground, trying not to attract too much attention, but her beauty betrayed her. As she walked passed Jon, he said, "Wait, come here, close to the lantern and let me look at you. What a beautiful face you have. Have you come down from the clouds to charm us poor fighters into surrender?" Jon made a big effort to smile but succeeded only in cracking the lines that ran down his cheeks.

Against her will Yahyu slowly raised her eyes and looked Jon in the face. She saw him blink suddenly and shake his head as his eyes showed recognition, but he quickly turned away. Showing great tact that belied the desperation of his situation, he said, "Nona, you come with me. Let's get the keys to the car." He gently took her arm and pushed her before him to the door.

When they were outside, Jon caught Yahyu by the shoulders and turned her round to look into her face. "So, it's my Nona of the river come to rescue me. I didn't recognise you; you've grown healthy on the fat of the land. How come the little scarecrow that I wanted to recruit has ended up the owner of a Jeep and a friend of the good Father? Perhaps you found gold after all. Good for you."

Yahyu felt uneasy about his possible reaction to her new situation. She forced herself to explain immediately and directly. "Jon, I don't know what to say. I have a child now and I'm going to be married soon."

Jon fell quiet and seemed rather disappointed or possibly embarrassed; Yahyu wasn't sure. Jon carried a permanent air of loneliness with him and Yahyu felt a twinge of pity for his solitary life. Driven fanatic though he was, he still had a kind heart and Yahyu wanted to comfort him. She opened her mouth to speak but Jon interrupted her.

"You are even more beautiful now than when I last saw you.

You probably won't believe me but I have spent many lonely nights dreaming about you. We would have made a great team, you and me. We could have shared the struggle together. Who's the lucky man? I hope he deserves you."

Yahyu realised Jon was speaking without guile, almost like a romantic teenager although he was dressed as a fighter. But she did not want him to know about Jim or the plantation. She wanted nothing to interfere with the life she had mapped out for Peter, Jim and herself. Jon was a good man, perhaps too good in his pure but naive belief in justice for oppressed people, but because of his innocence he was dangerous.

"No one you know, Jon."

"Have you ever thought of me since we parted on the river bank?"

"Yes, often. I remember you with kindness. You were a good friend to me and you left me some beautiful memories. I still think of you with affection."

Yahyu left him slumped in his loneliness against the bonnet of the Jeep while she fetched the keys. In some ways so strong and in others so weak, she thought. I must be careful not to upset him.

On her return, Jon came up to her. "Is your husband someone who works for Pak Jim? I see the name of his tea plantation on the side of the Jeep. If I'm not mistaken, this is Pak Jim's own Jeep. I recognise the stripes down the side. He once gave me a lift several years ago when it was raining. He didn't know who I was but he stopped in the dark and let me ride in the Jeep; a brave man to do that for a stranger. Is it Pak Jim you are going to marry?"

She simply replied, "Yes, he is. He's a good man."

Jon's face changed rapidly from disappointment to a kind of admiration as he studied Yahyu's expression. "Pak Jim has good taste. He's a lucky man to get you, Nona of the River. He's a strange man, your Pak Jim. We've been looking at his plantation for a long time but the workers seem loyal to him. They say they want to create a Javanese community in the middle of Sumatra, with all the mythical mumbo jumbo that goes with it. Pah, don't have any patience with that."

Yahyu didn't feel it necessary to inform him that she was the basis for the mythical mumbo jumbo. Instead, she asked him quietly, "What are you doing? Who are you fighting for?"

"We wanted a better world, a socialist world where everyone would have equal opportunities. There has been a coup in Padang and we declared independence for Sumatra, but Jakarta sent troops to crush us. Even the communists want to crush us. We're on the run now; they want to kill us in case our ideas spread. I don't know how this is going to end."

Jon looked hesitant, as if unsure whether to proceed, then changed the subject. "There's much more to you than just your beauty. Over the past few years you have changed from a tramp into a beauty queen and found yourself a good man to marry. Can I still trust you? You aren't a landowner type but you are going to marry one. That makes you my enemy, Yahyu, although I could never fight anyone as beautiful as you." Jon tried to smile and again failed, but his eyes were alive as they flickered over Yahyu's face, trying to pick up every sign of understanding in her expression.

Yahyu was wary; she wasn't totally certain of Jon's emotional stability. "I would never betray you. I don't understand your cause and I don't really want to, but the reason I won't betray you is because you're a friend. It's nothing to do with politics."

"Everything is politics for me," Jon spoke in a lonely voice while looking out at the windswept blackness that surrounded them, and Yahyu saw the contradictions written on his face. She thought he really meant the exact opposite of what he had said; he wanted everything to be politics for him but it wasn't. He was trying to be the political tough-man but failed. Yahyu's heart melted a little as she saw once again the man she had first met on the river, torn between his duty to be violent and his natural desire to be kind; not a good trait in a fighting commander.

Yahyu laid her hand gently on his arm. "You can trust me, Jon, and you can trust Jim, but please be careful. I now have a child to think of and involvement with you could mean trouble with the police."

Jon turned to look at her and spoke slowly and quietly, as if not wanting his own troops to hear him. "I can't take your Jeep. If I do, the police may trace it back to your plantation, and then you and your new man will be in trouble."

Yahyu saw in his expression the struggle between his humanity and the political dedication that constantly haunted him. "Why don't you take the Jeep quickly into the forest, bury your comrade and then come straight back here and wash the car. You and your friends can then disappear on foot. As long as no one sees you, we will be alright."

Jon still hesitated.

"What are you afraid of?" Yahyu asked him. "You once told me you weren't afraid of death, just of failure. Is that what's worrying you now?"

"My troops may not like me bringing the Jeep back here. I mustn't appear weak in front of them." Jon looked slowly around the hospital compound before continuing with a subdued voice. "When I left you on the river bank all those years ago, I was going on a mission and I failed. I was supposed to kill some people. I set the ambush well but when I saw them arrive, I ordered my men to retire. The targets were all women; I couldn't do it. I told my men that killing women would alienate the people, but they knew the truth. I've had to live with a big question mark over my political commitment ever since and I'm no longer trusted by my commanders in Palembang. They say I lack the toughness to carry out difficult tasks."

Jon looked at Yahyu as if trying to gather her support. "I couldn't hurt you, even if it meant another failure."

"I know but you must act quickly. As long as you bring back the Jeep we shall be alright. If things go wrong, I can say you took the Jeep by force."

He continued to hesitate.

"Go, Jon, just go. The longer you wait, the worse it will be for all of us."

He smiled briefly before abruptly turning away and jumping into the Jeep.

***

Yahyu waited until she saw Jon and his colleagues carrying the dead body to the Jeep before returning to the priest's house. She found Father Tomas and Dr Sirait speaking quietly together whilst being overseen by a guard.

Father Tomas looked up as she entered, his face distraught with worry.

"They've taken the body away," he said.

"I know; I saw them carrying it. Do you think this will get us into trouble, Father?" Yahyu asked.

"Yes, I'm afraid it will. But what can I do? I can't refuse help to an injured man. And your Jeep—I hope no one sees it being used."

Dr Sirait intervened. "We may not be able to keep this secret. Even if they bury the body without being seen, someone here in the church or the hospital may have seen us and they will talk. The police give money for information and many of my patients are poor; they're easily tempted. I think we should inform the police after these guards have left us. It won't harm them as they will be long gone but it may protect us. We can say we were forced to shelter them. What do you think, Father?"

"No, I don't want to do that. They will put a guard on the church doors and then neither parishioners nor patients will dare come in. Let's trust to God and pray that no one here saw what happened."

They waited tensely for several hours and the guard became agitated as time wore on and nothing happened. He was an uneducated village boy, albeit a well-armed one, and didn't know what to do. Every few minutes he got up, walked to the door and stared out at the black, windy night. Something had gone wrong and that meant trouble.

Yahyu tried to calm the boy. "Don't worry, they will be back soon. Would you like some tea? I can make it in a couple of minutes."

The boy looked at her in surprise. He tried to adopt an expression of toughness but failed miserably as he said, "Yes, please. No, don't move; wait for the commander."

"Come on, we can't wait like this all night. Let's have tea." Yahyu smiled at his youthful face that showed such indecision. "I think the Father's got some cakes in the pantry. Shall I get them?"

The boy stood up straight and in too loud a voice said, "You feed the Father and the Doctor. I may join you later, if I feel like it, but if you try anything funny, I shall shoot you." He blushed slightly and checked his rifle with exaggerated care.

Before Yahyu could get to the kitchen, there was a knock at the door; three taps followed by two taps. The guard looked up with a relieved expression on his youthful face and he shook his head at Yahyu, telling her not to leave the room. Yahyu guessed he didn't want to be seen by his commander munching cakes with his prisoners.

He opened the door and Hans walked casually into the room. Yahyu gasped in shock and held her hand to her mouth to stifle the noise. The guard, however, did not appear surprised but stood to attention as if to salute him. Hans gave no time for any association to take voice; he pulled out his revolver, as if to threaten the three prisoners, then turned and shot the young guard in the chest.

Yahyu screamed as the boy's body jerked with great violence and he slumped back against the wall without a murmur and collapsed on the floor, his body still twitching in its death throes. Hans walked over to the boy and, to Yahyu's horror, recocked his pistol and shot him again. His body jerked violently once again and flopped back on the floor, lifeless.

There was a gasp from all three watchers. Yahyu kept her hand tightly over her mouth but her knees gave way and she had to sit. She had never seen a man shot before and the violence of a bullet hitting a body at close range was a shock, but the greatest shock was the casual brutality of Hans. They all stared open-mouthed at him as he casually put his pistol back into his belt. He didn't even look at the dead boy but turned straight towards Yahyu.

"He was a rebel," Hans said. "If I hadn't shot him, he would have shot all of you. We caught the rest of them in your car. Only the leader gave us the slip. I persuaded one of his men to tell us what happened before I shot him. I then rushed here to save you, but I must ask myself whether you are worth saving. I can believe your Jeep was stolen or I can believe you gave them the Jeep. I can believe whatever I like and everyone will believe me." He spoke only to Yahyu; the Father and Dr Sirait were totally ignored.

Yahyu felt as she had when she first realised she was totally lost in the rubber forest with Rusdi; a rising wave of panic at the desperation of her position and a feeling of complete helplessness. She tried to speak but Hans stopped her with a dismissive wave of his hand and pulled her into the kitchen.

"You have two dangers facing you and you don't even know it. You should be afraid of the separatists who may believe you tipped us off and they will repay you with violence, and you should also be afraid of the police who may believe you helped the separatists. I came here to help you. What would you like me to believe?" He looked at Yahyu with an expression of triumph on his brutal face. "I can do anything I like with you and with your English tea gardener. I could kill you both or I could play with you. Which would you prefer?"

Yahyu wanted to slap his face but knew how ineffective it would be. Her mind raced around the possible facts as she realised that, intentionally or not, she was caught in a trap. She sat on a stool, head in hands, trying to think while Hans stood triumphantly in front of her.

Yahyu was a slow and methodical thinker and she needed time. Her instincts told her that something was not natural but it took several minutes to work out what it was.

"You know that none of us are involved in any way; we are victims. The police are supposed to protect us and I presume you are working with the police. Why did you shoot the boy? He could have given you information." She gave extra intonation to her question, which forced Hans to look at her sharply. He tried to smile but sometime during his debauched youth his facial muscles had forgotten the art and every expression came out as a leer.

"We shall tell the dear captain of police that the three of you were kept hostage until I rescued you. But don't take this as a sign of weakness. Both you and the English tea gardener are in my power. Don't forget it." Hans placed his hand around the back of her neck as he spoke, forcing her face nearer to his. She could feel the sweaty palms trembling, but whether through desire or exhaustion she could not tell.

Hans continued, "I have other urgent work to do now so I shall leave you. The police chief may come here tomorrow or, more probably, the day after. You must wait for him. If you get any trouble, tell him I rescued you. And show him the dead body. It's evidence of your innocence and my action to protect you."

Hans pulled Yahyu after him as he left the priest's quarters and walked towards the gate. "I see contradictions and I see lies. I wonder why you came here today. I wasn't expecting to see you here until that stupid rebel told me. I'm surprised by coincidences and I don't like them. Don't ever think you can fool me. You knew those rebels were here even if you don't want to admit it. But don't worry yet, I'm not going to tell this little secret to anyone. I've got other plans for you."

Yahyu felt her fear rising again but held herself tightly, saying nothing as Hans casually continued the conversation. "I know beauty when I see it and I know that all men, rebels also, are tempted by beauty." He squeezed Yahyu's arm as he spoke and she could feel the continued trembling of his palms. "It's not that English tea picker that arouses my interest, Yahyu, but you. You were once arrested by our gallant captain of police but you persuaded him to release you and that idiot you call Rusdi. You appear out of the mists, holding a baby, and immediately start sleeping with the English tea gardener. Then we have the socialist leader, Jon, using your Jeep. Do you realise what I could do to you if I take you to the police cells?"

"Let go of my arm. You know I'm not interested in politics. I just want to get married to Jim. What's wrong with that?" Despite her fear, she spoke with real anger and Hans seemed to recognise the emotion, although he pretended not to.

"In these times truth may not protect you. In war only the strong win, not the truthful. Your English tea gardener lives in the clouds with his romantic dreams while the forces of violence gather around him. He's a baby, Yahyu. When the great test comes, he will fail you, then you will need a strong man to protect you."

Yahyu had no doubt as to whom Hans was referring. She looked at him with disgust but also with some anxiety. Hans spoke with authority, perhaps warning her of some unknown danger still to come. She tried to ignore the cancer of doubt growing in her heart. "Don't underestimate Jim. He's a good man, and God protects good men," she said, but less confidently than before.

"Goodness is not enough; only strength will save you and your Peter. He is your son, isn't he? One of my men looked into Bungo's business and he's certainly not the father. So, who is the father? It can't be Jim or else you would have said so. How did you ever convince him to marry you with that baby in your stomach? You must be a really powerful little witch to do that. I respect power."

He saluted Yahyu as he spoke, although his face showed only mockery. "So, who is it? Is Jon the father of Peter? I know Jon and I wonder why he came here at the same time you did. He could have let his men bring in that injured man without coming himself. When you were arrested in Muaraklingi a few years ago, there was also an attempted ambush of some government leaders carried out by Jon close to Muaraklingi. He failed, of course. Did you come across him on your travels, Yahyu? Did he befriend you? Did you cast your spell over him as you did with the English tea picker? Did you get him into your bed so you could talk politics together?"

Yahyu felt her knees shaking so she squatted on the ground, avoiding his eyes. He was following his own logic but she could not tell if he believed what he said or whether he was simply trying to scare her. Whatever the situation, it was getting dangerously out of hand.

"If you were clever you would look at Peter and realise he's an Indo." Yahyu spoke quietly. She didn't like bringing Peter into the picture.

"Ha ha, a good point, Yahyu. So you are clever but not as clever as me. Jon's grandfather was a Dutch soldier, so he's quarter belando himself."

Hans caught hold of Yahyu's arm and pulled her to her feet, not violently but with purpose. "Listen to me. I know more about you than you realise. I can imprison you or release you at my will. What matters is what I choose to tell the police or the army. They will do whatever I tell them. I can even make our police chief act on what I don't tell him. He wants to be noble and honest but he's blind; blinded by his notions of honour for his country. You and I, Yahyu, are not blind, are we? We know what we want: we both want power. You want power to protect Peter and I want power for the joy it brings me. We'd make a great team."

He looked at Yahyu intently as he spoke and she saw his desire. It distorted his normally bland expression. He tried to smile at her but once again failed, producing only a parody of friendliness that did little to hide his lust.

Now that his desire was in the open, Yahyu suddenly felt dirty. She wanted to be beautiful in the way that Jim admired her, as a beautiful dancer or a beautiful princess. The thought of the loathsome and violent Hans wanting to be with her and to do things to her made her feel her beauty was shameful. She shuddered again at the thought of him touching her but she did not try to move away from him.

"What you say is laughable. The police chief knows better than you and so does Jim. You're just trying to scare me." She spoke with a confidence she did not feel. What had really upset her was not just Hans's desire for her but his subtle understanding of her. He was causing her to doubt herself and her future together with Jim.

"Times are changing, Yahyu. There will be a time when you need a strong man to protect you and then you will come to me and ask for my help. I'm not an animal. I understand you and I acknowledge your beauty; a beauty that can defeat armies. I want you too, but only from a position of power. When you come to me asking for help, as you will, you will find that it's not for free; I shall want something in return. In the end, you will love me and you will give me everything. It will be my power that will seduce you, Yahyu, not some romantic notion of honour or rightness."

As he was leaving her, he let his hand slide along the curves of her thighs. Yahyu was too confused to react.

***

Yahyu walked back to the priest's house deep in thought. Hans had upset her more than she was prepared to admit. He had the animal dynamism of a tiger; wild, brutal and powerful but also unpleasantly exciting. She felt as she had when she was still a virgin being seduced by the Dutch rubber planter so many years ago, a feeling akin to vertigo—the fear and thrill of falling into an abyss. She tried to put Hans to the back of her mind. She didn't want to awaken those animal feelings ever again. Jim was clean, pure, human and sensitive, and she loved him and she loved his dreams and, most of all, he loved her and Peter. She must never give in to sexual temptation again. Jim offered her and Peter a future; Hans threatened her with degradation. She hated him for tempting her.

***

Yahyu joined the Father and the doctor in the hospital complex where they spent the rest of the night together, fearing a knock at the door that would herald a police inspection.

"This is not what it appears to be," Father Tomas whispered as they sat in the doctor's office. "Did you see the reaction of the guard when Hans came in? He was calm, as if expecting to see him, so why did Hans shoot the poor boy? Why not keep him alive for interrogation? It isn't natural.

"Yahyu, what do you know about Hans? I've only met him once or twice. Last time he called me an interfering old fool because I wouldn't let him inspect my hospital. I told him he would probably catch leprosy if he came in and I wouldn't treat him." The Father chuckled at his own bravery.

"He's a bad man," Yahyu said. "He comes to the plantation with the police chief and he's always rude. Jim says he's an animal but a dangerous one. The police chief seems to trust him, or maybe he's afraid of him. We can't work it out."

"What did you talk about with him just now?" the Father asked.

"When we were outside he made rude suggestions to me; that's all. He's disgusting."

"We need to have a common story before the police come," Dr Sirait said.

"For us, that is the doctor and myself, it's easy," said Father Tomas. "The rebels came into the hospital with their wounded leader and forced us to operate on him, but he died and they kept us under guard while they buried the body. I think we may be under suspicion but I don't think our new police chief will take it any further. He's an intelligent man, not the like the other thugs in the police force. But the case for Yahyu is more difficult; police don't like coincidences." He turned to Yahyu while he was speaking but she stayed silent, waiting to see if he detected anything about her relationship to Jon.

Father Tomas continued, "You were a long time outside with Jon while you were getting the keys for the Jeep. What did he say to you?" Such an innocent question could be the death of Yahyu if it was asked in front of the police chief.

"Please let's not say anything about that. He just wanted the keys and it took time to start the Jeep. He said nothing to me, not that I can remember. I was too scared to speak to him."

The good Father gave Yahyu a questioning look. He was not a stupid man. "Understood. He forced you outside to get the Jeep. That won't tax my conscience too much; it's almost true."

***

Yahyu spent the night in great agitation although she controlled her emotions in front of the other two. Her grand plans for Peter and herself were suddenly under threat and the spectre of her past had come back to haunt her. In her dreams that night, while stretched on the floor of the doctor's office sleeping next to Peter, she was running through the rubber forest looking for Jim but Rusdi kept pulling her back and she could not find Jim. She cried out several times in her disturbed sleep until Father Tomas came over to see what was happening.

"What's the matter, Ibu Yahyu? Did the death of that poor boy upset you so much or is there something more here than just the boy's death? Do you want to talk to me? I hear many strange stories from my parishioners, both men and women; there's not much that can shock me."

"Father, in your religion, is it a sin to have a child outside of marriage? I know it's wrong, but is it a sin? I made one mistake in my life and now everything seems to be against me. I thought when I met Jim that I had escaped from that mistake but now, with this problem of Jon and Hans, it looks as if I am going to drag Jim and Peter into trouble. It's not fair. God has no mercy." Yahyu spoke not with anger or bitterness but with deliberation, as if stating a fact that she had discovered and against which she was considering how to fight.

Father Tomas looked at her kindly, "I know what you're saying. Jim told me a long time ago about your affair with the belando man on the rubber plantation. But everybody now presumes Peter is the son of you and Jim. Jim plays along with it because it will make things easier when you get married. It's only you who wants to pretend you are not the true mother of Peter; nobody else cares. When a girl gets pregnant outside of marriage, it's a big thing; it causes family embarrassment. But people get used to anything. It's unlikely anyone is going to bother about the biological facts of who is and who isn't the father and mother of Peter. As to whether it's a sin, I should say yes, but at the same time I can't. How could young Peter be a sin?

"But this is not the moment to discuss morality. I think there is a problem between you and Jon. I saw the way he looked at you. I think he probably took a fancy to you. Don't let that show in front of the police chief. He may see more into it than you want."

Yahyu looked at the ground as the Father spoke. She knew more about Jon's desire for her, but she wasn't going to tell the Father, or Jim, or anybody else, especially now that Jon was in Curup as a wanted man.

Father Tomas continued, "I think it's the price you have to pay for being so beautiful. Beauty is a great asset but it creates desire which is not always welcome.

"One more piece of advice; about Hans. He also looked at you in a special way. I suppose I should say in a lustful way. Please be careful. We once had to treat a woman, a Jaipong dancer, who was sent to us by Hans. She was pregnant and someone had tried to give her an abortion that failed and she nearly bled to death. After she had been with us for only a few days, Hans sent the police to pick her up. They said they would take her to the House of Young Bamboo in Linggau. It has an awful reputation. Hans is involved in some very shady dealings with its owner, Ibu Efi."

After Father Tomas had left, Yahyu sat on the bed thinking. She formed her plan slowly in the early hours of the morning. She would warn Jim of the danger and then they would come straight back to Curup and get married immediately. That way the future of Peter would be assured and her marriage would protect her from Hans and from any other man, including Jon. Jim would swear to be the father of Peter and no one would know. If anything happened to her, then Jim would take care of Peter. Her task was clear. It was to protect Peter and to do that she must protect Jim; her own life was of secondary importance.

***

The police chief did not come the next day. The three of them spent the day anxiously watching the main gate, waiting for the sound of the policeman's car. However, on the following day, as they were discussing in the doctor's office, the police chief suddenly arrived. He strode in briskly and smiled. "Don't look so glum. Hans has already filed his report. It seems you were all the victims of rebels and Hans was forced to shoot one of them. All I need from you is a few facts. Yahyu, you first. Please come with me."

He took Yahyu to a separate office. Despite his smiles, Yahyu did not feel at ease. She remembered her last interview with the Captain; it had resulted in the mutilation of Rusdi's hand.

"Sit down, Ibu."

The Captain walked behind Yahyu before he spoke. Yahyu remembered this tactic from her previous interrogation. She found it difficult speaking to a person standing behind her because she could not see his face and the height difference was intimidating.

"Why did you go to see Father Tomas? I know Jim is a friend of the good Father, and so am I, in my own way. I respect his dedication to the poor people in my country. Answer my question, please."

Yahyu looked ahead of her, not daring to turn for fear of appearing scared. "Jim thinks we should put Rusdi in Father Tomas's care. I went to discuss it with the Father but I didn't have a chance. Those rebels were here and they wouldn't let us speak together."

"They took your car but they were caught by one of my road blocks. Your car's a write-off but that's not important. Several of the rebels got away in the shoot-out, which is a shame. But what I want to hear about is the guard they left with you, the one that Hans unfortunately shot. Did he chat to you? Did he say what he was expecting to happen?"

"No, Captain. He only told us to shut up," she said.

"What happened when Hans burst into the room? I want this in detail please."

"The guard was a peasant boy. He said nothing. He looked nervous when the others didn't come back. When Hans came in, the boy looked confused. I thought he was going to salute but instead Hans shot him in front of us. It was awful. Nobody said anything."

"Do you have any contact with Hans outside of his official duties?"

"No, of course not. I don't like him and neither does Jim." Yahyu's voice faltered slightly as she spoke and the Captain, quick to perceive weaknesses in his subjects, raised his eyebrows slightly. The conversation had not taken the direction Yahyu had expected. The Captain had not even alluded to Jon—maybe he didn't know who Jon was—but was more interested in his own adviser, Hans.

The Captain brought up a chair and sat next to her in a friendly manner. "We are both Indonesians and we are both dealing with foreigners; we should work together in the interests of our country. Hans has been showing a lot of interest recently in Jim and in Jim's plantation. Do you know why?"

"I have no idea," she said but her voice was not totally convincing and the Captain glanced down into her eyes.

"If I may give you some friendly advice, please don't go playing with fire. This situation is more complex than it seems and even I don't fully understand it yet. Don't get mixed up in it; just marry Pak Jim and leave the rest to us."

This was a new side to the Captain, but Yahyu was unsure how much she could trust him.

"I will take you home," he said. "I would like to chat with Jim."

On the journey both Yahyu and the Captain were silent; both thinking about Hans, albeit for different reasons. Yahyu noticed that the Captain was a surprisingly considerate driver, slowing down when he came across village women walking under their burdens of firewood carried in wickerwork baskets strapped to their foreheads. He also carried an assortment of sweets which he threw out of the window to children in the few villages they passed through, much to the delight of everyone.

When Peter complained he was getting no sweets, the Captain stopped the car and fetched a new packet from the back. "These sweets I keep for special children," he said to Peter. "Are you going to be a policeman when you grow up?"

Peter looked up at the policeman, his mouth full of sweets. "I don't know," he said. "I have to ask Mama first."

Captain Supriyono laughed as they drove on. "It's for people like you and Peter that I fight this battle. I want you and all good people to live in peace. These gangsters and politicos are disturbing us for their own ends. We shall crush them and then you can marry Jim and live happily ever after."

It was difficult for Yahyu to reconcile the ruthless policeman who broke Rusdi's hand in a pointless interrogation and his kindly behaviour. In many ways, she thought, Captain Supriyono was as fanatic as Jon, albeit in different political spectrums. The main difference was that Jon was weak whereas the Captain was ruthless.

When they got to the house, Jim was not there, which was not unusual; most days he visited some part of the plantation. Yahyu asked the Captain to wait on the veranda until Jim returned while she took Peter to the domestic quarters.

She returned to the Captain and they sat on the veranda waiting but Jim did not appear and the plantation workers seemed to be avoiding the house. Even the domestic workers looked at Yahyu with suspicion when she asked them to bring the Captain some tea.

Something was happening on the plantation. She went to find Ibu Wati.

"Ibu, what's going on? I can feel that something's wrong but I don't know what it is."

Ibu Wati looked at Yahyu with sympathy rather than her normal resigned expression of a mother looking after a wayward daughter. "I'm not sure. Tuan Jim went towards Curup, looking for you, and hasn't come back yet. I can't tell you more than that but I've sent two of the young workers to run down to the gate and report back to me. If Jim's still on the plantation, they will find him."

Yahyu tried to get more information but Ibu Wati was evasive, saying, "Let's wait till the runners get back."

As the sun set over the plantation, Yahyu came once again to the veranda to find the police chief sitting in a chair with his feet on the railings, reading one of Jim's novels.

"Jim has a nice library here; Western-induced decadence, of course, but in good taste. Where is he?"

"I don't know, Captain. He usually returns before dark. I expect something happened to his Jeep, or maybe there's a problem somewhere on the plantation." She tried not to sound worried.

"These are not good times to be out after dark, even if it is his own plantation. Doesn't he know that the communists are working this area, as are the army and the remains of the separatists."

"Why don't you go home, Captain? Jim and I will come to Curup tomorrow to see you, I promise."

"I think you want me to be gone, so I shall do so. It's not good for a young lady like you to be alone with me at this hour. I'm glad you have such respectable manners. I expect Jim's absence is pure coincidence but I shall expect you to keep your word. Come and see me tomorrow in the police station."

***

Jim did not appear that night. Around midnight Yahyu heard gunfire in the distance, which was not unusual but it added to her anxiety. The next morning one of the workers came to see her. He looked exhausted and his face streaked with mud and sweat.

"Ibu, there's been a problem. Tuan Jim has been taken by the army. They shot him but he's not badly hurt. They took him away but I don't know where."

In times of crises Yahyu's real strength shone through. She did not rush out to the Jeep and dash off to Curup; neither did she burst into tears. She told the worker to wait outside while she sat in a corner to think. She saw Hans's hand in this. The combination of Jon and Hans were conspiring against her, although she could not work out in what way. She would not go straight to Curup because that was probably what Hans wanted her to do. She would stay on the plantation and send a letter to Captain Supriyono asking for his help. He seemed to be the only honest man in this mad world. The irony of it being a policeman that was honest was not lost on Yahyu. In the meantime, she would guard Peter and the plantation.

Chapter 7

I presumed Yahyu had stayed overnight in Curup, which was unexpected but not worrying. However, the night was disturbed by intermittent gunfire which, judging from its intensity, must have been between the army and ... gangsters, separatists, communists? It was difficult to tell; so quickly did the politics change. I barricaded the door, placed a revolver by the bedside and fell into a fitful sleep.

The next day I waited at home but Yahyu never appeared. Looking through my binoculars at the long track leading to the house, there was nothing; no Yahyu and no movement. The plantation seemed to be paralysed and I could feel the suspense. Even the insects that usually offer the background music to the forests were silent. I needed to shake off the lethargy, break the suspense and act.

As I was getting into the spare Jeep in preparation for driving to Curup, Ibu Wati came running out from behind the house. "Tuan, Tuan, don't go," she yelled as she came towards the Jeep.

"I'm going to Curup to look for Ibu Yahyu. What's the matter?"

"Nothing's the matter; just don't go, Tuan. Not now. Go tomorrow." She was wringing her hands in agitation. "There may be a problem near the big gate. Don't go there, Tuan."

As she spoke, she fumbled inside her sarong and brought out a crumpled piece of paper. She kept it tight in her hand as if uncertain whether to give it to me. "Tuan, forgive me. This note was sent to the foreman earlier today but he's not in. I read it, Tuan. I'm sorry. Don't go. It's a trap."

I took the wet, crumpled paper from her hand. It was a simple note written in pencil in bad Melayu: "*Send the Tuan to the main gate now.*" It was signed, "*Hans*".

"You can't trust this foreman, Tuan. He's not what he appears to be; he's got bad friends. They come here at night and drink and gamble and discuss how to get rid of you. That man Hans also comes here secretly in the middle of the night and leaves before morning. Hans and the foreman are very close and I don't trust either of them. Stay here, Tuan. Don't do what Hans wants."

My heart lurched and missed a beat. My immediate reaction was fear, not for myself but for Yahyu. She could be driving through the main gate at any time and if there was a trap set by Hans, she would drive into it. I felt the adrenalin start to rush. It was many years since I had last prepared for battle and I found the sensation exhilarating after the hours of passive waiting. I would find Yahyu, and Hans could go to hell.

"I can handle Hans; if he's a problem I can always report him to Captain Supriyono."

"You don't understand, Tuan. Hans is bad. He's already got blood on his hands. We don't know what he wants but we don't trust him."

I left her standing by the well, waving to me and, as far as I could tell from a distance, crying to herself. I had never thought Wati capable of such emotion.

Driving through the plantation, I was struck by the absence of workers. It was surreal; there was total silence and no movement except the wisps of cloud climbing up from the valley and caressing my tea bushes. Where was the world hiding? I was driving through a landscape that was suspended in time.

I passed an old man walking alone along the muddy path, but he quickly dashed amongst the tea bushes and would not come down to talk when I called to him. This was really worrying. I felt a cold sweat forming on my back as I looked at the grey clouds gathering over the mountaintops giving a sombre tone to my beautiful plantation.

Rain drummed on the canvas roof of the Jeep as I approached the outer reaches. Only in Curup, reputedly the wettest town in Indonesia, does it rain like this. The rain was so heavy that peering through the windscreen was like looking underwater, but I managed to see the outline of a cart lying on its side, blocking the road. I braked hard and slithered to a stop, swearing profusely.

Before opening the door, I looked around and saw vague shapes appearing through the torrents of water falling on the windscreen. They moved towards me in crouched, catlike postures. I recognised immediately the cautious approach of the professional soldier. I froze, heart pounding, adrenalin flowing. My service revolver would be no use against well-armed professionals and it was technically illegal to carry firearms, although everyone did. I slid down the window on the side away from the oncoming soldiers and hurled the revolver into the tea bushes, hoping the heavy rain would hide my actions.

Two soldiers stood crouched in front of the Jeep, rifles pointed straight at me. There may have been others nearby but the rain restricted my vision. As I saw a third figure approach from the side, I knew what to expect so I flung myself flat over the front seats as a rifle butt crashed through the side window and a guttural voice shouted in heavily accented Melayu, "Get out of the fucking Jeep."

Several pairs of hands dragged me out and forced me to lie on the cold muddy track while someone tied my hands tightly behind my back. There was so much water rushing down the road I thought I would drown, but when I tried to turn over, I was kicked in the ribs by several pairs of boots. I couldn't scream because I didn't have enough breath. I lay still, concentrating on breathing whilst trying to ignore the pain in my ribs.

There was no talking; these soldiers were professionals. Short, squat peasant boys recruited for their toughness and endurance, well adapted for jungle fighting. They knew what they were doing and I knew enough of soldiering not to interfere in their activities.

I wasn't really scared at this stage; had they wanted to kill me, they would have done so immediately and without questions. They were acting under orders and, as far as I knew, there was nothing against me. I might get mistreated but I didn't fear more than that.

After the soldiers had searched my pockets and found the keys for the Jeep, they started arguing amongst themselves. They hadn't realised I spoke their language. It was a good two-hour hike to the main gate and they wanted to use the Jeep, but none of them knew how to drive.Eventually a couple of them came over, dragged me to my feet and cut the ropes around my wrists, motioning me to get into the driver's seat.

With the soldiers hanging onto various parts of the Jeep, we slowly descended the bends in the muddy track that served as the main road through my plantation, heading towards the main gate. They laughed as they rode. Despite their sodden uniforms and the seriousness of the situation, the ambush had turned into a picnic with the added advantage of a belando acting as their chauffeur. One of them stuck a cigarette in my mouth and lit it with a grotesque smile of kindliness. "Have a smoke Tuan, maybe your last." He made a sign of cutting his throat and they all laughed; so did I. What else could I do?

I saw the humour of the situation but I had seen enough military action to know that these smiling peasant boys would just as quickly turn their guns and shoot me without so much as a change of expression on their bland, smiling faces. Feelings had been bashed out of them in their hard training in the forests and swamps of Sumatra. It was best to humour them but stay detached.

As we approached the gate, I saw a larger collection of troops, maybe twenty or thirty, and a smaller group of dejected-looking young men and women sitting on the ground, some of them bleeding from wounds. An officer walked towards the Jeep. He looked young and had the fine features of an educated Javanese. I stopped the Jeep, quickly jumped out and walked up to the officer with a smile, holding out my hand in greeting. It worked, as I guessed it would, for the boy soldiers hung back in front of their officer, smiling to hide their embarrassment.

"Hello, Lieutenant. What are you doing here on my plantation and who are these people?" I said, pointing at the dejected group squatting on the ground.

"You must be Pak Jim," said the officer. "Pleased to meet you.

My apologies for this disturbance, but this group of rebels were caught crossing the bridge; probably going to stir up trouble on your plantation. How're your workers? You get any trouble from them?"

"Not that I know. My workers are a quiet bunch. The main problem is our closeness to the gold trail from the Lebong Donok mines to the coast. We get a lot of bandits hanging around looking for a quick kill."

The officer seemed quite relaxed and friendly so I also began to relax, thinking my previous brush with his troops was just a mix-up.

"Get any trouble with my troops?" he said amiably. "They've had a tough few months. We've been patrolling the gold trails. Good loot but hard work." He laughed as he spoke but I could guess at the ruthlessness with which he would have carried out his tasks. He would probably pocket any gold he could lay his hands on from both legitimate and illegitimate travellers, giving a small proportion to his troops to buy their loyalty and then killing any witnesses.

The officer and his troops would probably not care who won or who lost; they would change sides overnight if they had to, as long as they made money. They were typical of the opportunists who were attracted to Sumatra at this time; men dressed as soldiers but acting like bandits, and bandits dressed as such but acting like soldiers. It was impossible to say who were the legitimate armed forces until the fighting stopped. The winners would be legitimate.

"Where were you going?" the lieutenant asked me.

"To Curup. I want to pick up my wife."

The lieutenant gave me a strange look. "At this time of night? You're either very brave or very stupid. My men could have shot you. They have orders to shoot anyone who doesn't stop. I think a couple of my men should escort you to Curup. There's trouble brewing and you might get caught up in it." I wasn't sure if he wanted to protect me or to keep an eye on me; probably both.

"What about the wounded here" I said, pointing to the group squatting on the ground. "Can I take the injured to the hospital?"

"Why?" said the officer with a bland expression on his youthful face.

I looked again at the group. They were wet and shivering and several of them looked bruised and bloodied, whether through fighting or their treatment in detention I couldn't tell. "Some of them look as if they won't survive much longer. If you want, I can take them and your soldiers into Curup."

As I was speaking, there was scuffling and muffled screams came from the group on the ground. Two of the older soldiers were walking amongst the prisoners, looking carefully at the women squatting on the wet footpath. They selected one and dragged her, shouting and screaming, into the tea bushes. The officer looked mildly embarrassed but continued speaking smoothly. "We'll take good care of the wounded, don't worry. You go on to Curup but take a couple of my soldiers with you."

As I moved towards the Jeep, I saw Hans talking with the soldiers who had brought me. I hadn't realised he was here, but then I remembered the note he had sent to my foreman, so I suppose he had been expecting me. I continued walking steadily. I had no wish to talk to him. Although I could not see Hans, I could feel his eyes on my back. I think he was playing with me, waiting to see what I would do.

"Tuan Jim," he shouted with extreme sarcasm. "English tea picker, come here."

I turned back to face him and saw several of the boy soldiers advancing towards me. I could tell from their posture they were hostile; they approached sideways, keeping my gaze in their eyes to prevent me studying their movements. They were trying to keep me occupied until they were in a position to strike. They probably thought I was still armed and were more wary than they need have been. I froze. I couldn't escape anyway.

I looked over to the officer who stared back with a blank smile on his face.

Hans said quietly to the soldiers around me, "Don't kill him. He's no good to me dead." The circle of soldiers sidled in, still cautious but with deceptive smiles; they were enjoying themselves and knew they would win, so why hurry.

Strong hands grabbed my legs, slammed me onto the muddy pathway and tied my arms tightly behind my back. I remember the shock of the fall and then being dragged along the ground but my face was so covered in mud I couldn't see where we were going. They tied me into a bamboo cage which was only big enough to stand in. My arms were forced back through the bars and lashed to a bamboo pole. The action had been too fast to feel fear and I was concentrating on the pain in my limbs as the knots cut deep into my wrists and ankles.

With a parody of friendliness, one of the soldiers patted me on the head. "Enjoy your rest," he said, before disappearing into the pouring rain and leaving me to contemplate my fate.

I looked around with some difficulty as my head was bound to a bamboo pole. There were two others to my left, both men, locked in separate sections of the cage. They looked as if they were in more agony than me; one was only semi-conscious, which was probably a blessing. I whispered to the other, "Pak, what's happening here? What's going on?"

The man could not turn his head as it was tied between two bamboo poles but he managed to speak in very broken Melayu. "I don't know, Tuan. Last week, men with guns come and ask for food and we gave it. They told us to bring more food to the footbridge over the river. If we not bring it, they would burn down our village."

"Were they the separatist troops?" I asked.

"How do we know, we're just farmers, we don't know about politics. We just wanted to protect our village."

"What happened?"

"We wanted to hide our women and children in the forest before bringing the food, but the army got to us first. They accused us of feeding the rebel forces. They are evil, Tuan. They will kill all of us. They've got a belando with them."

I stopped talking; it was too much effort for both of us. I still couldn't understand what was happening. No one could believe I was supporting any rebellion: I was a most un-commercial foreign capitalist. If Hans was really a foreign agent then he should be anti-communist and, presumably, pro-separatist. Maybe he was just a mercenary for all sides. It was a confusing time.

A guard come up to me as I squirmed in the cage; a sergeant of one of the local militia hired to terrify villagers. "Tuan, how do you like your palace? We're going to cut your throat tomorrow." He grinned with the pleasure of power. "But I want to help you. You got gold buried on your plantation. Where is it?"

Greed is a powerful weakness; I picked on it immediately.

"I promised that information to Hans last week. He knows approximately where it is but he needs me to show him tomorrow morning."

The sergeant looked suspicious and uncertain.

"You know us belando stick together. Hans needs me to guide him to the gold. You better be careful cutting my throat. It may annoy your boss."

The sergeant snarled and kicked the bamboo bars of the cage. "If you're lying to me, you die."

"If you want the gold, you'd better let me out of here so I can show you before Hans gets his hands on it." The sergeant hesitated, his big ugly mouth wide open as he stared at me. I continued, "Come back when everyone's asleep and let me out of this bloody cage, then I will show you. But if you double-cross me, I will make sure Hans gets everything."

I was left to myself for several wet, sweaty hours. The man next to me fell into unconsciousness only to come back to life some minutes later with a pathetic moan, "Yani, help me. Where are you, Yani?" I tried to speak to him but he was too far gone to understand or even notice me. I wanted to lose consciousness myself, to escape the torment of cramped limbs, but I couldn't.

As I was wriggling in the confined space, I heard the bushes rustling behind me, followed by heavy breathing. "How are you, English tea gardener?" Hans was behind me, whispering into my ear. I could smell his stale breath. "We've got a lot of talking to do if you want to leave this cage alive."

Hans walked around the narrow cage so as to face me. He was smoking a damp cigarette that spluttered in the rain. Behind him I could see two boy soldiers smiling in their half embarrassed way that hid depths of violence it was better not to know about.

Hans put a lighted cigarette between my lips and the nicotine immediately revived my ragged nerves. He put his face close to mine so he could speak quietly. "I know you are innocent of any crime, but that's meaningless here. Innocence itself is a crime. The only truth is that of strength and, at the moment, you don't seem to have much of it."

I tried to stand straight, to show strength, but it was impossible; movement just tightened the knots.

He continued, "These farmers we've captured here, you know what we're going to do with them? I'll show you tomorrow. The good lieutenant doesn't care if they are guilty or innocent; they are just peasants getting in the way. It will teach other peasants not to support rebels or anyone else except, of course, us. But, my dear Jim, I expect you are wondering who 'us' is. Ha ha, well, I'm not going to tell you. Not yet. Maybe you will find out later, if you live long enough.

"In your position I don't think you can really worry too much about who we are. All you want is to get out of here." He spent a long time looking at me before continuing. I could see he was sweating, more than the steamy night justified. I presumed he was nervous but, hell, he couldn't be nervous of me; I couldn't move a limb.

"What would you do, Jim, if one on these handsome young men …". He stopped and pointed to the two soldiers lolling behind him smoking clove cigarettes that sparked and fizzled in the night air. "If they got hold of Yahyu and brought her to this jungle camp for a few nights?"

I froze, as far as it's possible to freeze when movement is already impossible. "You can't do that," I yelled.

"In a way, you are right, Tuan Jim. I can't, but not for the reasons you are thinking. I can, physically, do anything I like. If I nod my head to one of these dumb soldiers, he will kill you instantly or slowly, depending on what I ask of him. But, no, I can't give Yahyu to the soldiers. You see, I want her for myself. She's a beautiful little thing and has caught my fancy. I could easily force her but I would prefer she came to me from choice; her choice, not mine. I have arranged it already. There's nothing you can do about it. She will be in my bed in a few days and you will be a forgotten dream."

I spat the cigarette out of my mouth, aiming at Hans but I didn't have the power to spit far enough. "What're you doing with Yahyu? What the hell's going on?" I tried to sound tough but it's difficult to achieve when you are trussed up like a pig.

"She's OK. She spent last night with me in Curup. Not in bed; not yet. She knows who's powerful in this shit awful island and she now knows it's not you. She's a bright girl. I could use a girl like that."

I knew Yahyu would never be a lover of Hans but ... these were dangerous times and anything could happen. I was the bait to tempt Yahyu into a trap. Yahyu and I had discussed what she should do if these troubles ever parted us. She would go north to Medan and stay with Bunggo until things settled down.

"Just let me out of here, Hans, then we talk. I can't move."

"I will let you live if you don't cause me too much trouble but you will also see your beautiful Yahyu with me. You don't believe me but you will see. Power is greater than love, my friend. What do you have to offer her? A romantic vision of gardening on a mountaintop.

Pah! In these times only the strong will survive."

As Hans turned to leave, he bent down to pick something up. I couldn't see what it was because my neck was tied too tightly and prevented me looking downwards. "You want proof of my power," Hans said with a grin. "Then I give you this present."

He thrust into my face the severed head of the militia sergeant I had tried to bribe earlier. I regret that I screamed in horror; I wanted to squirm away from the revolting thing but I couldn't move my head. One of Hans's soldiers placed it on a cross-section of the bamboo poles in front of my face and stuck a cigarette between the dead lips. He grinned at me as he patted the grotesque head. "Enjoy your chat with him. Maybe you will meet him soon."

I spent many hours trying to avoid the dead eyes. It was so close to me, I could smell the corruption. Up until that moment I still had some confidence but now I realised, all too late, what I was up against.

***

Several hours later, one of the guards let me out of the cage. Constant pain is similar to addiction; a hatred of the drug but a fear of its sudden withdrawal. When I was dragged from the cage, my cramped limbs went into agonising spasms. They had to drag me because my legs refused to cooperate.

I was kept loosely tied that night, although under close guard. During the night, several of the women prisoners screamed. I tried to stuff my head in a pile of leaves to hide the sound but to no avail. I imagined Yahyu at the mercy of these animals and it scared me to death. I was totally powerless.

The morning brought a sombre scene. It was wet and misty, and the prisoners lay in a miserable heap on the ground quietly moaning. The soldiers had tired of playing with the women and sat around their cooking fires chatting and smoking. Hans came over to me.

"Sleep well, tea gardener. Hope you are going to co-operate today, otherwise you're in for a very uncomfortable time."

After the soldiers had breakfasted, they kicked the prisoners to their feet, roped them together in groups of three or four and led them in the direction of the footbridge. A soldier tied a rope around my neck and pulled me along with them.

The prisoners were brought onto the bridge and the first group forced at bayonet point to climb on the parapet, where they were pushed into the rushing water below. The rest shouted and screamed while trying to run away, but the ropes entangled them and they fell over each other in their panic. The guards laughed loudly, while Hans and the officer watched from a distance, smoking and chatting.

All the prisoners were thrown over the bridge; screaming, crying, fighting—it made no difference. Some of the prisoners may have survived the fall and the water. It didn't seem to matter much. Life or death was a lottery. I wondered how someone like Father Tomas managed to keep faith amongst such random deaths.

I hoped the revolting scene hadn't been enacted to impress me. I doubt it. I think it was a random terror patrol subjecting the local population to its will. I should have felt horror and sympathy but I didn't. Sometimes extreme emotional shock can be so great it numbs the soul, leaving no feelings at all. Whatever the cause, I managed to cut myself off from the suffering around me and concentrate on plans for the survival of Yahyu and Peter.

We were standing by the bridge when Hans came up to me. He

took a revolver out of his holster and said, "Is this yours?"

Hans must have gone back to the ambush site during the night and searched the area for evidence and had found my revolver.

"Yes, it's mine." There was little point in lying.

Hans cocked the revolver and aimed at my left shoulder. I never heard a sound but I remember hitting the ground and thinking how hard it was. The pain of a bullet wound comes some minutes after the shot, but the shock to the body is immense. It's like being kicked with enormous force. I lay bleeding on the damp earth as Hans casually lit another cigarette.

I looked up at Hans who seemed to have lost interest. "You bastard," I yelled up at him.

He turned in my direction and equally casually kicked my shoulder. The pain was excruciating but so was the humiliation.

I was pushed into an army truck and taken to the police jail in Kepayang, a small town between Curup and Bengkulu. A place, Hans explained, where Captain Supriyono wouldn't be likely to find me for some days.

***

I was shivering from the shock of the bullet and from the drenching I received while confined in the bamboo cage as they dragged me into the police cell. I sat on the wooden shelf that served as a bed and looked around the sordid little cell. It was made of brick but with rotting plaster falling off the walls. It stank from a hole at one end that was presumably the latrine. There was no window, but through the barred grill that served as a door I could see Hans talking to one of the policemen. However, my attention was drawn to the far end of the cell where I saw, squatting in the corner and holding his head in his hands, a figure I knew only too well: Rusdi. I suppose Hans had sent his troops to pick him up as soon as he knew I was captured by his troops but I couldn't think of any reason why Hans would be interested in him. Rusdi was gurgling to himself in the corner. I don't think he even realised I was there. Rusdi's response to danger was to squat, stay still and hope no one would notice him. A sensible thing to do; maybe I should copy him.

I didn't disturb Rusdi but lay back on the bed to ease the pain in my shoulder which had progressed from the numbed but sickening pain that immediately follows a sudden wound into a dull throbbing threat of instant agony at the slightest movement. However, Hans walked in, a grin creasing his sweating cheeks. Rusdi looked up and caught my eye. He showed no recognition of me, but I saw cunning in his face as he quickly averted his eyes. Hans stood for a long time looking at the pathetic figure of Rusdi squatting on the floor and salivating as he stared blankly at the ground. He then turned to stare at the equally pathetic figure of myself lying on the bed and trying not to shiver because it hurt my shoulder.

"So, I now have the two best friends of Ibu Yahyu," he said. "One carries an empty sword scabbard but the other one comes to meet me carrying a loaded revolver. What does that mean? I think you wanted to kill me or perhaps you wanted to kill someone else. You failed, of course, but this crime cannot go unpunished. Maybe we shall shoot you. You can die in this squalid little cell now if I choose so. Nobody will know. Nobody, except perhaps your little Yahyu, will even care. But don't worry, I will take care of Yahyu. I know her little secret. Not the secret of her son but the secret of her soul. She is not the strong lady you think she is. There is a chink in her armour and I have found it."

"Let Rusdi go Da'eut. I take Nona to Da'eut." Rusdi stood up and danced in front of Hans. He knew what he was doing, whether through intellect or instinct I could never tell. He was playing Hans at his own game of bluff and counter-bluff, which took some of the attention away from me.

Hans turned away from me with a dismissive wave, took hold of Rusdi's hand and led him out the cell, telling the guard to lock the door behind him. I saw Hans talking to Rusdi in a friendly manner and Rusdi responding with apparent enthusiasm. He gave Rusdi coffee and patted him on the back. Eventually, Hans gave him a few coins and let him out the door. I heard Hans shout after him the fatal words, "After you get back, I shall take you to Da'eut. Be a good boy and bring her here."

"Hey, tea gardener," Hans called to me in a voice full of humour. "I thought you should know that Rusdi has gone back to the tea plantation. I think he will probably ask Yahyu to come here and ask for my help." Hans smiled as he talked but his eyes watched me intently; he was enjoying his triumph.

I could have stood up and yelled, I could have cried, I could have shaken the bars, but why? I lay back on the trestle bed, trying to lose myself in painful oblivion.

Later that afternoon, my shoulder throbbed badly and I felt the sinister chills that creep through the body giving a gloating warning that malaria is about to strike. I knew the symptoms of old and I hated the predictable process. Like Hans, the malaria knew what it was doing; it slowly advanced, searching for the weak spots before attacking in full force. As I slipped into deep fever, I saw Hans flying in the sky. Then I calmed down and saw the real Hans on the ground. I didn't know which was worse. He was dominating my hallucinations as I fought to retain control of my sanity.

During the height of the fever, I dreamed I was in a prison camp in some grimy industrial town in Northern England, surrounded by sinister figures waiting for me to make a mistake so they could kill me. I knew Yahyu and Peter were in the camp but I didn't know where. The camp had no walls and no fences, so I walked out into the grey town, thinking it was too easy; all I had to do was run and nobody would ever find me. Then I realised that Yahyu and Peter would get into trouble if I escaped, so I returned to the camp and was immediately watched by the same sinister characters. My prison did not consist of bars but of feelings.

I remember vaguely Captain Supriyono coming to see me during the night and questioning me, not about my revolver or my intentions, but about Hans.

"Why did you go to the gate when you knew Hans was waiting for you?" he asked.

"I wanted to get to Curup to find Yahyu. I wasn't concerned with Hans," I answered in short, sharp sentences. Talking is difficult when teeth are chattering in fever.

"He tells me you were carrying a revolver. Why was that?"

"You know that no one travels unarmed at night in Sumatra. I had no intention of seeing Hans."

"No, maybe not, but Hans had every intention of seeing you. Why was that?"

"I still don't know, but I think it's to do with Yahyu."

The Captain looked shocked although he quickly hid his reaction behind the inscrutable smile of the oriental aristocrat. "Interesting," he said.

The Captain left my cell and I heard snatches of a heated argument between him and Hans. The Captain was demanding to know by what authority a foreigner like Hans could arrest anyone in Indonesia and Hans responded calmly and smoothly with the simple words, "Jakarta authority." I fell into a semi-coma to the sounds of the Captain's disdainful accusations and Hans's silky assurance of higher authority in Jakarta.

The rest of the night was full of fevered dreams of tigers laying in wait on the path to my house and me being afraid to move in case they attacked; a kind of frigid fear where any movement will bring instant destruction. I woke in the morning covered in sweat and staring up at the dirty plaster on the ceiling. My shoulder was causing serious trouble and was probably infected, but I could not summon the energy to look at it. I lay on the shelf trying to preserve my strength for whatever ordeal Hans had in store.

In the morning the captain came back to my cell and sat beside me. "Don't worry," he said. "I shall write to Padang to ascertain Hans's true authority. In the meantime I shall instruct the doctor in Curup to come here and treat your fever and your wounds." I noticed he was sweating as he talked and he looked distracted. His normal air of natural authority had disappeared and been replaced by genuine concern, not for me, I think, but for his own authority and his understanding of what was happening in his area.

***

I was woken by someone gently calling me, "Jim, wake up, Jim."

I couldn't at first understand where I was. In between fevers and the pain in my shoulder, the sordid little world of the prison cell had grown shadowy and unsubstantial. I wasn't sure if I was conscious or still in a nightmare as I slowly gazed around the dirty walls trying to get a grip on reality.

It took some time to focus my eyes and it was an agonising effort to sit up. I held my shoulder with my right hand to prevent it jarring. Then I saw Yahyu standing by the bars. She was dressed in traditional Javanese style, and the contrast between her elegant beauty and my sordid little cell and wounded body was striking. I stretched out my hand to her but couldn't reach the bars.

Yahyu did not speak at first but stayed still, looking at me between the bars. I couldn't read her expression, which meant she was holding something back.

"Jim," she said quietly but with a faltering voice. "You've got to concentrate. There's something I have to tell you."

I tried to get up to move towards her but my foot had been manacled to the wall and I fell back on the shelf.

"Yahyu, come here." I panted for breath; the effort of trying to stand up and speak was too much.

"I can't, Jim; they won't let me come in. You must concentrate on what I have to say."

I looked towards her and saw tears slowly trickling down her cheeks.

"Listen carefully, Jim. I've got to make a decision and it's one neither of us ever wanted." She faltered again before continuing. "If we live long enough, you will understand why I am doing it and then

I hope you will forgive me."

I was still trying to keep a grip on reality but found it hard to concentrate. Yahyu kept floating out of focus until I wasn't sure she was there at all.

"What's happened Yahyu, what's going on. You must tell me."

"We've been trapped. Hans says he will kill you if I don't ...". She broke down completely, holding a handkerchief to her mouth as her body slowly wilted to the ground.

"Yahyu, you're strong, you can get out of this. You don't need to think of me. Run to Bunggo, take Peter with you. I can look after myself."

Yahyu stood up once more and reached through the bars towards me, but our hands couldn't touch; it was a few inches too far.

"Rusdi came to me last night. He brought a note from Hans saying you would be released as soon as I arrived here, but if I didn't come, he would shoot you and send Peter away from me. So I've done exactly what Hans wanted. I didn't know what else to do." She started crying again but with a great effort she pulled herself together.

"I didn't come straight here. I went first to Curup to ask for help from Captain Supriyono. He was kind but evasive. He said he couldn't get involved; that it was in the hands of the authorities in Jakarta and that you were caught carrying guns. He said he expected Hans would not shoot you but would probably ensure you and Peter were expelled from the country. So I left Peter with Ibu Wati and came here."

There was silence between us. She was grappling with an immense problem which I was only just beginning to understand.

"What happened when you arrived here? Sorry, I don't even

know what day it is. I think I've been unconscious for some time."

"You've been here for three days," she said. I arrived yesterday and tried to speak to you, but you were unconscious. I got them to send for a doctor who gave you something for the malaria, but he said your shoulder is serious and will get infected. Hans refused to let him treat you further."

"Hans! Is that bastard here now?"

"Yes. He's waiting outside. I refused to speak to you if he was listening. He's won, Jim. He's worked it all out and I'm the cause of it."

"What? You're not the cause of anything. Hans is an animal. What does he want?" I knew the answer but didn't want to admit it.

Yahyu looked at me sadly. "I wish I could reach you but they won't open the cell door. They said I must speak to you from here."

Yahyu stopped speaking briefly and I could hear her taking deep breaths to control her voice.

"Jim, I know what I must do but I don't have the strength to carry it out unless you help me."

"Of course I will help you, but you need to get out of here; go to Bunggo. It's easier for me if I fight this battle alone."

With another deep breath she came out with her plan. "The only way you can help is by going away, back to your own country."

"I'm not leaving you and Peter here. You know what Hans is like."

Yahyu was crying again and her voice grew faint, but she still found the courage to continue. "Try to understand. It's not for me that I ask you to leave. You and Peter are all that I live for; I don't care what happens to me. You go and take Peter with you. If you don't, then Hans will shoot you and put Peter in a bad house in Linggau. Hans promises that you can both leave the country together but I must stay."

I looked in astonishment, my brain trying to catch up with events.

"I have made a deal with him," Yahyu continued. "He will let you and Peter go but I must stay." Yahyu fought back tears while she spoke and her elaborate eye shading began to smudge, but she held herself under control—just.

"Hans cannot force me to go. We'll stay here. We'll fight him together. The Captain will help us."

"The Captain will not help us, although he will not harm us either. He cannot touch Hans. If you stay here and they shoot you, then I will be left with Peter and I cannot defend him against Hans. He's evil. We must save Peter; you are the only man in the world who can save him. Please do this for me and please understand the reasons why I want it." Yahyu gripped the bars as she spoke.

"Hans wouldn't harm Peter. There's no point, no reason. I don't even know what Hans does want, other than to get rid of me."

"You must go, Jim, and take Peter with you. Leave me behind and forget me. Look after Peter and tell him his mother died in Sumatra. Don't let him know what will happen next." As she spoke, I looked into her large oval eyes and it shocked me. Sadness was the only expression, the end of all her dreams.

"Even if I do agree to go, what's to stop Hans killing me and Peter on the road."

"Me. He won't do it because he wants me and I won't go near him until you and Peter are safe. After that ...". That's all Yahyu said. She couldn't continue. She stood outside the bars, striving to look strong and decisive but beginning to crack. It was too much for anyone to take.

"Yahyu ...". I wanted to say I loved her, but I couldn't; it stuck in my throat.

She knelt by the bars so she was level with me and stretched her arm out to touch my hand, but still we couldn't reach.

"Whatever is going to happen," she said, "Remember that I am doing it for you and Peter. It's not what I ever wanted." Tears rolled down her cheeks once more as we both finally succumbed to the realisation of what she was about to do.

We stayed for a long time, looking at each other but not speaking and unable to touch.

Reality and dreams intermingled in my weakened state. Yahyu seemed strong but sad as I drifted in and out of delirium to the strains of her soothing voice.

¤ ¤ ¤

Our dreams were interrupted by Hans who came quietly into the police station followed by a couple of guards holding Rusdi who looked at me slyly from the corner of his eye; he seemed uncertain of his reception. Unusually for him, he spoke almost immediately. "I bring Nona here. Tuan Hans says he will take all of us to Da'eut. We'll all be happy together." Rusdi did not speak with his usual idiotic grin. He was serious but hesitant. Perhaps he was wishing it to be true but doubting it. Hans interrupted him gently.

"Rusdi, my friend, you speak the truth in a way," Hans spoke softly to Rusdi whilst keeping his eyes on Yahyu and myself, studying our reactions. "Some of us will find Da'eut, although some may not.

It all depends what we want our Da'eut to be. I have certainly found my Da'eut, haven't I, Nona."

Rusdi looked at him blankly and then at Yahyu and me. "Tuan Jim," he said, "I help Tuan and Nona to find Da'eut. We all be happy together." His face showed real concern. Perhaps a part of his mad soul realised he had sold Yahyu into Hans's hands but he did not want to believe it; he was still desperate for the happiness which was represented by Da'eut.

Hans turned to me. "Has Yahyu told you of our deal? Did she tell you all of it or only part of it? I am offering you and Peter the chance of a new life in your cold, wet England where you can drink tea until you die. If you don't go, you will be shot as a rebel sympathiser and Peter your son, at least I shall presume he is your son, will be given to my friend Ibu Efi in the House of Young Bamboo in Linggau. She knows how to look after orphans and to reform them from the bad influence of rebels. He's a good-looking boy. He'll be popular with some of her special customers."

At the name of Ibu Efi and her infamous brothel, Yahyu rose quickly and slapped Hans hard in his face but then refrained from following up. Hans smiled at her. I think he enjoyed seeing Yahyu's fire.

Hans turned to the guards and nodded. They opened my cell and carried me to a waiting Jeep. I tried to reach out to Yahyu but a guard pushed her away. My strength was spent; I wanted to fight but I couldn't.

Yahyu called out and started to follow me to the waiting Jeep, but at a nod from Hans she stopped and turned her back on me. As we drove off I saw her back heaving; she was crying.

***

Hans, Rusdi and a couple of guards sat in the Jeep with me and we drove at high speed in the direction of my plantation.

"We're going to pick up Peter," Hans said with a smile of success. "No need for the mother to see his departure. How do you feel, Tuan Jim, although I don't think anyone will call you Tuan again. You accepted Peter into the bosom of your family; how noble you English are. Now I'm going to give you a chance to be together for the rest of your lives. You get Peter and I get the mother; fair deal."

I tried to punch the dirty smile off his face, but I was too weak. He ducked the blow and one of the guards returned the favour on me, leaving me staunching blood from my mouth. Everything hurt: body, soul, pride.

Instead of turning into the main gate of my plantation, we drove on for another half an hour to where the road abruptly stops by the banks of a river.

"OK Rusdi," Hans said to him. "Time to get off. If you go over that river and up the bank, you will see Da'eut before you."

Rusdi looked up quickly, his face shifting between delight, suspicion and fear.

"I don't see Da'eut," he said. "And I go Da'eut with Nona and Tuan. Don't want to go Da'eut alone."

"They go to their own Da'eut," Hans said with what appeared to be genuine sincerity. "You must go to your Da'eut alone. Just follow the path over the river and up the mountain."

"No go Da'eut alone. Rusdi promise Nona to look after her."

Hans soon tired of the game. He nodded to one of the guards

who pushed Rusdi off the Jeep.

"Go, Rusdi. Go find your mama. I guarantee you will see her in a few minutes."

This was too much for Rusdi. "Mama," he yelled as he ran down the path. "Mama, Mama, where are you?"

I heard a rifle bolt click behind me and I turned to see one of the boy soldiers taking aim. I tried to lean over and push the barrel up, but I was too weak and fell from the Jeep as he fired. I didn't see Rusdi fall but I could hear his screams from somewhere near the river.

"OK," Hans said. "Job done, let's go."

"You can't leave him screaming like that, at least put him out of his agony," I spoke angrily, but my weakness made me sound flat and helpless.

"Alright," Hans said. "Here, English tea gardener. Take this pistol and one bullet. You're a kind man; put the idiot out of his misery. But don't try shooting me first. These guards will kill you before you even cock the hammer."

I took the pistol and stumbled towards Rusdi but I wasn't sure what I'd do when I got there.

I reached Rusdi and found him grasping his stomach. Stomach wounds are always the worst. They cause intense pain and it can take hours, sometimes days, to die. I expect the guard shot him there purposely. He could easily have aimed higher and ensured a fast kill.

"Tuan, where's my Mama. You must go to Da'eut and find my mama. Tell her Rusdi needs her."

I looked at Rusdi gasping on the ground; what a wasted life. He was born to be a good farmer; get married, have kids, grow rice. Instead he had led a life of madness from his childhood and now he was dying a slow, painful death whilst thinking he was almost in shouting distance of his long-lost mother. I couldn't leave him there to die alone.

"Rusdi, you will be with your mother soon, in Da'eut, I promise."

"Rusdi also want to be with Nona and Tuan. Nona good to me, she helped me."

This was going to be hard. I placed one hand softly over Rusdi's eyes while telling him to wait for his mother who was coming to help him. I placed the revolver next to his heart and shot him. His body jerked violently and then flopped back in death.

I couldn't look at him. I sat beside his dead body, head in hands for what seemed like hours. I had lost Yahyu to a fate which may have been worse than death and I had just killed a harmless idiot who had been part of my family for the past few months.

I staggered back to the Jeep to find Hans watching me with interest. I managed to stand up by leaning on the Jeep's bonnet and turned towards Hans. With one violent movement I threw the pistol in his face. I had the pleasure of seeing blood spurt from his nose before I felt a sharp pain which knocked my head to one side. I presume one of the guards had hit me with a rifle butt.

The rest of the journey was a blur of pain, fever and anger. I remember being carried into my house on the plantation and meeting with a very distraught Peter. "Where's Mama," he demanded. Then, seeing my weak condition he quietened but asked in a whisper, "Are these bad men? That big man, I don't like him. I saw him putting his hands on Mama once. That's not allowed, is it?"

There was a long journey by Jeep but I remember little of it except for Peter's resilience and plucky spirit. I lay in the back of the vehicle when Peter crawled up to me and whispered in my ear, "When we next stop, you kill the guard, Papa, and then we steal the car and go back and rescue Mama."

"I can't, Peter, my shoulder's too bad. Let's wait till we are out of the country, then Mama will escape by herself and run off to Uncle Bunggo's place, then we will rescue her from there."

"OK Papa," he said dejectedly.

I prayed that what I said was going to be true, both for his sake and mine.

I eventually came to full consciousness in a hospital in Palembang where I was chained to a bed, with Peter sleeping on a blanket on the floor. He whimpered at night and called for his mama, but in the daytime he was defiant and tried to stop the guards coming to me, only to be pushed aside.

When the guards had gone, Peter came and sat on the bed. "The big man, the one that smells bad, told me we are going in a big ship. Is that true?"

"I expect so Peter. Let's wait and see."

***

I was carried on a stretcher to the big ship that turned out to be a dirty little tramp steamer chugging up the coast of Sumatra and spewing us onto the docks of Penang in Malaya. I stayed in hospital for some months. They amputated my arm at the shoulder. My emotions were in complete turmoil and Peter was my only link with the past, my only link with my beautiful Yahyu.

Chapter 8

Yahyu turned her back on the departing figure of Jim but she heard every sound he made; his faltering steps as he was led to the Jeep, his cry of "Yahyu, trust me, I'll be back", the sound of the Jeep door slamming and the engine fading as they slowly disappeared down the track that led into the mountains.

She could not turn and look at him. She didn't have the confidence to see him depart and not run after the car. In exchange for the freedom of Jim and Peter she had sold her body to Hans and her soul to the devil. She felt herself spinning out of control; her emotions a confusion of anger at her fate, frustration at her own weakness and sadness at the loss of all she had learnt to love and cherish. The nobility of her sacrifice was of little comfort in the expectation of the degradation that was soon to follow and the emptiness that stretched out before her. The rock that kept Yahyu sane was the thought that once Jim and Peter were safe, she would murder Hans or kill herself. He'll only have me for a short while, she thought, then ... death.

A police officer took her gently by the arm and led her to a waiting police car. "It'll be several weeks before your husband leaves the country," he said quietly. "If you take my advice, you'll just give in to Tuan Hans until they're gone. What does it matter if you share a bed with him for a few weeks? You'll be free afterwards to go anywhere you want but you won't be allowed back to the plantation. We're going to torch it tonight. There'll be nothing left tomorrow. I'm sorry, but we got orders from above."

Yahyu looked at the officer in confusion, a cold sweat creeping down her back as she realised the implications of what he said. "Stop the car," she yelled, nearing hysteria. "Let me out. You can't burn my home. There'll be no where for Jim to come back to." She shook the door handle in vain.

"Ibu, the doors are locked; you can't get out. I'm really sorry but Tuan Hans says we are to leave you with nothing but the clothes you're standing in. It's not my choice. I'm just obeying orders. And don't go thinking too much about your Tuan Jim. He's never coming back, not as long as this government stays in power. He's branded as a separatist rebel. You got to get used to a new life now."

Yahyu sat in the backseat staring blankly at the passing countryside as doubt crept insidiously into her heart. She gripped the seat in panic. Have I really saved Jim or just betrayed him and myself? Maybe there was another way? Will he ever want me after this? Will Peter still love me when he grows up and knows what I am about to do?

She didn't care where she was going as the policeman led her upstairs towards her hotel room. She didn't hear him lock the door from the outside after he left. She fell on the bed in a confusion of emotion and expectation of what was to follow. In a perverted way she wished for total degradation; she wanted it to be fast and violent because that would absolve her of any hint of complicity or guilt.

Yahyu spent the night in a state of expectation. She lay on the bed listening for the sound that would warn her of Hans's approach. A creaking of the stairs or a sudden cough or laugh from outside the window and her heart pounded as she cringed on the bed in fearful anticipation. She was confused as to what she feared most, the arrival of Hans or the sickening emptiness of her life. Father Tomas had once told her that hell could only be understood as the absence of God; Yahyu's hell was the absence of everyone dear to her. Maybe it was the same hell as that of Father Tomas. But thinking of God made Yahyu angry. She had prayed to every god she knew and none had helped her. I hate God, she said to herself; no one with mercy could wish this on me.

As several days passed and Hans did not appear, Yahyu began to think more calmly about him and her situation. He was obviously not a hasty man, she thought. He had laid his plans well and he was going to obtain a complete victory over her. She was resigned to that fate although determined it would only be temporary. She was his reward for winning the battle with Jim and he was going to appreciate her in the same way a connoisseur enjoys a good bottle of wine; to be savoured slowly so the taste of her would linger on his tongue and excite all his sensations. Why else had he left her alone for several days, locked in her hotel bedroom? With renewed courage, born out of anger, Yahyu was determined that what would linger on his tongue would not be the taste of her but the marks of her teeth. Once Jim was safe, she would seek revenge and she would make him suffer as he was making her suffer.

The week passed in boredom and despair. The only person she

saw was the guard who brought her meals. The unnatural isolation made her crave company, even that of Hans so she could exert her anger. Anything would be better than the limbo into which she had been carefully trapped.

***

Yahyu heard whispering outside the door. There was a gentle tap followed by the sound of keys and the door slowly opened. "Hello Ibu Yahyu," said a cheery voice as an old lady walked respectfully into the room. "Ooh, you got a nice room here," she said, turning to Yahyu. "And I heard that Tuan Hans is going to pay all your bills. You lucky girl; wish I was young and beautiful again like you. Maybe he would look after me then. But no one wants an old crone like me."

Yahyu looked at the old lady as if she were a ghost. After a night of nightmares and anguish, she couldn't understand what the old lady was doing. "Who are you?" was all she could say.

"My name don't matter to you, dear. Just call me Ibu. Now, don't go moping around on the bed like that. You're a noble Javanese lady or so I'm told. We Javanese don't go giving in. Where's your pride? You got the chance to benefit from Tuan Hans and he's one of the most important men in Sumatra. He's a friend of the new governor and he knows important people in Jakarta. He's got power. You're a lucky girl, only you don't seem to know it yet. Most women in this town would give their right arm to get Hans chasing after them."

Yahyu stood up to look at the old lady. "But I've lost my husband and my son. They've gone away to England. Han's did that. He forced them to go." Yahyu's voice broke as she spoke and she slumped back on the bed, head in hands.

"I've lost many husbands," the old lady said. "Most of them I was glad to get rid of. Losers they was. I had to earn money every night out on the streets and they gambled it away the next day. Don't go relying on husbands; you got to rely on your own wits. When my last husband left me, I got a job cleaning in Ibu Efi's place in Linggau, the House of Young Bamboo." She glanced sideways at Yahyu as she spoke, looking to see if Yahyu was of that persuasion.

Yahyu shook her head in disgust. "I'm not like that. I don't want to go anywhere near that horrid woman or her disgusting bordello."

The old lady continued as if Yahyu had not spoken. "Efi's a good woman, always pays well and gives me loans whenever I need them. She and Hans are very close; not in the way of beds, if you get my meaning, but he's got business with her. They spend hours together in the back office. I thought they was doing things at first but they weren't. They were just discussing. I don't know what they talk about, but Hans always comes back to her, several times a month. It was Efi who sent me here to you. She said Hans wanted me to help you. Anything I can do for you, dear, or would you just like me to clean up a bit and keep you company until Hans arrives?"

Yahyu let the old lady carry on chattering. Her own thoughts were in such confusion she could not concentrate on what was being said. She saw little hope of using this situation to any advantage except to give Peter and Jim time to leave the country. She would be strong, she told herself, but not in the way the old lady meant.

That night there was no sign of Hans and Yahyu began to doubt his desire for her. Perhaps he was not as licentious as she had at first imagined or was it all part of his game? She wasn't sure whether his absence gave her confidence or disappointment. She wanted to get it over with, to know what she had to put up with, to know what sort of man he really was. She was lying in limbo and the strain started to tell in sudden outburst of frustration and anger at the slightest cause. She had been expecting, possibly even needing, an immediate struggle with Hans, but instead there was nothing; only a locked door to prove he was still controlling her. She felt she was losing her way and also her sanity.

The next day the old lady came again and cleaned the room. "I expect Hans will come and see you in a few days," she said.

Yahyu nodded and continued to look wistfully out of the window that faced east, towards Palembang, where Jim and Peter were probably in a hospital or waiting for a ship to take them to England.

The old lady continued to chatter despite Yahyu's apparent lack of interest. "Can I give you a tip, love? I got this tip from one of the nice ladies that Hans used to know in the House of Young Bamboo. He likes a squealer, if you know what I mean."

Yahyu looked at her in total incomprehension. "What do you mean?"

"You know, he likes to hear the girls squeal when he's with them, in the bed when he's doing things to them. It gets him really excited and that way he finishes earlier. Good tip, that; if you squeal for him, it's less work for you and he gets off you quicker. Mark my words, if you listen to me, I can tell you how to control men like Hans. Like all men, he thinks he's powerful, but we women know he's only powerful among other men. When he's with us women, we can control him easy. Give him what he wants, make him think he controls you and then, slowly, slowly, you will control him because he won't be able to live without you. You're the most beautiful woman in this town and you got class, so there isn't much competition, is there?"

Yahyu listened intently to the advice of the old lady but she did not reveal her real fear. She couldn't even admit that to herself. It was too disgusting, too confusing, too much of a betrayal of all that she and Jim had built together.

***

Later that afternoon, Yahyu heard the key turning in the lock and the door slowly opened. She saw Hans standing in the doorway chatting to the guard while holding a bottle of whiskey. He came into the room with a smile and nodded to the old lady to leave them.

When the door was closed, Hans sat on the sofa and looked at Yahyu. "You are just as beautiful as ever. You look even more beautiful when you cry. Will you ever cry for me?"

Yahyu tried not to look at him but her eyes were dragged back to his fat, sweaty face with his small, intense eyes boring into her and asking questions which she did not want to answer. She knew what was expected of her but she didn't know how to start. She had expected a quick attack, to be flung on the bed and forced to submit to Hans's superior strength, but that was not happening. In front of her she only saw Hans relaxing on the sofa, drinking whiskey and smiling at her; although with Hans the difference between a smile and a leer was so minuscule she could never be sure.

"We're going out tonight, you and me." He spoke slowly and calmly as he sat back to watch the shock and confusion on Yahyu's face. He continued, "I am taking you to see the army commander. He's visiting Curup at the moment. I told him that my new consort, a beautiful Javanese princess, was going to dance for him, although in practice I expect you to be dancing for me; he will just be a casual admirer. So please dress up. I told the police to bring your clothes here. I had them rescued before your house accidently burnt down. Get changed and I shall pick you up in two hours.

"Oh, by the way, Jim is in the best hospital in Palembang but he has not left the country yet. A few more days. I always keep my word, both the good words and the bad words. So you'd better be well behaved or else he might never make it."

This was to be her first time outside her luxury prison and it would be her final goodbye to Jim and Peter. The evening would be the saving of her family but the death of herself as a wife and a mother. She had few illusions as to what would follow her public appearance as the concubine of Hans. The tingling sensation in her stomach was like a battle cry; if I'm to do it, then let's get on with it and do it properly.

She took great care with her make-up, looking into the mirror as she outlined her eyes in black and carefully brushed her long curled eyelashes. I'm doing it for Jim and Peter, she repeated to herself as if to justify her behaviour and quieten the excitement mounting deep inside her body.

True to his promise, Hans came to her a couple of hours later and she was ready for him, dressed as a classical Javanese beauty. Hans stood back to admire her as he told her to turn around so he could view her from all angles; her glistening black eyes, her small but shapely bosom, her curved back and well-rounded bottom. She was the epitome of high Javanese culture: beautiful, controlled, calm.

"You're the woman I want," he said as he sat back in his chair and surveyed his latest possession. "I'm going to keep you at whatever cost. You're different from those other women. I'm going to preserve you just for me."

Yahyu looked at him blankly but Hans was razor-sharp and noted the slight reddening of her cheeks as she struggled to maintain a bland expression.

"Excitement getting the better of you, my dear?" he said casually as he turned her round to view her again.

"Stop it, Hans. Let's just go and get it over with." For all her brave words, Yahyu knew she was falling into an abyss of her own making. Hans was pressing all the right buttons and her previous image of him as an animal was changing to one of masculine power. Her knees grew weak, but she managed to pull herself away and make for the door.

Hans helped her into his Jeep and they drove to the house of the Mayor where the dinner and the performance were to take place. Hans was sensitive to her feelings and indulgent towards them. "Don't worry," he said. "You look stunning; the most beautiful woman in Sumatra."

After some moments he turned to her once more and added, "But I'm not foolish enough to presume you dressed like this to impress me. You just like dancing; a real professional. I'm supremely confident in your dancing ability and I'm looking forward to seeing you on stage. You'll be great. They will love you. And, although you may not be dancing for me, the guests will think you are and that's good enough for me. Later on you might find that you like performing for me." The innuendo was not lost on Yahyu but she pretended not to notice.

"Tell me where Jim and Peter are," she said.

Hans's face fell slightly at the reference to Jim, but he quickly recovered his composure and his charm. "I told you, he's in the best hospital in Palembang, at my expense."

"How do I know they're still alive if I can't contact them?"

"For that you will have to rely on my word. But Jim is free to write to you, care of me, after he has left the country if he still wants to, which he may not. It takes a big man to desire his wife when he knows she is enjoying herself with another man and I doubt if Jim is a big enough man. I've spent the past few months seeing you with Jim. It didn't worry me because I knew that in the end I would win and you would come to me. I doubt if Jim has that strength. He will just run away and, like a good Englishman, act with great nobility looking after your son whilst you are having fun in bed with me."

This was too much for Yahyu. It was a gross distortion although there was a grain of truth in it. Hans knew her vulnerability and he had hit it. She turned her face to him, eyes flashing fire as she slapped him hard across the left cheek.

Hans smiled as he dabbed a drop of fresh blood from his lip. "I like to see your fire, Yahyu. Your eyes flash when you're angry and your cheeks redden. Quite delightful. I don't like passive women. They are very boring both in bed and at the dinner table. But you, Yahyu, have both beauty and fire. What a lucky man I am that you chose to stay with me."

Yahyu's shoulders drooped in recognition of her failure. A Javanese must never show anger but she had let her feelings show in front of Hans who saw it the Javanese way, as a sign of her weakness and his superiority, and it obviously gave him much pleasure. She felt humiliated and she hated him for it. He had planned the destruction of her family and had carried it out with total ruthlessness. Now he had planned her total seduction and he was in the process of carrying it out equally successfully, and she felt incapable of withstanding his advances.

When they arrived at the Mayor's house, Hans showed charm and courtesy to the guests. He introduced her to the important people as if she was his consort. The General was immensely impressed by her beauty and slyly passed her his telephone number during the course of the dinner. The Mayor kept eyeing her but was obviously too scared of Hans to do anything about it. There was a group of Chinese businessmen who seemed to be very friendly with the General; probably gold smugglers or gangsters who were paying him off to ensure his troops stayed out of their business. They ignored her. Money was more important than beauty. There were several important police officers whom she vaguely recognised but they also ignored her. All except Captain Supriyono, who sat at the far end of the table looking disdainfully at the Chinese businessmen. Unusual for a policeman in Sumatra, he hated corruption. He caught her eye several times during the meal and gave her the inscrutable smile of the true Javanese aristocrat, a smile that said absolutely nothing.

After the meal, Hans announced that Yahyu would dance for them on a small stage on the Mayor's lawn and they slowly wandered onto the veranda to get a good view. Yahyu noticed that Hans stood directly in front of the stage as if guarding his property. Perhaps the old lady was right, she thought, and Hans's possessiveness could be turned into a weakness that she could control. Turning to the audience, she spoke in a loud voice, "This dance is for my husband, Jim."

As she climbed onto the stage, she saw anger momentarily pass over Hans's face and it thrilled her.

It was a long time since she had danced in front of a serious audience. The General, for all his corrupt lechery, would be familiar with the Javanese classics. She had often danced for Jim and his workers but that was more a form of light-hearted fun. This was to be serious.

She tried to lose herself in the drama of the ballet but she couldn't. In the past, when she danced in front of big audiences, they had ceased to exist after the first few movements as she became totally absorbed in the artistry of her dancing. But this time she could not ignore Hans's eyes studying her. His eyes followed every subtle movement of her hands, every sway of her hips, every angle of her bosom, every blink of her long, beautiful eyelashes, and every flash of her big, black eyes. He seemed to be truly admiring her as no man had ever done before. It was hard for Yahyu to concentrate. This man who studied and admired her was also the man who had threatened to sell Peter to Ibu Efi and had shot her husband, but she still yearned for his admiration.

When she finished her performance there was much clapping. The General was effusive in his praise for the most perfect Javanese dancer in Sumatra. Hans positively beamed his pleasure. The General patted him on the back and congratulated him on his good luck in getting such an exquisite consort. Everyone seemed impressed except Captain Supriyono who kept his disdainful distance. He was happier cleansing the world of the destructive influence of communism than observing sleazy affairs between foreign men and one of his own kind.

While Hans was involved in a private conversation with the General and one of the Chinese businessmen, the Captain nodded to Yahyu to join him on the veranda. "Aren't you disgusted with what you're doing?" he snapped at her, his expression showing his contempt. "You're selling yourself and your culture to a dirty foreigner. I could understand your feelings for Jim because he was a true gentleman, almost polite enough to be one of us, but Hans … it's too much."

Yahyu looked in despair at his serious face and felt her cheeks blushing once more. "Do you know what he threatened to do to Jim if I didn't stay with him?" she snapped back at him.

"I don't know but I can guess. But I still think you could do it with less display of enjoyment."

Yahyu tried hard to suppress the tears that formed under her eyelids. She had never guessed that her ambiguous feelings would be so obvious to the ever-observant eyes of the policeman.

"Do you remember when we first met, in Muara Enim?" he said to her. "I knew there was more to you than meets the eye and I was right. I was also pleased when I saw you with Jim. I liked Jim and I liked you, even when you were a dirty little scarecrow." He allowed the ghost of a smile to flicker over his serious face. "But I don't like what you are doing now. It's not honest to your culture, to Jim or to your son Peter. I know it's not your choice but a true Javanese queen would die rather than be touched by another, especially a foreigner."

Yahyu looked at her feet in shame and confusion. "What do you suggest I do? I have to keep Hans happy until Jim and Peter have left the country."

"I understand that. In fact I am beginning to understand a lot more. While I was in Padang, I picked up some interesting information on our Mr Hans. He may not be so influential in the long run. You may be backing the wrong horse. Can you do something for me? Something that may badly affect Hans."

Yahyu was taken off guard. "I don't know," she said. "I'll do nothing until I know that Jim and Peter are safe. After that ... I don't care what happens after that."

The Captain looked at her kindly. "I'm glad you said that. I wouldn't have respected you if you had jumped at the chance of revenge on Hans regardless of your family's safety. I know you are acting out of necessity, but pleased don't look so happy when you're doing it. It offends me as I am sure it would offend Jim, if he knew about it.

"What I want from you is information on Hans's movements. Who he sees and what he does. Get him to talk to you, to tell you what he does in the daytime or when he's away from you. I am particularly interested to know what he does in Linggau. He goes there every month but I don't know why. He doesn't need the whores there; he has enough whores of his own."

He suddenly stopped talking and looked at Yahyu's pained expression. "Sorry Ibu, I didn't mean it that way. I know you are no whore. If you help me, I promise to protect you. You can trust me. I'm Javanese like you, and I want to see a proper Javanese rule of this country, not this corrupt anarchy we have now."

"I know one thing," she said. "When he goes to Linggau, he always stays in the House of Young Bamboo and spends hours in the back office discussing with Ibu Efi until late at night. Nobody knows what they talk about but he goes there every month, sometimes more."

The Captain gave her a long inscrutable stare. "Um, interesting. That rogue Ibu Efi is involved in all sorts of filth. She gets involved in anything and makes money from everything. That's exactly the sort of information I wanted to know. Tell me when he next goes there please. I'll replace the policeman guarding your door with one I can trust. His name is Yoga. You can pass messages to me through him but please don't discuss anything with him. This may be more dangerous than you realise. And be careful of Hans; he's not the stupid animal he pretends to be."

Yahyu was both confused and excited by the Captain's words. At least the excitement of the intrigue would fill the terrifying vacuum in her soul. If she could harm Hans on the way, then all the better. She began to feel a tinge of confidence coming back to her heart. She could trust Captain Supriyono; he seemed to be incorruptible and ruthless.

On the way back to the hotel Hans was full of compliments for Yahyu and her performance. "Your beauty stunned them. The General even offered me money to spend the night with you but I refused, of course. You're mine now and I'm going to keep you. Don't think for one minute that that little shit the Captain can help you. I saw him talking to you this evening, asking for information about me, I expect. He can't help you, Yahyu. I can destroy him whenever I want, but it amuses me to see so many men lusting after you. I shall let him lust away for the time being."

On arrival at the hotel Hans held her hand as he led the way to the bedroom. The door he carefully locked from the inside. "For my own protection," he said. "Not to keep you in."

Yahyu looked at his face, watching for signs of animal lust but she could see none. Hans sat on a chair studying her, looking at her reactions to his every word and every action. His was a psychological seduction which Yahyu found hard to resist. His power at this moment was absolute and, to make it worse, he did not exploit it. Instead, he was concerned with admiring her beauty and grace, which was not what she expected or wanted. She wanted to see Hans as a brute animal lusting after her body but he wasn't. He was refined, sophisticated, subtle. He was forcing her to respect him. She could not hate his considerate manners or his genuine admiration of her beauty, but she had to hate him for what he had done to her family.

Hans gently but firmly removed her clothes whilst looking only into her eyes. "You are my beauty, Yahyu. You are so beautiful it's a shame to spoil you with anything so sordid as sex. But I must explore all of you and I must possess your soul and, to do that, I must make love to you in all ways known to man. I want your body as well as your soul, and I believe you want the same, although you can't yet admit it to yourself."

Hans did not drag her to bed or leap on top of her. When she was completely naked, he slowly ran his coarse but powerful hands over the curves of her figure, showing genuine delight at the refinement of her body. When he considered she was ready for him, he gently lifted her onto the bed and lay beside her, smiling into her eyes while caressing her breasts.

Yahyu's resistance began to wane; she returned his kisses with interest. She grabbed hold of him, pleading with him to enter her and get it finished, but Hans would not. He kept her on the brink for a long, long time until she was gasping for him as if dying from thirst.

"Hans, please, just do it. I can't go on. Do it now. Please."

Hans slide himself on top on her and gently, so very gently but firmly, started to make love to her. She felt her madness rise and she encouraged speed but he would not comply. He was controlling the pace, not her. Somewhere in the back of her mind she heard the old lady saying, "He likes a squealer." She squealed quietly at first, but then, seeing the effect on the increased pace of his love-making, she squealed and sighed louder until Hans lost himself in his delight of her.

When she came to her senses, she realised she may have won a battle but had lost the war. She had won the initiative in love-making but at the price of submission to her own secret desires.

***

Over the coming months Yahyu developed a craving for Hans despite, or perhaps because of, her imprisonment in her comfortable hotel room. Hans was her only visitor and her only contact with the outside world and he only visited her once or twice a week; his absences serving to increase her desire. When he came to her after an absence of two or three days, it was her, not him, that forced them onto the bed as she pushed his hand down her blouse or his mouth onto her breasts. Even Hans, for all his debauched experiences, was surprised at the extent of his conquest and of Yahyu's insatiable desire for him. What he did not know was the extent of her descent into despair that followed his departure in the morning, when Yahyu cried to herself and swore never to touch him again. But the next time he visited her it would start all over again. She was beginning to hate herself.

Hans eventually made a fatal psychological mistake; he stayed with Yahyu during the daytime. After a night of frenetic love-making, he did not leave in the morning but stayed with her and chatted, mainly about himself. Yahyu did not like that. She had hardly said a word to him over the previous month. She preferred to see him as pure sexual power, not as an ordinary person. But as he chatted casually to her, she saw him as he really was; an ugly, corrupted man going to seed while desperately trying to maintain the vestiges of power and youth. His pale, spotted belly suffered from heat rash, his hairy chest was unwashed and his breath smelled of decay. She felt her anger rise as he sat naturally beside her as if he was the equal of Jim. She wanted to kill him because of his ugliness and because of her desire for him.

At the end of his stay he told her he would be away for a week in Linggau and that she could go out into the town with the police guard stationed outside her door. So confident was he of his conquest over Yahyu that he forgot to check which guard was guarding her.

**

Yahyu knocked on her door and asked the guard to come in.

"I can't, Ibu. The Captain told me never to come into your room."

"Are you Pak Yoga?" she asked him and he nodded. "In that case please tell the Captain that Hans has gone to Linggau. He will understand what I mean."

"But I can't leave you here unguarded. Hans would kill me if he found out."

"I promise not to tell Hans or to run away. Please go to the

Captain now. It's important. And tell nobody else what I have said."

"OK Ibu," he said and locked the door before Yahyu heard his boots going down the stairs.

***

Nothing happened for several weeks. Hans kept his visits down to one or two nights a week and Yahyu was occasionally allowed out with a police guard during the daytime. Yahyu's desire for Hans continued unabated and her morning feelings of despair and emptiness increased in their intensity. It was as if Jim and Peter had ceased to exist, so total was her obsession with Hans in bed and so great her hatred of him, and of herself, on the following morning. The harder she tried to suppress her desire the stronger she reacted when he eventually came. She told herself many times that the next time he came she would shoot him or jump out the window but she never did. As soon as she heard his steps on the stairs the madness began once again.

One evening, after a longer-than-average absence, Hans took her to a formal reception with the local General and some Chinese businessmen. It was only the second time they had been together in public. After the meal she was approached by Captain Supriyono. "Walk with me in the garden, please," he said to her in Javanese, a sign there was something important he did not want prying ears to understand.

In the garden he led her gently by the arm as they studied the orchids in the beautifully crafted flowerbeds. Very casually he spoke to Yahyu but without turning to her, as if he was speaking to the orchids. "Yahyu, I have a little job for you. I know that Jim and Peter have left the country. I got the report from the steamship company. They are safe in Penang. According to my reports, Jim will need some serious medical attention before he's fit to travel further."

He stopped speaking as he looked enquiringly at Yahyu. She knew this information already from Hans but it was good to get the Captain's confirmation. But she sensed it was not the main purpose of the Captain's talk.

"Thank you Captain. Please go on,"

"You should not thank Hans for what he has done. He may have kept his side of the bargain, but the bargain itself was not fair. If you hadn't agreed to it, he would have killed Jim and got you that way, although you may have been less enthusiastic," he said with some bitterness. "The guard outside your door reports to me what goes on. I don't like your enthusiasm for him. I find it disrespectful, but that is none of my business." He paused briefly and looked at Yahyu's mortified expression.

"That's not fair," she said in great bitterness while trying to avoid the Captain's stare.

The Captain chose to ignore her reaction and continued. "Don't think that Hans has done you any favours because he hasn't. When he gets tired of you, be that next week, next month, or next year, you will end up with all those other spoiled Indonesian women in the House of Young Bamboo, selling your body to anyone with enough money to buy it.Do you want that?"

Yahyu knew the truth of the Captain's statement; she had known it from the start. She hated Hans more than anybody else in the world but the strength of that hatred was matched by the strength of her delight in the indulgence of depravity. Only the night before, during one of their long love-making sessions, Hans had taunted her with the statements of, "Thinking of Jim now, are you?" as he increased the pace of his love-making to match Yahyu's insatiable desire.

"I want to kill myself," was all she said in reply to the Captain.

"But there's a better way," he replied. "Why not help me and your country get rid of this foreign devil who speaks like an animal and corrupts all those who meet him. I want you to help me kill him."

Yahyu caught her breath in astonishment. "But why me?" she said. "You can kill him on your own. You don't need me."

"Not everyone in authority understands what Hans is doing. Many of them are in his pay, directly or indirectly. He is well protected by the money of the gold smugglers and arms dealers. Will you help me?"

"What would happen to me if he was killed? Would I be free to go?"

"Of course. No one will suspect you and no one will be interested in you. If Hans is dead, you should run away. I can help you run, if you want to. I can get you to Medan to stay with Jim's friend, Bunggo. I checked up on him; he has a history of shady deals but he's not a bad man and he may be able to help you contact Jim."

Yahyu saw her chance. Through all her desire and depravity she finally saw a way out and she must grab it before she succumbed to total madness. Taking a deep breath, she said, "What do you want me to do?"

"When the time comes for you to go home, which will be at about ten o'clock, you must find an excuse to stop him getting into the car. Start to leave with Hans, but as you get outside the door, tell him you must go to the bathroom, or say you left your purse on the table and must go back to get it. Do it in such a way that he is left outside the door on his own for several minutes. That's all you do. You don't need to know anymore."

"OK," was her only response.

During the course of the evening, and after Yahyu's customary dancing performance, Hans took her to one side of the veranda to talk to her privately. "Yahyu, you've been good to me," he said, and he kissed her gently on her cheek.

Yahyu could smell the whiskey on his breath, which stimulated her passion despite her burning hatred. She breathed his animal perfume as she struggled to control her racing heart.

"I've got a present for you. No, that's not true. I've got two presents. I've now got so much confidence in you that I'm going to give you your freedom. Your door will never be locked again and you can go wherever you want. I shall be interested to see if you try to run away or stay with me. I think we both know the answer to that one. In the mornings you will run away and in the evenings, when your little breasts get lonely, you will come running all the way back to me."

Yahyu's cheeks reddened in embarrassment and anger. "Don't, Hans. That's not fair. You made me what I am now. Why can't you just treat me decently?"

Hans laughed as he put his hand into his pocket and drew out a small package. "This is your second present, my little princess," he said as he placed the parcel in Yahyu's delicate hand.

Yahyu's fingers shook as she took the parcel and opened the tortoiseshell box. Lying on purple velvet was a silver tiara inlaid with black pearls surrounded by small diamonds. She held it to the light from the paraffin lantern. It sparkled a thousand stars as she turned it around. No one had ever given her such a gift. The most beautiful tiara she had ever seen.

"Let me put it on you. You are mine and I want to make you even more beautiful than you are now." Hans placed the tiara on Yahyu's head, adjusting it to show her flowing black hair in its true magnificence. He stood back to admire her and then led her to the heavy ornate mirror hanging by the door where she was dazzled by the beauty of the sparkling lights twinkling in the light from the lanterns that seemed to set her glossy black hair on fire.

Hans led her back into the dining room where several of the older women gasped in delight as they came up to Yahyu to admire her new ornament and to compliment her on having such a thoughtful lover. "You've really won his heart," one of them said. "First time he's ever kept a woman more than a few months," whispered another whilst hiding her mouth behind her hand.

Yahyu tried hard to control her emotions. She loved being admired and she loved beautiful things that enhanced her beauty. But he was not a beauty. He was a beast, albeit one with a refined sense of beauty that belied his ruthless nature. She looked over at Hans who was smiling to himself as he stared at her, revelling in the envy of his fellow men.

Hans came over to Yahyu. "Come on my dear, time we went home before one of these lovely ladies steals your tiara."

Hans held her around the waist and she felt him trembling, which she knew from experience was a sign of sexual expectation, but his face showed nothing except rapture at the envy he had caused amongst the little circle of corrupt officials and rich gangsters. Then she froze as she saw Captain Supriyono staring at her. In the whirl of excitement and attention, she had forgotten she was supposed to be leading Hans to his execution. She might not be the person pulling the trigger but she would be as guilty as he.

The room swayed in front of Yahyu's eyes; the twinkling chandeliers were swinging as the sparkles of light leapt from the long silver tentacles. Yahyu felt her body being relentlessly pulled towards the door. She heard the tender words of Hans whispering something about making love under the sparkling light of her new tiara. Yahyu's soul seemed to rise out of her body as she looked down on the scene. She saw herself next to Hans, slowly and reluctantly walking towards the door. She saw the Captain watching them, tense and expectant. She felt sorrow for herself as if she was a detached spirit pitying the person below her. It was the time of ultimate decision. From above, she saw the sparkling diamonds of the silver tiara twinkling over her black hair. She felt herself wilting. Without any apparent control over her own actions, she saw herself talking urgently to Hans, but he was laughing at someone else and seemed not to hear her. As they got to the door, and the servant opened it for them, Yahyu felt her knees buckle and Hans gripped her tightly to stop her falling whilst still walking slowly but surely towards his death.

As if she was being controlled by an external body, Yahyu suddenly straightened as she felt rather than saw the gunman in the shadows; a sinister, still figure kneeling under a banyan tree in the garden, full of menace. She felt the rifle being aimed. She felt Hans's warm, living body next to her. She had no control over her actions but she saw herself from afar as she pushed Hans away as the crack of a rifle shot resounded from the garden and the sharp hiss of a bullet passed between them, smashing into the glass door which shattered behind them.

Hans was quick to assess the situation. He looked at Yahyu with an expression of confused distrust, realising immediately that she had known in advance of this attempt on his life but had nonetheless saved him at the last minute. "You …" he yelled as he dived into his waiting car which drove at high speed through the gates and out into the dark night.

There was shouting and screaming from inside the house. She heard the Captain urgently ordering his police guards, "To the left men, check the lower garden," as he pointed them in a different direction from where the shot had been fired. The Captain had time to glance at her as he rushed past, a look of incomprehension on his face. Yahyu was lost in the rush and the shouting.

She was now calm as she realised she was truly alone and the thought filled her with excitement. Now's my time to go, she said to herself as she quietly slid out the back gate of the garden and away from the light and the noise. Within a few minutes she was in the paddy fields walking precariously along the bunds that separated the fields. She took off her high-heeled shoes and felt the sensuous paddy mud slipping between her toes and cooling her feet. She felt like the person she had been so many years ago; a tramp but one who was free to go wherever she wished.

Now I shall find Da'eut and see Rusdi there once more, she joked to herself as she walked lightly over the fields heading for the dark shadows ahead. Within an hour she entered the forest and she knew from her previous experiences as a tramp that no one would be likely to find her there. She was free and she was happy to be free.

Chapter 9

Yahyu was floating on air as she skipped over the tree roots on the muddy footpath that wound its way deep into the dark, sombre forest that clad the foothills of Mount Api. The steeper, the darker, the more treacherous the footpath, the lighter was her spirit. She didn't know where she was going but she revelled in the delight of the cool air caressing her body and the joy of complete freedom as she glided her way into dark oblivion.

I want to remain a tramp all my life, she said to herself, a free spirit. I shall be Sita no more; never again will I be a consort to a king or to anyone. Never again will I be a slave. I don't want to be in this world. I want to fly to the next one and live with the memories of Jim and Peter and Rusdi, as we were in Gajah Tiga. I will find my own Da'eut.

After many hours walking as if in a dream, with the track climbing ever upwards, Yahyu began to notice her surroundings. Dawn was breaking high above the forest canopy and the dark interior pierced by shafts of pale orange sunlight reflected on the rising mists. The coolness of the air calmed Yahyu's fevered imagination as she slowly came to the realisation that she was totally lost.

Yahyu sat on a tree root and looked at the giant tree trunks towering over her, their dark canopies cutting out the sunlight. She wasn't scared, not at this stage, although she felt a tingling on her back which was her warning signal to be alert. A forest is a dangerous place for those who are not prepared, and it was many years since Yahyu had wandered on strange roads and footpaths. She had to sharpen her senses and relearn her survival skills quickly.

Despite the apparent desperation of her situation, Yahyu remained calm. Anything was better than the degradation of the past few months. The freedom to look around and know that she could walk in any direction she chose, be anyone she wanted, think any thoughts she desired; this was what kept her so happy. The nagging feeling in her stomach that suggested the start of hunger pangs was not yet an irritant to her good feelings.

She wanted to sleep, but it was cold and damp and there was nowhere to lie down. She remained sitting on the tree root with her back resting against the trunk, listening to the forest as it woke from the long night while waiting for the sun to warm her. Forest animals wandered past as she dozed by her tree. None of them bothered her for she was obviously not a threat to anything. She heard the distant crashing of a troop of monkeys as they swung through the trees on their way to morning eating. She heard snuffling which could have been wild pigs, but they never came near. Her passive form was protected from harm that morning. Yahyu was eventually disturbed by hunger, not by wild animals. She had spent too long living with three meals a day and her body was no longer accustomed to the intermittent eating opportunities of the vagrant.

Her stomach told her it was time to move. There was only one obvious direction to go and that was to follow the indistinct outline of the footpath. It didn't seem to be much used but presumably it would reach a hut in the forest or another footpath. As she prepared herself for the journey, she thought she saw a shadow moving in the forest behind her, but she wasn't sure. Mustn't start getting scared of shadows, she laughed to herself as she started on the footpath that wound its way laboriously up the mountainside.

After several hours hard walking, Yahyu found her path blocked by a rushing mountain stream. She could not remember how she had got there. She was still living in her dream of freedom. The stream wasn't deep but the path did not appear to follow on the far side. She stepped into the stream; the water was cool and refreshing but the current strong. She slowly made her way upstream and then slowly downstream, but she could find no evidence of the continuation of the pathway. She couldn't understand. She crossed back over the stream and sat on the bank to think; her feet dangling in the cold water that rushed past her.

Yahyu shuddered as if a shadow had passed over her and the forest slowly fell silent. She looked quickly around and saw nothing, but she could not shake off the uncomfortable feeling of being watched. Her back suddenly felt vulnerable. There are many wild animals in the Sumatran highlands and she had once seen the body of one of the tea workers who had been mauled and partly eaten by a tiger. She tried to suppress such thoughts but her heart beat faster in the realisation that she might not be alone; but who or what was watching her she could not tell.

She stood up slowly as if to go once more into the stream but turned quickly. She jumped in shock as she saw two young men standing several yards behind her, partly hidden by the dense undergrowth, holding machetes and staring at her with blank expressions on their tough peasant faces. Whilst keeping eye contact with the two men, Yahyu nimbly jumped to one side and rushed into the surrounding forest. She ran blindly in panic, falling over tree roots and slipping on rocks until she could run no more and fell down behind a large tree, panting for breath and with heart pounding.

She lay in silence, fearing pursuit, but there was no sound. Her heart slowly stopped pounding, and after many minutes with no sound of pursuit, she started to relax. She didn't mind exhaustion, hunger and thirst, but she didn't want any more involvement in sex and, in her current situation, she presumed that any man automatically meant sex. She was not ready to handle this yet. She wanted freedom for her body and her mind.

After several hours lying in silent vigil, she planned her next move. Night was coming and Yahyu had never been able to overcome her fear of the dark. Last night had been different; that had been lived in a dream, but now real night was coming and real danger was close at hand. She got to her feet and started to hobble back the way she had come. There was nowhere else to go.

The dark had descended when she found the stream and eventually stumbled onto the footpath just as a storm burst, drenching her and the surrounding forest. She sat down once more on the cold, wet forest floor, shivering in fear and exhaustion. She had forgotten so many lessons she had once learnt during her months as a vagrant.

With a jolt of panic, Yahyu saw a pale flicker of fire approaching her. She tried to get up but couldn't; her ankle twisted and gave way, causing her to crash to the ground. The two young men holding the blazing lantern walked cautiously towards her, holding their machetes loosely in their hands. As they held the lantern aloft to study her more closely, Yahyu noticed that one of them was leaning on a roughly hewn crutch and his body was twisted in deformity. The older and bigger of the two young men spoke to her in a rough, guttural language which she did not understand.

She replied in Melayu, "I don't understand you, brother."

The smaller of the young men, the one with the crutch, replied in good but halting Melayu, "Sorry sister, we didn't want to startle you. We been looking for you all over the place, but you disappeared into the forest like a deer. We don't see people on this track much. You hurt?"

The lame boy moved toward her but Yahyu held up her hand, "Don't come closer. I can manage myself."

The two boys hung back, smiling with embarrassment while fidgeting as they watched her. "Excuse us sister, but we lit a fire a few hours ago in the hope you would see it. You must be cold in all them wet clothes. Why don't you come to the fire?" The lame boy spoke with earnest concern on his deformed face. Yahyu did not like the reference to her clothes; that could hide a desire for them to get her to undress. But the boys looked so clearly uncomfortable that she doubted her fears.

"Come on," the lame boy said. "Follow us. We'll walk slowly so you can keep up. It's not far. Oh, by the way, I think this is yours. It must have fallen off when you was running." He held out her tiara which twinkled in the light from the lantern. "It looks really valuable. You must be one of those princesses from Java that we hear about." As he gave the tiara to her, Yahyu noticed his face glowing in the light of the lantern. He had the strong, thin face of the mountain dwellers but she also noted his twisted expression. He was drooling and constantly dabbing his mouth with a dirty rag to get rid of the spittle. Yahyu felt her distrust decline at the sight of the unlikely boys, so polite and considerate in the middle of the forest.

It was not far to their camp. The fire was still spluttering and hissing from the damp wood, but the boys were experienced foresters and soon got the blaze going. Yahyu sat on a log and watched them. The bigger of the boys was older and stronger but yielded to the suggestions of the younger boy. The younger boy was badly deformed. His left leg was like a stick and probably useless, his spine slightly twisted and he was still drooling at the mouth.

"My name is Koko," the lame boy said. "And this is my cousin, Usman."

Usman smiled but looked embarrassed and rather lost. He was probably overawed by her beauty and apparent wealth. Koko, however, had intelligent eyes that smiled at her and belied the deformity of his body.

"We don't want to pry, sister," said Koko. "But we want to ask if we can help you. Very few people use this path and my brother Usman is supposed to guard it." At the mention of his name, Usman looked at the ground with an embarrassed smile. When Yahyu did not reply, the boy continued. "This path is the back way into our village. We hid the path after the stream because we don't want them gangsters or army people coming up behind us and raiding our village. You've got to go about half a kilometre upstream to find the continuation. My brother's job is to warn us if they ever find where the path starts again after the river. I just come here to give him some rice."

Yahyu was at a loss for words. What could she say; tell them she was running away from an attempted assassination on her forced lover who was also one of the most powerful men in Sumatra? She didn't want the two boys to run off and leave her; she needed them.

As Usman constructed a rough shelter, Koko sat at her feet and continued to talk. He proved to be an interesting companion and a most unusual person to meet in a forest. "I'll bet you've read lots of books, haven't you?" he said

Yahyu was too surprised to answer right away. No one in this part of Sumatra ever read anything. How could an uneducated peasant boy know anything about books? "That's an unusual question," was all she could say.

"I read a book once. Found it on a bus. Don't know where it came from and it didn't have all the pages but it was wonderful. I can read quite well, my uncle taught me, and I managed to finish it in a couple of weeks. My heart would fly up and down with the success and failures of the hero. He had a girl in the book. She was wonderful, a real beauty, a bit like you I suppose. Wish I could get a wife like that."

"You are an unusual boy, Koko. Do many people in your village read books?"

"No, no one does. Only me, and I only read the one book because that's all I've got. Don't know where to get any others."

Yahyu laughed, "I'm delighted to meet you. You are a fellow artist like me. But I'm a dancer, not a reader."

Koko looked rather disappointed. "I can't do anything like dancing," he said. "Because of my leg." With an expression of suppressed frustration he got up to wander into the forest, leaving Yahyu feeling confused; she hadn't meant to disappoint him.

During the night the boys took excessive care of Yahyu. They offered her their only spare sarong to use as a blanket and they both slept outside the shelter so as not to disturb the princess sleeping within. Yahyu slept well. Her confidence of finding friends in the most unlikely places had returned.

***

The following morning, after a meal of cold rice and chilli, the boys slung their wicker baskets from their foreheads and set off in single file along the narrow forest track leading to their village, Yahyu in the middle and Koko in the rear. She followed them up the steep, slippery path until they came to the top of a ridge where the trees parted to allow a view of the long valley below. Part way down the mountain she could see the outline of a large village set amongst clumps of trees and surrounded by rice fields climbing up the steep hillside.

The boys stopped and unslung their baskets. "That's our village," Koko said proudly. "Talang Salak it's called. My uncle's the village headman."

The boys promptly sat on the ground, lit a cigarette and started intimately inspecting each other's legs, arms and bodies. Yahyu was taken aback. "What are you doing?" she said with suspicion.

"Removing leeches, of course," replied the crippled boy without looking up from his task.

They carefully inspected each other's bodies and burned off the leeches with the glowing end of the cigarette. Each leech was carefully cut in two amongst a spreading pool of blood. Koko looked at Yahyu as if to do the same to her when he suddenly stopped and blushed as he realised what he was suggesting. After a furtive conversation the two boys gave her the lighted cigarette and tactfully turned away and pointedly stared in the opposite direction whilst pretending to discuss the forthcoming harvest.

Koko very tactfully called over his shoulder, "Just leave the leeches on a tree root. I'll kill them later." He was probably making sure that Yahyu understood what was expected of her.

Yahyu smiled to herself. Had any knight in shining armour ever before offered such a service to a damsel in distress?

Yahyu inspected herself and was surprised to see so many leaches in different stages of enlargement clinging to her legs. She had been used to leeches before but had grown soft in the ways of the forest and the sight of the plump little worms gorging on her blood disgusted her. She bled profusely as she burnt them off; a sign that her body as well as her spirit had grown accustomed to a softer form of life.

***

As they approached the village a crowd of children gathered around them shouting in a language Yahyu could not understand. Everyone spoke at the same time, creating an impression of total chaos. Koko led her proudly amongst the admiring stares of the young men and women who came to look at the beautiful princess.

Yahyu stared around her in amazement and delight. She had never been in a highland village before. The houses were large wooden structures perched on stilts some ten feet off the ground; water buffalo were kept in enclosures under the houses. Each house had a substantial veranda suspended over the pathway where families gathered to stare at the strange visitor who had come into their village. The women called out to her in their own language and laughed; there was no hostility in their tone.

As she walked through the village, side by side with Koko, she saw a complex system of bamboo pipes criss-crossing the main pathway leading through the centre of the village supplying constant running water to every house. She felt she was in a foreign land. The clean, efficient-looking village was a long way from the scruffy migrant village from where she came, where the farmers scratched a living from the unforgiving clay soil. Talang Salak seemed timeless; untouched by the outside world.

Koko led her to the wooden steps of a substantial house in the centre of the village. "This is my uncle's house. It's where I live. My father died a long time ago. He was not from here."

Yahyu stopped at the foot of the stairs, peeping up at the veranda some ten feet above her, before taking a deep breath and following Koko up the steep steps. Koko's family were gathered on the veranda chatting and calling out to their neighbours. A thin, wiry old man came from inside the house and smiled at her while saying something in Rejang. After Koko had informed everyone she was a Javanese princess who only spoke Melayu, the old man laughed and pointed to a wicker mat on the floor of the veranda, saying in fluent Melayu, "You are most welcome, Nona. Please come and sit with me. You can call me Pak Lukman, I'm the village headman."

On the veranda there was a chaos of children and laughter. It was not often a princess visited their remote village. The girls felt her expensive clothes and held her hands, marvelling at their softness. They had rough peasant hands, accustomed to hard work in the rice fields, but they also had a tough and healthy beauty with firm, hard bodies, and the cold mountain air gave their plump cheeks a rosy tint.

The old man turned to Yahyu and spoke softly. "Welcome Nona, we have few visitors in our village but those who do come usually walk up the main path from Muara Aman, two days away from here. Few ever choose the back route; it's difficult to find. I expect you have a story to tell but there's no rush. You must eat first and maybe wash yourself."

He stopped briefly as he saw Yahyu blush and look at the ground as she realised the contrast between her expensive clothes but dirty appearance. "Sorry Pak, we spent last night in the forest and ...". She blushed even more deeply at the suggestive comment. "No, I mean I've been travelling a lot and ...".

The old women sitting at the back of the veranda laughed loudly. "Lucky princess, got two of our young princes hooked, although one of them is only the crippled Koko."

Yahyu glanced at Koko who seemed not to be offended by their disparaging comments. He also sat at the back with the women, looking admiringly at Yahyu.

The old man raised his hand for silence as he continued. "Don't be offended, young princess. We mean no harm. Some of our grandmothers have vivid imaginations; probably wishing they were in the forest for a night with one of your young princes from Java." The old women screeched in enjoyment as they slapped their thighs in delight.

The old man laughed again at Yahyu. "Later this evening we will hold a meeting and you must tell us your story. But don't worry; you are under my care now. Nobody will harm you in this village, and

I know that Usman and Koko are honourable young men. No one will suspect anything of them or you despite the imagination of our grandmothers sat at the back."

***

Several of the young women took Yahyu away, leaving the men to speculate as to what it all meant. They formed a small, serious circle around Pak Lukman as they questioned Koko and Usman carefully. These were dangerous times and even their isolated village was not immune from the gangsters involved in the gold smuggling. Yahyu seemed harmless, but no one ever used that back route. How did she know it existed? How did she find the way? Why did she want to come here? It was a mystery, and mysteries are not welcome in times of strife.

"How did you find her?" one old man asked Koko.

"She just appeared, kind of sudden. We followed her for a bit then when she saw us she ran as fast as a deer into the forest and disappeared. We tried to follow her but she was clever in forest craft and we lost her. Then, about evening time, we heard a crash close by and there she was again. Come back to the same place but with a bad ankle; just twisted it a bit, nothing serious."

"And what did she say? Where was she going?"

"We don't know but she seems lost. I think she's running away from something. She didn't know how to find the path after the river crossing."

The old men murmured their disapproval. There must be something more suspicious than just running away. Their village was well hidden by dense forest and travellers didn't come across it by accident.

The village leader raised his hand for quiet. "Koko is a shrewd young man, even if he doesn't often show it. I see nothing suspicious in the young woman's eyes. We give her the benefit of the doubt until she has had time to tell us her story. She's in my house and I take responsibility for her behaviour." The old men nodded their grudging assent.

***

The village girls led Yahyu to a small veranda at the back of the kitchen area where the bamboo pipes gave an unstoppable supply of water. Much to Yahyu's embarrassment they helped her undress, marvelling at the beauty of her clothes and the softness of her skin, feeling and pinching every curve of her body as they chatted and laughed at her nakedness. Yahyu tried to resist but their openness was too natural to succumb to her modesty. They bathed her and pampered her whilst talking continuously in their coarse, guttural accent interspersed with rough, friendly laughter. None of them spoke much Melayu so conversation was limited, but that didn't spoil the enjoyment of the occasion.

Yahyu finally succumbed to the delight of fresh water pouring over her sweaty skin and refreshing her naked body. The girls pushed her head under the endless stream of cold, fresh water and rubbed her hair with oil until it shone in the afternoon sun. The girls had found Yahyu's tiara and tried to put it on her head for the evening meeting but she managed to refuse. She didn't want to display too much wealth in front of the village elders.

***

In the evening the women sat in the kitchen eating rice and vegetables, whilst the men sat together on the floor of the main room in a big circle and ate among themselves whilst exchanging news of the day. The main news was the appearance of Yahyu whom they now presumed was a noble Javanese lady on the run from her family.

After food and when the paraffin lamps had been turned up, Yahyu and the other women came into the main room and sat at the back, waiting for the men to start the proceedings. Everyone wanted to hear about the new visitor but none of them could speak good enough Melayu to question her properly, except the headman and Koko.

Pak Lukman smiled at her before speaking. "Don't be frightened. Everybody here is curious to know about you and they are pestering me to ask you to tell us your story. You don't have to tell us but they will not leave me alone until their curiosity is satisfied."

Yahyu smiled in return but said nothing. It was not easy to tell her story and, if they ever guessed the truth, they would probably kick her out of the village as being both dangerous and immoral. She needed to invent a personality and a history for herself. She desperately wanted to tell someone about Jim and Peter but she realised that she could never explain that without creating suspicion about herself. Despite the awkwardness of the situation, she felt safe in the village with Pak Lukman in charge. It was like a haven of sanity in a mad world and she didn't want to be forced to resume her travels again.

Everyone waited but when no story was forthcoming the old men asked questions directly, using Pak Lukman and Koko as translators.

"Firstly, what's your name, Nona."

"I am called Yahyu," she said, modestly turning her eyes to the ground. "My father comes from central Java."

There were murmurs of excitement as this simple and obvious information was translated, analysed, dissected and further questions formulated.

"Are you a princess?"

"I don't know. I don't think so. But I have been taught to dance like a princess."

Murmurs of interest arose and some of the younger women looked up expectantly. "Who taught you to dance?" one of them asked, but the old men motioned her to be quiet; they were seeking more immediate information.

"Where's your family, Nona? Why do you travel alone?"

This was the difficult question that Yahyu did not want to answer. Any hint of Jim or Hans would involve her in issues of politics and morality, neither of which she felt capable of answering, so she lied. "I am an orphan. I was sold to an old lady in Linggau to clean her house. She treated me badly so I ran away and went to dancing school in Palembang, but my money ran out. Now I've got nowhere to go. I was in Curup when some men chased me and I ended up in the forest where Koko found me. I don't know where I am."

Her story was plausible but the villagers of Talang Salak were not stupid. They noted her fine clothes and soft skin and her graceful Javanese manners. They didn't believe the story but were too polite to say so. Their main concern was that she was neither an evil spirit from the forest nor a woman of bad repute come to corrupt their men and steal their gold.

"Nona Yahyu," the headman said quietly as the audience hushed to hear him better. "We don't totally believe you but no matter. We suspect you have run away from a love affair or a bad marriage. The women who went with you to wash, they noticed your stomach. We know you have had at least one child."

Yahyu gasped and held her hand to her mouth. She felt her cheeks reddening as she once more looked at the ground.

"Don't look so perturbed, Nona, or I suppose I should say Ibu. We've had young women from this village get pregnant and run away with their lovers. It usually doesn't work out and they come back here with their baby. We accept them back into the community even if their father doesn't want them in his house. I'm the village head and I won't allow anyone in distress to be neglected, even if they have made a mistake in their lives."

Yahyu wanted to speak. She wanted to tell Pak Lukman what a wonderful man he was and how much she respected him but she couldn't; her emotions wouldn't allow the words to come out.

Seeing Yahyu's embarrassment, Lukman quickly continued, "Whatever the true story, I see no harm in you and you may stay in my house until you decide what you want to do. I shall appoint Koko as your guardian; he speaks Melayu well."

One of the older women called out that she wanted Yahyu to dance for them. Several of the other women joined in, "Come on young princess, do your stuff for us."

Pak Lukman called for quiet. "No, not today," he said. "Ibu Yahyu must be tired. Look at her ankles; they're still bleeding from the leeches. Let's wait until after the harvest, when we have lots of rice, and then we will celebrate and all the young girls will dance for us. Perhaps Yahyu will train them in advance?" The statement was met by great applause from the women.

***

For the first time in many months Yahyu slept well. Rejang sleeping habits dictated that young men slept together at the front of the house, married couples slept together in the middle and unmarried girls at the back, usually with an old woman to guard them. At night they released their dogs to guard the village and young men were appointed to walk around the village boundaries to guard against attack from both men and animals. These were dangerous times but the village was well organised and took no chances. All the young men slept with their machetes close to their hands, although they were rarely called upon to use them in anger.

During the night Yahyu thought of Jim and Peter. The feelings of security created by the good headman gave her the time and space to think of her past and her future. She wondered what they were doing, whether they remembered her, whether Peter was in England and how he adapted to the cold climate and different food. She had no doubt as to the reliability of Jim to look after him and she told herself time and again that Peter was better off without her; he would be ashamed to know what had become of her. Now he was in England with Jim he would get a good education. But she could never hope to meet Jim again, not now, not after what she had done with Hans.

She cried slowly to herself not so much in sadness but with nostalgia for what had passed and regret for what could have been.

***

Yahyu stayed in Talang Salak for many weeks. In the mornings she followed the women to the fields and worked on the steep slopes gathering the paddy harvest. She had grown soft over the past few years and found the hard physical labour exhausting. After a few hours perched on the steep slopes the pain in her calves gnawed into her brain until she stopped to rest, much to the raucous amusement of the other women. They called out to her in bad Melayu. "A young princess from Java is too precious to work in the fields. You should keep your soft, pale skin for the hands of a handsome young prince. Why don't you rest in the shade?"

After several weeks of hard work, Yahyu's body toughened until she could work with the best of them. Her life of dancing had given her great suppleness and once she had learnt the knack of standing on steep slopes, she could keep up with the experienced women and join in their laughter, although she never understood what they were laughing about.

Koko often accompanied them but because of his deformity he could not join in the harvesting. The older women treated him kindly but he was always an outsider. He couldn't work and therefore was not a full member of society. The village had little room for passengers although no one was allowed to starve; poverty was shared hence there was none. But poor Koko was destined to be an outsider from birth.

In the late afternoons, after work in the fields, most families gathered on their verandas high above the pathway to chat to each other and shout to their neighbours on surrounding verandas. This was the news system of the village. Koko rarely joined in the banter although he always listened with rapt attention, except on Friday afternoons when he was glum and distant. Friday was football day and the young men paraded through the village kicking a small rubber ball on their way to the village green and the younger girls whistled to them from the safety of their verandas. Yahyu saw Koko's eyes following their progress with tears rolling down his cheeks and his puny fists clenched tightly on his lap. She spoke softly to him but he shrugged her away and then turned to apologise. "I want to go with the boys to play football but I can't," he said.

Yahyu's kind heart reached out to Koko's loneliness. She remembered the feeling of being shunned when she was a dirty tramp and she knew it hurt. "No, Koko, you can't play football but you can talk well and you are an intelligent boy. Girls also like that."

Koko looked at Yahyu with suspicion in his eyes as if suspecting her of mocking him. Yahyu looked back at him and smiled the smile that had melted a thousand hearts when she was on stage and, true to form, Koko's heart also melted.

***

The night of the post-harvest feast was a great success. Yahyu had easily picked up the simple rhythmic Rejang dances and became the best dancer in the village. She led the village girls out to dance to the sound of the gongs and bamboo flutes, and it was her that the young men stared at. After each dance there was a queue of highly embarrassed young men coming to ask her to walk with them around the village but she declined with a smile and went back to the dancing area.

She stared often at Koko sitting forlornly at the back, unable to join the fun. None of the dancing girls wanted to walk with him. It would look too ridiculous. His eyes remained glued to Yahyu, hoping and praying she would not go walking with one of the fit young men who surrounded her. She knew his yearning and would do nothing to hurt his sensitive feelings.

During the evening, Pak Lukman asked Yahyu to dance a Javanese ballet. He had seen Javanese dancing when he was a student and he wanted to see it again. As she entered the dancing circle a hush fell throughout the audience. Everyone wanted to see a touch of Javanese culture brought into their isolated village.

Yahyu danced from her soul, so lost was she in the ecstasy of performing to an audience of friends. The villagers looked on in awe at the beauty of her performance. They may not have understood the story behind the dancing but they appreciated beauty and grace which they compared to their own harsh physical existence. It was an outstanding success and Yahyu became a star in the village, liked and respected by both men and women. She went to sleep late that night feeling satisfied and accepted.

During the night her dreams were disturbed by thoughts of Jim and Peter. She awoke many times thinking about what they were doing and what they would think of her if they knew she was living in an isolated mountain village. Had they been with her they could all have had so much fun, but, in her experience, fun was always transient. The feeling of fun could never survive the remembrance of those she had lost and, after her depravations with Hans, those she hoped never to see again.

The following morning she awoke with a feeling of sickness in her stomach. She thought it was a result of over eating and too much excitement. Later in the day the sickness went away, only to occur again the next morning. Over the next few days Yahyu realised that her worst fears may have come true; she was probably pregnant and it could only be Hans who was the father.

***

It was Koko who first noticed Yahyu's change of mood. She tried to hide her pregnancy, as much from herself as from the villagers, but she could not deceive the observant eyes of Koko. He had suffered too much during his short tormented life not to notice distress in others. He tried to get Yahyu to talk about it but she wouldn't; Yahyu withdrew into herself as if hiding a great secret from him and it hurt him. He was only sixteen and too young to understand the infatuation he felt for a beautiful girl who was so far from his grasp but so close to his understanding.

Yahyu felt herself emotionally crippled after her experience at the hands of Hans, and she felt empathy with Koko in a similar way that she had understood the tortured soul of Rusdi. But Koko was very different from Rusdi. Koko had developed a sharp intelligence that was often misunderstood because of his habit of dribbling when he talked. His isolation from mainstream social life had led him to much introspection and, in his rather boyish way, he was a shrewd observer of village life. He knew Yahyu was in trouble but his limited experience of life would not allow him to guess why.

Yahyu carried on as before, trying to pretend to herself that she was not pregnant, that it was just a trick of her body to deceive her and to punish her. She refused to believe that God could allow her to bear the child of that murderous animal who had so completely destroyed her life and then seduced her into a state of slavery to her own desires. But when her second period was due and nothing happened, she had to admit to herself that it was true.

She went off to the forest to sit and think. She had hoped to slip out without Koko seeing her but he was too observant. His intuition was as sharp as his intellect and, understanding Yahyu's need for solitude, he sat some distance from her, waiting in case she needed his help, hoping she would call him.

Yahyu sat by the small stream that fed the bamboo pipes of Talang Salak's plumbing system. This was the second time in her life she could be thrown out of a village for immorality but this time she would tell no one. She did not wish to embarrass the good Pak Lukman who had showed her so much kindness.

She stared long and hard into the rushing stream, wishing her life could have turned out better. She felt sick in her stomach, not just from the baby but also from her repugnance at the thought of bearing a baby from the person whose name she had hoped never to utter again. She didn't want to think of him or to acknowledge his existence in any way and now she was bearing his child, and every time she thought of the baby she had to face up to the depravation of her own behaviour.

Where was Jim to help her? She knew she could not reach out to him and that he would probably not want her now. He had accepted Peter as his own but could any man be expected to accept a second child, especially one conceived by his enemy and in a situation where Yahyu was the instigator. She knew she could have run away from Hans long before she did. She had stayed because she craved his attention. Her madness had come back to haunt her and now she was trapped.

Koko could stand the suspense no longer. He quietly walked over to Yahyu, calling her name. She looked up at him and smiled at the pleasure of seeing his crooked but concerned face. She had so few friends in the world that anyone, even this crippled boy, was like a gift from heaven.

Koko did not know how to begin. He felt rather than understood Yahyu's anguish but felt inadequate to help. He only knew his village; he had no experience of someone as complex as Yahyu. "Why don't you tell me what's the matter?" was all he could say as he sat beside her on the river bank.

"There's nothing wrong with me," she lied and immediately saw the disappointment in Koko's face.

"I know there is. Maybe you're lovesick for your boyfriend back in Java."

Yahyu smiled at Koko's concern. "If only it were that simple," she said as she got up to walk back to the village, but she turned back to look at Koko sitting dejectedly by the river. "You come with me Koko, back to the village. You are my brother, aren't you? You must look after me."

Koko was silent for some minutes as he looked up at Yahyu and gathered his courage to speak. "Come and sit beside me. I want to ask you something. It's something important but I don't want you to tell anyone else that I asked you."

Spoken by anyone else Yahyu would have been suspicious, but Koko was so sincere and so feeble there was nothing to fear.

"I promise," she said.

"You got to tell me honestly what you think of me. I know I'm a cripple and I don't look good, but you got to tell me as a woman. Not as my woman. I know you aren't that and you never will be because you're a princess. But I want to know what women really think of me. I love beautiful women but I can't expect them to love me in return. Not with this leg of mine and my twisted face."

Yahyu smiled at the crippled boy but hesitated before replying and Koko instantly knew she would tell him a lie. She said gently, "You have the ability to understand people; women like that. You know how to admire beauty and how to love and women like that too. You have beauty in your mind although not in your body. You need to find a special woman somewhere; one who looks deeper than just your body. You will find one, I'm sure of that."

Koko looked at her with suspicion. "I won't ever find a girl like that in this place. Will you take me with you to Java? I could be your servant and I would meet different people. Maybe one of those Javanese girls would like me."

"I wish I could take you but you would not want to go where I have to go. I must leave Talang Salak soon although I don't want to."

Koko and Yahyu got up together and walked slowly back towards the village.

***

Yahyu planned her departure carefully. Pak Lukman and his family had been too kind for her to run away without a word, so she spoke to him one day when Koko was away in the fields.

"Pak, I need to speak to you privately."

"In that case we must go for a walk. Nothing can be said in this village without a thousand ears hearing it and another thousand pretending to have heard it. Let's go up the hill towards the forest. There's a wonderful view of the valley from up there."

When they got to the ridge, Lukman sat down and motioned Yahyu to sit beside him. He surprised her as he came straight to the point. "I know what you're going to say. My wife is a bit of a witch in her spare time. She casts all sorts of spells, reads tea leaves, all those sorts of things and she's sharp. She told me some days ago that you are almost certainly with child." Yahyu looked at him sharply but he put his hand on her arm to steady her and continued. "And I think you don't know what to do about it."

Yahyu looked at the ground as the tears flowed down her cheeks. She didn't know what to say.

"It's a secret between me and my wife. Nobody else suspects it yet but your behaviour of late has been odd and sooner or later other people will come to the same conclusion. What is it you want to do?" He spoke kindly but his meaning was clear; he expected her to do something.

"I must leave you," she sobbed. "I can't stay with this ... this baby in my womb. It would cause you trouble and you have been so good to me."

Lukman waited for her to compose herself before continuing. He was a kindly old man but not a soft one. He knew what he had to do. "I think you are right, Ibu Yahyu. We all like you but you cannot stay here in this situation. People in these parts are very conservative and suspicious. I am afraid they would suspect me of being the father and I cannot allow that. My advice to you is to go to the town to have your baby. I'm told there are foreign nuns in some towns that take in orphans. You can leave your baby with them and return to us after the birth if you want. We will always be pleased to see you and we could then find you a suitable husband. Although I doubt if any of our young men would be brave enough to court you; they're a little frightened of you."

He waited patiently for a response but when none was forthcoming he continued softly, "We will equip you well before you go. You can take as much rice as you can carry and we can give you a spare set of clothes. I don't think you will be able to shake off Koko so easily. He's taken quite a fancy to you. Let him come with you for one day so he can guide you back to the footpath you came on. He will appreciate your trust in him."

"I'm sorry Pak. I wanted to stay here but I know I can't, not now."

"Is there any way you could go back to the father of the child? Is he the same man as with your first child?"

"He's not a man, he's an animal and I don't want his baby," she said angrily.

Lukman looked at her for some time before getting up and walking back towards the village, leaving Yahyu sitting alone amongst her thoughts of Jim and Peter and the new, unwanted baby in her womb.

***

It was announced quietly in the village that Yahyu was going back to her family in Java. No one suspected anything different. They put her odd behaviour down to her reluctance to leave them. They held a feast on the evening before she was due to leave but it was a sombre affair, eaten in silence.

The next morning Yahyu got up early to prepare herself for the journey. Parting was bitter; she had fallen in love with Talang Salak and everyone in it and it was difficult to say goodbye. She shook the hand of Lukman and walked briskly down the steps and up the hill towards the end of the village, Koko hobbling after her. She did not look round. She looked at no one, not even Koko. There were tears in her eyes as she walked and she couldn't trust herself not to break down and plead to be allowed to stay. She walked for several hours, not turning, not talking but aware of Koko's shuffling gait behind her as she left the rice fields and entered the dubious comfort of the tall, dark forest.

When they came to the stream where the pathway had been changed, Yahyu stopped and turned to Koko who was standing behind her, leaning on his crutch.

"Koko, you are my best friend and my brother but it's time we parted," she said to him.

Koko looked at her pleadingly. "Why? Why do you have to leave? I thought you were going to stay with us forever. You're my best friend. You're my sister. I don't want you to go. Or rather, I want to go with you." He cried as he spoke.

"I'm sorry too, Koko. I wanted to stay with you but now I can't. It hasn't turned out the way I wanted but I can't explain to you. You must trust me. I'm your sister, Koko. One day, if I am able, I will come back here again, I promise. But you can't come with me now. It's going to be hard enough to feed myself without having two people to feed."

Koko looked sorrowfully at her and at the surrounding forest. "I don't think you can manage without me," he said. "I know this forest. I can look after you. Without me you will get lost."

Yahyu held his hand as she spoke to him. "Koko, I can see you have great understanding. You are a wise man although you are still only a boy. You understand me better than the others do and I think I can understand you too. You must realise that there is something I must do but I can't tell you what it is. I don't even know myself how to do it but I know I can't do it in your village. It's my problem and my burden and I must carry it alone.

"You are an intelligent boy. Why don't you go to Muara Aman and go to school. Perhaps you could follow your uncle and become a school teacher."

Koko glanced sharply at her. "You're not the first person to say that to me. Are you one of them too? You know, one of those socialist rebels."

Yahyu recoiled in shock. "What do you mean?"

"I know these forests. I spend my time wandering around on my own because I can't keep up with the others when they walk fast. I know everyone here. I meet the rebel patrols sometimes. They are good; both men and women. They tell me about their beliefs but I don't see much in it. What they say is no different from life in our village. We don't have starving workers in our village; my uncle wouldn't allow it. So I don't know what all the fuss is about. But they are different. They treat me as an equal. They say I need an education and when they have won independence they will ensure that all people like me get an education. I don't believe them but I like them. I can talk to them."

Yahyu smiled at the boy's story. She could see Jon righteously telling the young man of the wonders of a classless society. "No, I'm not one of them, but I like some of their ideas. I think you should go to school like they said. If I am ever rich, I will come back and send you to school."

Koko looked at her in hope. "Do you mean it? Honest. I would love to go to school."

"Now I must go. Goodbye, Koko. You've been a real brother to me when I needed one. I won't forget you."

"Wait, Yahyu. Give me something before you go, please. Give me a lock of your hair. I love your hair when you dance; it glistens in the lamp light."

Yahyu laughed as she cut a length of her hair and placed it in Koko's hand. She held his hand a long time but when she felt tears welling up in her eyes, she turned her back and walked purposely down the footpath until he was lost from sight in the tangle of trees.

Yahyu walked quickly. She knew what she had to do and she wanted to do it quickly. She would avoid Curup, because of Hans, and go directly to Bengkulu and sell her tiara, which must be worth a lot of money. Then she would go north to Medan and go back to the convent where she had given birth to Peter. The nuns there liked her and they would look after the baby if Yahyu could help with the cost. She might even contact Bunggo and see if she could write to Jim and find out how Peter was. She doubted that Jim would ever want her back but she craved news of Peter.

In the evening she stopped on the pathway and built a small fire. She was still scared of the dark and she needed the light as much as the heat. She stared around her at the gathering gloom and thought with nostalgia about the communal fun and company of Talang Salak. She missed Pak Lukman and his wife. She also missed the faithful company of Koko.

***

After years of lonely roaming around the forests of Mount Api, Koko knew every root and branch. He was also surprisingly nimble with his crutch; the result of years of practice. He had followed Yahyu and was now squatting in a hollow where he could see her fire and hear every movement she made. He would not desert her. She was his sister.

During the night Koko became agitated. He could hear nothing unusual and see nothing unusual but he could sense danger around him. He had the hunter's sixth sense born of many nights spent alone in the forest. Danger can be felt before it can be seen. He felt the prey's awakening of all the senses as they searched for the source of danger. The rush of adrenalin as his body prepared for action and the prickling of hairs at the back of his neck told him to beware. But it was his sense of smell that first gave him an indication of the danger to come. He smelt cloves and, a little later, stale tobacco and that could only mean one thing: it was either the army or the police because only they could afford the expensive clove cigarettes imported from Java.

Koko saw several figures as they rushed at the sleeping form of Yahyu. There was a stifled scream as rough hands grabbed her and bound her tightly. Koko could sense another soldier lying outside the circle of the fire, waiting to see if anyone came to her rescue. When they were sure she was alone, the soldiers put more wood on the fire so they could study their catch.

One of the soldiers laughed. "Hey look what we've got here. It's a bloody woman and a good looker too. What a catch; we're going to have some fun tonight. I'm first because I'm the one that caught her. You can come later if you want."

Koko stifled a gasp of fear and with shacking knees he moved closer. There were three of them; two privates and a sergeant. As they took off Yahyu's gag to see her face better, the sergeant stood up quickly. "Oh fuck me," he said. "It's the Javanese tart of that foreign bastard, Hans. I saw her once when I was guarding the Mayor's house. If we lay a hand on her, he'll kill us."

Another soldier intervened. "I also heard she was mixed up in some rebel plot to kill the Mayor, or something like that. Whatever it is, she's dangerous. We'd better be careful and bring her back to Curup for interrogation. I bet Hans is going to enjoy interrogating her. I know I would." They laughed as they killed the fire and arranged themselves into a circle to give all-round protection during the night.

Koko was a quick thinker. His years of solitude had given him an independence of mind and he was able to act with resolution when required. He knew Yahyu was in great danger. He had suspected for some time that she was probably one of the rebels and he knew the army normally shot rebels. If he didn't help her, they would shoot her too.

Koko knew the location of the temporary camp constructed by the rebel forces, only a few hours' walk from the footpath. If the camp was occupied, he could tell them what had happened, and if Yahyu was one of them, they would rescue her. His mind made up, he crawled quietly away from the soldiers and then rushed as fast as his crippled body would allow through the dense forest in the direction of the well-hidden jungle camp.

As he got closer to the camp, he rustled branches and whistled to attract the attention of the guards and give assurance that he wasn't dangerous. Danger in the forest always came silently. Within minutes Koko was met by a challenge.

"Stop," was the only word spoken.

Koko was known to the local rebel forces and his crippled body was easily recognisable. They didn't totally trust him because he wasn't one of them but they didn't fear him either. They respected his lonely wanderings and knew him to be a reliable source of information on local affairs.

"I've got to see your leader. Quick, it's urgent," he said to the guard who led him into the makeshift camp.

The rebel leader was awoken with a gruff, "Commander Jon, wake up. There's news."

The commander was tall and wiry with a lean, bespectacled face. "What is it that's so important that you wake me and half the forest animals in the middle of the night?" He looked keenly at Koko. "I've seen you before, haven't I? You're that young crip ...". He hesitated momentarily before continuing. "You're that young boy from Talang Salak who wanders alone around the forest. What have you got to tell me that so important? And how did you find our camp? I can see you're a seasoned hunter." He smiled at Koko. He had little to fear from the boy and he had genuine respect for his ability to find their camp in the middle of the night. He could be useful to them in the future.

"Pak, my sister; they got my sister. Three army men got her on the footpath and tied her up. They said she was important and they would take her to Hans for interrogation."

At the name of Hans, Jon sat up and looked sharply at Koko. "Who's your sister? Tell me, quick."

"She's new. I met her on the footpath a month ago. She's a princess from Java. She came to my village and she's now my sister.

She can dance. She said she had to go home to Java so she walked off, but I followed her and I saw the army men catch her and tie her up."

"What's her name?"

"Yahyu."

Jon was not surprised. He had heard about the assassination attempt on Hans which was blamed on a rebel plot, although Jon knew otherwise. He had also heard that Yahyu had disappeared and the rumour was that someone had spirited her away and hidden her in the jungle. Jon had guessed correctly that Yahyu had run away alone and headed for the closest forest in which to hide. He had come to this jungle camp on the offchance he would hear something of her.

"OK boy, you've done well. You're a brave lad and you deserve a reward. We need boys like you."

"But you must do something quick. They will shoot her. She's my sister."

"We leave immediately. We desperately need the ammunition and guns the guards will be carrying but you must stay here 'til morning, then you go back to your village."

"That's not fair," said Koko in great disappointment. "I never get to see the action. It was me that followed her and it was me that came for help. I've got to go and rescue her too."

Jon smiled kindly at the distressed face of the crippled boy. "You know that we will travel very fast and you will not be able to keep up with us. But you are a brave and resourceful boy; it took much courage to follow her and then come to find us. When we rescue Yahyu I will tell her it was you that organised the rescue attempt. I promise she will know."

Koko looked at Jon and understood the truth of his words. "You promise she will know. I don't want her to think I deserted her when she needed me."

"I promise. You can trust me."

* * *

Jon and his patrol left the camp at high speed. They travelled quickly and silently over the rough ground to cut off the soldiers' exit, before they could leave the cover of the forest. It was a well-trained and experienced patrol; there was little need for instruction or direction. Jon's only order as he set the ambush was, "Avoid the girl and shoot to kill. No gun battle; just a quick, clinical kill of all three guards and then we grab their ammo and the girl and run. Don't waste bullets. We don't have many."

His troops, a mixture of tough peasant boys from the lowlands and serious-looking students from Java, grinned at him. "You going to have a good night with this girl, Uncle Jon?" They all laughed together. It was a good-natured section of the military wing of the rebel government, well led by Jon and well disciplined. There was no playing with women when Jon was in charge.

Like a good commander, Jon rarely did any direct firing. He concentrated on leading his troop and setting up the right tactical situation. He knew that when it came to actual fighting his peasant soldiers were far more effective than he. He nominated three of them as snipers to shoot the three soldiers. The other members of the patrol were backup in case the soldiers ran or were able to fight back. They had confidence in Jon. He had never let them down. They lay in total silence, concentrating on the pathway ahead and the spot by the stream where they expected the soldiers to stop.

***

The soldiers had released Yahyu's legs so she could walk and they wouldn't have to carry her. Her hands were tied in front and they had put a noose around her neck so they could lead her along the path.

They had been walking for some hours when they came to the small stream. As Jon had expected, they stopped to fill their water bottles. They were experienced soldiers and only one man filled his bottle at a time, but they were not expecting trouble so close to the edge of the forest and they had started to relax; a fatal mistake in a jungle fighter.

Jon tapped a bamboo pole, the agreed signal for action, and three shots rang out, followed by silence. Yahyu was stunned in panic as she looked around and saw all three of her guards writhing on the ground. One of them was still able to move and he was crawling towards the forest edge when another shot rang out; he shuddered and lay still. A dark figure came out of the jungle, walking with the catlike agility of the seasoned fighter. He went up to the nearest body and raised his rifle to fire when an order rang out from deep in the forest. "No, don't shoot him. Use your knife. We don't have enough bullets."

To her horror, Yahyu saw the man pull out his machete and slice it violently across the soldier's throat. He went up to the other soldiers and did the same. Yahyu felt panic welling up inside her and she tried to move slowly towards the forest in order to run but, to her great surprise, she saw a familiar profile walking up to her from out of the forest; it was Jon.

"So, Yahyu, we meet again. You have a habit of getting into

trouble, don't you? I think it's time you joined us; you need our protection, although it's now us on the run. But things may change in the future."

Yahyu tried to throw herself at Jon in her relief and happiness at seeing him but her hands were tied and she fell against him. Jon untied her hands while instructing his patrol to strip the soldiers and take everything: clothes, boots, guns, ammunition, food, everything.

The dead bodies were left naked and bloody by the riverside as Jon led Yahyu and his troop at a good pace back into the forest.

Chapter 10

The glow of success that followed the easy ambush was quickly extinguished. They hadn't expected trouble. It should have been several days before the bodies were found, by which time they would be long gone, but something had gone wrong. As they headed back to their temporary camp, they heard gunfire.

The patrol quickly glided sideways into the jungle, one of the fighters leading Yahyu by the hand. They crouched, looking forward with concerned faces, searching for the cause of the firing and wondering whom it could be. The forest was their domain and few people ever challenged their supremacy. Jon sent one man forward to reconnoitre while the others formed themselves into a defensive block.

Yahyu felt no sudden onset of fear; it was an ongoing nightmare of which she only had a partial grasp. Still numb from the shock of her sudden capture by the soldiers, she just wanted the suffering to end. She tried to approach Jon but he motioned her to stay still. She tried to speak to the soldier next to her but he motioned her to be quiet. She moved behind a tree and squatted on her haunches, tending her wrists which were still raw from the ropes that had bound her, whilst trying not to think of the bodies of her captors lying cold and naked by the river.

She looked at the faces of the troops around her; a mixture of squat peasant boys with tough faces and ready smiles and a few Javanese students with serious expressions on their intelligent faces. She was too exhausted to judge or to fear. She accepted them as Jon's men, hence they must be good.

There was a stir amongst the fighters as the scout returned and reported immediately to Jon. "Our camp has been discovered. The area is swarming with troops. They're the bloody Batak battalion."

"Oh shit, not the Bataks," said a voice close to Yahyu. "Those three soldiers we killed in the forest were Bataks. I suppose they come from the same battalion. They're never going to give up until they catch us. They're vicious bastards."

Jon glanced at Yahyu. "It's good we rescued you when we did. That Batak battalion was sent to attack our camp and we'd have been caught like rats in a trap if we hadn't left it to rescue you. Thanks, Ibu."

He called his fighters to gather quietly around him and said tersely, "There's a traitor somewhere. There's no way they could have known where our camp was and they couldn't have known we are using it now unless someone informed on us."

There was a hushed whispering amongst the troops as they digested the ominous news.

Jon continued, "It may not be one of us here, maybe someone in headquarters, but traitors are the bane of a guerrilla's life. Stay vigilant and don't let your buddies out of sight. We've got to control the leak. But for now, we've got to act."

Jon looked into the surrounding forest as he quickly came to a decision. It was an obvious decision because his choices were so limited, but it was not an easy decision because it would involve great hardship. "We go to our main camp in Seblat, and we go fast," he told his troops.

There was a collective groan from the fighters and Jon knew they had understood the implications of his order. It was several weeks hard trekking to Seblat even if they went direct, which they could not because of the need to shake off their pursuers without revealing their ultimate destination. They had few supplies, their temporary camp being lost to them, so it was going to be a hard and hungry flight and they had the added burden of Yahyu to look after.

***

They were six days into the march and the rebel patrol pushed further into the forest, trying desperately to avoid the revenge of the Batak battalion. They firstly went east, into the high mountains to shake off pursuit and were now pushing ever northwards into the unmapped forests of the upper Seblat. Every day was the same: up before dawn to eat a small, cold breakfast of a handful of rice, and then constant trekking over mountains, through dark forests, over rushing rivers. Several times they lost their way and the troops had to hack their way out of dense undergrowth or climb high into the forest canopy to view their position. There would be a brief stop at lunchtime, but there was no lunch because food supplies were almost exhausted, and then more trekking until evening.

Yahyu was constantly wet and exhausted as she trudged after

the hardy patrol climbing the long, steep inclines that formed the foothills of the mighty volcanoes that ringed the Seblat watershed. In the evening she collapsed until someone revived her with a handful of boiled rice and hot water, but she could never recover her strength at night because of the difficulty of sleeping in the incessant rain. The soldiers were good to her in their own way. She was not expected to carry anything, and if she lagged behind, one of them fell back and marched with her. In the evenings, they did their best to make her comfortable, but theirs was a fighting patrol and they had few luxuries to share.

Despite Yahyu's determination to keep going, it became obvious she was flagging and keeping the others back. Every time she fell it took a little longer before she got to her feet. In her sodden exhaustion, she sat on the ground and waved the soldiers on; she needed rest or her heart would burst. But the patrol could never leave her, not just out of compassion but because they were not sure they had shaken off pursuit and they didn't want to leave anyone behind who could reveal their route to the Batak battalion which was pursuing them.

On the seventh evening Yahyu fell into a fever; it was probably only a minor lung infection, but in her exhaustion it felled her. She lay through the long night shivering on the damp forest floor with only a canopy of leaves to protect her from the rain and mist that came swirling up the valley in the early morning, coating the forest with a damp, glistening sheen. She could not get up and was on the brink of delirium.

Jon came to look at her and tried to wake her. "Yahyu, get up. You can't stay here; it's dangerous. We must keep moving."

Yahyu did not move. She moaned to herself and complained that her stomach hurt, but she made little sense to the concerned group of fighters gathered around her. She lay huddled in her damp shelter, one hand protecting her stomach. When Jon reached down to lift her, she fought him with what little strength she had until he withdrew in confusion. His life of hard action and political struggles had not equipped him to cope with the complexities of Yahyu's emotions. He sat on a tree root looking at her moaning on the damp earth. She needed his help, but his men were impatient to be off.

The patrol had been happy enough to bring Yahyu along so long as she was not too burdensome, but they didn't like to stay still, except in well-hidden and guarded camps. All their training had taught them that security lay in constant movement, but Yahyu represented a static problem.

One of the peasant soldiers voiced the concern of the others. "Pak, we can't stay here for ever and we can't leave her on her own. She knows too much if she gets found. We're running out of food; we've got to move. What're we going to do?"

Jon knew the implications. If he left one of his troop to stay with her he would almost certainly shoot her if she did not recover in a few days. That was their law, their custom; help was given to the afflicted but not at the risk of endangering others. But Yahyu was a non-combatant, and a beautiful one, and no one volunteered to stay with her because no one wanted the task of shooting her if she failed to recover.

Jon looked around at the tall, dark trees reaching up into the sky as he tried to decide on his priorities. The forest was his home and he felt comfortable in its dark secretiveness. He had been born in the city but since the struggle had begun, he had lived deep in the unmapped mountain forests of the upper reaches of the Ketahun and Seblat rivers; an area that government troops dare not enter unless in great force. His sensitive soul had never stopped marvelling at the beauty of the raw, untamed nature of the primeval forest.

He loved the life because it was natural and free from contradictions. The class struggle existed out there, in the cities and on the rubber plantations. In here, on the jungle-clad slopes, the struggle was simply to survive. He wasn't called upon to kill innocent people. The few villagers they met were treated as a source of supplies and information.

Although Jon was well equipped to cope with the hard, self-disciplined life that his position demanded, he didn't feel comfortable when faced with an emotional dilemma that didn't fit his narrow understanding of right and wrong. He didn't know how to handle Yahyu or his feelings towards her.

He bent down to her recumbent form and tried talking to her but to no effect. She lay on the earth, shaking and delirious, and wouldn't allow anyone near. Pity, the Achilles heel of Jon's emotions, rose in his heart as he looked down at her broken and pathetic figure, her once-beautiful hair matted with sweat and dirt, her face haggard. She looked very different from the elegant beauty he remembered from Curup, or even from the beautiful but skinny young girl he had met on the boat near Muaraklingi so many years ago. She looked to be close to death, both physically and emotionally. He saw Yahyu now as he had always seen her, an innocent victim who needed his protection.

Jon was still thinking when one of his troops came purposely up to him, impatience stamped over his tough face.

"Pak, it's time to go. We can't stay here and we can't carry her. We'll cut lots for who stays with her for maximum two days. If she doesn't recover after two days then ... you know the rules. We got to go. Those Batak bastards won't show no mercy if they catch us, not after what we done to those three soldiers of theirs." The fighter spoke in earnest, using his hands to emphasise the danger of their position. He had been brought up in a hard school that did not teach wilful violence but did teach total survival in a harsh environment where any weakness could mean death.

Jon came to his decision quickly. It was not one his troops would like and certainly not one his commander would approve of if he ever found out. He called the troops around him and faced them directly before he spoke. "I'm going to carry Yahyu on my back. If I slow you down, you have my permission to push on ahead of me."

There was grumbling in the ranks and looks of disappointment on some of the faces around him. Jon was a popular commander, they liked his fairness and concern for their welfare, but this was breaking the rules. "That's not right," one of the troops said angrily. "We agreed what we do if someone falls sick and we got to stick to it. I'll stay with the woman for two days then follow you, with or without her."

Jon was adamant, even at the cost of a loss of respect; he would not leave her. The Javanese ex-students accepted his decision with a resigned shrug but the peasant boys didn't like it and their anger showed as they prepared to move on. Their commander had gone soft on a Javanese woman and she wasn't even a member of the rebel party. However, they were a well-disciplined patrol and got ready to go as one of the fighters rigged a harness so Yahyu could be strapped to Jon's back.

They set off at a good pace, walking in single file with Jon in the middle. After several hours of grinding hardship ascending one of the ridges that separated the headwaters of the two great rivers, it became obvious that Jon could no longer keep up. He was a strong man but Yahyu was too heavy. He slipped several times on the steep muddy hillside and could not make it to the top, finally falling on his stomach, gasping for breath with Yahyu lying on top of him, oblivious to the hardship she was causing.

The troop stopped, uncertain what to do. No one wanted to leave Jon, their most popular commander who had led them through many gunfights and had proved himself a courageous leader. The student fighters argued for sharing the burden of carrying Yahyu but the peasant boys would not have it; they had been brought up in the forest and knew it well and their instincts told them the lame and the sick should be left behind.

"Commander," one of the peasant boys said. "This is breaking us up. You got to come to a decision. It's either the girl or us. We're not going to hang around here for her and starve to death or get our throats cut by them Batak bastards. We got to get to the camp."

"No one's following us," said one of the students. "Let's stop for a day. See if she gets better. It's not the end for us."

Jon saw the discipline of his troop disintegrating. It was his job to lead them and he was failing. "I'm sorry," he said wearily. "I can't leave her. You go ahead and I'll follow at my own pace. I probably won't be able to keep up with you but I'll meet you at the camp. You know the way. When you get there, tell the sentries to keep an eye out for us."

There was a stunned silence followed by angry murmurs of dissent which were quickly suppressed by one of the older fighters. "Jon's still our commander and he's letting us off easy. We got to obey and I wish him luck."

As they moved out, no one turned to say goodbye, it was not their way, but one of the peasant soldiers gave Jon a handful of rice as he passed. "Take this, Pak. It's almost the last of the stock. She'll die if she don't get fed soon. Shame, good looking girl too." They set off at a fast pace, leaving Jon standing over Yahyu as she lay semi-conscious on the wet earth.

Jon took a deep breath, lifted Yahyu onto his back and struggled after his fleeing patrol, but they outpaced him on the steep upward gradients and then lost him completely as they nimbly slithered down the slippery slopes until Jon lost all sense of their presence. There was no sound of his patrol and no visible pathway. He and Yahyu were alone in the forest with only a handful of rice and a few bullets for his pistol.

Jon knew it would be a fight to save Yahyu's life and he got to work immediately. He built a rough shelter and placed Yahyu's limp body inside before going to the ridge top to reconnoitre his position and work out a plan of action. He wasn't exactly sure where he was but he knew he must keep Dragon Mountain to his right until he hit the swampy land that signified the watershed of the Seblat River and then turn directly east towards the mountain itself. Their well-hidden camp was on that mountain slope. Once in the region, he could expect to be picked up by one of their patrols.

Jon climbed a tree to get his bearings. He saw, far to the north, the outline of a river that could only be the Seblat; they were too far to the west. It would take an enormous effort and a lot of luck to get Yahyu back to the camp.

Jon climbed down and sat on a tree root to consider his options. He knew from one of his many patrols that some nomadic Kubu groups, escaping from politics and soldiers, had set up temporary settlements down near the river where no one would bother them. The settlements were only occupied during planting and harvesting seasons and it was already late in the year, but some of them might still remain. The Kubu were primitive and timid and likely to run away if disturbed, but their temporary settlements were closer than the rebel camp and easier to get to. It would be a risk and also strictly against military regulations, but Jon had few options other than to let Yahyu die a lonely death in the dark forest.

He went back to the shelter and found Yahyu lying in a fevered sweat, moaning to herself and calling the name of her son. "Peter, Peter, come to Mama," she cried. "Come help your mama. I can't see you. Where are you?"

Jon went to her and tried to lift her, but she fought him with all the strength left in her failing body. "Go away. Leave me alone. I want Peter. I hate you." She swayed as Jon pulled her out of the shelter and she fell back once more onto the damp earth.

Jon may have been a clumsy innocent in matters of romance but in this situation, where action was called for, he knew what to do. With the instinct of a true leader, he took the only action that could save Yahyu's life. He built a strong platform of bamboo and branches so Yahyu could lie off the damp earth and get some protection from the wild pigs that roamed the forest floor. He boiled the small handful of rice which he rolled into a ball and wrapped in banana leaves. It was only a mouthful but it could save her life. Inside the leaves he placed a simple note that read, *"Gone for help. Don't move from here. Light fire at night. If you hear shouts, fire the pistol to attract us. Jon."*

He left her his water bottle, matches, pistol and torch; he left her all his tools of survival except his machete and compass. He considered kissing her hot cheeks in goodbye but dismissed the idea as unbecoming a true revolutionary. With a hasty, "Stay safe, Yahyu", he started his desperate trek at a slow but steady trot, following his compass directly northward towards the river and, he hoped, the camps of the Kubu.

***

Jon was icy cool as he calculated his chances of success. If it took him more than two days to find the Kubu, then Yahyu would certainly die, although he would probably still survive. If he could not find the Kubu camp at all then his own life might be at risk.

More difficult than finding the Kubu was the problem of finding his way back to Yahyu. He made deep cuts in the trees along his route so he could track back again. He kept strictly to his compass bearing even when it entailed walking deep into swamps or dense bamboo groves which required exhausting use of his machete. Against both his training and instincts, he made a discrete pathway to ensure he could find his way back to her.

In the early hours of the morning Jon came to the river. In his exhaustion he almost fell into it. He had been part-walking and part-running for twelve hours and he was too exhausted to go on. He lay down on the river bank and slept for several hours until woken by the early morning cold when he once again forced his aching limbs back into action. He had no idea where on the river the Kubu made their camp, so he climbed a tree hanging over the river and saw in the near distance the tell-tale signs of smoke that suggested a jungle camp of someone. In this isolated part of the forest it could only be the Kubu; no one else travelled in these remote regions.

He followed the river upstream as if in a trance until his inner instincts told him that something was not natural. He instantly fell to the ground as he found himself in the middle of a small, scruffy settlement of mean little shacks hastily constructed from branches and banana leaves. So well disguised was this habitation that he had stumbled into it before noticing where he was.

There were signs of fire but no people; they had probably fled at his approach. He got up slowly and sat on the ground to show his lack of hostility and made signs that he was hungry, but no one came. The settlement looked deserted but he could feel suspicious eyes looking at him from the surrounding forest. The Kubu were like forest spirits. They could appear and disappear at will but were rarely aggressive.

After many minutes of tense waiting, Jon began to sing. He was a lousy singer but no one, not even the Kubu, could mistake his attempt at friendliness. He sang Yahyu's favourite song, *Terang Bulan*. He had heard her sing it in the boat so many years ago. Luckily, the Kubu did not have a good ear for music, or maybe they were just polite. One old man walked calmly and slowly out of the forest and sat near Jon, not in front of him because that could have been confrontational, but slightly to the side, and lit a bamboo water pipe which he inhaled deeply before passing it to Jon.

Jon spoke to him in slow and simple Melayu but to no effect; the old man continued smoking. Other members of the group came to join them; first the children, then the young men carrying bows and arrows, and then the woman. They squatted on the ground, staring at him as they chatted amongst themselves, occasionally pointing at Jon and laughing.

Jon was desperate for action but he could not make himself understood with words as nobody spoke even simple Melayu. He slowly got to his feet, careful that no sudden movement would frighten the Kubu, and acted the part of Yahyu lying in the forest in a fever. He pointed in the direction he had come and made a show of carrying someone on his back. The Kubu were quick to understand and they began an energetic discussion amongst themselves.

The old man stood up in front of Jon and pointed at Jon's metal machete and held out his hand.

"What do you mean?" Jon said, and then mimed his confusion.

This time the old man took to playacting, much to the amusement of the surrounding Kubu. He made a motion of going to the forest and then picked up one of the watching women and carried her over to Jon, which caused screams of laughter from the others. He then went up to Jon and gently removed the machete from his hand.

Jon was equally quick to understand the play. His machete was to be part of the negotiation for Yahyu's life. He smiled and added a few loose matches, much prized by the Kubu, and the group nodded their assent.

Jon wanted to leave immediately but it was not possible; food had to be prepared for the journey and the Kubu women quickly got to work washing and roasting cassava roots which were wrapped in banana leaves. It was afternoon by the time the party of five young Kubu men packed their supplies into small bamboo baskets suspended from their foreheads and, together with Jon and a pack of small but fast hunting dogs, set off to find Yahyu.

Jon struggled to keep pace with the wiry Kubu who made light of the steep ascents and slippery slopes. They laughed at the trail he had cut and ignored the marks he had made on the trees. The dogs could easily follow Jon's trail without any need for extra signs.

***

Yahyu came to consciousness during the night and looked around at the deserted clearing and the dark, silent trees.

"Jon, where are you? Jon, anyone, where are you?" she whispered for fear that noise would wake the demons lying deep in the forest but there was no response. She hid her head under her sarong, telling herself it was a nightmare; in the morning her fever would be gone and she'd wake up to see the smiling faces of the tough peasant fighters.

Although she could cut out the sight of the dark, deserted clearing, she could not ignore the strange sounds of the forest at night, so different from the familiar sound of troops snoring or preparing breakfast. Plucking up her courage, Yahyu lifted her head from the sarong once more only to see the black menace of the dripping trees. Oh my God, they really have left me, she told herself.

The realisation of her total loneliness in the dark jungle gripped her bowels and she felt rising waves of panic fighting with her sanity. After everything she had been through, after all the trials she had endured and survived, she was now cast adrift in a remote part of the forest where no one ever came, where no one would know or care if she lived or died. She slowly put her head once more under the sarong, shivering from shock and fever. "Where's Jim," she sobbed quietly. Then, with a rush of energy, she shook herself awake and up into a sitting position on the bamboo platform and yelled at the top of her voice, "*Jim*, hear me Jim, I need you. Come to me, please come to me."

She was met with silence as her cry fell flat amongst the dripping leaves and her voice trailed off into a slow, gentle sobbing that shook her body. She fell back onto the platform. I don't want to live anymore. I want to die a quiet death amongst friends. This life's no good; I hate it, I hate this forest and I hate ... everything. What have I done that God treats me like this. All I did was get pregnant and now .... She stopped as she suddenly remembered she was pregnant again. She grabbed her stomach in rage and tried to punch herself and squeeze the baby out of her womb, but she was too weak and fell back once more panting for breath and crying herself back into a fevered sleep.

***

She awoke with her head still under the sarong. She had had a terrible nightmare and was glad it was over. She felt weak but the fever had subsided. She poked her head outside the sarong to see the wet trees shrouded in mist and the complete emptiness of the little jungle clearing. Slowly, very slowly, she realised that it had not been a terrible nightmare. She really was alone.

With shaking hands, Yahyu tried to pull herself up but fell back with a thump onto the springy bamboo platform. Why did I have to wake up? Why can't I just sleep forever? I don't want this life anymore. I can't cope with it. Yahyu's thoughts wandered down dark paths as she continued to hide her head in the comforting darkness of her sarong, but it began to rain heavily and she was forced to move.

Yahyu looked around her once more. The platform on which she was lying had been built with some care; it was soft and there was a rough covering of leaves and branches to keep out some of the rain. Then she saw the pile of things Jon had left her, including a small packet of banana leaves which she opened and found the ball of cooked rice crawling with ants. With the decline of her fever she had begun to feel hunger and she bit into the rice, spitting out the ants as she slowly ate.

The smell of the rice ball reminded her of the happy evenings she had spent on the veranda of Koko's house in Talang Salak and she began to cry, not out of fear or frustration but out of pity for herself. Pity that she could not live the simple village life that she had been brought up to live. Her beauty and her dancing had been her downfall. She envied Pak Lukman's family and wished she was a simple country girl living in a well organised family in a well organised village. Instead, she was pregnant from a man whose name she couldn't bear to utter and she was alone in a strange forest and didn't know the way home.

As she slowly ate the cold, lumpy rice she saw Jon's note lying amongst the banana leaves and suddenly a seed of hope sprang in her heart. She read the note many times and tried to work out when it was written, but she had been in a fever for so long, she had lost track of the days. She sat listening intently for the sound of rescue that would surely come but there was only the mysterious music of the forest to keep her company.

Towards evening, when Yahyu was quietly talking to herself to ward off loneliness, she heard the faint sound of a whistle. She looked up and strained her ears but could hear nothing more. She could wait no longer. Afraid that whoever it was would pass by without finding her, she reached for Jon's pistol. She had never fired a gun before but she had seen how Jim cleaned his weapon and understood the mechanics. She picked it up gingerly and aimed into the sky. With both thumbs on the heavy hammer, she cocked the weapon and squeezed hard.

The jolt of the weighty revolver jarred her hand and she dropped it, but the shot had clearly been heard by others. There was an immediate sound of dogs barking furiously and the shouts of men. She stayed where she was, hoping they were the right men.

The dogs came first and spotted their prey immediately. They did not attack but circled her platform barking and snarling. They knew they had to keep the prey still until the men caught up with them. They had done it many times while hunting pigs, deer and other wild animals. The men soon approached; small, dark-skinned figures standing before her with only loinclothes between their legs, holding bows and arrows but smiling. Seeing her confusion, but not understanding its meaning, the men laughed to each other as they squatted on their haunches and spat betel juice onto the earth.

After some minutes, an exhausted looking Jon appeared. He was struggling for breath and holding his side as if in pain. He looked haggard and tired. "I'm back," he said as he sat on a tree root with his head in his hands, panting for breath. Yahyu wanted to rush to him in delight but she didn't have the strength to stand and she felt embarrassed in front of the half-naked tribesmen squatting in front of her. They smiled and laughed and seemed not to care if she was ill or not. Perhaps they didn't even understand who or what she was. Maybe she was just another mystery of the forest.

When Jon had regained his breath, he walked over to Yahyu, still lying on her bamboo platform. "I hope you weren't too scared. I had to go. There was no other way." Jon looked forlorn despite the success of his brilliantly executed rescue mission.

Yahyu reached out and feebly clutched his arm. "I knew you would never desert me. I don't know how I will ever be able to repay you. Where are the others?"

"They've gone. We didn't have enough food for everyone, so I went for help and they went on to the camp."

Yahyu knew enough of Jon's dedication to his troops to understand the enormous sacrifice he had made to rescue her. She squeezed his arm. "Thank you, Jon. I know what it must have cost you."

Jon blushed and got up quickly, walking briskly into the forest.

Meanwhile, the Kubu got to work. They built a proper shelter, big enough for Yahyu and Jon, and started a fire whilst talking and laughing amongst themselves.

***

The Kubu stayed with them for five days while Yahyu built some reserves of strength for the forthcoming trek to the camp. Each day the Kubu went hunting and returned carrying a dead monkey or a couple of snakes. Yahyu hated eating monkey; the sight of their limbs roasting on the fire was too human. She felt sick when offered the meat, much to the delight of the Kubu who laughed at her, munching on the monkey bones and spitting on the earth. Yahyu could not relate to these strange young men. When not out hunting, they sat in the camp talking together, pointing at Yahyu and Jon and laughing. She couldn't understand anything they said.

On the third evening they heard the sounds of dogs barking in the forest and then the whoops and shrieks of Kubu women which were met by shouts from the men in the little jungle clearing. Four half-naked women came into the camp carrying baskets of cassava, much to the delight of the young men who danced around them.

The men had never touched Yahyu; they had pointed at her, studied her from every angle, laughed at her, talked to her, but they had never touched her. The women, however, had no such inhibitions, much to the acute embarrassment of Yahyu. They came over to her lying on the bamboo platform and, with much laughter, prodded her and felt her. They held her breasts and admired them, they felt her thighs and ran their hands over her silky skin with admiring nods and wide, open smiles that revealed their red betel-stained teeth. However, when they started kneading her stomach, they fell quiet and withdrew, making signs of a growing stomach.

As soon as they discovered that Yahyu was pregnant they stopped their antics and called over to their men while the oldest woman sat beside Yahyu, holding her hand and pointing at her stomach but with a questioning smile on her face. Luckily, Jon was not in the clearing; she did not want him to know about her pregnancy. The Kubu, however, not only found she was pregnant but also seemed to know there was something unusual about it. Maybe they sensed Yahyu's repugnance at the thought of what was growing inside her, but they could not communicate except by smiles and a growing indulgence towards her. The men came to help her whenever she tried to get up, whereas previously they laughed at her weakness. At meal times the women gave her more food than the others and the men fed her titbits of meat that were normally reserved for them or, presumably, for pregnant women.

***

After several days, when Yahyu was already able to walk, she and Jon woke to find the clearing deserted. The Kubu had vanished without a sign or a sound but they had kept their bargain; in return for Jon's machete, they had left a small pile of cassava.

Jon searched around the camp looking for signs of them but returned quickly to Yahyu. "I think they just wanted to go. There's no sign of them but they don't seem to have left in a rush. Maybe it was just their time to move. They helped us a lot. You owe your life to these Kubu; without them I couldn't have helped you."

Yahya did not answer immediately. She had grown accustomed to the presence of the Kubu but now she was acutely aware she was alone with Jon and she felt awkward. She had often observed his detached infatuation with her from the way he looked at her when he thought she wasn't watching and his brisk dismissal of her whenever she went near him in front of other men. It had not mattered before because there were his troops around them, but now it was different. When she looked over at Jon she saw that he was over-actively packing up supplies, so perhaps he too was conscious of their loneliness and was hiding his awkwardness.

"What do we do know? Do we walk to the camp?" she said

lightheartedly. "I'm ready to move. I'm not looking forward to the hike and I'm not sure I have the strength for it, but the sooner we move the better. I just want to get it over and get back to some sort of normality. I don't want to see any more killing."

Jon made as if to reply but his voice caught in his throat and he started coughing. Jon smiled deprecatingly at Yahyu's clumsy attempt to stifle a laugh. He promptly got to his feet and Yahyu recognised his immediate response to the threat of intimacy: instant action.

"We move out today," he said. "I must climb a tree and get a compass bearing. We can't afford to get lost." He promptly dashed out of the clearing, leaving the branches swaying in his wake as he disappeared between the trees.

***

The journey was more difficult than Yahyu had expected. They were constantly climbing steep, slippery inclines for many agonising hours, always expecting to find the summit at the next ridge, but there was then another, higher ridge calling for an even greater effort. At the top of the ridges there would sometimes be a spectacular but daunting view of the forest canopy as it stretched uninterrupted for miles in all directions. The slippery downward stretches were even more difficult and Yahyu had to concentrate hard to avoid slipping down the precipitous slopes.

In the mornings Jon was at his most taciturn, sitting dejectedly by the fire, shivering from the damp, cold mist. Yahyu understood his concern for deserting his troops and wanted to help, but his awkwardness in talking about personal matters made it difficult to know how to start. She decided to begin practically. Jon was always at his best when tackling practical problems.

"Why don't you find a tree to climb, so we can find out where we are?" she said to him from her position on the small platform he had built.

Jon looked at her as if not seeing her, but then suddenly straightened up and spoke in his usual short, efficient way. "Can't here. We're still going uphill. Wait till we get to the top and then I'll get a good view."

"How many more days, Jon? I'm can't keep going for ever."

"Don't worry. I think we've come a bit too far to the north. It should only be a few more days. We have a secret meeting point which has reserves of food on a river bank a few days' walk from the camp. If we can find the river, I'm sure I can find the food cache and then we could just wait for a patrol."

"How do you feel about going back to the camp? Are you worried about it?" Yahyu spoke seriously, as a friend, inviting Jon to confide in her.

Jon looked at her mournfully. "What I've done is unforgivable. If my commander ever finds out, it will be the end of me, and my troops will never totally trust me again. But what could I do? I couldn't leave you to die in the forest and you couldn't keep up with us. My troops were just as likely to find their way back on their own as with me. But it's the betrayal that hurts me; I betrayed them in a time of need."

Yahyu felt his despair whilst acknowledging her own part in his potential downfall. She wanted to show her gratitude by sharing his burden of guilt but she didn't know how. She moved over to the fire and spoke softly to him, "I think you're a good man and I think I understand the sacrifice you made. Is there anything I can do to help?"

Jon continued to sit by the fire. Usually he would leap into instant action to avoid a conversation that hinted of intimacy, but this time he remained, staring into the fire but saying nothing.

"I'm not worth it, Jon. You acted out of kindness and pity, but I'm not worth it. Jim took me in out of pity and now look what's happened to him: he's been banished from the land he loves and he's having to look after my son. He'd have been better off if he'd never known me."

Yahyu saw Jon raise his head and his eyes narrowed as he studied her intently. She suddenly put her hands to her mouth but it was too late; she had revealed too much.

"I thought Peter was the child of you and Jim," Jon said while stroking his chin.

Yahyu's embarrassment showed in her reddening cheeks and she tried to avoid answering Jon's question directly. Jon was very narrow-minded, almost puritan in his lifestyle and she doubted he could understand the complexity of her relationship with Jim or the sacrifice Jim had willingly made for her.

"I thought Peter was also Jim's child," he repeated.

"Well, in a way he is. Jim is the only father Peter has ever known and that's what really matters."

"That's not my understanding," said Jon. "The father is the one who … who makes the baby."

"Not for me, Jon. The father is the one who stays loyal to the family. Any man can make a baby but not every man can be a father. Now, come on, it's time we started to go. Why don't you go and check out the direction while I heat the last of the cassava."

Jon got up without a word, his drooping shoulders revealing his disappointment.

***

The last few days of their long march took place in silence as they trudged laboriously up the final slopes leading to the mountain camp. Yahyu could feel the tension within Jon; he exhibited a studied unawareness of her, as if he was acutely conscious of every move she made but strained every muscle to pretend he didn't. He trudged along the trail as if she weren't behind him. In camp he ate the food she prepared and went to sleep without even looking at her.

Yahyu felt utterly miserable at the pain she had caused him but was afraid to discuss the problem while they were still alone in the vast forests. Would he explode in anger? Would he treat her like a tramp or a whore? Would he try to seduce her? Yahyu wanted to maintain the unhappy but safe status quo until they got to the camp where she would be able to hide behind others and Jon's attention would be distracted by his troops. She might even have an opportunity to escape, but escape to where? Yahyu could not face that question. The current task was to reach the camp alive and without major incidents.

Yahyu did all she could to help on the long strenuous march. She organised the camps at night, she prepared the lean-to and the bed of branches and leaves, and she cooked. She gave Jon most of the little food that was left and went short herself, although she was conscious of starving the baby in her womb. She tried in the only way she knew to repay him for his sacrifice and to restore some of his confidence in her but Jon seemed oblivious to everything. His disappointment in Yahyu was exhibited by every refusal to recognise her presence or her actions.

* * *

They reached the rebel camp late one afternoon. No patrol had found them but Jon's navigation had been inspired. They had found the food cache and from there Jon correctly calculated the route to the camp. They were challenged by a sentry, as they approached but Jon was well known and they proceeded quickly.

"Hey, Commander Jon's back," yelled someone as a group of soldiers and women gathered in the central compound of the camp.

"Yes, we're back," Jon said wearily as he looked around.

"Who's the girl?" said a wild-looking woman pointing at Yahyu.

"Not one of your lot, thank goodness," said another woman with a snarl. "What's your name?" she said to Yahyu.

"I'm Yahyu," she said while looking in confusion at the surrounding groups. There was one group of fighters but two groups of women who kept themselves apart: rough peasant women with children and a smaller group of younger women who held themselves like fighters but looked wild and dangerous.

"Are you Jon's woman or are you going to join us?" said one of the wild women to the amusement of her colleagues.

"I ... I don't know what you mean," Yahyu stuttered, looking up at Jon for guidance.

"She's with me," he said. Then, turning to the troops, he raised his voice, "I'm back in command now, unless there is someone more senior here from HQ." He looked around at his troops, waiting for a response but no one answered.

"Come on," Jon repeated. "Is there anyone here more senior

than me?"

One of the older soldiers spoke up, "You're our commander and we respect you. But one of the young guards dashed into the forest as soon as he heard what happened to you and the girl. We think he went to HQ in Palembang to report against you. We don't trust them guards from HQ."

Jon took some time before answering but he found the energy to stand up straight and raise his voice once more. "I am your commander and I never run away. You know that. I stay here with you and see what happens. As from now, I'm back in charge and we're a fighting unit, so no slacking."

There was a murmur of assent from the troops who discussed amongst themselves for some minutes. Turning back to Jon, the older fighter said simply, "We're with you, Pak."

Jon glanced at Yahyu, "We stay over there, next to the office. Let's go."

Yahyu was almost too exhausted to move and slumped on the bamboo veranda outside Jon's office while he went inside with several of the fighters. One of the wild women came over to her. "You want food?" she said. "There's some cold rice left over from lunch. You want it?"

Yahyu nodded her head, "Oh yes. We haven't eaten properly for days."

"And you need a wash. Let me take you to the river. You can borrow one of my sarongs if you want."

Yahyu was followed to the river by several of the wild women whilst the other women scowled from their positions on the bamboo platforms that were erected throughout the camp.

After the delight of soap and hot rice, Yahyu had time to question Jon as he left the office. "What's my position here? And who are those strange women in the compound? They look at me strangely but they are friendly. I don't understand this camp."

"They don't understand you," Jon replied. "Just note that there are three groups in any camp. All the men are fighters although we suspect one of them to be a traitor. Then there are two groups of women. The normal women are camp wives and they cook and look after the sick. The wild women are really prostitutes although they sometimes fight. I don't like them and don't want them, but there would be a mutiny if I threw them out. I don't mix with them much and they don't like me because I don't give them any money. You should mix with the camp wives."

"But I'm not a camp wife," said Yahyu. "Where do I sleep?" She detected a reddening of Jon's austere cheeks as she spoke.

"Wait till this evening when I've got more time and we discuss then. For now you can doze on the veranda. I've got work to do."

Yahyu stayed on the veranda relaxing her aching limbs whilst waiting for Jon to pronounce her fate later that evening.

***

The camp was preparing for the night and the soldiers sat around their fires talking and smoking. Jon left his group and wandered over to Yahyu swinging in her hammock on the veranda. "Let's go inside my hut," he said but then hastily added, "just to talk in private."

Yahyu got up slowly, her limbs and back objecting to every movement as she followed Jon wearily into his hut.

Jon sat on the floor of the bare office and motioned Yahyu to follow him. "Yahyu, I know you probably feel uncomfortable here. There's no place for the likes of you in a fighting camp." Jon hesitated before he completed what he wanted to say. "And there may soon be no place for me either. We're both likely to be treated as outsiders once word gets through from Palembang. That guard who ran away when my troops got here, I've suspected him for some time. I was informed several months ago that he'd been spotted going to the House of Young Bamboo with Hans. I can only guess what he's doing now; probably telling Hans about us.

"Headquarters know Hans and they use him; what for I don't know, but I'm suspicious. I think he trades with both sides and he's got high backing. Whoever wins this war, you can bet Hans will be on the stage accepting the accolades of the winners and he will be the most vicious and vengeful to the losers because he'll have to cover his tracks. HQ won't like your association with him because it may compromise some of them, and I don't know what Hans will do when he hears you are here. If I can keep my post as commander I can protect you, but it looks as if they may punish me too, and they won't be merciful. It's not the first time I've failed them."

Jon's eyes looked sad and empty and he looked at Yahyu before continuing. "You stay with me Yahyu, in my hut, like we did on the march. I'm not going to touch you but I've been thinking. In a way we're both losers, you and me. We've got a lot in common now, although I would never have said that a few weeks ago. Funny how quick your fate changes, isn't it?

"I thought I was acting with true nobility in saving you, but then things turned out wrong. Firstly that bloody Batak battalion knew about our camp and then you fall ill. It's all gone wrong and now

I've got to take the blame. Never get out of the boat, Yahyu; best always to follow the flow. As soon as you leave the boat, you're on your own and then ... I don't know what'll happen then. It's all new to me. But you've been here before. You got out the boat a long time ago, didn't you?"

Yahyu had never heard Jon speak like this. She had doubted he understood anything other than politics and fighting. This was a new side of him and one she was eager to explore further. She wanted to answer him but Jon continued.

"We may as well stick together. We're as bad as each other in a way. Neither of us have any principles. We both give way to weakness when the big test comes."

Yahyu wasn't so sure she liked this last bit. She still wanted to believe she had always acted in Peter and Jim's interest. But then, after they had been expelled, the principle faded away as she submitted to her sexual desires. Jon knew nothing about her descent into madness, but he probably guessed she could easily be tempted because of her pregnancy before meeting Jim. In a way she supposed Jon was right: they were similar. He had strong principles but was seduced by his pity for her.

Jon wanted to continue so she sat back, leaning against a bamboo pole, and waited for him.

"If we live together then maybe the troops will understand. They'll think I'm soft on you but that doesn't matter. They understand the need for a woman. They use those women over there." He pointed to the group of fighter prostitutes who were sitting on the ground chatting and laughing to each other. Yahyu envied their freedom to say, "To hell with the world," and live day by day. She wondered what they did about pregnancy, but Jon interrupted her thoughts.

"We've got to act normal as if we're together, if you know what I mean. We got to make them believe I want you. The problem is that bastard, Hans. You don't understand him; he's dangerous. If they think I rescued you for any other reason than love, or sex if you prefer, then they may suspect I was involved in the attempt on Hans's life for political purposes. They might also think you've got a political agenda with that police chief in Curup. Everyone's under suspicion. Better they believe I'm totally besotted with you than to believe there's politics behind all this. And Hans ...". Jon was stuck for words to make Yahyu understand their predicament. "I don't fully understand him but he seems to be playing one side off against the other. HQ doesn't trust him completely but they think they can use him. He brings in guns and ammunition and protects the leaders from the army. He also supplies them with women from Ibu Efi's place in Linggau. No one is safe from his corrupting influence.

"If he wants you back, he may persuade HQ to kill me. Then again, he may persuade HQ to kill both of us, although that's unlikely. There's not much I can do at the moment. I'm not going to run and you will never find the path out on your own. Our best defence is to stay together and be seen as lovers."

Chapter 11

A runner came into the camp with news that a friendly patrol was approaching and could be expected before nightfall. Jon's heart missed a beat as the news was relayed to him; the patrol would be carrying his fate in their hands. He immediately sought Yahyu and found her sitting around a fire talking to a couple of girl fighters. They seemed to have taken a liking to her, although they did not accept her completely into their group. Jon didn't like her mixing with those girls and grimaced when he saw her. He had at first seen Yahyu as an innocent girl fallen on hard times, but when he learnt that Peter was the son of yet another belando man, he had begun to doubt her. But Jon was an honest man and had noted her steadfast denial of any physical relationship with him or with anybody else in the camp. Jon had almost wanted her to be decadent so he could punish her for her former immorality, for destroying his image of her beautiful innocence, but he had to admit he could see no immorality in her current behaviour.

As he reached Yahyu, the girl soldiers got up to leave. They knew Jon didn't like them and they didn't much like him either, although they respected his fighting qualities. There was no money to be made out of men like Jon and such puritanical virgins could be troublesome.

"Yahyu, let's go for a walk."

The girls laughed as they walked away. They weren't afraid of officers and they enjoyed making fun of Jon's innocence. "Comrade Jon's found the courage to do it at last. You'll be alright Yahyu. The quiet ones are usually the easiest. You don't have to do so much work with them. Make sure he pays the full amount."

One of the other women, a wife of one of the fighters in Jon's troop, shouted at them, "Shut up you whores. We're better off without you. You can't even fight proper and you don't do any honest work. Just here for the money."

The girls laughed even louder as one of them opened her blouse and shook her breasts at the woman. "You're just jealous because your man wants us and not you. You're too fat to be one of us."

Yahyu looked at the ground. It wasn't her fight; she was just a temporary observer trying to understand the complex camp relationships. She was conscious of the contradictions in her inclinations. She felt that her allegiance should be to the wives or partners of the guerrilla fighters, but she preferred the company of the fighter prostitutes who had an easy-going attitude, free of moral judgements or constraints, with a camaraderie she had not met before. She kept her head down, determined not to show preference for either side.

When they came to the small stream that provided water for the camp, Jon stopped and motioned Yahyu to sit with him on the rocks beside the stream. "Do you still remember the first time we sat by a river," he said to her whilst looking wistfully into the forest across the stream.

Yahyu looked at him carefully. She remembered well the enthusiastic young commander she had met on a boat lazily going upstream past Muaraklingi. It seemed so very long ago when she was a much younger and more innocent girl. She also remembered his suppressed attempt at romance and wanted to laugh but was unsure of Jon's confidence in himself. "I remember it well. We were both young and innocent then."

"No, we weren't," replied Jon as his face took on the haunted look that both appalled and fascinated Yahyu. "You were pregnant at the time, or had you forgotten?" He spat out the sentence as if in disgust but then quickly changed his tone. "I wasn't innocent either. I was on my way to assassinate some reactionaries. I failed, so in some ways I'm worse than you. I wanted not to be innocent and failed, whilst you also wanted not to be innocent but you had the courage to carry it through."

Yahyu felt the bitterness of his words and it stung her. She wanted to explain but she could not find the words. What he had said was true. She touched his arm but he flinched away, his automatic response to any shows of affection, so she gripped him more firmly. "Don't Jon. Don't torture yourself. We've both made mistakes but that doesn't make us bad people. We're together in a very different way than you or I ever expected. In some ways I feel closer to you than to anyone, except of course Jim. I respect you and I think respect is more important than love, or maybe it's the same thing, I don't know. Every relationship is different. I once thought I would marry a king, like Sita in the Ramayana, but now I know the world's not like that. Everyone is fighting and everything is upside down. I don't know any longer what's right and what's wrong. I was involved in the attempt to assassinate Hans but then I saved him. I think I was wrong to save his life. It was weakness, not goodness, that made me save him. It's strange, isn't it; to save someone's life is a weakness and to kill is a strength."

Jon nodded as Yahyu spoke. "I was wondering what part you played in that scene. So perhaps you are as weak as me."

Jon spent some time looking into the forest before continuing in a subdued voice, "I once pictured you as perfect innocence and I wanted to protect you, but ... I disgraced myself. Do you know why I was so keen to rescue you?"

Yahyu felt Jon's arm trembling in her grip. This wasn't like him; he was an action man, albeit a most awkward one. She stayed silent.

"Well, do you want to know or not? It's not very honourable," said Jon with a sign of resignation.

"You don't have to tell me, not if you don't want to. I know you well enough to understand that you saved my life twice and it was a great sacrifice for you."

"I'm talking about the first time. I'm talking about rescuing you from those Batak soldiers."

Yahyu didn't immediately reply. She had enough experience of men to know that some things are best left unsaid although mutually understood, but Jon seemed to have a need to bare his soul to her. As Jon stayed silent, waiting for her response, she said quietly, "Please tell me if you want to but I will never judge you; how can I judge a man who has saved my life twice?"

"News has just come in. There's a patrol on its way; expected any time. I know what this means. They've probably come to arrest me, or worse. We may not have much time left together so I want you to understand the truth, the whole truth.

"When you told me about Peter not being the son of Jim, but Jim still accepting you and Peter into his family, it got me thinking. At first I wanted to hurt you because I felt you had also been unfaithful to me. Don't laugh. I was infatuated with you when we first met on the boat. To be told later that you were already pregnant from a foreigner was a shock. I felt you had betrayed me. But what you don't understand is that I had also wanted to betrayed you."

Yahyu looked puzzled. "How could you have betrayed me?"

"I saved you because of guilt. It's not something I'm proud of but I think the time has come for honesty. If I'm going to die ...".

Yahyu sat up straight and her heart missed a beat. "Don't talk like that. You're not going to die. The worst is that you may be demoted. Nobody is going to kill you." But she remembered Father Tomas's statement that when his patients were about to die they wanted to confess everything, even things they never wanted to admit to themselves during their lives. She wondered if she would ever have the confidence to confess all her sins as Jon was about to do. She doubted it.

Jon sighed and reached out to hold Yahyu's hand. With much tenderness he continued, "Listen to me, Yahyu. You don't know these people; I do. They may decide I'm a liability, in which case they will put the party before my life. If I'm going to die, I at least want to die honestly and that means telling you the truth. You are the only friend I have left in this world. When we met on that boat, I had never been with a woman before. In all truth ..." Jon hesitated before continuing and Yahyu noticed a reddening of his cheeks, "I still haven't."

Jon looked away from Yahyu, but when she tried to intervene to lessen his embarrassment, he motioned her to be quiet. He was determined to speak, even if it meant demeaning himself.

"You probably don't understand. When I met you, it was like two strangers passing in the night. I liked you, you were beautiful and I knew we would never meet again so I thought ... I wanted to be with a woman and I thought you would be, um ..., appropriate. I could have gone with you and then continued with my mission but I failed on both accounts. I couldn't make love to you and I couldn't shoot those women. I seem to fail with all women, both in loving them and in killing them. I think mine is a strange fate."

Jon sat on a stone, looking at the ground and occasionally glancing up to Yahyu, looking to see if she was laughing at him or shocked by him. He was wringing his hands in awkwardness as he said, "What do you think of that?"

One look at his tortured face was enough to kill any amusement. She relaxed the grip on his arm and smiled at him. "Jon, you are so honest. Many young men think like that but few of them could ever admit it. You shouldn't be ashamed. If you had tried anything, I would just have slapped your face." She laughed as she spoke, in the hope that Jon would relax but Jon would not be distracted from his confession. He wanted to wring out every drop of guilt in his desire to atone for his self-assessed sin.

"But I wanted to use you, Yahyu, and then to leave you afterwards, pregnant or not. I've felt guilty ever since. Then when I had the chance to rescue you, it was like atonement. If I saved you, I wouldn't have to feel guilty anymore and then maybe we could ...".
He didn't finish the sentence but quickly changed direction. "But then

when you told me you were pregnant at that time, I felt betrayed. But that's not fair to you because I wanted to betray you too."

Yahyu noticed that Jon had forgotten to blush when talking about sex; a sign of his intense concentration.

"I suppose we're both failures, aren't we. Maybe we deserve each other," he said.

Yahyu looked at Jon's haunted face as he sat by the river thinking of his dramatic and hard life as a series of failures and her heart went out to him. He had admitted to her what she could never admit to him: the failure of her own soul when she yearned for Hans. Jon, she thought, was a more honest person than herself. She was lost for words but quietly squeezed his hand and simply said, "What's going to happen now?"

"I expect they will escort me back to Palembang for trial. They will probably let you go but we shall be separated. It would be dangerous for you to follow me and there's no point in you doing so; we're not together in that sense. I shall ask them to take you back to Linggau and let you go, but they may want to keep you for a bit, until the Batak battalion has moved on. They may not like your knowing about the camp, even though you don't know where we are. But you know a lot about us and the Hans relationship will make it difficult. I hope I haven't saved you from one fate only to lead you to destruction in another."

***

There were shouts in the camp as Jon and Yahyu walked back to their hut. The expected patrol had finally arrived. They looked tired and dirty, but they walked briskly enough through the centre of the camp, heading for the office. Then Yahyu gasped in horror and clutched Jon's arm.

"Look there, at the back of the group," she whispered to Jon. "It's Hans. How can he have come here? His ghost seems to follow me everywhere."

"Oh no," was Jon's only comment as he visibly drooped by the side of Yahyu.

Yahyu continued to stare in morbid fascination at her most hated enemy and most coveted sexual partner. Hans staggered at the back of the group; he was overweight and sweating profusely. He must have noticed Yahyu and Jon looking at him but ignored them as he followed the officers into the camp office.

As soon as the door of the office closed, two guards came up behind Jon and held his arms. "OK Pak, come with us. Don't struggle; it'll only make it worse." They made as if to walk Jon to the office but Yahyu kept hold of his arm.

"Leave him alone. He's done nothing wrong," she yelled at the guards but her yell was met by silence from both the guards and the onlookers. Yahyu looked around in panic, "Help us, someone, help us," but nobody moved.

"Leave it, Yahyu. There's nothing you can do. Stay strong," said Jon as he gentle prised Yahyu's hands off his arm and followed the guards with as much dignity as his wounded pride would allow, leaving Yahyu standing with her hand to her mouth, unable to move.

One of the women fighters who disliked Jon came up to her and put an arm around her shoulders. "Don't worry, love. Plenty more fighters here you can hook up with. We'll look after you." The girl spoke with genuine concern despite her disrespect for Jon's sexual capabilities. Yahyu said nothing but tamely followed the girl to her section of the camp, her eyes staring blankly at the ground.

***

Jon was kept in the office for several hours while Yahyu sat on the veranda with a couple of the girl fighters watching the door of the office, waiting for Jon to appear. The girls offered her tea and then rice, but she refused with a distracted shake of her head. In their own way the girls felt sorry for Yahyu. They had also been in love once, many men ago, and they hadn't forgotten the feeling. They may have laughed at Yahyu and despised Jon, but in their hearts they also envied her. She was still a real person, even in this god-awful struggle which none of them expected to survive, although they never discussed it amongst themselves. They wanted to help Yahyu but it was long ago since they had had such feelings and they'd forgotten how to help.

Jon was pulled out of the office between two guards, his hands tied behind his back. Yahyu stood up and advanced towards him, hands outstretched. "Jon, why? What's going to happen?"

One of the guards pushed her to the ground. "Get out of the way, slut. You've caused enough problems."

Yahyu fell heavily in the mud of the camp compound. She looked up, her face covered in mud which she wiped away as she tried to focus on Jon's face, trying to understand why he wasn't responding to her. Both his eyes were puffed and blackened and he was obviously having trouble seeing. He was tottering between the two guards, walking hesitantly as a blind man, afraid of what he would meet.

Yahyu put her hand to her mouth to stifle a scream when one

of the women fighters came up to her. "You got to expect this. We hear that you're Hans's woman. Hans don't allow anyone to touch his women, at least not as long as he's still interested in them. I'll bet Hans was the one who beat him up. But don't worry, he's still alive, although you better not go near him as long as Hans is here; you'll only make it worse."

Another guard came out of the office. He was short but heavily built. He wandered over to Yahyu, holding his rifle in one hand, and with a dirty leer on his face he said, "You're wanted in the office, you Javanese whore. Get over there quick. We want to see how you perform." He laughed as he pushed Yahyu in the direction of the office, but the group of women fighters had heard him and immediately intervened to protect Yahyu as if she was one of their own.

"Don't call us Javanese whores, you Sumatran pig," one of them yelled.

The girls surrounded him and one of them tripped him as the others pushed him to ground. These women were small and compact and had been brought up the hard way. They may have been prostitutes but they had learnt to behave as fighters and knew how to work together as a team. They laid into him as he fell on the ground and stamped hard on his groin. For the girls it was a quiet battle; they didn't yell and shout but held his arms and legs as they methodically reduced his groin to pulp. The guard screamed in pain and indignity, much to the amusement of the onlookers. He was a headquarters man, hence despised by the fighting troops, so no one came to his aid.

An officer came out from the office demanding to know what all the noise was about. As he saw the guard writhing on the ground amidst an angry group of girl fighters he burst out laughing. "Hey, guard, are you getting raped by a load of whores?" he yelled. "Serves you right. Now girls, don't get upset and leave my guard in one piece. We know what you do for us and we show our appreciation. Stay calm and let this poor soldier, idiot though he is, do my bidding. I want that Yahyu girl in my office now."

The women fighters were not so easily subdued. Unlike their male counterparts, they were not inhibited by officers and didn't take much notice of hierarchies. For them, all men wanted the same thing and officers were no different.

"You let that little shit insult us again and we leave. Plenty more troops we can work with. You don't keep proper control. Yahyu's one of us; she's Javanese and you aren't going to touch her."

As the girls were talking, several more guards came out of the office. At a nod from the officer they quickly strode over to the girls and hit one of them hard in the face with a rifle butt. She turned away quickly, holding her bloodied nose in her hand as she dodged behind her friends.

The officer shouted from his position on the veranda of the office, "You've overstepped your mark, girls. That's insubordination; you don't realise what you're getting involved in. Get out the way before my guards really hit you." He was accustomed to dealing with difficult troops and he didn't fear insurrection from these girls. They were useful but expendable.

The girls knew when they were beaten and they weren't going to get involved in a fight they could not win. They withdrew together, in a group, telling Yahyu to join them after she'd finished in the office.

One of the guards turned to Yahyu and, grabbing her by the

hair, dragged her struggling and yelling towards the office. The officer stood on the veranda with a smile of benevolence on his face as he let them pass.

Yahyu was pushed roughly to the floor, her scalp stinging from the rough handling but she didn't cry or scream. She fought hard to maintain her sanity for the struggle ahead. She lay on the floor, steadying her breathing, telling herself to be calm and controlled. Never let them see you're scared, Jim had once told her; keep the initiative and fight back.

At the far end of the office she saw an officer with a hard, hatchet-like face, sitting cross-legged on the floor, staring impassively at her. Next to him sat Hans. Yahyu looked once more at the floor before taking a deep breath and rising to her feet so she could look down at the others.

The hard-looking officer looked intently at Yahyu before starting the proceedings. He neither smiled nor snarled as he spoke. "Nona, sit down. You've been accused of plotting with Jon to kill Pak Hans. What do you have to say?"

Yahyu looked quickly at Hans who was trying to sit cross-legged on the mat but his bulging stomach forbade it. "That's not true. Hans knows it's not true. I saved him when I saw the gunman aiming his rifle." She looked at Hans who looked back at her with a smile that said absolutely nothing. "And you're too fat," she said as an afterthought and was rewarded with an angry look from the grossly uncomfortable Hans.

The hard-looking officer intervened, not waiting for Hans's comment. "How do you expect us to believe you when you lie so obviously?" The officer spoke with no expression on his pockmarked face but his eyes bore into her, causing her to flinch away from his stare. "It was too dark that night to see anyone. The fact that you saved Hans at the last moment was due to your disgusting lust for belando men and their money. You are a whore with no morals and no ideology. Were you acting under instructions from Jon or from someone else? Answer me." The officer's face lit up with animation as he insulted Yahyu but his eyes never lost their hardness.

Yahyu sat on the floor wringing her hands and trying to concentrate. She raised her head and looked the interrogator in the face while pointedly ignoring Hans. "Jon was not involved in any way with that incident. I saw a rifle and I pushed Hans away. I saved him and you should thank me." Yahyu spoke with more confidence than she felt but she was buoyed by the thought that at least she could repay Jon by defending him.

"Really, then who was involved? Who instructed the assassin to pull the trigger while you kept Pak Hans waiting by the car?"

"How do I know? I wasn't involved. Someone wanted to shoot Hans; good luck to him. It's nothing to do with me."

"You and Hans were lovers, weren't you?" The officer shot out his question as if it was distasteful to him.

"I wouldn't call it that," she replied.

The officer ignored her sarcasm and continued. "You were lovers and your lover escaped unhurt and then you ran away. Why would you run away if you weren't involved?"

"Ask Hans why I ran away. Maybe it's because he smells too bad. He kept me prisoner against my wishes. I saw a chance to escape and I took it."

The officer looked at her with distaste before turning to Hans.

"Do you want to reply?"

Hans smiled. "I don't think that anyone who saw you in bed with me would presume you were doing something against your will."

Yahyu tried desperately but unsuccessfully to suppress the reddening of her cheeks.

The interrogator snapped back at her, "You ran away because you were guilty. I want to know who you were in league with."

"Why do you care about Hans? He kills your people. He's in with the police. Why is he here?" Yahyu spoke with passion but was met by blank faces from both the interrogator and Hans. Yahyu felt helplessness setting in; this interrogation was a sham.

"Unless you answer my question, I shall presume it was Jon that put you up to it. If this is true, then say so. We won't hurt you; you are small fry and of no concern to us. We don't hurt the innocent or the ignorant." The officer did not smile as he spoke. He stared at her through his thick spectacles as if she was a rather unpleasant object.

"That police officer, Captain Supriyono, he called me back as I was going to the car with Hans. Maybe he was involved."

Yahyu glanced at Hans and saw he had stopped smiling. He looked at her sharply as if this twist to the plot had not occurred to him and, judging from his expression, he didn't like it. He turned to the officer next to him on the mat and spoke quietly.

The officer turned back to Yahyu. "What you have just told us is most interesting but it makes Jon's situation worse. If you were in league with the police chief, then you are actively involved in political activities, and as Jon has been supporting you, it means that Jon is a traitor amongst us."

The officer got up to go. "Pak Hans has spoken well of you. He says you are obedient, but quite what he means by that I don't know. To me you are just a whore who sells herself to belando men.

"You stay here with him, but I warn you, don't try to leave the camp under any circumstances. I shall instruct my guards to shoot you if you try to escape." As he spoke he glanced at Hans, but Yahyu was unsure if he was seeking Hans's assurance or if he was warning him. Hans's position in the camp, as everywhere else in his life, was ambiguous.

The officer left Yahyu and Hans alone, facing each other across the bamboo mat. She had been trying to ignore his presence during the interrogation but on seeing him she drew strength. The enemy you see is less dangerous than the one you don't, Jim had once told her. She purposely looked straight at Hans as she analysed her feelings for him. Her infatuation had disappeared on the realisation that she was bearing his baby and that she hated the baby lying inside her womb almost as much as she hated him. But there was something else; she felt defiance welling up inside her. She would not be used anymore. Better to die and let the baby die in her womb than to succumb to the degradation of the man who had destroyed Jim and taken Peter away from her. Yahyu found strength in the understanding that she had no further to fall, or so she thought.

"That was an interesting little exchange of information, Yahyu, my dear." Hans lay back against the wall as he spoke, the better to ease the strain on his bulging stomach.

Yahyu stayed silent but she did not look down at the ground as was her normal reaction to embarrassment but stared Hans in the face.

He continued, "I know you saved my life, Yahyu. You saved me because you are really in love. Not in love with me, I wouldn't fool myself on that score, but in love with what I can give you.

"By the way, the truth as to who tried to kill me may not matter to these stupid soldiers but it does to me. I shall settle with that noble policeman, Captain Supriyono, when I get back."

"You know Jon had nothing to do with it so please let him go."

"Ha ha. My dear Yahyu, you are so naive, you have had many men in your life but you understand none of them. I know Jon's totally innocent of everything except his infatuation with you. But I won't allow infatuation." Yahyu noticed the tension in him as he spoke. His knuckles whitened as he gripped his knees.

"How did you know it was me that came here with Jon? Why don't you leave me alone?"

"There are many things you don't understand Yahyu. I was looking for you on that mountainside when you were captured. I'm not going to let you go now. Those soldiers that captured you were looking for you, under my instructions. They'll do anything for a few rupiah; they're not well paid. What you don't realise is that I love your obsession with me; best sex I've ever had. I doubt if you ever did for Jim what you did for me." Hans spoke with a sardonic grin, goading Yahyu to show her fire, but she was up to the challenge. She did not slap his face, as he wanted, but smiled at him in return.

"No, I never did. Not with Jim. It was different with him; he's a real person. You're just an animal; you have no soul." She spoke quietly but a sudden feeling of anger shook her and she snapped out at him, "You only know how to destroy and control. All men who have been good to me have suffered at your hands. You are evil and one day you will pay the price."

Hans studied Yahyu's face as she spoke. "You've grown up over the past few months, haven't you? Would you like to know how I first heard you were with Jon?"

Yahyu sat still, looking at Hans. She wasn't yet sure of her strength against him but she was prepared to fight, not so much for herself but for Jon.

Hans continued, speaking quietly so Yahyu had to lean towards him to catch his words. "I went with the Batak battalion into the forest looking for rebels. It's good for my image with the army to be seen ferreting out these rebels, although personally I couldn't care a shit if they live or die as long as I make money. My real reason, however, was to find you and bring you back; make you suffer a bit for plotting against me, but still to get you back.

"I was with them when they took the rebels' temporary camp, the one where Jon had been staying only a few hours before he rescued you. Shame we missed him then. It could have saved a lot of trouble later. Anyway, there were only a few troops left in the camp and most of them were killed in the first attack. Those Batak troops, they're really something to watch. They're ferocious; those poor bastards didn't stand a chance. I wanted to take prisoners for questioning but they didn't. They killed everyone, or so we thought.

"After we moved into the camp, one of the soldiers heard someone whimpering behind the bamboo wall of one of the huts, so he goes to investigate and dragged out a crippled idiot who called himself Koko."

At the name of Koko, Yahyu looked up sharply; an action not lost on Hans. Jon had not told Yahyu of Koko's part in her rescue and it shocked her that Koko was in any way involved. She felt sick in her stomach and her head began to sway as if the ground was moving under her. She took a deep breath, struggling to keep control of herself.

"We questioned him a bit. Didn't take much; those Bataks know how to make someone talk, and did that idiot talk. We couldn't stop him. Seems he was madly in love with you and followed you all the time. He saw you being captured by the soldiers so he went to his rebel friends and told them to rescue you. That's how Jon came to know where you were. The Bataks didn't like that. Those three soldiers Jon killed were part of the Batak battalion. They took their anger out on this crippled idiot. He screamed like a girl so we had to shut him up."

Hans stopped at this point, hoping to goad Yahyu into a response, but she didn't move. She was too shocked. She had almost forgotten about Koko in the rush through the forest, but she remembered him and his poor, crippled body with affection.

"He squealed and begged for mercy; said he'd lead us to you so we could get you back again. We didn't believe him, of course. Cowardly little bastard was just trying to look after himself. So they cut his head off with one swipe of a machete; beautiful stroke, only a Batak can do that. They stuck his head on a bamboo pole at the entrance to the camp; a warning to all the rebels that they shouldn't mess about with the Batak battalion."

Yahyu felt sick. She hung her head in her hands mumbling, "No, not Koko, it can't be. He was just a boy. He knew nothing. This is lunacy." She felt a wave of madness rising up inside her but her rage was impotent.

"I think you should know that we're going to shoot Jon in a few hours."

Yahyu shot back at him, "You can't. He hasn't done anything; not what you're accusing him of. You know he hasn't."

"I know that and you know that but they don't. They think he was part of the plot to kill me and then to hide you. He's too dangerous to handle. They'll have to shoot him and it suits my purposes to let it happen. I don't like the thought of you and him together. He should know better than to meddle with me or my woman. He will die because of his own stupidity and our rebel friends will believe he was in league with the police chief. That strengthens my position. The fools will trust me more now. Once Jon is dead and buried, there will be no one to prove otherwise. No one except you, but no one's going to believe you. We share a great secret, you and I; we both know I don't care a shit for politics but I'm investing for the future. It doesn't matter who wins because I will always be on the side of the winner and then ... well, then I shall be very rich and powerful and so will you, Yahyu, if you're sensible."

Yahyu hardly heard him. Koko had died a violent death and now Jon. How much longer could this evil man carry on? But was it really only him that was evil? She had encouraged his lust for her and she had encouraged the admiration of Koko and Jon, maybe not purposely but they had been encouraged all the same. Yahyu's stomach contracted until she finally retched over the mat.

"Come on Yahyu, get up. You've got to be stronger than this. There's a war going on and you've got to make sure you're on the winning side. Jon was a failure and these rebels will also be failures soon. If Jon doesn't die now, then he will soon when the army catches up with him. Those Batak soldiers never give up. They know his name and what he looks like. He's a marked man. I'm offering you the chance to win; to win with me.

"You've got to realise the world is changing and this country is changing. There's going to be a big backlash against these revolutionaries and you've got to be flexible enough to survive the storm. We can do it together if you join me. I need a beautiful Javanese wife to help me stay at the top with the new Javanese-dominated government that's going to come to power soon in Jakarta.

"I know you plotted to kill me, although I didn't know it was at the request of that puritanical policeman Captain Supriyono, but it doesn't matter. I also know that you couldn't do it. When it came to the final act you backed down. That means something. In return I'm offering you life, power, wealth. You can be my access into the new government and you will get all the attention you so badly seek. You can take up dancing again if you want. We can do anything we like."

Yahyu looked at Hans with contempt in her eyes. Never again would she succumb to the temptation of him. She stood up slowly, brushing the dust and vomit from her sarong, until she was looking down at him as he sat on the mat.

"I will come with you, Hans, but not because I like you or want you. I will never want you after what you have made of me. But I do want a favour from you. You grant me this favour and I will come with you."

Hans's face immediately took on a look of suspicion. He didn't like powerful women. One of the many attractions of Yahyu had been his ability to totally dominate her feelings. Hans motioned her to sit down, which she did, but opposite him in a purposefully confrontational position.

"Let Jon go free," she said.

"That I will not do. Even if I wanted to, which I don't, I couldn't let him go free. It was me that incriminated him in the attempt on my life. If I let him go, they will doubt my judgement or my honesty."

"Since when has honesty been a consideration of yours?" Yahyu felt the beginnings of excitement in her heart now that she had a purpose, but her confidence was born of desperation, not of logic.

"Honesty is a relative term. I am brutally honest with myself, which is why you find me so attractive, my sweet Yahyu. Jon will not be released; he will die. And, if you don't follow me, you may die with him."

"If you don't release Jon then you can forget me. Kill me, leave me, throw me out. I don't care anymore. I've lost everything because of you; family, dignity, everything. You think I'm scared of you? You think I'm scared to die? There's nothing left that you can do to me." Yahyu felt relief that she was finally able to confront Hans and talk back to him in the knowledge that she really didn't care anymore. However, her confidence was short lived.

Hans moved backwards so he could lean against the bamboo wall of the office. He was in no rush to show his hand, but Yahyu knew from the satisfied smile on his face that he had a trump card still to play.

"We, that is the police and I, intercepted a letter addressed to Father Tomas in Curup. It came from Penang. I have of course read it. It was meant for you. You can guess who it's from."

Yahyu drew her breath sharply and her hands shook. She avoided looking directly at Hans, trying desperately not to let him see her distress, but he was too adept at interrogation to miss her reaction.

"Then you should give it to me," she said.

Hans relaxed against the wall, looking at Yahyu as if he was about to eat her but said nothing.

"Give me the letter," she shouted at him. She got up as if to hit him but then drew back. She knew in her heart that the pleasure of hitting him would cost her dearly. She wanted the letter and would have to use subtlety to get it. She was no match for him physically but she would not give up trying. "What do you want from me?"

Hans continued to smile as he spoke, leaning against the wall of the hut and sweating profusely in the midday heat. Yahyu could smell the sweat on him and it made her feel sick. It reminded her of her despairing desire to lose herself in his animal sexuality.

"You'll get the letter, I promise, but not yet, not until I'm sure you're not going to start another plot to kill me. In a few days' time, after we have shot Jon, we shall return to Palembang and you must come with me. You don't need to know why. Come quietly and don't cause any trouble. You will understand the reason later."

With hatred in her eyes, but a firm control of her voice, she said, "You don't have to shoot Jon. I'll come with you when you leave, but don't shoot him. He's done nothing to you and he's no danger to you."

"I have to. You understand nothing Yahyu. It cost me a lot to follow these rebels to this camp. They think I'm on their side but that doesn't mean they're going to tell me all their secrets. This camp is one of their most secret hideouts. To persuade them to let me come along cost me a lot of money and a lot of convincing. They think the reason is my love for you, Yahyu. They laughed at me but who cares; even politicians understand the need for a woman." He laughed as he spoke, but Yahyu was not convinced by his story. There was something untrue in his tone; Hans was hiding something.

"So why did you come here? I don't believe it was just for me. You've got another reason and it's probably a dirty reason."

"You're growing up Yahyu. You're beginning to understand the world doesn't revolve around love as you young girls seem to believe. It revolves around power and you are going to become part of my power in the future. But, you're right, you are not the only reason I came here; you'll find out the other reason later."

Yahyu sat upright on the bamboo mat looking earnestly at Hans, trying to work out the dark and devious pathways of his mind as he contrived to maximise his power and benefit from every struggle and every agony of his victims.

"But what's it got to do with Jon. Why should he suffer," she said.

"Revenge is an important part of love. It's my way to convince our dear friends that I'm truly besotted with you. They already recognise you as the most beautiful woman in these parts, so they are beginning to trust me. But I need their complete trust and that involves the shooting of Jon, at my insistence. And ..." Hans stopped briefly as if uncertain whether to go on. "Believe me, Yahyu, his death by shooting will save him from a far worse fate later on."

"What do you mean?" Yahyu spoke sharply, demanding a reply.

"I will tell you later. Personally I don't care a shit what happens to him. He's too small to bother about. But it might be good for you to know that you should help us shoot him. It's in his interests. Unless, of course, you would prefer to see him die a slow, agonising death at the hands of somebody else."

Yahyu stood up, the better to shout her rage and impotence at Hans. "I don't understand you. You're just making up riddles to confuse me. You're going to shoot Jon for no other reason than revenge because he's a better man than you. He's braver and stronger than you are. He helped me when he didn't have to and he did it out of goodness, not because he wanted something in return."

Yahyu walked around the hut wanting to shout, wanting to hit Hans with everything she had but she knew it was pointless. Hans had won. He had won everything as he always did. He was right in a way; power is the only attribute that ensures success. Jim was the best man in the world but his rejection of the world and his isolation in his mountain kingdom gave him no power. When it came to a struggle, he lost.

Despite the desperation in her heart, or perhaps because of it, Yahyu felt her head clearing. The mist surrounding the events of the past few months dispersed and she saw Hans as he really was. The rebels were fighting for a cause; Captain Supriyono was also fighting for a cause, albeit the opposite one to that of the rebels; but Hans fought only for himself and reaped profit from misery. For the first time in her life Yahyu felt the exultant urge to destroy him for the benefit of all the future Jims and Peters of the world.

Yahyu quietly said, "OK, Hans. You win again," as she walked slowly but steadily out of the office and into the camp compound. She knew she had nowhere to go. Without Hans's protection, the rebels would probably shoot her as well as Jon. She would wait before exacting full revenge. In the meantime, there was the plight of Jon to think about.

Yahyu wanted to be alone so she could plan her strategy. Sita had once again returned to her soul and she would act with calculated deliberation, or so she thought. She tried walking out of the camp, towards the river, but a guard stopped her and pushed her back. She looked around for somewhere to be alone but the long camp barracks looked inwards towards the central compound. Privacy was a luxury of the forest, not of the camp. As she walked slowly towards Jon's end of the hut, hoping to find some privacy inside, one of the girl fighters came up to her.

"Why don't you come and stay with us," she said, leading Yahyu by the hand towards their quarters. Yahyu had never been in this section of the camp before but in Yahyu's current situation the maintenance of her reputation was not a priority. The girls gathered around her as they led her inside.

They were a sympathetic bunch; hard, tough fighters who would as soon stick a bayonet into any man as to make love to him, but they maintained a rough camaraderie amongst themselves. They felt an unspoken envy for Yahyu who had formed a relationship with one of the toughest commanders in the camp, even though he was known as a puritanical virgin.

"We don't know what's going on but this isn't the first time this has happened. Whenever any of the commanders puts his girl first, before the party, they usually get the chop. But don't worry, they'll just beat him up a bit and then demote him. He'll be alright in a few weeks as long as he protects his groin during the beating."

"They're going to shoot him," said Yahyu blankly, with no expression in her voice.

The news was met with disbelief. "That's not possible. They can't. They never do that. It's not as if Jon's done anything against the party." Then one of the girls said, "I'll bet that belando bastard, Hans, has got something to do with it. You were his girl once, weren't you? He wants revenge but they don't normally take much notice of foreigners, except to take their money. Why they want to do what he wants?"

The girls gathered into a huddle to work out tactics. They had their own code of right and wrong, and this was definitely wrong. One of the girls left the room while the others tried to find out more information from Yahyu but she wouldn't respond. She was afraid to tell the true reason about the accusation against Jon because it would only complicate matters and might even turn them against her.

The girl returned to the hut. "I found out where they've taken him," she said. "He's tied up like a pig in the bamboo cage behind the latrines, guarded by two men. Should be easy."

They turned to Yahyu who was sitting on a platform, looking at the ground, deep in thought. "Do you want to go and see him?"

"Yes, but the guards will never let me near."

"Don't worry about the guards; we can look after them." They laughed as they spoke. "We can guarantee you quarter of an hour. Can't usually keep the men active longer than that. But we can offer them a double dose: two women each. That might occupy them for half an hour. Don't worry dear; we'll do our best. We know how to control this lot." The girls laughed but their faces were serious. This was their battle and they were doing it for Yahyu whom they secretly admired.

As they were leaving, one of the girls gave a couple of pills to Yahyu. "Give Jon these when you leave him. It'll make him fly high tonight. Might as well spend his last few hours happy."

Yahyu walked casually in the direction of the latrines and then quietly slipped behind them and up the slippery path that led to the bamboo cages where they kept prisoners. When she arrived, panting for breath in her rush, she could see no sign of the guards, but there was one of the girl fighters lounging against a tree, presumably keeping guard. The girl gave Yahyu a thumbs up.

Yahyu saw the bamboo cage. There was only one prisoner tied up. Jon could not move; his arms were tied to a pole that ran over his shoulders, forcing his head forward so he could not look directly upwards into her face. She ran over to him as if to hold him but then stopped short as she remembered his awkwardness with physical contact.

Jon looked sideways. "Yahyu, please sit below me. I can't look up properly. Let me see your face."

Yahyu squatted below him. It was an awkward position which allowed neither of them to see each other's faces properly. Yahyu didn't know how to start but stared silently up at his puffy, battered face. He was still bleeding from the nose and the blood slowly dripped onto her.

Jon spoke first, his voice weak and strained; he had difficulty breathing because of the awkward position in which he was tied. "It's the end, Yahyu. There's no more. I wanted to die fighting. I wanted to be a martyr but now I die a traitor, shot by my own people." His voice gave way as he spoke but Yahyu couldn't tell if it was through emotion or the physical difficulty of speaking

Yahyu felt inadequate to the task. She had nothing to offer him, nothing to say to him. She gazed into his face but it was such a mess. She couldn't tell if he was crying or sweating or just bleeding.

After some minutes Jon spoke again while staring at the ground. "Yahyu, are you there. I can't see properly."

"I'm here Jon. I'm next to you." She stood up and held his head lightly against her. He did not flinch when she touched him. "I'm always with you," she said, her voice fading as she felt tears welling up. She wanted to hold him more tightly but she didn't know how badly he was injured and she was afraid of hurting him.

"Is there anything I can do for you?" Yahyu recognised the banality of her question but she could think of nothing else to say. Jon was going to die but she didn't know him well enough to comfort him.

"Yahyu, I've never been with a woman. Never. I thought when I met you on the river that I could experiment with you. That's not nice, is it? I tried to make amends, to be noble, to help. And now it's too late. I shall never know a woman. There's nothing like that you can do for me now." Jon tried to laugh but it came out as a sigh of bitterness.

Yahyu had never been able to imagine making love with Jon. He was too awkward, too prickly to think of in terms of physical affection. Instead she tried to show affection in her voice.

"I think you are a wonderful man. You saved me and asked for nothing in return. No man has ever done that to me. You don't deserve this fate. It should be me that they punish, not you. I shall always think of you as brave and strong; a true leader and an honourable man surrounded by violence."

"Will you think of me when I'm gone, Yahyu, or are you going off with that Hans and forgetting all this."

Yahyu noted the bitterness in his speech. He may have guessed more than she had realised of her relationship with Hans and it obviously hurt him.

"Of course not, Jon. Don't think about it. You are the one I'm thinking of now; nobody else."

"I've failed. I've fought so hard and given up everything for this cause and now they are going to kill me." He tried to turn his head to look at Yahyu but failed again. "Let me see your face, Yahyu. Wipe my eyes gently; I can't see anything."

She knelt before him and wiped the blood from his eyes. They were puffed and he probably couldn't see from one of them, but he recognised Yahyu and gave her a wry smile through his split lips.

"It's your lover that's going to kill me. He's corrupted you and he's corrupted the party. I wanted you more than I've ever wanted anyone. When I heard you were lost in the forest, I ran. I literally ran to try and find you. But now I must die at the hands of your corrupted lover. How can you live with yourself?"

Even in her most depraved moments with Hans she always knew it was wrong. She had started by trying to save Peter and Jim, but then she kept on doing it long after they had left. "I can't," she said. "I can't live with those thoughts. When I ran away from Hans, into the forest, I swore I would never think of him again. But then he came here, after me. I don't know why he came, but I doubt if I am the only reason." Yahyu wanted to change the subject, to talk about Jon and her, but he would not let the subject go.

"You must never go with him again. You're better than that. How can you degrade yourself? The most beautiful woman I have ever met. I understand you not wanting me, but to go with him .... He's evil, he'll destroy you."

As Jon spoke, Yahyu saw one of the women fighters signalling her to go; presumably one of the guards was returning. She tried to stop Jon talking, but he wouldn't stop and she could not force herself to leave him.

The guard came into the clearing and saw Yahyu beside Jon, holding his head in her hands. Yahyu expected him to tear her away but he didn't. He hesitated and then waved vaguely in her direction whilst lounging against a tree, talking to the girl fighter.

"I'm scared, Yahyu. I'm scared to die like this. I thought I would die in a hail of bullets, leading my men to attack the army. It's easy to die in battle amongst the shouting and the action, but this ... this lonely death carried out in total silence. I'm scared Yahyu."

Yahyu felt completely out of her depth. She held his head next to her breast and stroked his neck whilst crying to herself but saying nothing. There were no words she could find to describe her feelings.

There was the sound of movement from the camp. Someone was barking orders although Yahyu could not hear what was being said. Jon shook his head and tried to look up. "This is it. There're coming for me."

Yahyu just had time to slip the two tablets between Jon's split lips when the guard walked quickly over to them. "Sorry Nona, you got to go. The officers are coming." He spoke kindly, but when he saw that Yahyu was not moving away from Jon, he called over to the woman fighter, "Hey, Nona, give us a hand. I don't want to hurt her or him but she's got to go."

The woman came over and they gently but firmly dragged Yahyu away as the officer came into the clearing. He slapped the guard hard in the face and dragged Yahyu by the hair. "Get out you slut. You've caused enough trouble already." He threw her to the ground where the women fighters helped lift her up. Yahyu made to shout back at the officer, but at a sign from the girls around her she stayed silent, looking towards Jon.

"Make sure she attends the execution," the officer barked to the guard. "Good for her and everyone to see what happens when troops neglect their duty for a bit of skirt. Teach you all a lesson. The party will not tolerate weak fools who give in to tarts like her."

As Jon was released from the bamboo cage he fell heavily on the ground with a groan. "Drag him," the officer roared at the guard as he turned back towards the camp compound. Several more guards quickly converged on Jon, but they did not drag him. They lifted him with a few kindly words, "Soon be over, Pak. Stay strong."

Jon was lifted into the middle of the compound where the troops and the camp followers were gathered. It was hushed; Jon had been a popular commander and although they disapproved of his behaviour with Yahyu, none of the fighters wanted to see him shot. Yahyu tried to turn away from the sight of the execution but one of the girls whispered to her, "He'll want to see you at the end. Look at him. Show him you are supporting him."

When he came to the execution place Jon couldn't stand but slumped on the ground groaning. He tried to get up again but failed. The officer in charge was getting impatient but didn't know what to do. The regulations said that prisoners should be shot in public while standing but Jon stayed slumped on the ground as if oblivious to his surroundings.

"Get up, you fool. Stand up like a true man," the officer shouted but to no effect.

Hans walked into the compound. There was at first a hush and then a crescendo of hissing from the girl fighters that was quickly taken up by the men; they didn't like foreigners interfering in their affairs. Hans looked distinctly uncomfortable at what was turning out to be a farce but a highly dangerous farce that had to be solved quickly. The troops yelled at Hans's back, "Foreign pig, get out of our country."

The officer demanded silence but the troops ignored him and moved forward in a mass towards Jon lying on the ground. The troops had been through tough times with Jon leading them and sharing their hardships. They didn't like officers from the comfort of the headquarters office in Palembang coming into their camp and lording it over them.

"Jon, Jon, Jon," they chanted and Yahyu joined in, hoping there was still a chance to save him.

The chanting grew louder as the officer drew his pistol and fired in the air for silence but they ignored him. "Let him try to shoot us," a fighter yelled to his comrades. "Then he'll realise the anger of true fighters."

The officer called to his own guards, "Fire over their heads but don't for goodness' sake hit anyone."

The guards fired, much to the amusement of the fighting troops; they were too experienced to be scared of this pathetic bluff. They moved in slowly, towards the officer and Jon, chanting, "Jon, Jon, Jon."

Hans, despite his bulk, was nimble on his feet and quick to grasp the danger of the situation. He deftly ducked under the ring of chanting soldiers and walked up to the officer and whispered something in his ear. He then turned to Jon who was slumped on the ground, drew his revolver and shot him in the stomach at point-blank range. Jon jerked violently but the bullet didn't kill him instantly. He lay writhing on the wet ground, looking up at the ring of faces above him.

Yahyu had difficulty seeing what was going on; being smaller than the soldiers she could not see over their heads. But, to her surprise, they fell silent and moved away to let her pass. She walked over to Jon and knelt beside him. Hans tried to stop her but several of the women fighters broke into the circle and ran in a compact group over to Hans. With great accuracy and equally great force, one of them kicked him hard in the groin and he fell on the earth holding his crotch and crying in pain.

Jon never said another word as he died in Yahyu's arms. What he could not achieve in life he had achieved in death; to be held tenderly by a woman without flinching.

Chapter 12

For several days Yahyu sat silently in the girl fighters' hut, staring listlessly into the distance, oblivious to the men that came and went during the night. The men respected her sadness and went past quietly, some with a softly spoken word of comfort or a gentle pat on the shoulder. The girls recognised the change in behaviour of their nighttime visitors; the aggression was subdued and some of the men wanted to talk, which was unusual. The girls approved of the change brought about by the passive presence of Yahyu and they tried to help her in their rough, friendly way. One of them sat with her at all times, occasionally trying to get her to eat and drink but never pressing her presence.

The girls discussed Jon's execution and Yahyu's role endlessly, generally concluding they had underestimated Jon as a man but that Hans was more contemptible than they first thought. "That Hans won't be able to do much with a woman for a few weeks," one of the girls said. "Not after what we did to his balls. Serves the murdering bugger right and it'll give Yahyu a rest."

"Strange taste Yahyu's got," said another. "The most beautiful woman in this bloody forest, could have any man she wants and she goes for the camp virgin and that foreign bastard, Hans. Exact opposites if you ask me. Can't understand her tastes but I suppose we're not the ones to judge."

Her friends nodded agreement. The events of the execution had created a bond between them and the tragedy brought out their sentimental side, which was grossly exaggerated as if in compensation for the lack of sentiment in their nightly activities. Yahyu had been in love with Jon, and Hans had killed him; that was enough to earn their solidarity.

On the third day, Yahyu got up and tottered stiffly towards the door. Her self-styled guardian made to go with her but Yahyu turned her away, saying, "No, not now please. I've got something to do and I want to do it alone. I may be some time."

The girl let her go but sat on the veranda waiting in vain for Yahyu's return. She went over to her friends and asked for news of Yahyu, "She's been gone a long time. Said she wanted to be alone, so I left her. We don't want them guards to know she's gone or they might think it's an escape. Let's find her quietly."

One of the other girls intervened. "Maybe she's gone to those rocks up by the river. She used to go there with Jon. I spied on them once but all they ever did was talk. She may have gone there for, you know, to think about her lover or something like that."

The girls walked as a group, quietly but quickly up the hillside. They were skilled jungle travellers and moved with ease over the rough ground, skipping over the rocks that littered the riverbed. They spotted Yahyu from a distance, sitting on a rock overlooking the river, but what they saw caused them to rush towards her.

Yahyu ignored them, or perhaps she didn't notice them, although they made much noise as they gathered around. Her left cheek was slashed from eye to mouth and bleeding profusely, but she did nothing to staunch the flow. In her right hand she held an open razor, one of the fighting tools of the rebels. It was covered in her blood.

"She's slashed her bloody face," said one of the girls in horror. "What the hell she do that for? She'll ruin her good looks."

Yahyu turned to look at them. She wasn't crying and didn't seem to be in much pain, but her voice was faint and far away. "I don't want to be beautiful anymore. No one will want me now and I don't want anyone. I want men to leave me alone."

The girls slowly nodded in sympathetic understanding. Self-mutilation was not unknown in the camp, although usually it was a man who shot off a toe or a finger because he couldn't stand the jungle life any longer and wanted to be sent away, back to the town. But Yahyu was different; she was trying to be sent away from men forever. The girls tied a piece of cloth around the wound and led her back to the camp where they called the medical orderly.

Hans heard about the incident some hours later and came storming into the girls' quarters accompanied by a bodyguard. He went up to Yahyu seated listlessly on a mat, leaning against the bamboo wall, her face covered in a bloody bandage. Hans tore the bandage off and spat out his anger in Yahyu's face. "You stupid bitch. You've ruined yourself. You're no bloody good to me looking like that. No one's going to want to look at you now, not with that bloody great scar down your face." He raised his hand as if to strike her but the women were too quick and pushed him away.

"Leave her alone, you belando pig. Your balls not had enough yet?" they shouted at him. "You want another dose. You get the hell out of here. This ain't your hut and it ain't your camp. Bugger off back to your own stinking country and leave Yahyu alone."

Hans looked at the angry women and then at Yahyu with her bloodied cheek. His face showed his frustration and anger. His plans had been shattered and now he was left with a badly scarred woman who was no use to anyone. He left the hut and stamped across the camp compound, back into the office.

Later that night Hans came again to the girls' hut, but this time he came quietly and asked the girl guard if he could speak to Yahyu. "Suit yourself," she said. "But if you cause any problems, we'll cut off your balls and send them back to Palembang as a souvenir."

Hans found Yahyu still seated on a mat with several of the girls sleeping around her. "Yahyu, we've got to talk. It's important. Come with me. We can't talk in front of these whores."

Yahyu continued to stare at the wall. "They aren't whores. They're my friends."

"Who cares what the hell they are. We've got to talk now. Get up and come with me," he ordered.

One of the girls turned in her sleep. "Fuck off belando and leave her alone. She's with us now. Piss off back to belando land."

Hans backed off momentarily and then spoke slowly to Yahyu, pronouncing every word carefully so the full impact of what he was offering could be understood.

"Do you want to read the letter, Yahyu?"

Yahyu looked at him wearily, expecting another trick, but the letter was too important. She got up and walked slowly to the door and out into the night with Hans following her.

Standing under the moonlight in the camp compound, Yahyu turned to Hans and held her bloodied cheek as she spoke. "Where's the letter? I want it."

"It's not here. I left it with my kit back near the river. We can pick it up when we go back. We must leave tomorrow."

Yahyu looked at him suspiciously. "Your tricks are getting boring. I hope you rot in Jakarta because I'm not coming with you. Why should I ever trust you after what you've done to me and my friends?" Her cheek started bleeding again as she spoke but she let it drip onto her shirt.

Hans spoke indignantly, "I have never lied to you. I told you what to expect from me and you got it. I promised you will get the letter and you will, but we must leave tomorrow, early. I can't leave on my own; they might find it suspicious and stop me. You've caused a lot of trouble already with that scar and I'd like to dump you but I can't. Not yet. You help me get out of here and I will give you the letter and take you to Muara Aman. After that we go our separate ways. If you don't come tomorrow, it will be too late for both of us, and you will never get the letter from the English tea gardener."

"Tell me the truth for once. Why do we have to hurry? Are there more people you want to murder somewhere else?"

"You don't understand yet, but you will. I promise that when we get to the river, three days' walk from here, you will get the letter and then you will be free to leave or to follow me to Muara Aman. But if you don't leave this camp with me tomorrow, then I burn the letter."

"Give me your revolver first," Yahyu spoke with decision, putting out her hand to receive it.

Hans's face turned pale. "Why do you want it?"

"So if you trick me I can kill you."

Hans looked at her with an expression that was almost one of admiration. "No pistol for you. What you get is the letter. If you kill me, you will never know where the letter is and you will never read it. I will come for you at sunrise; if you're not ready, then I will try to leave without you and you can stay and meet your fate. It will be a violent one."

Hans walked off, confident that Yahyu would give in to the temptation of Jim's letter. As he turned the corner towards his hut, he stopped and called back to her, "Oh, by the way, that letter I told you about; it has a small photograph of a child attached to it." He quickly turned the corner, leaving Yahyu in confusion.

When Yahyu got back to the hut, she found the girls awake and talking. As they saw Yahyu they fell quiet but invited her to join them. "What did that bastard want with you? He shot your lover; you can't trust him."

"He's trying to bribe me to go with him. He has a letter from my husband, Jim. I want that letter."

The girls digested the news in a babble of chatter. They had not heard of Yahyu having a husband.

"You certainly get a lot of men. You're almost as bad as us," one of them laughed, only to be shut up by the others.

After much discussion, one of the girls, Tuti, got up to speak. "Yahyu's got to go with the foreign pig and I'm going with her. I'm fed up with this camp and the lousy money. I'll get more money with Ibu Efi in the House." She turned to Yahyu, "You tell Hans we're good friends and you're not going without me. I can shoot him after he gives you the letter if you want. I don't care; good riddance to him.

We'll protect each other." The girls nodded in agreement.

Yahyu felt good with her new friends. It was a new experience to be part of a sisterhood of fighters, even if their line of work was not one of much moral standing. Their feelings were real and, most importantly for Yahyu, they were unselfish. They wanted nothing in return.

"What can I do for you all?" Yahyu said. You've been so good to me. I don't know what to say."

The girls laughed. "Tell you what, darling," one of the girls replied. "When they come to hang us from the gibbet, you can seduce the hangman with your good looks and then we can all escape." They roared with laughter but quickly quietened as Yahyu put her hand to her mutilated cheek.

***

In the early morning, before the sun came up, Tuti took Yahyu to the river bank, some distance from the camp. "This is where we hide our secret cache of weapons," she said. "The men don't know about it but we need it in case things go wrong. If we're ever attacked, the men wouldn't come to our rescue. We have to look after ourselves."

Tuti reached under the roots of a large banyan tree and pulled out a small cloth package containing several pistols and clips of ammunition. She chose two; one large pistol for herself and a small one for Yahyu.

"You ain't much good with a firearm, I expect," she said to Yahyu. "So you want an easy one to use and one that's small enough to hide, so Hans don't find it. This one here, it's only a .22 calibre. That means it's got a small bullet and it only holds six of them. For a fat pig like Hans you'll have to use three or four bullets to kill him; one won't be enough."

Yahyu looked up in astonishment at Tuti calmly instructing her on how to ensure death in a victim. "But ..." she stuttered.

"Be quiet and listen or else you're going to get killed," said Tuti, as if instructing a dull pupil. "Get close, ideally only a few feet away, aim for his middle and fire fast. Don't shoot once and see if he's still standing because if he's not badly hurt he'll have time to run or draw his own gun. Just keep firing at him close up till he drops. Count the rounds and make sure you got one left. When he's down and not moving too much, point it close to his head and fire the last shot. Make sure the bugger's dead. I'm not being cruel but you can't half-kill someone and expect to get away with it. You either kill him proper or you don't try in the first place. You understand?"

"Yes, I understand, but I'm not sure I could do it in cold blood," said Yahyu, her face pale with anguish.

"Look, honey. You think any of us was born to this lifestyle; fucking men one night and shooting them the next? We're all here for a reason, not from choice, and you have to get used it. Either you adapt or you die young. If you kill that bastard, no one here will regret it. If you don't shoot him then I might, especially if he's got some money on him. I could do with a few foreign dollars. We can go to Jakarta together and forget this hellhole."

Yahyu walked back to the camp feeling qualms about her new friend and travelling companion. Her experience was too far removed from Yahyu's understanding but she was friendly and could probably be relied on in a tight situation.

***

Hans came to fetch Yahyu as the sun rose over the steaming forest. He looked pleased when he saw Yahyu ready to leave but his smile turned to suspicion as Yahyu told him that Tuti was going too.

"She can't come. She doesn't have permission. They will never let her come."

Tuti heard him and laughed. "Are you referring to that pockmarked prick in the camp office? Hey girls, which one of you is going to give him a free one so I get permission to leave?"

The girls laughed while shouting names at Hans. "Good riddance you fat pig. Don't come back here. You'll get nothing from us except the pox." Hans knew when he was beaten and walked back to collect his bags as the officer came out of the camp office, yawning. "Hey you, girl, what's your name? Where do you think you're going?"

Tuti stuck her chest out at the officer and smirked. "You get a free one tonight. Take your pick."

"Pah. You disgusting whore," said the officer as he turned back into the office, but he let her go.

The party left quickly to some hurried goodbyes from the girls. They were sad to see Yahyu go but they had forgotten how to cry. One of them held her hand, another gave her a ball of cooked rice, one even kissed her cheek. But there were no tears, just an uneasy silence as they disappeared into the forest.

***

The trekking was hard and it was difficult to keep direction amongst the dense trees, there being no footpath from the camp. They had been allocated two guides; one to lead and another to look after Hans who was struggling to keep up with the leader. Hans, for all his animal strength, was too fat for forest trekking and both Yahyu and Tuti took great delight in goading him as they nimbly followed the guide.

By the afternoon of the third day they came to a river and Hans abruptly stopped and sat on a rock. The leading guide came back for him. "Come on Pak, we got to go. We can't stop here. It's too open. We stop in a couple of hours when we're away from this river."

"I can't go on. We've got to stop." Hans spoke wearily but Yahyu knew him too well and detected a sly change in his tone. She looked at Tuti to see her reaction but Tuti apparently noticed nothing.

"No, we've got to go on," the guides both insisted. One of them offered to carry Hans's pack for him.

"I can't. I'm half dead. We stop here for tonight." Hans looked weary but, to Yahyu's eye, not too weary to continue. What trick was he up to now, she thought.

The guides were edgy as they argued between themselves. One of them tried to pull Hans to his feet but Hans contemptuously pushed him away. "I'm the important one here," shouted Hans imperiously. "You look after me or else we'll see what your commander does to you when we get back. We camp here. I'm not going one step further."

The guides grudgingly gave in but refused to light a fire. When Hans fetched some branches and set light to them, one of the guides hit him hard in the face. "You fucking idiot. You want every bloody soldier in this forest to find us. What're you up to?"

Hans pulled out his revolver and shouted back at the guide, "Do as I tell you or your commander will kill you if I don't."

The two guides conferred together and sat far from the fire, on the edge of the clearing, clearly unhappy with this grave breach of their training.

Yahyu was also thinking about what Hans was up to. She remembered his insistence that they must leave the camp or else she would suffer. She went over to Hans. "Where's my letter. You promised when we reach the river you will give me the letter. Where is it?"

"I will keep my promise. You will get the letter tomorrow morning but not now."

"Why not now? You promised."

"You will find out tomorrow. Now, I'm tired and need to sleep. You can sleep with me if you promise to hide your disgusting scar." He spoke with contempt; Yahyu was no longer the beauty he desired.

"I've got new friends now. Girl friends," Yahyu spat back at him. "I don't need you anymore. But if you don't give me the letter tomorrow, I'll kill you."

Hans laughed as he turned over to sleep.

Yahyu whispered her concern to Tuti as they lay together, away from the men. "He's up to something. He's not acting naturally. He's got some dirty plan up his sleeve."

"Yeh, maybe. The guides don't like it either. What do you think we should do?"

"I don't know, Tuti. You're the fighter, not me."

Tuti looked at Yahyu. She was proud of her fighting ability and proud that Yahyu recognised it and needed her. "We got to stick together. Let's go deeper into the forest and sleep far away from them and from the river."

***

In the night it rained hard, and the lack of a fire left them cold and shivering as the sun rose over the sodden forest. Tuti was accustomed to the life and didn't seem to notice her wet clothes and lack of sleep. She was awake and vigilant, staring towards the river, listening to the sounds coming from the men's camp. She held her revolver ready for action.

Yahyu came up to her and whispered in her ear, "What's up. What's all that noise in the camp?"

"It's Hans calling our names, but he knows we're close by. Why's he shouting? Let's go to the camp quickly before he wakes up every soldier in this bloody forest."

As they walked back to the men's camp, Yahyu noticed that Tuti was still cautious. She had put her revolver away but was walking with care, like a cat ready to spring away at the slightest sign of danger. On arrival they found Hans arguing loudly with the two guides, one of whom was yelling back at him.

"We got to go now," the guard yelled. "Why are you hanging around here, you stupid belando. It's dangerous by the river in daylight; it's too open. We've got to get moving. Now get your fat arse off the ground and come with us before I stick my machete in your fat gut."

The guide was really angry but Hans sat in stubborn refusal. He raised his voice further, "I said we wait for these two beauties. They need to eat before we leave, don't you?" He pointed at Yahyu who remained unmoved.

The guide turned towards Yahyu and opened his mouth but there was no time for him to speak. A loud crack resounded around the clearing and his head split open, spurting blood over Yahyu's face.

There was quick movement behind them as several small, tough-looking soldiers leapt onto the other guide and pinned him to the ground. More soldiers came into the clearing until they were completely surrounded.

Hans stood up and looked at Yahyu. "Now you understand why we had to leave the camp, you stupid bitch." He turned away from her and moved towards an officer who had come into the clearing.

"Leave the scarred woman alone; she's mine," Hans said. "The other one you can play with if you want." The soldiers around them laughed but took no action, looking towards their officer for instructions.

The officer looked with contempt at Hans. "We didn't come here for the women. You play with them if you want. We've got other work to do." He nodded to the two soldiers holding the guide. "Make him talk. I want directions and I want the camp layout. Don't kill him; just make him talk. If he dies, I'll eat your bloody liver."

The officer turned back to Hans and they walked away from the struggling guard.

Yahyu and Tuti were left alone in the middle of the small clearing, watching more soldiers file past them. They were small, swarthy men. None of them smiled and none of them leered but they marched with determination written over their tough, sweating faces. Their business was not with women but with retribution for their three dead comrades; this was the Batak battalion and revenge came before everything.

"It's the fucking Bataks," Tuti whispered to Yahyu. "God help our troops if they find our camp. That bastard Hans has set up a trap. This is all his doing. I've got to run back to the camp. If these Bataks get there first, they'll slaughter everyone. They don't have no mercy for us and we don't have no mercy for them. If they knew I was a fighter, they'd kill me too. You got to help, Yahyu. It's your friends as well as mine who're going to get killed."

Yahyu thought quickly. Now was her time to repay some of her debts to her friends. "Let me go to the officer," she said with determination. "I'll undo my blouse and flirt with him which will annoy Hans. If they get distracted, you can slip out the back and do what you can. Can you outrun these troops?"

"I don't know. They're travelling fast, but I got to try. I don't care about the men in the camp but I can't let my sisters die like pigs. These Bataks are cruel; they'll kill everyone."

Yahyu was not afraid. She wanted to die and all the better to die in a good cause. She walked over to the officer squatting on the ground talking earnestly to Hans. She unbuttoned the front of her shirt as she walked, revealing a small amount of breast; enough, she hoped, to tempt an officer.

The officer looked up with distaste at the scarred beauty before him. "Get out of here you slut. We've got work to do."

Yahyu did not move. "Are you in the pay of this foreign pig?" she said to the officer while pointing at Hans.

"What's that got to do with you?" He got up and slapped her hard in the face, splitting open the scar on her cheek which started bleeding profusely. As she fell backwards from the blow she heard a single shot behind her, but in the confusion of her fall she couldn't tell who was shooting.

Several soldiers left the long column and moved quickly to where Tuti had been standing. Hans was sitting on a tree root, his pistol in his hand, looking towards Tuti. "Is she dead?" he called out to the soldiers. Then, to the officer he said, "She was moving backwards, into the forest. Probably wanted to run for it. Can't take any chances."

There was another shot and a voice called over to them, "She's dead now, Pak."

Yahyu held her breath and felt her knees giving way. Tuti, the despised prostitute, had died defending her sisters in crime while Yahyu had done so little to help. She looked once more at Hans and swore in the name of Jim and Peter to kill him.

The officer looked back to Hans. "And what about this one? We kill her too?"

"No, leave this one with me."

"OK. You know the way back to Muara Aman from here?" the officer asked. "Follow the river south for about ten kilometres until you find a path on the other side, next to a white rock. It's hard to find the start of the path so keep your eyes open for the white rock and then just follow the path for five days. There're a couple of villages on the way and then you get to Muara Aman. Thanks for your help. We're really going to give those rebels a bashing they'll never recover. And we'll remember our friends, Pak Hans."

The officer got up to go without looking at Yahyu, who was left alone with Hans in the jungle clearing. The troops vanished like ghosts, the only evidence of their passing being the dead bodies of Tuti and one of the guides.

Yahyu sat on a rock looking at the river, her mind oblivious to the horror around her. Death was a better option than this life but she still had one more job to do. She gritted her teeth as she looked over at Hans walking towards her.

"Now we part company," he said. "I'm going back to civilisation and you can do what the hell you like. But there's something I want from you first."

He pushed Yahyu to the ground as he tore open her partly unbuttoned shirt and grabbed her breast. "Last one, Yahyu, but this time I don't want to look at your ugly scarred face. Turn over."

Yahyu did not obey him, but she did not resist him as he roughly pulled up her sarong and forced her wounded face into the muddy ground. Hans may have thought that her mad desire for him was still alive but he was wrong. Yahyu acted out the part till the end. When Hans lay back panting for breath, she was icy cool as she planned her act of murder.

The rape didn't matter; nothing mattered to her except her hatred of the man before her and the need for him to die. She turned back to him as if to embrace him once more whilst her hand slipped down her waist and pulled out the small pistol. With one hand she pulled Hans's face towards her to kiss his lips while with the other she thrust the barrel into his stomach and fired once.

Hans shuddered from the impact of the bullet and he clutched his bloody stomach. His eyes looked in surprise at Yahyu as if he finally understood her. "But ..." he said. "Why didn't you ...".

Yahyu, shaking with suppressed excitement and fear but remembering the instructions of Tuti, aimed again at Hans's stomach. "This is for Peter," she shouted as she shot him again. "And for Jim and Rusdi and Koko and Tuti and all the others." She screamed as she pumped bullets furiously into Hans's body. He shuddered with each impact and slumped backwards, his eyes losing their focus as he finally lay still on the muddy ground.

Yahyu looked at the dead body in front of her and felt ... nothing. She simply didn't care; she had shot him and that was it. She left his bloodied body lying in the mud and walked slowly towards the stream where she sat on a rock for a few minutes listening to the sounds of the jungle. She looked around her and spoke softly to the spirits of the forest, "I'm sorry, Jim, sorry for everything. You should never have got mixed up with me. Look after Peter for me."

Slowly, and with great care, she placed the pistol next to her heart and pulled the trigger. There was a click but no shot. In anger she threw the empty pistol into the forest and ran downriver shouting to herself, to the trees, to the birds, to anyone. Life was madness; death was better than life.

As her breath ran out and the cold rain beat on her hot cheeks, she began to cool until, quite suddenly, she stopped and put her hand to her head as if in great thought. Like a robot, with no control over her actions, she turned around and walked back the way she had came, back to the scene of death.

Back at the clearing she saw the dead bodies lying exactly as she had left them, twisted in the artistry of death. She walked over to the carcass of Hans. He was not moving, he would never move again of his own accord, but his body was covered in ants, which gave a strange sense of chaotic movement to his carcass.

Yahyu ignored his dead face as she emptied his pockets, brushing away the ants in a frenzy to find her treasure. She found a small bundle of banknotes, which she took and put inside her sarong, but it was not money she was after. She tore open his shirt and searched inside until she found an envelope. It was dirty and bloodstained but she recognised the writing immediately; it was from Jim.

She didn't open the letter. She kissed it before putting it carefully inside her shirt. She didn't want to read it in the sordid clearing amongst the rotting corpses. She struck out south, following the river while looking for the white rock that the Batak officer had described to Hans. She would read the letter that night when she was alone in the forest.

***

It was dark by the time Yahyu found the white rock. It was not the only white rock in the riverbed and the path that led on from it had been well camouflaged. Her fear of the dark had given her the strength to push on during the darkening evening to find the path. Once on the path, she knew where she was and the wild animals of the forest might give it a wide berth if humans used it. But as the sun quickly sank and she heard the sound of heavy rain advancing over the leaves, she began to panic. She quickly made a rough shelter of branches and collected firewood that she stored under the leaves to keep dry. She remembered well the lessons Jon had taught her about survival in the jungle.

She sat under the branches waiting for the rain to stop. The noise of the falling raindrops hid the mysterious noises of the jungle at night that always terrified her. But as the rain declined in volume, the forest noises increased; some repetitive, others sudden and terrifying. But Yahyu's main fear was simply the darkness; the vague outline of the tall dark trees and the deep shadows beneath them that hid all kinds of unspeakable horrors. She quickly lit her fire with Jon's precious waterproof matches and huddled close to it.

As she sat looking directly into the flames and trying to avoid thinking of the dark emptiness of the forest around her, she thought of Jon. His simple gift of matches was far more precious than that of Hans's diamond-studded tiara. Why value beauty when a fire could give life. The light from the flames gave her the comfort of keeping out the darkness, and Jim's letter in the breast pocket of her sweat-sodden shirt gave her the comfort of knowing she was not alone.

Sitting beside the fire she took out Jim's letter: this was what she had been waiting for. She didn't tear the letter open but kissed the bloodstained envelope. Then she smelt it, turned it upside down and looked at it from all angles. She fingered the envelope and felt the hard outline of a small photograph. But she still didn't open it; the excitement of holding Jim's letter was great, but she had a nagging fear that the gods who had treated her so unfairly might have turned Jim against her. What if the letter told her that he didn't want her anymore or that he had found a new mother for Peter?

She felt the still-raw scar on her face. There was blood and puss seeping from under the bandage. Would Jim still want me if he could see me now, she thought. But in her heart she knew it would not be her scar that would turn him away but the decay in her soul and the baby in her womb. Her behaviour with Hans had been depraved but now she was also his murderer. She didn't feel guilt or regret about murdering him, her emotions were dead towards him, but she felt dirty; contaminated by his seed in her womb. She had moved far, far away from Jim in the six months they had been separated and she no longer had the confidence to face even his letter, let alone his person. She didn't deserve him any longer.

The night was dark but quiet. Yahyu moved closer to the fire until it filled her vision and kept the dark shadows at bay. She slowly opened Jim's letter and felt first for the photograph which she carefully removed from the bloodstained envelope; it was of Peter, taken in Penang on his fifth birthday.

She looked intently at the small photograph, but the tears in her eyes distorted her vision and she continually wiped her eyes to allow her to gaze at the small photograph. This was her flesh and blood. Whatever had happened to her since they had parted, he was still hers and nothing could ever change it. She might be a Javanese whore as Hans had called her and she might be a murderer, but she was also a mother. Nothing could ever remove the pride she took in Peter, her Peter.

Whore, murderer, mother: Yahyu knew what she wanted to be but circumstances and her own beauty had not allowed it. How would Jim characterise her? Would he understand the difference between her heart and her circumstance?

Yahyu thought also of the girl fighters whose simple actions had done so much to help her. They would probably all be dead soon, killed in the savage revenge of the Batak battalion. Those girls had also once been lovers, sisters and mothers at some time in their lives, as they had also become whores and fighters now. How would they be remembered and who would remember them? Probably no one. Their bodies dumped in a communal grave at an unknown location deep in the forests of the Seblat watershed. She remembered the words of Tuti: "None of us was born to this lifestyle. We all came to it in different ways." Yahyu had also not been born to be a whore or a murderer but she had become one through the will of Hans.

Yahyu gently unfolded Jim's letter. There was blood on the page and sweat marks had caused the ink to smudge but it didn't matter.

She could still make out the letters. She held it close to the fire to read by the flickering light.

Yahyu yang tersayang (most loved),

We've been in Penang now for several months waiting for my arm to heal. It had to be amputated at the shoulder but I'm managing quite well with the other one.

Peter and I talk of you all the time. He asks where you are and I tell him you are a great heroine who helped us to escape. Every night we pray to your picture; we pray that you are well and Peter tells Jesus to look after you because you are his mama.

Yahyu, I know what you did for us and I find it hard to think about what you must be going through. I don't want to know what you are doing as it's too hard to think about, but I want you back and I will always want you back, regardless of what has happened to you since we parted.

I desperately want to come to Sumatra and rescue you, but at the moment I can't. I must take Peter to England first and then, when my health has improved and Peter is safe, I shall come back for you. I am afraid to leave him here because if anything should happen to me, he would be lost.

We have to be strong. You gave up everything for Peter and me and I shall wait for you, search for you, move heaven and earth to get you back. Never give in, Yahyu. You are strong, stronger than you think, and you will survive and we will be together again. If you are able to escape from your present situation, make for Medan and go to Bunggo. I have written to him and I know he will help you. I may not be allowed to come to Sumatra, but Bunggo can get you onto a boat to cross the Malacca Straits. Once in Penang you can contact St Theresa's hospital and convent. I'm staying there now with Peter. They know us well and they will help you.

Our parting in that sordid little prison cell in Kephayang was so sudden, we didn't have time to settle anything. But I am true to my promise to you; I shall guard Peter as my own. I am the only father he has ever known and we get on well together. I'm teaching him to play cricket and he loves it. It's his fifth birthday today and the nuns made him a cake and we all said a prayer for you.

I asked Peter to send you a special message. He thought about it all day and he says, "Tell Mama to stop being a hero and come home. I want her to see me playing cricket. And tell her to bring my toy soldiers that I hid in the hole under the mango tree in the garden."

That's Peter's message to you. He cried a lot at first, but we have grown close to each other and I think he understands that you have important work to do and will join us later. Don't worry about him; he's a great lad and I'll make sure he gets a good education in England.

Yahyu, I fear for you. I cannot bring myself to write the name of that man you are with but I know he's dangerous. He will grow tired of you eventually and then you must escape and go north to Medan and Bunggo. Whatever you've been forced to do will make no difference to me, although I still can't think about it properly. I know you did it for me and Peter.

You are a princess and if I can't have you in my kingdom in Sumatra then I shall make another kingdom somewhere in England and you can be my princess there.

Remember us as we were; sitting on the veranda in Gajah Tiga watching the sun go down over my beautiful plantation. That's how I always think of you. You are mine and I shall claim you back as soon as I am able.

Be careful. Keep your soul intact and think of us as we are thinking of you. We miss you deeply.

Love from Jim and Peter.

Yahyu sat still, holding the letter and staring into the fire, her thoughts dark and melancholic. She wanted to get up and walk around, but the sight of the dark, silent forest scared her. If Jim really knew what happened between me and Hans, he wouldn't want me back, she told herself. I must never tell him; he'll never know. But how can I keep the secret of Hans's baby waiting to be born? How would Jim react to that? He thinks of me as a princess but I'm just a whore and a murderer. And Peter, will he ever know what I am? Would he be ashamed to know what I've done? Better they never see me again. Better that Peter never knows how low his Mama has sunk. Better they both remember me as I was, not as I am now, a pregnant, murdering whore who's no use to anyone.

Yahyu could not sleep. She sat on the ground with her head in her hands, only moving to put more wood on the fire, and that only because of her terror of the dark. The more she thought, the more she convinced herself that the memory of her four or five years with Jim and Peter was more important to her than anything in the future, and for her to return to them in her present condition would destroy everyone's dreams. Better to die a quiet death in the knowledge that her own flesh and blood was in the good care of her only true love. Nothing else mattered. She could not bear the thought of the disappointment she would see on their faces if they realised what she had become. Tomorrow she would kill herself and the dreadful seed of Hans would die within her, but she needed to find a way to do it gently; a way that didn't hurt and where she would not be alone.

***

Next morning she got up early and headed into the valley of the Ketahun River. Once she found the footpath, it was easy to follow and she hurried along, fearing the return of the Batak battalion. She walked for several days, stopping only as the sun went down, when she rushed to collect firewood to keep out the terrors of the night. Every night she read and reread Jim's letter and spent long hours studying Peter's picture, looking for similarities with herself. At night she convinced herself they were better off without her; better they keep their memories of her rather than see the reality of her current condition. But in the mornings when she looked for ways to kill herself, her courage failed. She wished she had kept one bullet for herself rather than shooting them all into Hans. A bullet is easy; one squeeze of the trigger and it's all over. Other ways seemed difficult and failure could result in great pain. Yahyu walked on, quickly and quietly, oblivious to her bleeding feet and the cries of hunger from the baby in her womb.

Yahyu came to a small village but skirted around it, not ready to meet other people who might question where she had been and what she was doing; her scarred face being enough to raise doubts about her. She moved on further down the steep valley, but the area became more populated with small hamlets and farmsteads and she found it hard to avoid contact. In one village there was a cheerful, "Hi, stranger, come and chat." In another, an old woman shouted, "Are you one of those rebel women. Don't want you here. Not with that great scar on your face. Clear off." She hurried on, not knowing, or particularly caring where she was going. Her one thought was to kill herself but she didn't know how.

As she approached the small market town of Muara Aman, she caught up with a group of brightly dressed young women sitting beside the pathway, resting their sore feet.

"Hey Nona, where are you going?" one of them called out. "Come over here with us. We're going to Muara Aman."

As Yahyu walked wearily towards them, the same girl looked at her face with surprise. "My God, what happened to you? Your man run amok and cut you up? What are you doing here all on your own? It's not safe."

Yahyu sat on the pathway next to the group of six women, all in their mid-twenties, and one man who was older and had a battered and scarred face. "My name's Yahyu," she said to the girl who had first called out to her.

"Mine's Nining. I'm from Yogya. You're Javanese too, I guess. Where're you from?"

"My father is from Wonosobo but I was born in Sumatra."

"And what are you doing on your own? This is a really dangerous area although it's got money from the gold workers. Are you one of us?"

"I'm just travelling. No special reason. What do you mean by one of us?"

Nining looked quickly at Yahyu before answering. "Nothing special, just asking. We're Jaipong dancers, touring around this area making money. That fat oaf over there is our guard; he's called Budi. He makes sure we get paid proper and then keeps half the money for his boss in Linggau. But he's alright. Just does his job and doesn't bother us too much."

"I'm a dancer too," said Yahyu. "I'm a classical dancer. I used to play Sita. I performed in front of the governor of South Sumatra once. That was a few years ago."

The girls looked at Yahyu in admiration. A classical dancer was the height of their ambition and they respected her immediately. "Shame about your face," one of the girls said. "You'd be real beautiful if it wasn't for that scar. What happened to you?"

"That doesn't matter," Nining quickly intervened. "We can hide that with powder and make-up. Why don't you join with us? You look a bit down on your luck. You're all dirty and your clothes are torn and there's dried blood all over your shirt."

"I've never tried Jaipong dancing but I love to dance."

"Jaipong is easy. All you got to do is two steps to your left, stick out your bum, then two steps to your right, stick out your bum, and so on; and don't forget to move your hands gracefully. That's all there is to it. It's nothing, compared with your Ramayan dancing."

"I'm happy to try. Will you let me join?"

"Of course. We're performing in Muara Aman tomorrow, provided we get there tonight. We heard there's been a gold convoy come down from the mountains. Should be a lot of desperate men with a lot of gold; rich pickings for us."

"How do you charge for the dancing?" Yahyu asked.

Nining looked at her rather strangely. "You don't understand, maybe. You classical dancers are different. For Jaipong they throw coins at us as we dance. If no one throws any money, we dance real slow. Then someone throws some money at us and we speed up for a bit, but only a minute or so, and then we slow down again till the next man throws some money. It's not bad. We split it half-half with the boss in Linggau. But it's afterwards that we really make the money."

"What do you mean?" Yahyu asked.

"You really that innocent?" Nining said with a smile. "Well, I suppose we all was once. These men been on their own with no woman for months and they got money. The dancing gets them all excited and they pay for us afterwards." Nining spoke in a matter-of-fact voice as if describing a day at the office. "And we got the oaf Budi in case anyone gets rough. He knows how to deal with the rough ones."

"I don't actually need money. I've got a wad here." Yahyu moved her hand towards her waistband where she kept the money taken from the dead body of Hans.

"No, don't take it out here," Nining said urgently. "We're a good bunch of friends, but money's different. It can tempt people and then they do bad things. Better not to show it here but you can buy us dinner in Muara Aman. Haven't eaten a hot meal in days. These villages around here are poor pickings. We're half starved."

"Hey girls, Yahyu's going to buy us food tonight," she yelled joyfully to her friends.

"Good for you, Yahyu. You can be one of us. Anyone who fills my fat gut is my friend." The girls laughed in their rough, unrestrained way; very different from the classical dancers that Yahyu had mixed with. They were a happy-go-lucky bunch of young women, living from their dancing skills and their wits. Yahyu liked them although she was not going to join in any antics after the performance. She may have prostituted herself once to Hans but she wouldn't do it again.

She walked down the pathway holding hands with Nining. She needed a friend and Nining had a happy smile and seemingly a good heart.

The performance in Muara Aman went well. Yahyu picked up the simple but graceful movements of Jaipong dancing very quickly. On the first evening the other girls noticed her skills and gave her the lead. She set the tempo and the other girls followed. Nining in particular was very proud; she treated Yahyu as her friend and her property and took pride in Yahyu's dancing. However, very little of the money thrown by the men was thrown at Yahyu. She noted with some pleasure that the unhealed scar on her face was keeping them at bay and she was grateful for it.

After the performance, the girls gradually disappeared with various customers to their seedy hotel rooms on the muddy alleyways behind the bus station of the small town. None, however, came for Yahyu or for Nining. "It's because of our faces," Nining said. "You got that ugly scar and me, well, I'm just plain."

"You're not plain," Yahyu said in all sincerity. "You've got a lovely smile."

"Ha ha. I don't think it's the smile that these men are after. They've been without a woman for months up in those goldfields. I expect one will come for me soon, when they realise the others are occupied."

"I don't want one. I don't need their money," Yahyu said.

"Good for you, but I do. I got a kid. She's only five. I leave her with her grandma but they need money. Grandma's too poor to look after her and now's she's starting school. I want her to get educated so she don't have to follow me."

"How did you end up here?" Yahyu asked.

"We all got here by different routes, but as for me, I got pregnant and the man buggered off. How're we supposed to bring up a kid on our own when we're poor? We all start off like you: only dancing and not going with the men afterwards, but in the end most of us just give in. We do it for the money but the money's not for us. We send it home to our children.

"No one does this work from choice but you get used to it. I couldn't do anything else now and no man would ever want to marry me, not after what I've been doing. All the girls are the same; that's why we get on so well together. If I don't get a customer tonight, one of the other girls will share her takings with me. I do the same to them too, only I don't get so many customers as they do. That Wati, the one with the big breasts, she goes through three or four men a night if she gets the chance. She's strong and generous. She always buys us breakfast afterwards."

Yahyu and Nining stayed in the same room. They talked long into the night about their children. Yahyu respected Nining's dedication to educate her only child, even if it meant her living this lifestyle.

The next morning the girls slowly returned to their hotel, tired but happy. "Great takings," said Wati of the big breasts. "But my tits are bloody sore. Those miners have got rough hands." They laughed together.

"I vote we return to Linggau. We're all loaded now and I want to send cash to my mum before I spend it all, or before some bastard comes and steals it." The other girls agreed. They'd been on the road for several weeks and were tired.

Wati turned to Yahyu. "You coming with us? You're a good dancer even if you don't attract the men. But when that scar heals you'll be a hit with the men as well."

"I don't want the men," Yahyu replied. "But I'd like to come with you. I've got nowhere else to go." She did not tell them she was pregnant.

Wati quickly decided for them. "That's it then. Let's get the bus for Linggau. I could probably still manage a quickie with the bus driver if I get a chance. That way we all go free." They all laughed again; it was holiday time and for a few days they could relax and look after themselves.

"Where are we going to stay in Linggau," Yahyu asked Nining. "Have you got a house there?"

"We stay with Ibu Efi. She runs a restaurant and bar. It's got nice clean rooms out the back and we stay for free, as long as we help her in the House.

"Ibu Efi," Yahyu said in disgust. "What's she like?"

"She's OK. A bit rough sometimes but we ain't got much choice. Can't live in the street and don't want to spend our money on hotels. We've all got children to support. She runs a good house called the House of Young Bamboo. Ever heard of it?"

"Oh," said Yahyu in a flat voice, but she followed them onto the bus travelling towards the delights and horrors of that infamous

House. One death is as good as another, Yahyu thought to herself. At least I'll have friends there. After the birth I shall look for something else.

She looked at Nining sitting beside her, chatting with her friends. "No one will force me to go with men, will they?" she asked.

"No, 'course not. No one will force you to do anything, but you got to work for your keep; either dancing or waitressing. But we all started off saying no and now look at us. You can get used to anything in time. It ain't so bad. Just keep focussed on why you do it. Not for yourself but for your kid. Don't want them to end up like us, do we?"

Yahyu sat on the bus thinking of the baby growing in her womb and wondering what sort of life it would have. Her feelings were ambiguous; whenever she thought of the baby, she was reminded not so much of Hans, but of her role in the relationship with him and the feelings of guilt and disgust that went with it. She couldn't reconcile her love for Peter with her feelings of revulsion for the forthcoming baby. Both babies were a result of her actions but she loved one and hated the other. The fact that her baby was likely to be born in or near the most infamous House in South Sumatra was not lost on Yahyu. She hoped desperately that the baby would be a boy and so would not be able to copy her disastrous descent from fame to ignominy, but in her soul she felt the baby would be a girl.

They arrived in Linggau late at night and the dirty little streets were still muddy from the afternoon downpour. The girls alighted from the bus in high spirits; Wati of the big breasts had kept to her promise and earned them all a free ride, much to the delight of the rough-looking driver. They walked quickly towards the House, skipping over the muddy potholes, and entered a quiet, dark suburb lined with trees hiding large, colonial houses set well back behind locked gates.

Nining nudged Yahyu, pointing to the left. "Over there, behind that clump of trees. That's where we live."

Yahyu advanced with trepidation towards the flickering lamp that cast a pale orange light over the ornate doors to the House of Young Bamboo. "Nining," she said in a hushed whisper as they waited for the doors to be opened. "I could never go with the men here. I only want to dance, nothing else. Will they force me to do other things?"

"No, of course not," Nining said with a smile. "Because you're such a good dancer, they'll keep you for dancing."

The door was opened by a burly Madurese guard dressed in formal sarong and smart short-cut jacket. Yahyu followed Nining into the dim interior lit only by a shaded red lamp at the end of the hallway.

I expect Jim and Peter will think I'm dead by now, she thought to herself, and I hope they do.

Because, in a way, I am.

More books set in Indonesia

If you enjoyed *Jaipong Dancer* by Patrick Sweeting, you may like to read other books set in Indonesia and published by Monsoon Books:

Island of Demons by Nigel Barley (Historical Fiction)
Rogue Raider: The tale of Captain Lauterbach and the Singapore Mutiny by Nigel Barley (Historical Fiction)
In the Footsteps of Stamford Raffles by Nigel Barley (Biography / Travelogue)
Sold for Silver: An autobiography of a girl sold into slavery in Southeast Asia by Janet Lim (Memoir)
You'll Die in Singapore: The true account of one of the most amazing POW escapes in WWII by Charles McCormac (Memoir)
The Shallow Seas: A tale of two cities – Singapore and Batavia (Vol.2 in "The Straits Quartet") by Dawn Farnham (Historical Fiction)
Bali Raw by Malcolm Scott (Nonfiction)
Remembering Josh by Brian Deegan (Nonfiction)
Malayan Spymaster: Memoirs of a Rubber Planter, Bandit Fighter and Spy by Boris Hembry (Memoir)